"I never once met a woman like you before," Austin told her. "I guess I've never really met one I wanted to stay with. You've got more strength than a number of men, yet you're as tender as a flower."

"We must stop," Shadow said immediately, brushing his hands away and rising to her feet. "Only a short time ago I would have killed you. Now I let you touch me. I feel very strange."

Shadow moved out from the patch of aspens and stood in the grass and flowers of the meadow above the trail. With one hand she held the hair back from her face while gazing far out at high, snow-covered peaks in the distance, trying to understand what had just happened to her, trying to understand what the Long Knife Austin had done to her, why these strange feelings had come over her. She turned back to see him making his way up the slope toward the horses that were now grazing peacefully. She watched him climb the hill with long, powerful strides, his leg muscles bulging beneath his buckskin pants, his strong arms moving gracefully to propel him along. Yes, he was a man of confidence and, it seemed to Shadow, unusual understanding.

"Today there are possibly a scant dozen writers of the Native American experience who really understand and feel its spirit. One who must be included on that short list is Earl Murray."
—Don Coldsmith, author of *Ruin* and *The Spanish Bit*

SAVAGE
WHISPER

EARL MURRAY

A TOM DOHERTY ASSOCIATES BOOK
NEW YORK

This is a work of fiction. All the characters and events portrayed in this book are either products of the author's imagination or are used fictitiously.

SAVAGE WHISPER

A Forge Book
Published by Tom Doherty Associates, Inc.
175 Fifth Avenue
New York, NY 10010

Forge® is a registered trademark of Tom Doherty Associates, Inc.

ISBN: 0-812-53886-2

First Tor edition: May 1998

Printed in the United States of America

0 9 8 7 6 5 4 3 2 1

To Agnes Wright Spring,
a good friend and a wonderful lady

SAVAGE WHISPER

Prologue

1846

SHE AWOKE WITH a start.. Hardly more than a girl, the young Indian woman arose from her bed, her heart pounding, and cautiously peered through the early morning light into the shadows of the forest around her.

From nearby came the voice of her Indian mother, who arose from her own robes. "What is it, my daughter?"

Her father, a white man, one of the Long Knives who had come into the mountains many snows past to find the beaver, then also sat up, as did her younger brother.

"What is it?" her mother repeated.

"I don't know, Mother. It is a feeling I have. A bad feeling."

It was the first day of the Moon of the Service-berry—July. Though she had counted but fourteen winters, this was to be the day that would forever change her life, the day when she would become known to all the Indian peoples of the mountains. This day her name would change. She would no longer be called Mountain Flower, the name given her at birth, but take a new name, a name of great courage.

"What is your bad feeling?" her father asked.

"Someone is nearby," she said in a low whisper. "Enemies!"

Then came the high, shrieking cries of enemy warriors. The young woman could see them now, making their way on galloping horses across a nearby meadow toward their campsite among the trees. The war paint on their bodies and that on their horses glittered in the new sun that rose over the mountains.

They were Siksika, the Blackfeet, age-old enemies of the young woman's people, the Salish of the Bitterroot Valley. Riding with them were four Long Knives.

"Company men," her father said, speaking of the powerful American Fur Company, who held in great disfavor any and all who would compete with them for the fur trade business in the northern Rocky Mountain region.

"Besides the Long Knives there are many Siksika," the young woman said. "Maybe as many as the fingers on two hands."

Her father quickly took up his Hawken firestick and removed the hobbles from his horse. "Get next to the streambank, among the willows."

The young woman took her small brother, Little Bear, to her mother's side. The boy, having learned as an infant to be silent in the presence of enemies, held his small mouth firm and clutched his mother's doeskin dress.

"Do not go alone, Jim," the girl heard her mother plead. "I will leave Little Bear with Mountain Flower and fight with you."

"No, you haven't gone to war since the children were born. Keep them low in cover. I'll keep to the timber. That will make it harder for them." He quickly rode out from the campsite.

The young woman found herself blinking in horror. There was no way her father could be victorious over an enemy so strong in number. He would die; and then they would search until they had found everyone.

From among the possessions her father had with him, she took a bow and a quiver of arrows, a present to her father from a warrior friend among the Salish. They were intended as weapons for Little Bear, when he came of age.

"Mountain Flower, what are you doing?" the young woman heard her mother ask.

"I must help him, Mother. If he dies, we all die. And he cannot fight them all."

"No!"

"Mother, you must not fear for me. You know I can certainly shoot this bow. And well, for you have taught me the use of all weapons with your very own hand. Perhaps you somehow knew this day would come."

"But you have never faced an enemy," her mother said. "It is not like shooting elk, or even buffalo."

"This I know. But that day in your village, when you were a young woman, you had never fought before. Still, you fought the Siksika hand to hand."

"Oh, my daughter." She saw tears well into her mother's eyes.

"Stay with Little Bear, Mother. I must go!"

The young woman, her every nerve on end, made her way through the thick growth of trees to where she saw her father taking a stand with his horse. Already the Siksika and the company Long Knives were starting into the dense growth of pine, feeling within themselves that they would have a victory soon.

The sun was rising ever higher into the sky, and the young woman knew she would have to help her father soon, before the light filled the spaces between the trees, which were still in shadow, taking from them the one advantage they now possessed.

She heard her father's Hawken boom, followed by the yell of a Siksika warrior. Fitting an arrow to her bow, the young woman took position and waited, watching her father take his horse back deeper into the trees to reload. She slipped silently through the trees, close to the trail he had used, knowing the enemy would soon ride right to her.

She sang a low song to Amótkan, the Great One, the Maker of All Things. It was a song in reflection for the gift of life, and an earnest request for her life to continue.

One of the Long Knives came first, his Hawken pointed through the trees ahead of him. He was yelling, "Ayers, we got you now. Your hair is as good as gone!"

In an instant, a feathered shaft zipped through the air and made a dull, slicing sound as the metal point was driven through his upper chest and out through his back, leaving only the notched end visible at the front of his buckskin shirt.

"Aghhh!" The Long Knife halfway moaned, halfway screamed three times as he looked from his blood-covered chest to the trees around him, unable to understand who had caused his life to pour from him. His Hawken rifle fell from his hands and discharged beneath the horse's hooves. With a sudden bolt, the horse threw the Long Knife to the ground, where he tried unsuccessfully to come to his knees, coughing up a mixture of saliva and blood.

Close behind, a Siksika warrior stopped his horse, unable to understand what had happened just in front of him. By this time the young woman had moved soundlessly through the cover of pines to another position. Again an arrow was shot, placing itself into the warrior's side, just below the last rib.

Twisting atop his horse, his hand on the painted shaft, the warrior turned his horse toward the open meadow, motioning for those behind to get out of the trees. His breath gone, the warrior could not shout, and his words were drowned out by the war cries and yells of the other Siksika as they spread out to try to surround the campsite, each calling out that he would have glory this day. Only a few saw him fall from his horse into the meadow, where he lay writhing in the grass. Soon they were pointing into the trees and talking among themselves.

Suddenly the young woman heard her name being called. She turned to see her father, on his horse nearby, peering curiously into the trees, unable to see her but aware that it was she who had killed two of the enemy.

A blast from another Hawken was heard, and the young woman saw her father's horse lurch forward, as if touched by a hot iron. The horse began to squeal and thrash about in the trees. She heard her father's voice as he tried to calm the horse, and the laughter of another Long Knife, who called out, "You're done, Ayers. Now, I'll have your hair!"

Suddenly the young woman froze in horror. Her father's horse had collapsed, with him underneath. The horse struggled to get up, and she saw her father drag himself away from under. He then somehow made it to his feet, his right leg hanging at an awkward angle. He was yelling, "Mountain Flower, do not move! Stay where you are!"

The pain of the shattered leg then caused him to black out. It saved his life, for the sound of another Hawken blast was heard, and the young woman saw the ball slice through pine needles where her father's head had been. Another arrow ready, the young woman again moved into position to get a clear shot at the Long Knife through the trees. She wanted to cry out for her father, to scream. But she dared not give herself away and end her hopes of saving her father and her family.

Finally she had a clear shot. The Long Knife was sitting his horse over the fallen form of her father, yelling behind him in the Siksika tongue that he had killed Jim Ayers, that he had slain the enemy.

His cries of victory were cut short as another arrow from the young woman's bow made its way into his upper stomach. He cried out in pain and surprise, grabbing a tree to steady himself upon the horse. The horse, his head lowered into a large bunch of pine grass, seemed uncaring as his rider stared in disbelief as the young woman rose from her hiding place and shot another arrow point-blank into his throat. He toppled sideways, thudding into the boughs of a fallen pine, his horse continuing to graze.

The young woman knew she must hurry. There were other Siksika warriors coming, though others were calling to them that something evil lurked in the trees, something that was killing them. She shot quickly at an oncoming warrior.

The shaft came to rest in a tree, just in front of the warrior's face. He stared in shock. He gave the signal for silence and hiding, and they all slipped from their horses. The young woman now felt real terror; the enemy now knew they must fight a hard battle and would be very cautious.

Then, from just above the tops of the trees, came the cry of an eagle. It swooped low, its huge wings clearly visible through the tops of the pines. As it passed, a sweeping shadow passed silently through the forest, giving the eerie feeling of a winged spirit.

The young woman watched as the eagle folded its wings and dropped like a rock at the far edge of the meadow. The Siksika warriors, terrified, got back on their horses and made their way out of the trees as quickly as possible. Soon they were all gathered around the fallen warrior, looking into the skies for the eagle, pointing back into the trees.

The young woman heard movement. The call of the small chickadee told her that her mother had come to the aid of her father.

"I will drive them away from this place forever," she told her mother.

"Do whatever you feel you must," her mother told her. "The spirits are with you this day."

The young woman made her way to the edge of the trees and showed herself in the meadow. The Siksika warriors placed their hands over their mouths, and the two remaining Long Knives leaned over their horses and stared.

"Yes, I am the she-eagle." The young woman made the sign boldly. "I am angry that you have come here with evil Long Knives. I am giving you this chance to leave this place. It is not for you to kill the Long Knife called Jim Ayers, nor to destroy the fort-lodge on the Stinkingwater." She pointed to the two remaining Long Knives from the company, both still unable to believe what was happening. "If I fly over my lands and see you again in the company of these evil ones, I will bring dishonor to your lives. Now go!"

She backed into the trees, watching as the warriors made their horses ready for travel, staying away from the two Long Knives. Then, from the far edge of the meadow, the eagle rose. In her claws was a young wolverine, who clawed and spat as its life flowed out where the eagle's talons pierced deep into its ribs and chest cavity.

Turning their eyes from where the young woman had lost herself among the trees to the sight of the eagle, the Siksika warriors began to call to their spirit helpers to save them from the wrath of the large bird. The two Long Knives, unwilling to risk another venture into the trees, followed the praying warriors down off the hill.

The young woman fought back tears as she made her way to where her brother and mother knelt over the unconscious form of her father. Her feelings were mixed: She knew that by helping her father, she had saved all their lives; yet had her father not known she was fighting with him, the evil Long Knife might not have had the opportunity to shoot at him, killing his horse and causing his leg injury.

"He will live," she heard her mother tell her as she knelt near her father. "His leg is broken badly, and his mind is now in darkness from the pain, but his life in this world is not in danger."

The young woman, tears now streaming down her

cheeks, could no longer control the tremors of nervous release that racked her body. She had pressed her mind and her flesh far past any limits she had ever realized she could reach. She hugged both her mother and her small brother, thanking Amótkan for sustaining the gift of life.

"This is a day of great honor for you, my daughter," her mother told her, brushing the tears away from her own cheeks and those of her daughter. "You showed more courage in this short part of the sun's crossing the sky than many strong warriors do in an entire lifetime. And you were chosen to become special. The she-eagle came to be with you and to make her kill, so that her strength might also be yours. Her shadow passed through the forest, bringing the silent wings of death to the wolverine. And you moved so silently yourself, like the she-eagle's shadow, bringing death to our enemies. From this day on you will be called Eagle's Shadow Woman."

"Am I worthy of such a name?" the young woman asked.

"The she-eagle has proven she wishes to be your guardian," her mother answered. "Now you must always listen to the ruler of the skies. Yes, you are worthy of such a name. Because of you our family still lives in this world."

Shadow had by now calmed herself. Upon hearing what her mother had just said, she had let her body relax. Her time of trial had passed, had come and gone before she could allow her thoughts to fully comprehend what had taken place. She had been victorious this fine day; such a day comes but to a special few.

Little Bear, her brother, had been staring wide-eyed at her for some time. Though only three winters had passed in his life, he fully understood what had taken place. He came to her from his mother's arms, and Shadow took him to her lap, where he kissed her and pulled her close with his little arms.

"She is a special sister," Shadow's mother told Little Bear. "But now you must let her help me dig roots to prepare a broth for your father." She looked to Shadow. "I must set the bones in his leg. It will be the passing of many, many suns before we can leave this place and travel back to our fort-lodge on the Stinkingwater. There is plenty of game, and the waters flow clear and cool. We will live well." Then she looked far up from the trees where they stood to the rock walls that rose to high peaks above the valley floor. To her daughter, now called Eagle's Shadow Woman, she then said, "And you, my daughter, can spend time thanking the spirits and your new guardian for your victory this day."

Shadow followed her mother's eyes to the rock walls far above, where the piercing cry of the she-eagle echoed out across the forest. A strange feeling of association overwhelmed her, a sense of closeness to this majestic bird of prey, the ruler of the skies over the mountains. This day she had grown much in both body and spirit. Time would cause her to grow even more, bringing to her the life of a woman. She hoped she could someday find the sort of man that her father was, strong and brave; and caring far beyond the limits of most men. But Shadow knew she would not worry! The she-eagle knew her every thought now. This big bird would from this day on be her protector and her source of courage. She would come to the she-eagle in times of need, and for strength. And, yes, her guardian helper would surely lead her to the type of man whom she could stand proudly beside. Though more winters would have to come and go before this could come to pass, the feelings of a woman had already started. When the day came for her to meet this man, she would surely know it, for the eagle would be there with her, soaring against the blue sky, leading her onward to the fulfillment she would know as a woman.

Chapter One

———

THE WIDE, SURGING river pushed relentlessly against the barge as the men pulling her with the rope struggled in the day's heat. Austin Wells stood at the front of the boat, his piercing green eyes studying the country from under a broad-brimmed frontiersman's hat, his lean, well-muscled body relaxed in dark buckskin.

Summer had come to the upper Missouri River, the age-old flow of water that marked the vast, sweeping buffalo plains below the jagged line of the northern Rocky Mountains. To Austin, this land was far different from his native Kentucky, whose wooded slopes and valleys held their own fascination but seemed closed in by comparison to this land whose hills and sky pushed past the imagination.

The trip upriver from St. Louis had gone rapidly and without incident. A steamer had taken them as far as Fort Union, where they had reloaded their provisions onto the barge for the remainder of the journey toward the mountains. It was an exciting feeling for Austin, now almost at his destination. He pulled the letter from his pocket, addressed to him from his two uncles, and carefully read it again:

August 23, 1852

Dear Nefew Austin,

I hurd yor aunte June took up and died sorry to her thet. Yur uncle wolf and me want you to cum on out to the mountins and trap with us. You kin mak muny and you kin work for the amercun Fur cumpny puttin buflo down. You wont get kilt or los yer skulp the blackfeet is frendly. fergit the white diggins and cum out after the snow. Yer uncl Jake. Fort Benton.

Austin put the letter back in his pocket and moved away from an Indian woman who was rubbing against him, her hands having found their way under his buckskin shirt. She had been trying to stay near him since she had come aboard at Fort Union. Her man, an old French trapper, thought it funny, as usual.

"You can use her for tonight," he said to Austin through a laugh. "But I'll take that Kentucky rifle of yours in trade."

Austin felt more pity than anger. Many of the Indians who frequented the forts and boat stops along the river now lived their lives begging for trade whiskey and meager rations of food. This Indian woman was no doubt younger than she looked, but years of abuse and dependence had destroyed her. These Indians, a separate faction from the rest of their people, were called "blanket Indians" and were looked upon with scorn and contempt by their own race, who still lived wild and free.

The Indian woman eyed Austin for a short time, thinking better than to resume her chase after him. Austin could feel her probing, admiring gaze, the way her eyes traveled over his rugged frame. Then she turned and went over to the French trapper, who pulled her down beside him and began to fondle her breasts while she tilted his jug of whiskey high over her head.

Austin turned his eyes back to the grassy hills that rolled up sharply from the river bottom. He had been around Indians a lot back in Kentucky. In fact, he sometimes felt more at home with them than members of his own race. There was no real way to account for it, he had decided, unless it was the fact that he had a natural aversion for closed-in spaces, people in large numbers, and dwellings with solid roofs. He liked the smell of an open campfire and the taste of food roasted in hot coals. He liked the feeling of solitude, of roaming the trails and pathways of the woods alone, hearing the squirrels chatter and catching glimpses of deer as they ran through the bottomland, their white tails waving like large, furry flags.

It had been this way for him since the age of eight, when he had lost his mother to illness. That same year his father had been lost at sea and he had found himself with his Aunt June, a kindly woman, busy with her clothing store in a small settlement. Austin's days had taken him to the woods, and it had become his natural home. Though his days in school had been productive and he had learned a great deal, he still felt no comfort in tight-fitting coats or pants.

Austin turned to again see the eyes of the Indian woman upon him. He was also used to this. His looks could have gotten him anywhere, he knew, beyond Kentucky and perhaps onto a lavish estate on the East Coast, the husband of a fine lady with money at his disposal. Often he had turned to see women staring from under lace hats, or from inside carriages. But his way of life had isolated him from most women. Beyond the physical need there lingered a deeper hunger, a psychological demand for the right woman, someone who could love him and understand him at the same time, someone who did not necessarily follow the style set for ladies of the day. Those who catered to every whim of a man seemed, to Austin, to lack what it takes to keep their eyes forward and not down. To him, these women seemed in need of direction all of the time. It was too bad that independence in a woman was snuffed out at an early age. This was a trait he wanted in a woman as well as the qualities that would make her loving and caring. Some day, he knew, he would find such a mate.

There was a shout from the men pulling the rope, and all eyes went to the bluffs above the river. There, standing out against the backdrop of deep blue sky, was Fort Benton. The edge of the bluff below the fort, overlooking the river, seemed to come alive with men who shouted and waved. Cannons within the fort sounded a welcome to them, announcing their arrival to all.

The boatmen pulled ever harder, laughing and shouting among themselves, rejoicing that their struggle against the big boat and the river itself was finally over. They reached the shore below the fort, now lined with American Fur Company men stationed there as well as a good number of Indians.

Austin shouldered his large duffel bag and cradled his rifle in the crook of his other arm. As he waded through the shallows toward shore, a number of Indian women shouted and rushed toward him, holding out pairs of finely beaded moccasins and tailored buckskin shirts. Austin knew that this was their way of offering themselves to him as a wife. If he took any of their offerings he would be obligated. He crowded through them, shaking his head no.

Two men then approached him. One of them, showing yellow teeth and a graying crop of stubble beard, asked, "Would you be Austin Wells?"

"Has to be," the other man answered for him. He was a bit older, and much bigger. He had but one good eye. The other was closed and sunken in, with a deep scar trailing down his face from the socket, no doubt the work of a knife. "He's got them green eyes we was told about."

"You would be my uncles, Jake and Wolf Beeler?" Austin asked.

"Yep," the smaller of the two said. "I'm Jake and this here is your Uncle Wolf. We got your letter that said you was comin' out as soon as the snow left. Good to see you made it without your hair goin' to some Injun's war lance, or some such thing."

"There were no problems," Austin told them. "We ran into a few windstorms just out of Fort Union, but nothing other than that."

"Strappin' enough, ain't he," Jake said to the bigger, one-eyed Wolf. "I'd bet a plew of furs he could work a good lick if he had a mind to."

"He'll have a mind to," Wolf said, eyeing Austin as if he was sizing him up for quickness and strength. "He'll work right good for us."

"Work good for you?" Austin asked, surprised.

Jake, ignoring what Austin had just said, introduced two other men who had just walked up. "This here is Baldwin and Fenner," he said to Austin. "You'll likely be workin' with them for a spell right off."

Austin looked to the two men, both of whom were staring at him without expression.

"You can start out first light tomorrow," Jake went on. "First off, you got to work until you get your grubstake paid back to us. Then we'll talk wages and such."

Austin looked from Jake to Wolf and back, shifting his weight from one foot to the other and tensing a bit. "I don't quite understand," he said. "I thought I came out here to work for the American Fur Company. That's what I was led to believe in your letter."

"You did, my boy, you did," Jake said quickly, clapping Austin on the upper arm. "But the thing is, we got you some possibles and some gear to start you out. You got to pay us back for it. Then you can work for the company."

"I'll pay you for it now," Austin said. "I brought some money."

"How much?" Wolf asked, his one good eye opening some.

"Enough, I'm sure," Austin said. "But, now, that's really none of your business, is it?"

"No need to get riled. No," Jake again said quickly. "We just got you some things from the supply house here. I don't figure old Culbertson wants to handle any cash for it, though. He ain't set up for it."

"Then I'll just pay you two for it," Austin suggested.

"Well, maybe," Jake said after some hesitation.

"But you'd likely get a better deal if you was to just work it off."

"This isn't at all what I expected," Austin said. "Nor is it what I was led to believe."

Wolf then stepped forward a bit, hunching up his big frame and narrowing his one eye. He stuck his chin out toward Austin and said, "You're here to do as we say. You'd best understand that from the start. Then things will go plumb good."

"I'll tell you what," Austin said. "You two can just keep those supplies you got for me. I didn't order them. I'll just talk to the man in charge of the fort here and see if I can get on."

"Aw, come on now," Jake said to Austin. "We ain't out to do bad by you."

"Hush, Jake," Wolf said, his voice turning to a growl. "Maybe this young whelp needs a sizin' down."

"Now, Wolf." Jake stepped in. "We're all kin here. There ought not to be no trouble."

Austin, ready to move in an instant, stared at Wolf without expression.

Jake went on, noticing the coiled muscles under Austin's buckskins.

"Sure, Wolf. He didn't mean nothin'. We got to work together if we want to do good here. Austin, here, is one of us now."

After a moment Wolf curled his lips into an odd sneer. "I reckon you're right, Jake," he said. He was looking at Austin as he spoke. "Looks like your Uncle Jake, here, has taken a likin' to you. Best be thankful, boy. I would have tore you apart."

Austin, irritated with the circumstances as they now were, was not about to take anything from anybody. He knew it would take little or nothing to put Wolf

on the spot, to make him have to back up his last
remark. He had said it in front of everybody. Austin
crossed his arms in front of his chest.

"You'd best be careful how you talk to people,"
he said to Wolf. "Someday someone is going to teach
you some manners."

"By God not you," Wolf said through gritted
teeth.

He lunged with more quickness than Austin had
expected. But Austin was fast enough himself to
dodge a big fist. Surprised, he shuffled his feet to
brace himself against Wolf's strength as the big man
tried to wrestle him to the ground. With a burst of his
own strength, Austin managed to twist away from
Wolf, throwing him sideways and into a sprawl near
the shallows of the river.

"Ha, ha!" Wolf growled. "I ain't finished. Not by
a long sight."

Wolf was up quickly and at Austin again. This time
Austin was taking nothing for granted and positioned
himself as Wolf came on headfirst.

Austin sidestepped Wolf's initial lunge and swung
hard at his uncle. The blow glanced off the top of the
big man's head as he ducked and grabbed Austin's
shirt at the same time. With a yell and a mighty throw,
Wolf had Austin down on his back.

Wolf began to howl with glee as he placed his
thumbs into Austin's eyes and began to press. Austin
struggled, twisting his head, but he could not force
the big hands from their grip. Pain shot through his
eyes and nose. In desperation he reached on the
ground beside him, feeling, probing, until his fingers
found a rock.

With all his force, he slammed the stone into
Wolf's face, hearing his roar of pain and rage. With

the thumbs out of his eyes and the weight of his uncle shifted backwards, Austin struggled out and to his feet, blinking uncontrollably.

The rock had smashed into Wolf's nose and upper lip, smearing blood all across his face and stunning him. Austin, his eyes beginning to focus once again, did not wait for his uncle to recover fully.

Wolf had begun to struggle to his feet, getting ready to rush Austin again. In a single, powerful motion, too quick for Wolf to react, Austin slammed his fist into his uncle's face, just below the ear. The jaw popped from its socket with a sharp crack, and Wolf slumped back to his knees, bawling like a bear.

Jake quickly stepped between them. "You done him in good," he said to Austin. "That's enough."

"Out of my way!" Austin bellowed, his eyes still blinking in pain. He threw Jake aside, sending him tumbling into the men who had lined up to watch.

By now Wolf was bent over on his knees, supporting himself with one hand while he held his dislocated jaw with the other. Austin looked into the faces of the men. They all said that he had a right to do whatever he wanted but that he would not gain any respect for it.

Austin picked up his rifle and duffel bag, anger still boiling within him. He worked his way through the crowd back to the boat, where a man was ordering them to get back to the work of unloading the cargo.

"Culbertson is my name," he said to Austin. "Not everyone who stops here causes as much commotion as you."

"When does the boat leave again?" Austin asked.

"Leave?"

"Yes, to go back to St. Louis. I've made a mistake."

Culbertson raised his eyebrows. "I'm afraid your 'mistake' will cost you about six months' time."

"I thought you had pelts and buffalo robes to send back to St. Louis," Austin said in surprise.

"Not until early next spring. Those from last year are long gone already."

Austin took a deep breath, his frustration mounting again. He looked over to where his two uncles stood staring at him, Jake helping to hold Wolf up while Wolf held his injured jaw.

"That's quite a pair you came out here to work for," Culbertson said. "You look to me like you know the hills. How did you get into this mess?"

"I got played for a greenhorn," Austin said. "They said I was going to work for the American Fur Company, that you were hiring."

"I've got more men than I need now," Culbertson said. "I have to watch them close or they drink up more than they're worth."

"How about my uncles," Austin asked, "do they work for you?"

"Well, we don't carry their names on the roster. They earn their keep and maybe they'll do a few things nobody else has the stomach for. Follow what I mean?"

Austin knew perfectly well what he meant. His uncles were nothing more than troublemakers for hire to anyone who wanted their services. Usually it would be other fur companies that were in competition. Austin had gotten himself into something there seemed to be no way out of.

"If I can't work for you and I won't for my uncles,

what other choices do I have?" Austin asked Culbertson.

Culbertson shook his head. "Don't ask me for advice. I've got my own troubles to contend with here, too many of them. I don't need more." He turned and made his way up toward the fort from the river.

When he had left, Baldwin and Fenner, the two men his uncles had introduced him to, made their way over. It was Baldwin who did the talking.

"You put quite a lick on Wolf. He ain't likely to forget it. Never."

"I didn't come clear out here to be somebody's troubleshooter," Austin said. "I was told I would be working for the American Fur Company. I was lied to. Now I'd like to go back to Kentucky."

Baldwin looked impassively at Austin. "Can't see how that's possible, sonny."

"Austin. Austin Wells."

"Yeah, well I still don't see how you figger to turn tail and run from your uncles."

"Turn tail and run?"

"Jake and Wolf grubstaked you. High-priced goods at that."

"I don't need them. I don't want them."

"It ain't that easy. Forget your money. You've got to work it off. They've got jobs for you. Jobs for you to help me and Fenner, here, with. You can't just quit."

Austin took another deep breath, trying to control his resurging anger.

"And I wouldn't think about just pullin' out, either," Baldwin went on. "Them two know a passel of trappers and traders up and down the river. I ain't sayin' everybody takes a likin' to them. But just the same, there's plenty that do. If you run, word will spread clean down to St. Louis like wildfire. They'll make it hard on you, Jake and Wolf will. By the time the story hits St. Louis, why it might even sound like you stole goods from the Company. You wouldn't want that hangin' over your head.''

Austin took the letter from inside his shirt. He crumpled it into a tight ball and tossed it out into the river. The current caught it immediately, and Austin watched it bob atop the water as it was carried with the flow, wishing he had never even bothered to check his mail. It seemed the perfect opportunity to push the past aside and start out fresh. Kentucky had nothing to offer him now, and he had already grown attached to this country. During the trip upriver from St. Louis, each day had brought him a little closer to the wide, free land, to the herds of deer and elk that lined the river, and now to the vast numbers of bison that blackened the grasslands where they grazed. His heart had hammered within him when he had first gazed upon the high, snow-covered peaks that were the Rockies. And now he longed to climb to their towering heights, to see what life below looked like from the top of the world. That day would come, he knew, as he turned his eyes back to Baldwin and Fenner. But first he would have to figure a way to get out of his current situation.

''You carry a real wallop, Austin.''

It was the voice of Wolf. Both he and Jake had made their way over after watching Austin talk to Baldwin and Fenner for a time. Wolf's jaw was back in place but had already swollen considerably. As he spoke to Austin, his voice sounded like it was coming from the hollow of a cave.

''You got me a good one,'' he said, trying to sound

like he had accepted the fact that Austin had fought him with good cause. "Ain't many can put me down like you just done."

"We picked you right, sure enough," Jake then added. "You're a tough one. That's good. We need that. Now, what say you and your Uncle Wolf smooth over the rough spots between you, and we'll get on to the work that needs tendin' to."

Wolf extended his hand to Austin as if it had been rehearsed beforehand. They shook, and Austin looked hard as Wolf kept nodding his head while Jake spoke, without even the slightest hint of a smile in his eyes.

"We should all do right good by one another," Jake was saying. "Lucky thing your Auntie June died, otherwise you likely wouldn't have had the chance to come out here."

"Nobody ever whupped me like you did," Wolf managed to say, pain evident in his face. "You cater to fightin', do yuh?"

"When I have to," Austin said. "I don't look for it, but I'm not one to back down, just the same."

"That's what we like to hear," Jake said with a laugh. "You'll fit in real good, I've got a feelin'. And we've got just the job for you. Baldwin and Fenner, here, they got a little trip planned. You'll be goin' with them. Tomorrow."

"Maybe we'd better discuss the terms of our business arrangement first," Austin said. "Things seem a bit unclear to me."

"Unclear?" Jake said.

"Your letter said I'd be working for the American Fur Company," Austin told him. "I understand now that the company had no intention of putting me on."

"We work for the company," Jake said. "You work for us. Same thing."

"Not quite," Austin said quickly.

"Now don't be sore about it," Jake said. "We'll treat you right."

"We haven't gotten off to a very good start," Austin said with a little laugh.

Jake licked his lips nervously. "What say we just forget that."

"Well, I just don't feel very good about coming out here under different circumstances than I had planned, that's all."

"You mean you don't want to work for us?"

"Not really."

Jake thought on it a moment. "That kind of hurts our feelin's a bit."

"I'll bet it does," said Austin. "Culbertson told me you two aren't the same type of worker he would have talking trade with the Indians, or something like that. You do other things. I came out here to trade with the Indians."

"We do that," Jake said. "Maybe just on our own, is all. Not for the company."

"What do you do for the company?"

"Well." Jake shifted a bit, looking to Wolf and back before he spoke. "I guess you could say we look out for their best interests. Yeah, that's what we do."

Austin looked to Baldwin and Fenner, who had been listening to it all with smiles on their faces. They knew Austin had no choice but to go along with his uncles, no matter how he personally felt about it. In a land where a man's word carried a great deal of weight, anything they might say about him to others would do him a great deal of harm if they wanted to spoil his reputation. Being a stranger, Austin knew no one and could not defend himself in the manner he might if he had been in the country for a time. Austin knew the best thing he could hope for would be to get out from under the debt to his uncles as quickly and peaceably as possible.

"I didn't come out here to go into debt right away," Austin told his uncles. "But since you two have put me there to start with, I'll work for you until I'm out from under it. Which I intend to be by the time the snow comes."

Jake seemed delighted. "That's just fine," he said, clapping Austin loudly on the back. "You get square with us, you can stay or leave. How's that?"

"But I'll be square with you by winter?"

"Sure, sure," Jake said with a forced smile. "You'll likely have us paid back by then. Like we said, you got a job to do with Baldwin and Fenner, then maybe a little tradin' with the Blackfeet. You'll think this was the best thing ever happened to you before you're through. Wait and see. Maybe you won't want to quit us."

Austin knew a lot better than that. He had an eerie feeling about working for them as it was. The sooner he could part company with his uncles, the better. There was no question, they were trouble. He could only hope that what they wanted him to do wouldn't give him a worse reputation than just up and leaving.

"What is it you want me to do with Baldwin and Fenner?" Austin asked.

"That's the spirit!" Jake laughed. "What say we all go up to the fort and find ourselves a jug? The day's near passed, and you ain't even tasted the best part of this work."

Baldwin and Fenner yelled their agreement. Even Wolf, with his jaw as swollen as it was, seemed to forget his pain when he heard the word jug. Austin decided he would just have to forget about the answer to his question for now and go along with things as they were. He had no choice, and he knew things could get worse.

Chapter Two

―――

IT WAS HER father's pride, the fort-lodge they had called Madison. For Eagle's Shadow Woman, who had just seen the passing of her twenty-second winter, it was a source of comfort and happiness.

They had left their old fort-lodge in the land of the Shoshone, along the river called Stinkingwater, and had come north into this land, where the buffalo were plentiful. Shadow had left many fond memories behind: She had grown up along the Stinkingwater and would always love the narrow valley that rose high to rock peaks all around.

But this land was also beautiful, this place known to all who lived in these lands. This river, Madison, from which the fort-lodge had taken its name, joined with two others, called Jefferson and Gallatin. The three came together to form the waters of the Big Muddy, now called Missouri by the Long Knives.

This place, the Three Forks, was a major gathering area for the buffalo, who relished its lush, grassy bottoms and fresh water.

Shadow had not been unhappy to move to this place, for she understood that it was a necessity if her father was to compete for the trade of the Indian peoples in the Rocky Mountain region. "We've got to move on," she had remembered her father saying. "Nobody wants a beaver pelt for anything anymore, and there's none left anyway. If we want to stay with the tide, we've got to look to buffalo, and there's a lot more of them north."

This valley, the Three Forks, was also known as a battleground. Since it was a favorite place of the buffalo, the Indian peoples of the land came here to hunt just before the coming of the cold moons, so that they would have meat to carry them through the days of snow and cold. There came the Crow and Shoshone, from the east and south, and Shadow's people, the Salish, now commonly called Flathead, who came from the mountains to the west. But the Blackfoot Indian nation had claimed this valley as part of their hunting grounds for the passing of a great many winters. The other Indian tribes held that the Great One Above had blessed this valley with much game and that one single tribe could not claim it as their own. These words meant nothing to the Blackfeet, whose three divisions, the Siksika, the Kainah, and the Pikuni, were mighty and powerful warriors. Many died here with the coming of each fall hunt.

Shadow knew her family had nothing to fear by building their fort-lodge along these waters. Though her people, the Salish, and the Blackfeet were bitter enemies, there remained a strong bond between Shadow's mother and the war chief Walking Head, a powerful leader among the Siksika Blackfeet. Shadow had always been proud of her mother, from whom she had learned the ways of war. Her mother had herself been a woman warrior and had saved the great chief Walking Head's life during a fierce battle many winters past. He, in turn, had then helped Shadow's mother and father when they had become lost on the desert near the waters of the Snake, in a land which lay south. Shadow knew Walking Head would welcome them to this land, for the bond of friendship was still very strong.

Shadow hoped there would be no trouble in this new land, for she knew that continual fighting made it difficult for peace to grow within the heart. She often thought back on that time when she had first fought. That day she had saved the lives of her family, but it had marked her as a special person among all those in these lands. The Eagle Woman, she was now called; she who has the power of the great winged warrior of the skies. Since that first day she had fought at various times, to defend her family's possessions against those who would try to drive them from these lands. Her fame as a woman warrior spread far and wide, and there were those who said she had acquired even more power than her mother had had when she was a young woman. Her arrows flew straight to their mark, and her courage withstood any test an enemy might give it. There were many who feared her powers, even great warriors, for when a person, man or woman, is given special powers by the Above Ones, the spirits of the mountains and sky, then it was foolish to test their abilities.

Once during the Story-Telling Moon—November— a Salish elder watched the sun rise across a frost-

covered forest and came back to his village with these
words about the Eagle Woman:

The wind calls, the day has come.
Upon the clouds the warrior sails.
Her heart is strong;
She holds the skies.
And her call is heard throughout the land.

It was true, Eagle's Shadow Woman was someone
special. The spirits had so far been very good to her.
She had been blessed with great beauty and had been
given great strength of mind and body. She was the
envy of all the young Indian women of the mountains.
Stories of her courage had spread from village to village, and it was said only a very few came into this
life possessed of such stunning grace and power.

Besides those outside her family who looked upon
her with awe, there was her younger brother, Little
Bear. He was now approaching eleven winters of age,
and his eyes showed great pride in having a sister
such as Shadow. He worked hard at learning the skills
which his sister used so well. His days were spent
practicing with the bow which he considered a special
present, the same bow which his sister had used during her first fight to save the family from the evil
Long Knives and the Siksika warriors. He spent much
time stalking game as swiftly and silently as possible.
To him, Shadow was an unusual sister of great power
from whom he could learn and gain power himself.
No other boy his age could boast of such luck, and
he relished his situation more with each passing day.

Though many considered Shadow a spirit who had
come back to live again in this life, she had now
become a woman, and her feelings as such had de-

veloped fully. The one thing yet to come into her life
was a deep love of the heart, a love for a man with
whom she could unite and live as his wife. She had
heard the songs of many a young man's flute and had
smelled the fragrance of many a love charm, but none
of the smells or songs had ever won her heart. Three
winters past she had met a young Salish warrior with
whom she had spent much time. She had learned
much about the ways of a man from him and had
come to know the intimate closeness of a man and
woman. But a little voice inside had told her that this
warrior was not to have her, for she was to meet another, farther on in time. It was a relief to her; for she
had come to realize that her feelings for him had been
merely infatuation and that he did not really love her
but wished to have her for the glory and honor that
he would gain.

There were many questions, though, among those
who did not understand, for a woman of Shadow's
age should have gone to a warrior's lodge many winters before. Shadow's mother did not question her in
this matter, nor did she ever put any pressure on her
daughter to marry. She knew that Shadow needed a
special man: a man like her father, who was strong
and brave, yet understood the independence a woman
needed to be happy with herself. Shadow needed a
man who could show her love and respect as well as
strength and guidance. It was hard for a woman to
find such a man, for he owned all that he desired and
could win. He owned everything completely, and
those whom he owned obeyed his every command.

Though Shadow longed for the closeness she saw
her mother and father share, she did not worry. She
did not try to hasten the day when she would accept
a man as her own forever, for she had always known,

since the time when she had first fought against an enemy, that her spirit guardian, the majestic golden eagle, would take her to find this man when the time was right.

Austin sat with his uncles, Jake and Wolf, among a large group of men around a fire inside the fort. He ate and took his turn on a jug that was being passed around and listened to stories the men were telling. The majority of the stories were about the early days of the fur trade, of men like Jim Bridger and Tom Fitzpatrick, of Hugh Glass and John Colter, whose run from the Blackfeet was a feat that would be forever etched in time. They told of fights in those days with the Blackfeet and the Crees, the Assiniboin and Gros Ventres. The big bears called grizzlies were everywhere then, and the encounters were many. Often men were killed or torn and crippled for life.

"Them days is gone forever," one of the older men said sadly. "The mountains is spoilt and that can't change." He looked directly at Austin while he finished. "There's newbloods aplenty, and they don't know Blackfoot sign from Crow. Seems like there'll be nothin' left afore long."

"I came out here to be free and enjoy this land," Austin told the old trapper. "Just like you did. When you first came, maybe there was somebody out here then that felt the same way about you."

The evening wore on, and the light from fires inside the fort walls showed the sudden expressions on the faces of the men as one of the sentries called, "Blackfeet ridin' in!"

"Ever seen Blackfeet?" Jake asked Austin.

"There were a few in St. Louis," Austin answered as they walked outside the fort with the other men to watch the Indians ride in. "But they sure weren't dressed like these."

"They heard your boat was comin' upriver," Jake said. "They've been camped this side of the Great Falls for over a week. Looks like they brought plenty of furs for tradin' and such."

A large assembly of Blackfoot warriors, together with a good number of women and children, made their way toward the fort. Major Culbertson walked out from the group of men and extended his hand in the sign of greeting and peace. The Indians stopped, and a warrior at the front of the group moved his horse forward a few steps and raised his hand in recognition.

"It's Walking Head," Jake told Austin. "Look at him close, boy. He's—"

"Austin! My name is Austin. Remember?"

"Well, take heed of what I say. Walking Head is the most powerful war chief in the entire country around here. Every Blackfoot in these parts thinks he's Gawd A'mighty."

Austin studied the famous war chief of the Siksika Blackfeet. He appeared to be in middle age and was no doubt at the height of his power and authority. He wore a bearskin headdress, to which the head of a great horned owl had been attached, its beak open and the empty eye sockets in the skull wide and glaring. Attached to the back of the headdress was a group of eagle feathers, notched, trimmed, and painted in various ways to signify the many victories he had attained and the glory and honor that had been bestowed upon him. His elkskin war shirt was painted with many red, black, and yellow designs, as were his leggings. His war shield and lance were trimmed with ermine tails, which stood out white against his clothing. His face was solemn and lined with a thousand deep creases.

"He must be some leader," Jake said. "There's a whole bunch of Piegans and Bloods with him and his people."

"Who are those two on either side of him?" Austin asked.

"His twin sons. The one on his right, with just the one feather and the simple look on his face, is Standing Elk. He wouldn't hurt a fly. Too feebleminded. The other one, the mean one, is Badger. Now, that one's a different story."

Badger, whose eyes were hard, was dressed in a war shirt similar to his father's but lacking as many designs. His hair was adorned with a number of feathers, signifying he had become a respected warrior and had gained many honors in battle. He had been studying the crowd of trappers that had come out of the fort to watch, and his eyes settled on Austin.

"He sees somethin' he wants," Jake told Austin. "Most likely that rifle of yours. You'd better count on him lookin' you up later. It appears to me like he wants that rifle bad." He laughed.

Austin did not find it as humorous as Jake. "If he comes to see me," Austin said to his uncle, "then I'll just send him on to you. I'll tell him that you have many horses which you wish to give him, just because you are his friend. Then, when you can't come up with the horses, I'll laugh at you."

Jake quit laughing and glared at Austin.

"I know more about these Indians out here than you give me credit for," Austin said.

Before and during his trip up the river from St. Louis, Austin had made it a point to learn as much as he could about the Indians of the Rocky Mountain

region. He had come to St. Louis well before spring,
knowing many of the trappers and traders who had
quit the mountains now spent their time around the
riverfront and in the many saloons and grog shops
that populated the town. The extra time had been
more than worth the effort, for he saw many Indians
as well as frontiersmen and studied their ways and
the way they communicated. He had found an old
trapper whose joints were too stiff to ever again sleep
on the ground and supplied him with rum and food
in return for detailed lessons on sign language and its
use. The making of sign with the hands was the most
widely adapted form of communication on the fron-
tier, and it bridged all language barriers among the
native tribes. By the end of the two weeks, Austin
was convinced that this was the most important in-
vestment of time and money he had ever made.

Sign language was only one of the many things
learned by Austin from the old trapper. Just being in
the old man's presence was an education that would
have taken years for him to learn on his own. The
endless stories, detailed in character and location,
were vivid portraits of the lifestyle that was to be
encountered. Austin would sit, fascinated, for hours
on end while the old man's eyes would wander back
into the past, to the years spent as a young man on
the trails that threaded the mountains and plains. He
knew all the tribes, their customs, the ones most
feared, and the ones considered to be allies. He took
Austin up and down the waterfront, showing him
robes and furs that had come in from the West, showing him the good from the bad. After three weeks with
the old trapper, Austin was even more aware of the
value experience made in a land where life and death
were always only a moment apart. The old trapper

had known more than one lifetime of adventure, and when Austin had boarded the steamer for the trip up-river, the old man had bid him a fond farewell.

Walking Head and his twin sons got down from their horses and sat in a circle with Major Culbertson and some of the other men from the fort. They smoked the pipe of peace and began talking of trade while the women unloaded packs of furs from various animals and buffalo robes from the backs of the horses.

"It's bound to be a good night for tradin'," Jake told Austin, his eyes wide as he looked at all the valuable furs and robes. "I just wish we was gettin' all that fur instead of Culbertson."

Austin looked at his uncle. Since Wolf had gone off elsewhere to try to bargain with one of the Indian women, Jake was careful not to say anything that might make Austin mad. He could not understand the strange look Austin was now giving him.

"Do you work for Culbertson or against him?" Austin asked.

Jake frowned. "What's so bad about wantin' to be rich?"

Darkness soon fell and fires sprang up all over out-side the fort. It had become policy not to trade within the fort walls, so many of the trade items were brought, a few at a time, for Walking Head and his sons to inspect. When the trade talk went to buffalo robes, a quantity of whiskey was brought out, and a whoop went up from the Blackfeet.

The trading seemed to go well, and Austin watched carefully, learning how delicate an operation it really was, with both sides bartering heavily in favor of themselves. But soon the whiskey made the dealing easier, and many of the buffalo robes changed hands for nothing more than a jug of the burning water.

When the trading was concluded for the night, many of the Blackfeet gathered around the fires and began to gamble for the trade items they had just received. Jake had been with Austin the whole time, trying to make amends for what had happened earlier in the day. Austin listened but knew the words were hollow and contained no real truth. The longer he thought about it, the more he wished he had never even heard of Fort Benton and the fur trade on the upper Missouri River.

Then, from out of the shadows, Badger appeared. With him was his brother, Standing Elk, and two other young warriors. Badger's eyes appeared glazed and they settled on Austin's rifle.

"That is a good rifle you have," he made sign to Austin. "Since you are a brother to the Siksika Blackfoot people, maybe you will trade with me, so that I may have the rifle."

Austin made sign back. "This rifle will always belong to me. It is close to my heart, and I will never trade it, not for anything."

Badger's eyes narrowed, and he stared hard at Austin, who stared back, unflinching.

"It is not in his heart to trade," Jake then made sign to Badger. "But maybe he would care to gamble, maybe play the game of hands."

Badger's eyes lightened up. "That is what we will do. I will wager my bow and arrows and five buffalo robes."

Austin turned his eyes on Jake, who was trying to conceal a laugh. "One of these times," Austin told his uncle, "you're going to make me very angry. And then I will take your scalp. You can count on that."

Jake took a few steps backward, his face turning

white at the cold stare Austin was giving him. Finally he composed himself and said, "I just wanted to humor him some, that's all. We got to humor these Blackfeet, you know."

"Humor, nothing." Austin spat. "I'm getting so I don't care for you much at all."

"We play now," Badger told Austin.

Austin nodded and made sign back. "We play. But this is a very good rifle. You will have to wager your bow and arrows, plus seven buffalo robes. Not five."

Badger nodded agreeably, a confident smile parting his lips. "I will wager what you wish."

Austin and Badger took seats opposite one another near a fire. They sat cross-legged, three or four feet apart. From within his quiver of arrows, Badger produced two bones, each small enough to be grasped and covered entirely in the palm of the hand. To distinguish them, one had a deep notch carved in the middle.

There was confidence in Badger's eyes as they got ready to play. But Austin knew his own capabilities at the game and did not worry in the least. The hands game was ages old and handed down from generation to generation, passed from tribe to tribe, coast to coast, in various forms. During his stay in St. Louis before the trip upriver, Austin had seen it played on a daily basis. The old trapper had given him many valuable lessons.

Jake looked at Austin, puzzled. "I didn't even think you knew what this game was."

"There are a lot of things you don't know, Jake," Austin told his uncle. "Maybe you'll find out that trying to take advantage of me is going to get you into a lot of trouble one of these days. Maybe tonight."

"What do you mean?" Jake asked.

"When I beat him, he is going to be angry. I'll just tell him you knew how good I was and wanted to cheat him out of his bow and the buffalo robes." This time it was Austin who was smiling and Jake who was frowning.

Austin was blessed with a quickness of hand, which was what the game was all about. As he watched Badger place five small stones in a line in front of each of them, he knew that it would likely be a long game, but he would eventually have all of the stones in front of himself and would win the game. To do it he would have to use all his quickness. He would need to juggle the bones from hand to hand with skill so that Badger would not know which hand contained the notched bone. Each wrong guess by Badger would allow Austin to take one of the small stones from in front of the Blackfoot warrior and add it to his own string. Badger was showing a lot of confidence, and Austin knew he was also a good player.

Jake held a jug of whiskey out for the warriors. Standing Elk refused it, saying that the burning water made him do crazy things that he did not remember the next day. Badger quickly took the jug and drank a long swallow before giving it back to Jake. His eyes became more enlivened and wet, his confidence greater.

"You must not care a great deal for the fine rifle that you have," Badger made sign to Austin. "You do not know my abilities at the hand game. The rifle will soon be mine, and you will have to watch me carry it away." He laughed, his mouth wet from the whiskey.

Austin kept his composure and smiled back. "Your

bow is well made. It will last me many snows. And
the buffalo robes that I will also win will be the envy
of all who have come here to trade.''

Badger nodded, his smile widening. ''I will even
let you have the bones first. Let the game begin.''

Chapter Three

AUSTIN RETURNED BADGER'S broad smile of confidence. Instead of taking the bones from him, he pointed to the bow and quiver of arrows resting on the ground.

"You will soon have to make a new bow," he said. "It would be only fair if I let you juggle the bones first."

Badger eagerly began to juggle the bones from hand to hand. "Whose rifle am I about to win?" he asked.

Austin slowly pronounced his name in English for Badger. After fumbling with the word for a short time, Badger set the bones down and made sign. "I cannot speak the Long Knife tongue, and I cannot say your Long Knife name. But you look like your name should be Green Eyes. So I will call you Green Eyes. I am called Badger."

Austin nodded and watched as Badger again picked up the bones and began to juggle them and move them from hand to hand. Austin did not bother to watch his quick hands but instead looked into his eyes. Finally Badger held his hands out for Austin to guess. With a little smile, Austin pointed to Badger's right hand.

Badger's eyes widened, the smile gone. He opened his hand to reveal the notched bone. Then the smile reappeared, and he said, "The green-eyed Long Knife makes a lucky guess. Let us now see how quick your hands are."

Austin took the two bones from Badger and began to juggle them, first in the air in front of him, as Badger had done, and then to one side and then another. The crowd began to murmur and then rave in astonishment as Austin tossed the bones over his back and caught them before placing his two clenched fists in front of Badger. Without looking at either of his hands, Austin then fixed his gaze on the Blackfoot warrior.

Badger blinked in astonishment. He looked from Austin's face to his closed fists and back for a time before finally choosing the left hand.

Austin opened his fist, revealing the cut bone. Badger's eyes again widened, but he quickly smiled and said, "You are indeed quick, Green Eyes, but it is hard to fool Badger."

"Yes." Austin laughed. "Perhaps it was you who was lucky that time. But as the night goes on, we shall see who has the quicker hand. Luck is never victorious over skill."

The game went on for a long time, each taking stones but losing them again when the other guessed correctly. By now all had heard of the young Long

Knife with the green eyes who was giving Badger a hard game, and onlookers pressed to watch. Late in the night, after more whiskey, Badger finally watched his last stone go over to Austin. The smile had long since left his face, and his eyes now became hard.

"I have been beaten only once before," he told Austin. "I was beaten by one of my own people. I do not like being beaten by a Long Knife."

"You would have gladly taken my rifle," Austin told him. "And you did not care then that it belonged to a Long Knife. You should have considered that your bow might belong to a Long Knife."

Badger threw his bow at Austin and quickly got up from his seat. "Maybe you have the luck this night, Green Eyes," he said. "But your luck will not always be good."

The crowd of onlookers parted for Badger as he pushed his way toward his own family lodge. His twin brother, Standing Elk, then made sign to Austin: "It is only that he is angry for losing. The bow you have won is special to him, and he knows it would not be an honorable thing to refuse you, not after you have won the game of hands."

Austin studied the bow. It was well made, of elk horn spliced and glued together, then wrapped tightly with otter fur, to give each arrow that was shot a swift send-off.

"This is a fine weapon, and I will care for it well," Austin made sign to Standing Elk. "Perhaps another day will come when your brother and I can again play the game of hands. Maybe that day his luck will be good, and he will again have his bow."

Standing Elk nodded. "That would be good. Maybe you can come north soon, to where we will have our celebration at the end of the warm moons.

It will be at the foot of the Going-to-the-Sun Mountain. Then you can again play the hands game with my brother, Badger. Maybe we can even talk of trade.''

Before Austin could answer, Jake quickly made sign to Standing Elk. ''He cannot go to the Going-to-the-Sun Mountain. He works for us and will be traveling south, not north.'' Wolf had again come over and Jake pointed to him. ''The green-eyed one, here, is family relation to us.''

Austin exploded. ''When are you going to learn that you and Wolf have got only a short time to tell me what to do? You talk like I'll be answering to you for the rest of my life.''

''I didn't mean it that way,'' Jake stuttered.

''Then why don't you keep your mouth closed and let me talk for myself?'' Austin was glaring coldly at Jake, who looked up to Wolf for help. Wolf grunted and walked away again.

Standing Elk watched while Austin made sign to him, indicating that he would like to go to their camp at the foot of Going-to-the-Sun Mountain sometime after he had returned from his trip to the south.

Standing Elk then made sign. ''Will Green Eyes go south to the new fort-lodge called Madison? Do you intend to visit the fort-lodge just built by the friends of my father and our family?''

Austin looked to Jake, who had a surprised expression on his face. Jake quickly made sign to Standing Elk. ''Maybe he will visit the new fort-lodge, maybe not.''

Standing Elk nodded and rose to his feet. ''I will go to another fire and see if I have better luck than my brother at the game of hands this night.'' He looked at Austin directly when he added, ''I hope you can come to our village at the foot of Going-to-the-Sun Mountain. There will be dancing and much feasting.''

Austin rose to bid good-bye to the friendlier of the two brothers. ''I am glad that I have met Standing Elk and his brother, Badger, this night. Tell your brother, Badger, that I understand the feeling he has about loosing his fine bow. I would have felt the same had I lost my rifle. And I will try to come to your village soon.''

Standing Elk nodded and left to find his brother. Austin turned back to Jake and asked, ''What is all this about me going south? And does this new fort that Standing Elk spoke of have anything to do with my trip?''

''I'd say you'd best get some rest,'' Jake told Austin. He was visibly irritated at the discussion about Austin's work that had occurred in front of Standing Elk. ''You've got a lot of things you've got to get done before you can go to a Blackfoot festival.''

''Maybe we should understand what and how much work I'm obligated to right now,'' Austin said flatly. ''It seems to me that things have been altogether too vague up to this point.''

''Vague?''

''What am I supposed to do? What kind of work? Where? What's all this about another fort south of here?''

''Let's find Wolf,'' Jake suggested. ''We can all talk and then—''

''To hell with Wolf!'' Austin blurted. ''I know it's you who makes the final decisions on things. And you can't use him to scare me, you already know that.''

''I didn't mean that.''

''The hell you didn't,'' Austin went on. He took

his uncle by the shoulders, set him down beside the fire, and took a seat next to him. "Now you and I are going to arrive at some understandings, right here and now. Is that clear to you?"

Jake's eyes narrowed, but he saw that Austin was beginning to get mad, and he knew what that could bring on. Finally he settled himself and began to think in a more diplomatic fashion.

"Maybe we ain't been fair with you," he said to Austin. "Maybe it's time you knew what you was supposed to do."

"That sounds a little better," Austin said. "Earlier this afternoon I asked you what I would be doing with Baldwin and Fenner. You pretended you didn't even hear me and talked everybody into getting drunk. Now would be a good time to let me know the answer to my question."

"It figures in with that new fort down on the Madison, south of here," Jake confessed. "A man named Jim Ayers came up from the Stinkingwater, Shoshone country, and took it upon himself to build a fort right square in the middle of company territory. We aim to go down and pay him a visit. Ask him real polite-like to leave the country."

"And you want me in on this," Austin said. "Somebody I don't even know; somebody I've never even seen nor heard of. You want me to cause trouble for you, so you don't have to do it."

"It ain't that way at all," Jake said. "You see, Ayers killed our big brother, Ed, some years back down on the desert in the Snake River country. He knows me and Wolf are up here. We'd lose our hair sure as hell if we tried to ride up to that fort. His woman, named Whisper on the Water, killed a lot of Blackfeet in her day. But now they're friends with

Walking Head and his family, like Standing Elk just said, and the Blackfeet ain't about to drive them out. So we have to.''

"You mean I have to."

"You and Baldwin and Fenner."

"I thought you said we were just going to ask them to leave. Now you're saying we're going to get rid of them. I'm not going to kill anybody for you. I don't care what you think you have over on me."

Jake gritted his teeth. "Nobody said nothin' about killin'. Besides, you ain't goin' to tell me what's what. And if you don't think so, I'll just bring Culbertson over here to let you know what he thinks of you winnin' that bow from Badger. Word is out he's hot under the collar about it. Not good for tradin', you know.''

"There are other men who work for the company who've won things from warriors here tonight."

"Maybe. But not from Badger. He's strong medicine among these Blackfeet, and he's the son of a great war chief, Walking Head. You could have picked on anybody else and not had any trouble at all.''

"He picked on me," Austin protested angrily. "He wanted my rifle. And you thought it was all so funny."

"You'd best get some rest," Jake said. "The sun comes up early these days, and you got a job to do."

"What do I have to do?" Austin persisted.

"Baldwin will tell you when the time comes," Jake snapped. "Do I have to make trouble for you, or are you gonna listen to me?"

Austin looked around to see the Indians had begun to go to their lodges, while the men from the fort were also quitting their drinking and gambling for the night. There was little use in arguing with Jake anymore about the work they wanted him to do. Austin had committed himself to them by just getting off the boat, and there was no doubt that Badger had caused a stir among his people by having lost his bow. The smartest thing he could do now was try and rest. He would have plenty of time to sort things out better before he left with Baldwin and Fenner.

Without speaking to Jake again, Austin got up and went back inside the fort walls. He unrolled his pack and made himself as comfortable as he could on the ground near one of the stockade walls. Soon many of the men were laughing and drinking around fires within the fort walls, his two uncles among them. Austin was by now too physically and mentally tired to care what was going on around him. He felt despondent at being caged in by his two uncles and concerned about the mission he was now obligated to embark upon with Baldwin and Fenner. But for now sleep was something he sorely needed, and it came quickly.

He knew not when during the night, nor how it happened—Austin was to remember little of what occurred—but his sleep was suddenly a mass of pain and confusion as he fought to awaken. He heard a voice, hazy in his mind, saying, "Don't hit him again, you blamed fool! We ain't out to kill him!" After that his struggle to come to his knees was unsuccessful, and he blacked out.

Austin's next memory was the morning sun blinding his eyes after the feel of cold water on his face. He rose to a sitting position, trying to clear his head, while workers at the fort pressed around to see what had happened. He then heard Culbertson's voice, yelling at the men to get busy with their day's work.

Kneeling next to him was the fort doctor, who was now peering into his eyes.

"How did this happen?" he asked.

"Don't know," Austin answered.

"Do you feel sick to your stomach?"

"Yes."

"By Gawd you got whupped one, didn't you?"

Austin turned from the doctor to see the face of his uncle, Jake, as he tried to appear concerned over Austin's condition. Jake was trying to keep from laughing.

"That damned Badger must have climbed the walls to get at you. He must have wanted his bow back real bad."

Austin struggled to his feet.

"I'll need to have you come with me," the doctor told Austin.

"Maybe later," Austin said. "Leave me for a minute."

Though the pain in his head was like a continuous, pulsating drum, Austin began to gather up his belongings, which were scattered all over. His pack had been emptied, and many of his belongings were missing. He fought to control his anger, for it only served to increase the pain in his head.

Jake was following him. "I told you Badger would get owly about losin' to you."

"Why the hell should I think it was Badger?" Austin said coldly, glaring at his uncle. He held up his Kentucky rifle, which was still leaning against the fort wall where he had left it. "Badger wanted this rifle. Everything else is gone, but not the rifle."

"Well," Jake said, fidgeting around, "you know that Injuns can't work them rifles too good. Doubt if he had any use for it."

"What about my money?" Austin asked. "What use would Badger have for that? And how would he even know I had any?"

Jake shrugged. "Guess you'll have to find him and ask him. I heard they left. Goin' south to the new fort on the Madison is what I heard."

Austin had to fight from losing consciousness. The doctor came over and steadied him, then made him lie down on the ground while he summoned help and a stretcher.

"You've got to slow down for at least a few days," the doctor said. "You've no doubt sustained a concussion. How severe I cannot say. But you will be in the infirmary for a time."

"What? He's got work to do!" Jake told the doctor angrily.

"That will have to wait, I'm afraid," the doctor said. "He needs rest."

"He works for me, not you," Jake protested. "Now I say he comes with me."

The doctor took a deep breath as two men arrived with a stretcher. "I'll just call Major Culbertson," the doctor said. "I'm sure he'll be glad to hear that you are once again in the middle of trouble."

Jake huffed to himself for a short time before turning and leaving. Austin felt himself being lifted onto the stretcher and then off onto an uncomfortable wooden bed covered with buffalo robes.

Culbertson came into the room and conversed with the doctor for a short time, most of which Austin could not hear. But as Culbertson left, he could hear him say, "I have more trouble around here when those two Beelers show up than at any other time."

"I hope you aren't in a hurry to be somewhere," the doctor said to him as he came over with a large, deep bowl of steaming liquid. "I'm afraid I'll have to watch you for a few days, anyway. Drink this, all of it."

Austin sat up and took the bowl. It was warm and had a strong but slightly sweet taste to it.

"Willow bark tea," the doctor said. "It should ease the pain in your head considerably."

"Something you brought from back East?" Austin asked, trying to break a grin.

The doctor chuckled. "Some of the plants these Indians out here use have got our remedies beat seven ways from Sunday. Guess we could take a lesson or two."

Austin settled back and rested, knowing his rifle and those belongings he didn't lose were safe under the bed. Though his head had taken a bad blow and he would have to endure pain for a time, there was some consolation in the fact that he would not have to put up with his two uncles for a time. But there remained for him the challenge of getting out from under his debt to them. He was fully aware now that they expected him to destroy a fort and possibly kill for them. He realized he was indebted to them and that he would have to work it off in some way. But there were certain limits to how far he would go.

The sun had crossed far toward the western horizon when Little Bear rode into the fort to anxiously announce the coming of a large group of Siksika Blackfeet.

"It is your good friend, Walking Head," Little Bear said to his parents while Shadow listened. "And he brings with him the entire War Dancers band to visit and trade with us."

Shadow followed her mother and father out to welcome Walking Head and the others. Walking Head was dressed in his finest attire and was flanked by his twin sons, Badger and Standing Elk.

Shadow's father welcomed them in their native tongue, as he as well as Whisper and Shadow had all learned the Blackfeet language. "Peace to my good friend, Walking Head, of the War Dancers band of Siksika Blackfeet peoples. It has been many snows since we last ate together and smoked the pipe of peace. Your sons have become men, and I am sure that you are proud, as I am of my daughter and my son. Come inside and be our guests."

Fires were built both inside and outside the fort walls. The best cuts of buffalo, elk, deer, and antelope were placed for roasting and boiling with stews and broth. The pipe of peace was lit by Shadow's father and passed to Walking Head, his sons, and then to other higher members of the band who had joined with Walking Head to welcome the Long Knife, Jim Ayers, and his family to the valley of the Three Forks and to the lands of the Blackfoot peoples.

"I wish that I had more things to give you as presents," Shadow's father said as he passed out a collection of trade knives, some tobacco, some vermilion, and assorted beads of various sizes and colors. "But I will have more items to trade after the cold moons, when I can take robes and furs to the big Long Knife village called St. Louis, far to the east."

"We wish to see our good friends do well in this land," Walking Head said. "And to show that we are brothers always, I have brought many fine robes to give you as presents." He ordered horses brought forward that were heavily laden with many robes and furs of various kinds. "These will help you to get the trade goods you wish for so that you can always be in these lands and live in your fort-lodge.''

"I am grateful to my good friend," Shadow's father told Walking Head. "The day will come when I can repay you well."

"That I am not concerned about," Walking Head said. "But to the north, at the fort-lodge called Benton, there is much talk of you and this place. It is said that there are those who do not wish for you to trade with me and my people."

"Did you see two men there called Beeler?" Shadow's father asked. "One has hair on his face that is always scraggly, and the other is very big and has lost one eye to a knife. His face has a long scar upon it."

Here all eyes went to Shadow. Even during the talking, her striking beauty had held the eyes of both Badger and Standing Elk. But now, at the mention of the two Beelers, it was well known that Shadow and her father knew these two men, for she had killed other Long Knives and Piegan warriors as well that day many snows past. Shadow could remember their faces well, for they had both stared at her long and hard that day when she had come out of the forest and had proclaimed herself the Eagle Woman.

"Maybe your daughter, Eagle's Shadow Woman, should have finished those two with the others that day when she fought so bravely," Walking Head said. "Now I fear there will be trouble for you."

"We have had trouble before," Shadow's father said. "Maybe the two of them will not want to bother with trying against a fort as well built as this one."

"There is another with them now," Walking Head said, "though he does not seem to be of their kind. He does not seem to be evil and care only for himself. He gambles well and won a bow from Badger in the game of hands. He is very good at the game of hands and is also very strong. It is said that he beat the large one-eyed Long Knife in fighting hand to hand, without weapons. It is said that he hurt One Eye's jaw. My sons named him Green Eyes.''

The meat and stews were now cooked, and Shadow helped her mother as the two of them gathered with the Siksika women to feed the men. The talk went back to future trade relations and the upcoming Blackfoot tribal reunion at the foot of Going-to-the-Sun Mountain. It was to be a big event, with games and dancing and a celebration of life. The location had been carefully chosen by Walking Head and other elders among the Blackfoot nation. The area around Going-to-the-Sun Mountain was sacred, and it was some of the most beautiful country in all of the Rocky Mountains.

''It would make my heart glad if you and your family would come and be with us,'' Walking Head told Shadow's father. ''It will be a fun time for all.''

''We will come to the festival,'' Shadow's father said. ''My heart is glad that you wish us to come. You are truly a good friend.''

They began to eat, with each enjoying the fine meal provided by Shadow and her mother, with help from the Siksika women. Soon Little Bear had gathered with some boys his own age, and they began contests to see who could best shoot with his bow and arrows. Everyone seemed contented and happy. Then Badger spoke up.

''Do you have any of the burning water?'' he asked Shadow's father. ''I would like to have some of the burning water.''

Shadow's father thought for a moment. ''I usually don't bring the whiskey out during trading. What I have on hand is really not that good and—''

"I want the burning water!" Badger broke in. "Are you not a brother of the Siksika Blackfeet? Do you wish to deny me your hospitality?"

Shadow's father looked to Walking Head, astounded at what he had just heard. Walking Head said, "My son, Badger, is now a grown man and must speak for himself. He often says things that bring dishonor upon himself and his family, but his words are his own. You do not have to give him the burning water if you do not wish to. If you do wish to, that is your decision. Whatever you decide, you will always be my friend."

Shadow bent down to hear her father, who spoke to her in English. "Bring a jug from the storehouse. But dump half of it out, store and replace it with water."

On her way to the storehouse, Shadow thought on all that she had seen and heard already this night. The talk of the two Long Knives named Beeler and the new one with the green eyes began to trouble her greatly. There was no doubt that they meant harm to her family and the fort. She would need to find out more about it. Deciding how to find out was another thing that troubled her. As a child growing up, she remembered Badger and Standing Elk as two polite boys who were always at their father's side and always good to be around. It seemed things had changed, at least with Badger. Perhaps she could talk to Standing Elk, whom she remembered as being somewhat shy and usually quiet and reserved. Badger had always been aggressive but never intolerable, as he had now become. Her best chance was to talk with Standing Elk when she got the chance. She would need to find out all she could about the Beelers.

Shadow, after diluting its contents with water by half, brought the jug to Badger, who immediately grabbed it from her hands and brought it to his lips. He tilted it high, sucking loudly, pouring out more than he could take at one time. Rivulets of whiskey ran from the corners of his mouth, staining the fresh paint on his deerskin shirt. Walking Head continued to talk in sign with Shadow's father, his face showing visible anger at his son's behavior.

When night fell, fires were built and drummers began to assemble at the request of a number who wished to dance. It was structured so that singles could dance, or couples could come together. Badger took the jug with him and began to dance as a single, drinking when he felt like it. Soon he tired of dancing by himself and approached, one at a time, a few young women who either left the group at his approach or turned their backs and danced away. After a time Badger left in anger and went into the darkness with his jug.

Shadow found Standing Elk near one of the fires, eating chopped buffalo tongue from a clay bowl.

"It has been many winters since we last saw one another," Shadow made sign to him. "My family is honored that your family has brought your people so far to welcome us to these lands and to trade with us."

Standing Elk rose to his feet and smiled. "I am honored that the beautiful Eagle's Shadow Woman greets me. And it is good to see you and your family once again. My father always speaks with the greatest respect for your father and mother." He waited until she was seated before reseating himself.

"I wish to know more about the Long Knives at the fort-lodge called Benton, the evil ones named

Beeler,'' Shadow said. ''And the new one with the green eyes that is now with them. The one your father spoke of. Did you see or speak with any of them?''

Standing Elk nodded. ''I was there when the green-eyed one played the game of hands with Badger and won his bow from him. Though I had seen the other two before, the smaller one and the large one, I had never before seen the green-eyed one. It is said he came up the river on the boat that carried the many things that we traded for. It is hard for me to know about him. As my father said, he did not seem to be evil. But he is very good at the game of hands, and there were marks on his face from when he fought the large One Eye. It seems to me that he is very strong and very smart. If he is now with them and they wish to destroy your father's fort-lodge, then it will be hard to stop them.''

''How did Badger feel when the green-eyed one beat him at the game of hands and won his good bow?''

''At first he could not believe it. But he wanted the fancy rifle that belonged to Green Eyes. Now he has neither the rifle nor his bow.''

Shadow thought for a time. It seemed that maybe the Beelers had brought this new Long Knife up the river to help them fight her father. If this was so, they would surely be planning a strike as soon as possible.

''Did either of the Beelers or the green-eyed one speak of coming to this fort-lodge?'' Shadow asked Standing Elk.

Standing Elk nodded. ''The small one was with Green Eyes when Badger lost the game of hands. They spoke of traveling south, and the small one became angry with Green Eyes for some reason that I do not know. But then I left them, and when we left the next morning, they were not among the men from the fort-lodge called Benton who watched us break camp. So I do not know what they will do now.''

This gave Shadow more to think. Standing Elk had been very helpful, and it was good that he had seen, close up, this new Long Knife they had named Green Eyes and had even talked with him. It was good to know that they had more power. She knew now that they would be very difficult to fight.

"Do you wish for some of the burning water that Badger asked for?" Shadow said to Standing Elk.

"No," Standing Elk answered quickly. "I have vowed never to drink the burning water again. It makes me think with a strange mind. There have been times when I narrowly escaped death because of drink I had taken. I wish for those times no more."

Shadow nodded. She said nothing but could see in Standing Elk's eyes that he wished his brother, Badger, shared his feelings about the burning water.

"It is certain that you have noticed that my twin brother, Badger, is not the same person you knew when we were children many winters past. My heart is sad because of this. And it is all because of the burning water. He began drinking it as a very young man, and it has done something to him. Now I fear he will never change. Not in the life we have in this world."

"I am sorry," Shadow said. "I knew him as a fine, strong young man who was thought of highly. I will always hope that some day he can again gain honor among your people."

Shadow talked with Standing Elk little after that, for he seemed to lose the spark he had had earlier in the discussion. His love and concern for his twin brother were evident, and he felt hopeless in the face of a problem for which there was no solution.

Walking Head left with his family and the War Dancers band of Siksika Blackfeet after two more suns. Shadow spent the entire time thinking about what she had heard from Standing Elk concerning the Long Knives from the fort-lodge called Benton. She gained more knowledge about the trails that were taken when traveling to those lands which lay north. She found out that the trail toward the fort-lodge called Benton followed the waters of the Missouri closely and that there were places where the river had cut through the mountains. It was a place where enemy tribes would often ambush one another, as the forest was dense in this area. It gave Shadow an idea: Before she could think of traveling to the Blackfoot summer festival with her family, she would have to stop worrying about losing their fort-lodge to the evil Long Knives named Beeler. If the one called Green Eyes was now with them, they might have already left to come down to the Three Forks. Shadow would need to stop them, and she would need to hurry.

Chapter Four

AUSTIN STOOD IN the doorway of the infirmary, facing the early morning sun, while his two uncles spoke to him in anger.

"You've been in there on your back lollygaggin' around for near a week," Jake said gruffly. "That's wasted time. Now you'd best get set for the trip with Baldwin and Fenner."

Wolf added, "Walking Head and his band went down there to get things goin' with Ayers. If it hadn't been for that damned doctor, maybe you three would have beat them down there. Then we wouldn't have had to worry about any fort or Ayers, either one, for them to visit."

"Maybe you two should have thought twice about knocking me on the head and robbing me," Austin said. His head was much better, and though it certainly would be foolish, he wasn't about to take any abuse from his uncles now. "You should have known I would be laid up for a time."

"You got no call accusin' us," Jake said hotly. "You got no proof we did anything."

Austin knew arguing was not going to get him out of going south with Baldwin and Fenner. He had made up his mind he would carry this mission out but avoid, at all costs, any killing he might be expected to do. It had occurred to him many times that Baldwin and Fenner would likely have him do the main part of the work, thereby keeping themselves and his two uncles clear of any accusations by anybody who might be concerned about the new fort called Madison. Austin was determined not to let this happen.

"We got you a horse and some grub packed," Jake said to Austin, pointing to the entrance of the fort. "Baldwin and Fenner are waitin' for you."

Austin turned and went back inside the infirmary.

"Just what the hell do you think you're doin'?" Wolf roared from outside.

Austin came back to the doorway, his head beginning to hurt some from anger he was again building inside himself. One spark, he knew, and he would again be rolling in the dirt with Wolf.

"I intend to take all my things with me," he stated. "Now, I'm going back in here and get them."

"You can't ride with all that stuff," Jake said. "There ain't no call to try and pack that much."

"I'm not leaving it here," Austin said emphatically. "If either one of you don't like it, you can try and stop me. How does that sound?" His eyes were like two green embers as he looked from Jake to Wolf and back.

Wolf snorted and turned away while Jake got a

crooked smile on his face and said, ''Right perky today, ain't you? Good. Fort Madison ought to burn real
good when you get down there.''

''Then I'm through with the both of you,'' Austin
said. ''That was our agreement.''

Jake nodded and pointed into the room behind Austin. ''Just get to fetchin' your things and get on that
horse yonder. The sun's high already, and you ain't
got nowhere yet.''

Austin collected his things and went to the fort's
entrance, where Baldwin and Fenner sat their horses,
impatience evident on their faces. Austin took his
time, having little concern about the feelings of the
two men. If he was going to be used as a puppet, at
least he was going to make them pull some very tight
strings.

Shortly Austin climbed on the buckskin he had
been given to ride and followed Baldwin and Fenner
out across the flats, away from the fort and toward
the distant mountains. The trail followed an open
bench above the wide, twisting flow of the river. Ages
of use by buffalo, elk, and other larger game animals
had carved a deep, wide pathway through the heavy
sod. The bottom stretched out into rolling foothills
which, in turn, pushed up toward the distant mountains, their peaks glistening white through the deep
blue of the sky.

The first day stretched into the next, and Austin
made himself content enjoying the new land he was
just now learning about. A slight breeze, just enough
to cool the skin, brushed across the sweeping expanse
of wilderness, moving the mantled clusters of wildflowers into slow waves of crimson, blue, and white,
mixed with touches of pink and lavender. The air was
filled with their fragrance, and the valley ahead of

him, for as far as he could see, was alive with color.

They pushed onward toward the jagged, rising form of the mountains, across streams alive with wild ducks and geese, past roving herds of deer and antelope, seeing far in the distance to the east a vast herd of buffalo on the move northward to where the season's grass was yet ungrazed. They rode onward, past the ever-present expanse of the river, toward the place Austin knew only as Fort Madison, the unwanted new establishment owned by a mountain man named Jim Ayers and his family, a man his two uncles hated with all their being. Again Austin became aggravated at having been tricked into a mission he neither wanted nor cared to be a part of. If, perhaps, this man Jim Ayers was of the same breed as his uncles, then there would be no remorse in destroying this new Fort Madison. The fewer men in this country like his uncles, the better. But somehow Austin felt that Jim Ayers was likely a man of principles and integrity. To come in and establish a major fort for trading in the shadow of the American Fur Company was spitting in a giant's eye. Austin couldn't help admiring a man like that.

The sun was falling when they made their camp for the night at the mouth of a smaller river that emptied into the sprawling Missouri. The Dearborn, it was called, which pushed down from the endless forest to the west. They were now in the first stretches of the mountains, and their awesome beauty had captivated Austin. He only wished that he was traveling by himself; there was so much to stop and see. Earlier on he had once again become frustrated with his situation when they had come to a majestic landmark called the Great Falls, where the flow of the Missouri cascaded down over two sets of falls. Austin had stopped to watch a large flock of pelicans as they fished in the deep pools below the falls.

"Let's move, Wells!" Baldwin had shouted back at him. "We didn't come to bird-watch."

This second night provided him with little sleep, as had the first. The horror of the blow on the head was a recurring nightmare he knew he would not be rid of for some time to come. Though his head injury had come along quite well and his headaches were now minimal, his frustration, at times, became almost unbearable. He weighed the options from which he could choose: If he wanted no part of this, he would surely have to kill both Baldwin and Fenner, for they most certainly had orders to see that he went along with what he had been ordered to do. Though there was no telling what lay ahead, Austin finally decided the best choice would be to just wait and see what happened.

Austin felt a rough hand on his shoulder. It was Baldwin, and he spoke through a mouth full of pemmican in the predawn darkness.

"Get the hobbles off your horse. We're movin' out."

They were deep into the mountains within a short time. Austin held his head down to avoid the sweeping branches of pine trees as they made their way along a trail through the thick timber. He could hear the pounding of deer and elk as they left the trail for the cover of the trees. Here and there a squirrel chattered noisily, aggravated by their presence. Though the sun had by now began to climb into the sky, the forest was dark and shadowed.

They left the timber, holding close to the river. The sun climbed ever higher until it finally shone on high rock ledges on either side of the river. The Gates of the Mountains is what Austin heard Baldwin say this place was called. Above the rocks, echoing through the canyon, came the high scream of an eagle. Austin looked skyward, seeing the sweeping form of the big bird circling overhead. Ahead of him, Baldwin and Fenner began to sing a chorus of a lusty mountain song. The eagle continued to circle overhead, the piercing screams filling the cool mountain morning. Austin stopped his horse and looked skyward again, shading his eyes. That eagle sure is a pretty sight. *Real soon I'm going to be rid of these two and my uncles. Then I can begin to enjoy this country.*

Shadow remained motionless, hidden among downed timber and huckleberry along a trail near the Gates of the Mountains. She gripped her bow and arrows ever tighter as she began to hear and feel the hooves of horses somewhere back out of sight along the trail. Her enemy was coming. The time she had planned for so carefully was nearly upon her.

Overhead, the eagle continued her hunt, soaring across the sky in patterned, effortless circles, her sharp eyes scanning the meadows and openings below. Hearing the eagle's call, Shadow closed her eyes to gather strength and fitted an arrow to the string of her bow, fletched with feathers from the eagle, to send the shaft silently to its mark. These were most certainly the Long Knives she had been waiting for. Surprise would be hers this fine day, and her arrows would sing the song of death.

As she continued to wait for them to draw closer, Shadow fought to remain calm. She had chosen this mission on her own and had done so without the knowledge of her mother and father, who would surely be angry if they knew. She had counted over twenty winters, and yet they found it hard to see her as a woman, as a person now on her own. For this Shadow was happy, for no one could have more loving parents. But it was time they understood her decisions. And it was for them that she had decided to do this thing. After Walking Head's warning, they had slept uneasily during the time when the sun fell behind the mountains. Each night was now tension, waiting for the attack which would surely have to come against the fort her father had worked so hard to build and keep. This could not go on.

The Long Knives finally came into view. Three of them. And as they approached, Shadow could hear them singing. She did not want to rise up to see who they were, for it would surely give her away. There was little doubt it was the two evil Long Knives named Beeler and the green-eyed one who had just come into these lands.

The three Long Knives rode their horses along the trail until they were almost in front of her, singing and laughing. They had no notion of what was to come, no thought that they would meet death this fine day. They were yet a full sun's ride from her father's fort. Shadow had planned her mission carefully.

Screaming a Salish war cry, Shadow jumped from the brush along the trail and loosed an arrow into the chest of the lead rider. The Long Knife, his eyes wide and his mouth open, could only stare at the feathered shaft that had driven itself deep into his lung cavity. His horse bolted at Shadow's yelling and sudden appearance, and he fell sideways from its back, groaning loudly and spitting blood.

Shadow had quickly fitted another arrow and had released it with deadly accuracy before the remaining two could even begin to react. Unable to manage their horses, they were at her mercy, and Shadow watched the second iron-tipped shaft whiz under the arm and through the ribs of the second rider. His screams set off more panic in the horses, and the third Long Knife was bucked off, losing his Hawken in the fall.

Another arrow ready, Shadow let the terrified horses run past her. Planting her feet firmly, she made ready to again draw her bow against the third Long Knife.

But he was gone.

Shadow, suddenly realizing she was in grave danger standing unprotected in the open, crouched and lunged for the brush along the trail. At the instant she left her feet, she heard the report from the firestick and saw a puff of smoke rise from the trees opposite the trail. The ball made a buzz through the air where she had been only a slight moment before.

In the brush along the opposite side of the trail, Shadow could hear the third Long Knife cursing under his breath as he reloaded his long firestick. She thought of loosing an arrow but knew it would only be wasted because there was too much brush and thick cover that could deflect its flight. This Long Knife would be harder to kill, but she would succeed.

Shadow let out a sharp yell, then swiftly and without sound moved along the ground to another position, where she again hid herself and waited. The trick worked. No sooner had she left the old hiding place than there came another shot and the sound of the tiny lead ball popping through the leaves and low branches where she had just been. Shadow smiled to herself and waited.

But the Long Knife neither shot again nor did he move to give his position away. He knew the ways of battle. It seemed he had chosen to hide himself and gain the advantage instead of being hit by an arrow from her bow. He most likely had checked his long firestick to be sure it did not misfire, giving his position away, and waited a moment to shoot.

There was no sound from the brush on the other side of the trail. Only silence. The forest was still. The two Long Knives had ceased their wailing. They both lay motionless in their own blood on the grass, the leaves around them, her arrows sticking at angles from their bodies, their fingers frozen in death around the painted shafts.

Shadow now knew that these were not the Long Knives called Beeler, and it worried her. Neither of these men was big enough to be Wolf, nor were they missing an eye. But now she had killed them, and the third one wanted her life.

Shadow's eyes searched the brush in earnest, and she remained in her position of hiding. Still the Long Knife gave no indication of being there. Her eyes, trained to catch even the slightest twitch, saw no movement. But he was there. Her senses told her he had not run, he had not left but was there, waiting for her to move. This Long Knife was not foolish in any way. It bothered her.

The forest remained still, as if frozen in time. The eagle was gone, the birds and squirrels had long since stopped their sounds. The crickets felt unsafe. Yes, the Long Knife was still there, waiting to avenge the deaths of the other two.

Without moving her head, Shadow shifted her eyes to another position along the trail across from her. She had heard something loud and distinct. It had been a heavy sound; and as she stared at the spot from where the sound had come, she realized it had not been made by the Long Knife himself. No, it had not been the rustling whisper of branches and leaves as they move to the touch. Instead it had been dull and heavy, as if a rock had hit the ground.

She had been tricked! The Long Knife had thrown the rock to divert her eyes while he moved from his position. Shadow knew now that he was hunting her.

To her left, only a matter of steps away, a squirrel came out on the limb of a pine, keeping his body on the opposite side of the branch from something in the brush just below and to one side of him. He popped his head over the branch and looked down to a spot just to Shadow's right. With a jerk of his tail, the squirrel began to chatter in a rough, scolding tone.

In one motion, Shadow pulled her knife and leaped to the spot. The Long Knife was caught by surprise, and Shadow knocked the firestick from his hands. But he caught her hand as she thrust the knife toward his stomach. The squirrel barked in terror and scrambled high into the tree, weaving his way through the limbs and branches.

He rolled backwards with her, through the thick brush and out onto the trail, trying to flip her over him, refusing to let go of her hand. She screamed and struggled to twist her wrist from his grasp, to plunge the knife home. He also held her other hand, trying to keep her from scratching his face and pulling his hair. They slammed into trees, crashed through brush, rolled over fallen logs and branches. Finally he twisted her wrist just right, and the knife slipped from her hand.

In a surge of power, he swung her sideways and tried to force his weight down on top of her, fighting off her flailing, scratching hands and fists. She heard his grunts of amazement at her strength as she bucked him off time and again, bruising his ribs with her knees and adding to the welts and cuts around his mouth and along his face.

They continued to fight, their anger growing. Though he was much stronger, Shadow kept him from gaining full control. The thought of her family continuously sent surges of energy through her. She could not let her father's dreams be destroyed and their lives put in danger. This Long Knife would kill her before she let that happen.

"You will die, enemy dog!" she screamed. "You will never burn our fort. Never!"

The Long Knife tried to speak to Shadow, but her anger had taken her far past listening. She would stop only when this hated man had breathed himself empty in death. Or when she, herself, had lost all life.

Shadow began to tire, his strength wearing her down. He had paid many times over for coming to these lands. His face would show wounds for many suns to come. He would pay fully if only she could bring more strength to herself.

Their struggle took them back to where Shadow had lost her knife. It lay glistening where the sun's rays touched it on the forest floor. She reached for it, but he pinned her wrist to the ground. Then she felt the blade against her own throat and heard the words of warning from the Long Knife.

The Long Knife was bent over her, his hair tossled and tinged with blood. His lips and face were puffy and swollen, covered with cuts and scratches.

"I know you speak English," he said. "Now what do you mean by all this?"

"Dogs!" Shadow spoke without moving her head, forming the words through gritted teeth. "You only want to bring death to my family!"

Shadow continued to struggle for her freedom,

glaring up into his bloody face. He squinted down at
her through eyes a deep brownish green in color.
They would be attractive eyes, Shadow thought, at
any other time than this, and would likely be hard to
turn away from. She suddenly felt strange for her
thoughts about the one they called Green Eyes.

The Long Knife seemed to be looking at her
strangely, also. His eyes grew softer, the muscles in
his jaw eased from their tension. Shadow eased herself up a ways, to get her throat away from the knife
blade. He did not seem to care. Then she lashed out
again, the heel of her hand ramming hard into his
upper lip. He let out a whoosh of air. Shadow tried
to buck out from under him, but he caught her and
slammed her head back down. Again the knife was
at her throat, his eyes glaring. Shadow held her breath
as the blade pressed against her skin. A trickle of
blood ran down her neck.

"You're more wildcat than human," the Long
Knife said angrily. "It seems to me that you want to
put me under and be done with it. But I've got a few
things to say to you first."

With defiance and hatred tensing her every muscle,
Shadow said, "You are a fool if you do not kill me,
for it is in my heart to take your scalp back to our
fort-lodge along the waters called Madison, where I
would show it proudly to my father."

"Your father?" the Long Knife said. "A fort along
the Madison?"

Shadow closed her eyes, waiting for the pull of the
knife. But it did not come. Instead she felt the blade
lifting from her skin. She opened her eyes to see the
Long Knife with his own eyes closed and his hands
holding his head. With sudden swiftness, Shadow
pushed backward against his chest, putting him off

balance. She quickly twisted out from under him and grabbed the knife he had just dropped when she pushed him. She saw his green eyes grow large as she quickly jumped toward him. Now she would have the chance to kill this Long Knife before he could destroy her family's happiness.

Chapter Five

THE LONG KNIFE came to his feet, and Shadow raised the knife to strike. He stood before her as if to say that he had tried to speak to her, but she only wanted one of them to die, that she was a fool and would not listen. He was ready to try to block her attempt to drive the knife home, but his eyes showed not anger but frustration. Shadow held up and lowered the knife.

Shadow then watched as the Long Knife put his hands to both sides of his head and closed his eyes, as if he felt extreme pain. He staggered for a moment, as if he would soon fall to the ground, but he finally steadied himself and looked at Shadow.

"I guess I should have expected this," he said to Shadow. "I've about done all the fighting I can for one day. If I go on, I'll just kill myself. You might just as well do it. Use the knife if you want."

"You speak as though you are a coward!" Shadow spat at him. "You travel into these lands to try and sneak up on my father's fort. You would kill and steal when no one knows you are coming, but now you speak like a child."

"I said if I fight you anymore, I'll likely die anyway!"

Shadow looked at him for a time, then took a deep breath herself and placed her knife back in her belt. She shook her head at him.

"No. It is no longer in my heart to kill you. And I do not believe you wish to kill me, now. Something strange is in your eyes."

The Long Knife turned away, acting almost as if he wished she had decided to kill him. He looked at the two Long Knives who lay dead along the trail, then turned back to Shadow.

"Jim Ayers," he said, "is your father?"

Shadow nodded. "Yes. How do you know him?"

"Heard tell of him is all. From my uncles, Jake and Claude Beeler."

Shadow's eyes turned into a squint.

"It seems they and a party of Blackfeet came upon Jim Ayers's camp quite a few years back," Austin said in explanation. "But they got themselves shot full of arrows by some young girl." He was studying Shadow closely now, putting the story together. "Would that young girl have been you?"

"Are you a Beeler, also?" Shadow asked, avoiding his question.

"Austin Wells is my name," the Long Knife answered. "My ma was a Beeler before she married. I'm new in these parts, just out from Kentucky. Jake and Claude sent for me. They said they could put me to work out here, help me make good money in the hide business. I didn't set out to kill anybody. I was tricked into this. They set me up, that's all I can tell you.''

"Why didn't your two uncles come with you?" Shadow asked. "I thought it would be them who would come. I hoped it would be them. If they were now dead, I believe there could be peace at my father's fort-lodge.''

Shadow watched Austin while he wiped blood away from the corners of his mouth. After a moment he looked at her again and asked, ''Are you in a habit of fighting like this? I can't remember fighting too many men who gave me more trouble.''

"I'm fighting for my family,'' Shadow said. ''What did you hear about my father from your two uncles?''

"I've heard them talk about him. Seems your father killed their older brother, Ed, back when beaver was still good business.''

Anger returned to Shadow's voice. ''Your uncles tell lies. Their hearts are bad. Their brother met death at the hands of the Siksika, not my father. He died because he wished to take the lives of my mother and father, friends of Walking Head, the Siksika war chief who killed him. That is how he died, not by my father's hand.''

"But I heard that you are Salish,'' Austin told her. ''Your tribes hate one another. How could you be friends of the Blackfeet?''

"My mother once saved the life of Walking Head,'' Shadow explained, her hand pointing out over the mountains. ''It was far to the north, along the waters of the Big Muddy, the waters you Long Knives call Missouri. Walking Head possessed a deep love for my mother, but she loved my father, the Long

Knife Jim Ayers, and would have no other for a husband. Walking Head would not accept this and took my mother to his village against her will. To show her heart was not bad, she saved his life during a battle with the Crees, driving them away in fear. She was very powerful then. For this Walking Head was grateful. From that day on, he has respected my mother very much, and they have been close friends."

"Your mother fought in battle?" Austin asked.

"Many times. When she was young, she was called the Spirit Woman. She was known throughout these lands as a fearless woman warrior. But those days are gone, and she wishes only peace for our family. Now that you and your uncles are in these lands, I feel that peace cannot come. It makes my heart troubled. It brings anger to me."

Shadow stood in silence while the Long Knife named Austin studied her for a time. "Maybe my uncles weren't sure it was really your pa down here on the Three Forks. I guess that's what they wanted to find out. I always figured, from the way they talked, that your pa's fort was way south of here, clear down in the Shoshone River country."

"That is where the fort was until just two moons past," Shadow explained. "I wish we had not moved up into these lands. That land was far more peaceful, the land of my childhood. The Shoshone peoples were friendly, and they kept the Siksika and their brothers, the Piegans and the Kainah, from bothering us. And my mother's people, the Salish, could travel down to trade in peace. That was when the trade was for beaver. Those days were good, the days of my childhood. But the trade for beaver is past, and the robes of the buffalo are wanted. There are many more buffalo in these lands, so my father thought it wise to move here and to build another fort."

"But your pa knew this land was already taken, ground claimed by the American Fur Company. He knew he'd be stirrin' a hornet's nest."

Shadow grew tense with anger. "No man has the right to own any land. That is what is wrong with you Long Knives. The land belongs to all, to those who would use it and not take anything he cannot put back."

Austin nodded his head. "Maybe so. But that ain't the way the white man thinks."

"Long Knives are greedy," Shadow said with contempt. "Very greedy. Each one wants it all for himself. They kill in order to gain more and more. They never have enough."

"There's truth to that," Austin said. "It seems to me there's enough buffalo in this country to keep a dozen forts tradin' for good profit."

Shadow watched him as he touched his hands to his face and looked down, past the thick growth of brush and trees, to where a clump of aspen grew in a draw. She then followed him to the aspen and watched him kneel beside a small flow of water that bubbled out of the hill. He made faces and grimaced as he rubbed the dried blood from his cheeks and neck with the cold water. Shadow fought the temptation to kneel beside him and to wash his face for him, to tell him she wished she hadn't caused him the pain she had. She fought the desire to tell him she was sorry and that she felt bad as she watched him rub sprained fingers on both hands. And when he turned and looked at her, she quickly averted her eyes. They had met as enemies, and she could not make herself believe they were not enemies still.

But his eyes were on her, and she could not keep herself from turning back to him. She could see that he, too, wished they had not fought. His eyes spoke clearly, those eyes of green that were so deep and had just before been so hard but were now full of caring.

"Can't remember a time like this before in my life," he told her, trying to laugh. "Hell of a way to get to know somebody."

He was sincere in his words, this Long Knife named Austin. His words came from his heart. But he was not saying he shouldn't have fought her; he was saying he wished they had not met in the manner they had. She could sense his feelings were as hers: What had once been intense anger was now a feeling of attraction, and it made the senses confused. But he did not fight these feelings, this Long Knife named Austin, whose deep green eyes were reaching into her heart. Instead he spoke what was inside and had to come out. Shadow could remember no Long Knife 'she had ever met, other than her father, who presented such a strong, assured figure.

"Why did you not kill me?" Shadow asked him. "Why did you drop the knife and act as if something had entered your head?"

"I got my skull cracked early this week," Austin explained. "Somebody hit me with a club or something while I was asleep. But no matter, I wouldn't have killed you anyway."

"Why not? I would certainly have killed you."

"I couldn't see no real call for it. I had your knife, so you had nothing to fight with. And you thought I had come to kill you and your family. So, the way I see it, you had a right to do what you did."

"I cannot understand how you tricked me," Shadow said, thinking back on when she had heard the rock tumble through the brush opposite the trail from where she had been hiding. "You made me think for a moment that you had moved, then you snuck up on me. It is a good trick."

"It happened to me once," Austin told her, "back in Kentucky."

"Kentucky?" She had trouble saying the word.

"Back where I was raised. A long ways east of here, Kentucky is. I learned that trick as a kid. Never forgot it."

"You were so quiet," Shadow said. "It is not usual for a Long Knife who first comes to this land to be so quiet. It takes time to learn the ways of the forest."

Austin stared at her, as if mesmerized by her beauty. Finally he broke a broad smile and said to her, "I grew up in the woods. The trees have been my home since I was a kid. These are woods, too. Maybe a little different from Kentucky but still woods."

Shadow walked over to one of the aspens and let herself lean against it. The high state of energy she had sustained for so long had left her body, and she only now realized that she was very tired and that her body ached with a severe force that almost made her sick.

"A fight like we had, if you're not used to it, can wear you down to nothin'," Austin said, as if he knew exactly how she felt. "Maybe I can make things better for you."

Shadow felt herself being led over to a fallen log where Austin sat down and had her kneel between his legs with her back to him. She then let her head tilt slightly forward while Austin began to massage her neck and shoulders with his hands. She could feel his sense of commitment to easing her pain as he worked nimbly with his hands. She felt herself immediately begin to relax. There was no chance to fight the warmth that came over her as his strong fingers drove what remained of the anger and resentment from her. She felt herself swimming in a sense of total calm, a well-being that filled her with a strange desire to make him continue forever, to never stop.

"What is your name?" he asked. "No one ever said."

"Eagle's Shadow Woman. I am called Shadow."

"That is an honorable name for a woman," Austin said. "You must be highly thought of."

"How do you know about Indian peoples and their names?" Shadow asked.

"I've known some Indians," Austin answered. "There are Indians back in Kentucky. Maybe they're a little different than out here, but not a lot."

He continued to work his strong hands along her neck and shoulders while Shadow struggled with her inner feelings. It was hard to think of this Long Knife as the same type of man his uncles were. He did not seem to be deeply rooted in the idea that he would become wealthy, nor did he seem to care. Yet he was loyal to his uncles and the American Fur Company.

"Now you will go back to the fort called Benton," Shadow said, "and tell your uncles that this fort belongs to Jim Ayers. Am I right?"

"I will tell them I did not even reach the fort. That we were attacked by Indians. That's all I will say."

"If you do not wish to destroy my father's fort, why do you even go back at all?"

"I've got no choice," Austin answered. "I owe my uncles. I owe the company. My uncles brought me out here and gave me a new start. The company grubstaked me and set me up with supplies. I'm stuck until I pay it all back.''

"That is the way with you Long Knives," Shadow said. "You are all owned by someone. You cannot live your lives for yourselves. You must live them for someone else. This is very strange to me.''

"There's truth in what you just said," Austin remarked after some thought. "But that's the way things are set up. It's always been that way.''

"Not with my people," Shadow said quickly. "We live together, caring for one another, but we do not give up our personal freedom. We do not allow ourselves to be owned by another.''

Shadow had now relaxed completely, and the tension had left her, as if it had never been there. Though she tried to make herself reject the warm touch of this Long Knife, she could not. He had done something to her.

"I never once met a woman like you before," Austin told her. "I guess I've never really met one I wanted to stay with. You've got more strength than a number of men, yet you're as tender as a flower.''

"We must stop," Shadow said immediately, brushing his hands away and rising to her feet. "Only a short time ago I would have killed you. Now I let you touch me. I feel very strange.''

Shadow moved out from the patch of aspens and stood in the grass and flowers of the meadow above the trail. A breeze had begun to blow, and strands of her long black hair whipped across her face. With one hand she held the hair back from her face while gazing far out at high, snow-covered peaks in the distance, trying to understand what had just happened to her, trying to understand what the Long Knife Austin had done to her, why these strange feelings had come over her. She turned back to see him making his way up the slope toward the horses that were now grazing peacefully. She watched him climb the hill with long, powerful strides, his leg muscles bulging beneath his buckskin pants, his strong arms moving gracefully to propel him along. Yes, he was a man of confidence and, it seemed to Shadow, unusual understanding. He had a fierce nature controlled by good sense and a feel for the land. He, like herself, had grown up wild and free. Maybe that was why no woman in this far-off land he called Kentucky had ever held him and kept him from leaving to find these lands.

"I've got a long ride back," he told Shadow while he let the horses water at the spring. "My uncles will be none too happy to see me bring two dead traders in."

"I only wish those two were your uncles," Shadow said, her eyes squinting again. "I fear there will be much trouble now."

Austin tied the dead Long Knives on their horses and straightened the saddle on his own.

"That's the first time I've been bucked off a horse in a long time," he told Shadow. "You had us dead to rights."

Shadow watched him a moment. "You have not yet told me why you did not kill me when you had the chance," she said.

Austin turned to her, and his green eyes held their look on her. "Well, maybe I just couldn't bring myself to run that knife across the throat of the prettiest thing I ever saw in my life. Mad or not, you're more beautiful than any woman's got a right to be. And that does something to a man."

Suddenly, without warning, he took her by the shoulders and pulled her toward him, pressing her lips

to his. It was short yet forceful; and though it was
quick, it sent shivers of unexplained feeling through
Shadow. He released her and stepped back, his eyes
telling her he had been overcome by some strange
force. She stood and looked at him, unable to get
angry. Instead, the feeling within her grew stronger.

Shadow watched him climb atop his horse and lead
the other two back along the trail where they had
come. When the trees swallowed him up, she climbed
the hill to catch another glimpse. Somehow she could
not bring herself to dislike him, this Long Knife who
had brought strange feelings to her this day, even
though he was returning to the fort of her father's
enemies. When he was again lost in the forest and
out of sight for good, she started for the place, some
ways away, where she had left her own horse on
picket. She would now return to her father's fort and
would have to tell them where she had been and what
she had been doing. She did not yet know if she
would mention the young Long Knife, Austin Wells.

As she came down off the slope and onto the trail,
she again saw the vision of his warm green eyes and
his wavy brown hair. His poise and personality reminded her of her father: a man of intense strength
yet gentle in character. She looked high above, to the
rocks far above the valley. The she-eagle had finished
circling, having returned to her nest with her kill. She
was thankful for the strength the eagle had given her
and thought back to that day many winters past, also
during the warm moons, when she saved the life of
her father and her family. She remembered the words
her mother had spoken that day, how she had said the
eagle would be there the day she would meet the man
who would be most like her father, the man she would
wish to stand beside.

As Shadow prepared to make the trip back to the fort, she realized that the touch of this young Long Knife from Kentucky, Austin Wells, had done something to her and that he, without doubt, was the man the eagle had promised. But he was an enemy and that would make it impossible for them. She knew she would not be able to forget him. She knew her life had again changed, and new feelings, ones she had never really known before, were flooding over her.

Chapter Six

———

THE SUN HAD crossed to the top of the sky the following day when Shadow rode down from the hills and across the flat toward the fort. Tied behind her on her horse was a deer she had killed. She hoped it would seem to be a reason for being gone as long as she had. But somehow she knew there could be no good reason. She could only hope there was understanding in her wanting to defend their home.

"It will be more peaceful here." Shadow reflected on how often she had heard these words from her father. "There will not be as much fighting as there was on the Stinkingwater. Our friend, Walking Head, lives with his band not far from here. He's the best known Blackfoot chief in the mountains, and the most respected. He'll keep the Bloods and Piegans off our backs."

Shadow had known then that it would not be the

Blackfeet who would cause them trouble. It would be those Long Knives who had also just built a fort-lodge, known as the American Fur Company, along the waters of the Big Muddy, now called Missouri. They had been in these mountains for as long as her father, and they had never liked the competition for the fur trade, first the beaver and now the buffalo. Shadow would never forget her fight against them, the day she had shown the courage of the she-eagle, the day she had acquired her adult name, Eagle's Shadow Woman. Now, with these Long Knives so close, at their fort-lodge they called Benton, there would be more trouble as time passed. Shadow knew deep down that this would come to pass, especially since Austin's uncles were the same two Long Knives she had seen with the Siksika warriors the day she had fought so bravely. And they had come back into these lands to work for the American Fur Company.

At the fort, she got down from her horse to greet her mother, whose eyes were dark and whose arms were folded across her chest.

"It is a long time to be gone when only talking to your spirit helpers," she said to Shadow.

Shadow looked from her mother to the eyes of her younger brother, Little Bear. Now in early adolescence, he seemed to sense that his sister had again performed some feat of great quality.

"What do you have to say, my daughter?" Whisper demanded. "Is there some other reason why you left to go off into the mountains?"

"We needed fresh meat in our lodge," Shadow said, pointing to the deer tied across her horse.

Shadow saw her mother twist her mouth into a little smile. "There are deer along the river." She pointed.

"Even as we speak they browse tender buds from the berry bushes."

Shadow hung her head.

"I know there is something else," Whisper went on. "Your father and I both knew it when you left. You can hang the deer later. First we must talk." Then she turned to Little Bear. "Care for your sister's horse, please."

"But, Mother, I wish to hear, also."

"You will know soon enough. Now, care for the horse. See, he wants you to rub him down."

"He doesn't want me to rub him down."

"Little Bear, do as I ask."

Shadow watched her brother shuffle his feet as he walked over and began to untie the deer. He looked at his mother with a scowl on his face but said nothing. He let the deer fall in a heap on the ground, and Shadow watched him find a porcupine-quill brush before he took the horse to the meadow to graze.

"He will be a fine warrior someday," Shadow said. She followed her mother into their lodge, which stood just inside the fort walls.

"I wish to hear the whole story," she said to Shadow. "Leave nothing out."

Shadow related the events that had occurred, hoping for understanding from her mother. She spoke of how she had waited in ambush, and how she had killed two of the three. She mentioned Austin only as the third Long Knife who got away.

"This is a very foolish thing that you have done, my daughter, and you must give special thanks to Amótkan and your spirit helper, the golden eagle, for still having life in this world."

"I felt I must do this thing," Shadow explained.

"To do it on your own was wrong. Your father has

yet to return from looking for you. The sun has now crossed the sky twice, and I fear he will not return until he has found you."

Shadow's mouth fell open. "He went out to look for me?"

"Of course. You should have known he would. I have already told you that he knew, as I did, that you had gone for other reasons than to seek the spirits. When you had not returned in the proper amount of time, he went to find you."

Tears welled up in Shadow's eyes.

"Little Bear would have gone, also, but your father explained to him that he must stay here and help me. With most of the men gone from the fort, he did not want to go. But your father loves you very much."

"He should not ride any more than he has to with his leg," Shadow said. "That will only cause it to ache more."

"You do not need tell me this, my daughter. I pleaded with him to wait for a time longer."

"I must go and find him," Shadow said, standing up.

Whisper also stood up and quickly grabbed Shadow's arm. "I am tired of you thinking in a foolish manner. It is time you listened more to what is said and acted with the good sense I know you have." She paused a moment, letting her anger die down. "It would be better if Little Bear went to find him, for his father told him where he would be looking for you each time the sun crossed the sky."

"Is he not too young to travel these lands alone?" Shadow asked with concern.

"He is wise for his age," Whisper said. "He travels quickly and can move in silence. He has spent much time learning to do this. He says he has learned it from watching you.''

''He likes to hunt with me,'' Shadow said. ''He tells me always that his arrows fly truer than mine.'' She laughed.

''You must realize what you mean to him, my daughter,'' Whisper went on. ''He speaks often of your courage and how he someday wishes to have your powers. He has no older brother to look up to, but in his mind you are just as good. You must show him that your power comes from time spent thinking wisely.''

''I went out to stop the Long Knives only because I feared for our family,'' Shadow said, irritation showing in her voice. ''Would you have me do otherwise?''

''I understand, my daughter. But it would have been far better if you had not gone alone.''

''I cannot travel as fast with others,'' Shadow explained. ''It would have been hard for me. And well you know that I can fight as well as any warrior. To take others would have only meant failure. Can you understand, Mother?''

Shadow watched her mother take a deep breath, then turn and walk out of the lodge, where she turned her eyes toward the high peaks to the west.

''Mother?'' Shadow asked. ''Is something wrong?''

''I am only thinking back to when I was your age, and the many times I did foolish things. Many times my life should have been taken from me, but the spirits were always with me. I lived to meet your father and to have him take me as his wife. I have known the joy of your birth and the birth of your two brothers. It was destined that one of your brothers leave this life at an early age, but I have also known much happiness in watching you and Little Bear as you both have grown with each passing winter. I can only ask that you take care of your life and treat it with respect. I want never again to sing the songs of mourning for a lost son or daughter.''

Shadow took her mother in her arms, and the two held each other tightly for a time.

"I want only peace for us," Shadow said through her tears. "I want our family to know only happiness."

Little Bear came back from caring for the horse. When he reached them he pointed out into the meadow where two trappers were rubbing down their own horses, talking to each other and gesturing toward where Shadow stood.

"They have brought news from the trail," Little Bear said, his eyes sparkling. "They speak of how two Long Knives from the company met death in the canyon where the Big Muddy flows through the high rocks. They said a third escaped to tell of it." He paused shortly to look back out to the men in the meadow and then back to Shadow. "Did you take their scalps, my warrior sister?" he asked.

"Hush your questions, Little Bear," Whisper told her son. "You have talked before of finding your father, once some of the men returned to the fort. Some have returned. You may now leave to find your father, if that is what you wish."

Delighted, Little Bear quickly packed a skin bag with pemmican and found a rope for his horse. "Father and I have not been out on the trails together for the passing of many moons," he said. "Maybe we can do some hunting."

Shadow watched her younger brother leave, riding

proudly atop the two-year-old chestnut stallion he had
raised and trained himself. He now had his own bow
and quiver of arrows, the same weapons Shadow had
used that early morning now eight winters past. He
carried the bow with a certain reverence, for it was
his belief that the powers of his older sister were forever alive in the strong, curved wood and within each
straight arrow shaft that was touched to it. Shadow
knew Little Bear held for her a fascination rarely
found between brother and sister.

Hurry back, my brother. She let the words pass
unspoken through her mind as she stood beside her
mother. *My heart is not glad for having made our
father leave to search for me. Bring him back to us.*

"He will find his father soon," Shadow heard her
mother say. "I believe it will be this day, or maybe
early when the sun again climbs into the sky."

"He is so young," Shadow said.

Whisper smiled. "He thinks of himself as nearly a
man. And well he should. In the old days he would
already be preparing himself to go off in the forest
for a time by himself. It was the way then: It was the
way the elders could tell who the best and strongest
warriors would be and which among them would become our leaders."

"Little Bear will become a good leader," Shadow
said. "He is strong and wise beyond his years."

Whisper nodded. "Your words are true. And this
is good, though I hope he can understand the changes
coming to these lands. The coming of so many Long
Knives has brought a different feeling to me and to
all the Indian peoples of these lands. The Long
Knives who now come in great numbers are different
from your father. They do not know the land, nor love

it as he does. Most come only to take, with nothing to give.''

Shadow's thoughts went immediately to Austin, the young Kentuckian with the piercing green eyes and the strong hands that had so deftly taken the trembling from her body after their fight. She wanted to let herself dislike him, now. Even hate him. But she could not. She could not think of him as an enemy, though he had told her himself that he must work for the American Fur Company. She could only see his eyes and hear his words when he had spoken of her beauty. Now she could not forget him and knew within herself that he would always haunt her. She wondered if he had safely reached the fort-lodge called Benton, and what his uncles, the Beelers, said to him about returning with two dead comrades and no news of the new Fort Madison. Somehow, for reasons she could not understand, she wished she had told him there was a job open for him at her father's fort; that her father would welcome a man with his strength and natural knowledge of the land. She so wished for his presence near her again.

"What is it, my daughter?" Shadow heard her mother asking. "Have the spirits taken you to another world?"

"No, Mother." Shadow shook her head quickly. "Maybe I should find a good tree to hang the deer from." Shadow looked into the eyes of her mother, who seemed to have an intense curiosity about what she had just been thinking.

"My daughter, we have always spoken openly with one another," Whisper said. "We have never been afraid to discuss the things we felt as women. In your eyes I saw a look that comes to a woman when she has met someone special, someone who stays within her mind and will not leave. This happens when a special man comes into her life. Did you meet such a man while you were away?''

Shadow looked at her mother in amazement.

''I was a young woman once,'' Whisper said. ''I know the look that was just in your eyes, for I had the same look the day I met your father at the high mountain waters the Long Knives call Henry's Lake. I have told you before about that day.''

''You have, Mother,'' Shadow said, her eyes wandering back across the valley to the north, the direction of Fort Benton and Austin. ''Each time I heard the story, I thought how wonderful that feeling must have been. But now I know the real meaning of your words, and I think I know what my father must have been like when he was my age.''

''Then you have met a young Long Knife?''

''Yes. His name is Austin Wells. He is different from any man I have ever met.''

''He reminds you of your father?''

Shadow smiled. ''He is so much like him, in so many ways. He is untamed. He cares about the land and not about what he can take from it. And his heart is big.'' Shadow thought about the knife across her throat that Austin had chosen to remove. Maybe he, himself, had no good reason why he did not pull the blade; but he had chosen not to kill, even when he might have himself met death.

''I have not seen you like this before, my daughter,'' Whisper said. ''Many young Salish warriors wish for your heart, but you will not listen to the love tunes from their flutes. And it is true that you have made some of them angry, for many of them are very brave and would make any young woman a husband to be proud of. But it is good that you have a mind of your own. I can understand that you have always wished for the right day, when the right man would come into your life. And I am not surprised that he is a Long Knife. As you know from the stories I have told you, I once held great love for a warrior. But he was killed, and it was then that I met your father, who has made me as happy as any man ever could. At first, because he was a Long Knife, I did not know if I should love him; but then he would not leave me to myself. He said so many gentle things, as he still does, and my heart would not stop beating for him.''

"It is the same with me," Shadow confessed. "I do not know whether to hate or to love him. He is of the Beeler blood, but he is not like his two uncles. I wish I had not seen him, but now that I have I cannot keep from thinking about him. He spoke to me as he rode away, and I cannot forget the words.''

"What did he say?" Whisper asked.

"He said he wished to one day see me again, that to look upon me made him feel very good inside.''

"Did he offer you beads or vermilion for your hair? Did he hold up a mirror as he spoke?''

Shadow shook her head. "He did not try to win my affections by what he held in his hands. His feelings were deep and his heart was true. It is not that he simply wanted pleasure from me. I have seen the ways of those men before. This man, Austin Wells, did not wish only for a moment's closeness. He was looking past my eyes, to find out who I was deep within.''

"He said he wished to see you again?" Whisper asked.

Shadow nodded.

"And I am certain that you wish to see him again, also.''

Shadow nodded again.

Whisper smiled. "It will not be long until our good friend, Walking Head, of the Siksika, the Northern Blackfeet, takes his people to their camp of the warm moons. This time it will be where the waters of the giant spring flows, near the mountains of Big Snows. They are to have a celebration there, and I am sure your father will want to see them all and talk of the old times, and of trade with them. It is likely that those from the fort-lodge called Benton will be there also. Your young Long Knife will no doubt be with them."

Shadow smiled, feeling funny to know that her mother understood so well the strange sensations within her. It was very likely she would again see Austin when they traveled to visit their friends among the Blackfeet. She only hoped his words to her had not left his heart.

Shadow walked with her father along a forest trail just above the fort. He and Little Bear had come home just the evening before, to much rejoicing by Shadow and her mother. It had been a happy reunion, with each knowing that the other was once again safe and united with the rest of the family. But now, as they walked to the top of a hill and enjoyed the warmth of the sun and the beauty of the valley below, Shadow's father spoke to her in a serious tone.

"The story is out all along the trails," Shadow heard her father say. "Every campfire knows that two American Fur Company men were killed by the one known as the Eagle Woman."

Shadow wondered how they could have known it was she. Then she began to wonder if Austin had said something, if he had told them even though he had promised not to speak about any of it, except that he and the other two had been attacked by Indians.

"But how could they know it was me?" Shadow asked.

"You should have at least taken your arrows out of their bodies," her father said. "I don't understand why you didn't think to do that. You must have had other things on your mind. Your sign was all over those arrows. And everyone knows your sign after all the contests you've won shooting at targets in every camp in these mountains."

Shadow shook her head in disgust. How could she have been so foolish? Now it was known who had killed the two Long Knives, and it could only mean added trouble for her father and their fort-lodge. She breathed a sigh in frustration. Her attempt to stop trouble had certainly started more.

"I don't want to give you a long talk on why you shouldn't have done it in the first place," her father continued. "Aside from the fact that you could have gotten yourself killed, we've got plenty of men here. Three men wouldn't have stood a chance."

"This I understand, Father. But they might have made their attack at night and likely started a fire. We would not have been able to defend ourselves as well. Some of the men, or us, might have been killed or wounded. I just did not want a bad thing to happen."

"I'm your father." Shadow felt more relaxed and assured as he put an arm around her shoulders and pulled her close to his side. "I take considerable interest in your welfare. I know you did what you thought was right, and I don't fault you for that as much as not usin' your head about it. Men like those don't bat an eye when it comes to free-for-all and killin'. Woman or not, they'd have taken your hair, given half the chance.''

Shadow thought about Austin and his deep green eyes. She could not forget the way he had looked at her, saying without words that he did not want to fight her anymore and that he wished they had never fought in the first place. She remembered his touch, his firm but gentle hands taking the tension out of her neck and shoulders, filling her with a warmth she had never known before. She felt that same warmth now. Thinking of him, as she had often done since returning to the fort, made her mind lose its sense of place. It felt as though she was being taken to another land, where all was warm and at peace, and only the eyes and arms of Austin Wells could be seen and felt.

''I don't know what you're thinkin' about,'' she heard her father say, ''but just remember that I want to know about it the next time you decide to go to war. Understand?''

Shadow nodded. ''It was only that the stories told by Walking Head bothered me, and I only wanted to stop it all before it really got started.''

''Well, I guess you've done that job for the time being, anyway. Little Bear and I talked to a bunch of free trappers who had just left Benton, and they said that the whole bunch of them up there is scared to death to go out of the gates.'' He laughed. ''You put the fright in them good enough. Culbertson is fit to be tied. Nobody's gettin' any work done. It sounds like he is not sure if he wants to send anybody up to the Blackfoot get-together at the foot of Going-to-the-Sun Mountain, or even go himself. He's afraid you'll shoot him full of arrows.'' He laughed again. ''And he doesn't want to make an all-out strike against us because he knows that Walking Head is our good friend, and it would mean war with the Blackfeet. Looks like we've got him over a barrel.''

"I am still afraid the evil Beelers will try again,'' Shadow said. "And soon.''

"There was a young Kentuckian with those two you killed,'' Shadow's father said. "I understand he just got off a barge up from St. Louis. Your mother says you talked with him. And maybe took a liking to him.''

Shadow nodded her head, trying to hide her embarrassment.

"I wouldn't get too friendly with any of them,'' he advised. "You didn't kill one another, which seems odd to me; but if he's hooked up with the Beelers, I'd stay clear of him.''

"He told me he did not like his uncles,'' Shadow said. "He was tricked by them and did not want to come down to fight against us in the first place. He was forced to because he owed them for food and supplies he had gotten from them.''

"He told you that?''

Shadow nodded. "He does not seem to be evil like his uncles. I told him that you did not kill their brother, Ed, but that Walking Head and his war party were responsible for that. His uncles had told him that you killed their brother. I know he believed me when I told him his uncles had lied. No, I do not believe he is bad like they are. He could have killed me, but he chose not to.''

"Your mother told me that she saw some bruises on you, and that you said you didn't know how you got them. You must have fought him hand-to-hand.''

"He knows the ways of the forest,'' Shadow said.

"What did he say to you when he left you?''

"He said he hoped he would see me again. Perhaps at the Blackfoot summer festival."

"Well, I don't know if you should count on that or not. It sounds to me like he's left Fort Benton and may not even be in the mountains anymore."

"What?" Shadow asked. "What do you mean?"

"It seems he left about as soon as he got back to the fort with those two," he explained. "At least that's what I heard from that bunch on the trail. From what I can figure, young Wells told them he fought off the warriors that attacked them and that's why he wasn't killed and the other two weren't scalped. There were some Blackfeet at the fort who thought he had big medicine and were afraid of him. Then Culbertson told this Wells and his uncles to leave the fort and not to come back and cause any more trouble. Wells lit out and nobody seems to know where he got off to."

Shadow became concerned. Though she had done little more than just meet him, she felt responsible now for his welfare. She had caused this trouble for him and when he had not pulled his knife across her throat, she knew that he was not the kind who killed for the sake of killing. She could only hope he had not met death now because of what she had done.

"I can't figure how you knew where they would be," Shadow's father said. "There's a lot of country out there, and you haven't seen much of that up north yet. Not where you ambushed them."

"When Walking Head came to trade," Shadow explained, "I talked for a time with Standing Elk. We talked of his brother, Badger, and how his heart had changed because of the burning water. And we also talked of their trip to the fort-lodge called Benton to trade. Standing Elk said that he had been there when

Austin Wells won the bow from Badger in a game of hands. He said he had heard from Austin's uncle, the one called Jake, that they would go south, to our fort-lodge, very soon. Standing Elk then told me that the trails near the place called the Gates of the Mountains were thick with trees. That is where I chose to hide and wait for them.''

Shadow's father nodded. ''Well, that's all over now. We'll take things a step at a time from here. I don't know what the company plans to do now, but we can't worry about it. We'll just go on up to the Blackfoot camp at Going-to-the-Sun Mountain and set things up for trade with Walking Head and his band, and maybe other bands if we can.''

They started back for the fort, Shadow's mind again on Austin. This time she felt no peace or warmth; she felt grave concern. She felt she wanted to go and look for him, to be sure that he had not met with death. There was no doubt her days and nights would now be spent in a special kind of longing for him. If only she could see him again.

Chapter Seven

———

THE MEMORY OF Austin Wells continued to haunt Shadow. She could not help but think of him and wonder if he had decided to return to his own homeland, far to the east, or if he had perhaps met death somewhere along the Missouri River near the fort-lodge called Benton.

It was now late in the Moon of the Huckleberry—August. Shadow sat with her mother near their lodge along the waters the Blackfeet called Two Medicine. It was a beautiful place, not far from the camp where they would meet with Walking Head and the many bands of the Blackfoot confederation. They had traveled for the passing of many suns and had nearly reached Going-to-the-Sun Mountain. Little Bear and her father had gone hunting early that morning, and as Shadow sat with her mother, doing last-minute cleaning and mending on their celebration clothes, she let the worry of Austin depart her mind and concentrated on the worry she now had for her mother, who had neither eaten nor talked much during the entire journey.

The behavior exhibited by her mother was nothing new to Shadow. During this time of the year, for as long as she could remember, Shadow had noticed a disturbing silence that bordered on a deep depression. It was something her mother would never discuss, and when Shadow would ask her father about it, he would say, "She thinks about your older brother, White Feather, who died during this time of year."

Shadow could never get him to discuss it any further, for it seemed he had been as deeply hurt by the death as her mother, and neither of them wanted to remember it any more than they had to. In times before, Shadow had seen her mother cut off locks of her hair, as was commonly done by Indian peoples in times of mourning. Already the last joints of both little fingers were missing, one having been cut off in mourning for White Feather and the other many winters before when another child, yet unborn, was lost when she was hit in the stomach with a war club during a battle with Piegan Blackfeet.

Shadow realized her mother had suffered much sorrow in her life and, as each winter passed, seemed to become more moody with the coming of the warm moons. It caused Shadow more and more concern. Now, she thought, would be a good time to discuss whatever was causing her mother's unhappiness.

"Mother, I believe it is time that we had a talk about you. You were worried about me when I left to stop the Long Knives from the fort-lodge called Benton before they could cause us trouble. Now I worry about you, as I have during every passing of the Moon of the Huckleberry. I want you to tell me why you continue to grieve so over my lost brother, White Feather.''

Whisper lowered a doeskin dress she was sewing beads onto and looked at Shadow. ''Perhaps you are right,'' she said. ''Maybe it is best if I tell you, for you have a right to know.''

''Why would you not tell me sooner?'' Shadow asked.

''Because of the fear in my mind to relive that day. And, perhaps, because I feared the spirits, in their anger with me, would bring death to you and Little Bear, also. But I have that fear no longer, for the spirits look upon you with great favor; and I believe that Little Bear will also be favored by the spirits, as a young man and when he becomes a warrior.''

''I do not understand,'' Shadow said. ''I did not know that you thought the spirits held you in disfavor. Why do you think this?''

''I believe this is why White Feather died. He drowned, just before a terrible thunderstorm, and I believe the spirits were angry with me because I let him play with my medicine bundle. That is why I do not have a medicine bundle to this day, and this is why, when the Moon of the Huckleberry comes, that I feel afraid and saddened. I think of your lost brother, White Feather, and I worry that the spirits will again show their anger in some way.''

''What is the story of the death of my older brother?'' Shadow asked. ''Tell me the story, and perhaps I can better understand the feelings of the spirits toward you.''

Whisper took a deep breath. She bit her lip. ''It is a hard thing for me to talk about,'' she said to

Shadow. "So you must understand if I fumble with the words."

"I will understand, Mother."

"It happened in a place that lies to the east of these mountains, across the broad valley through which the waters of the Missouri flow, and over into another valley. That place is filled with the steaming pots of hot water which bubble up from the ground, much the same as those you have seen in the Burning Mountains, when you have journeyed there with us. But these pools of hot water do not make as much noise, nor are they feared to contain evil spirits as are the ones in the Burning Mountains.

"This place I speak of is called the Valley of White Medicine. Many of the Indian peoples go there to bathe in the waters, which contain a white medicine that is good for the body and makes those who are old feel young once again. It was while we were in this valley, after visiting Walking Head and his band of Siksika, that White Feather was lost to us." Tears welled up in her eyes and she bit her lip again.

"You must tell me how it happened, Mother," Shadow insisted. "You must once again relive that day, so that I might be better able to help you with your feelings."

"I will tell you," Whisper said, taking another deep breath. "We had started our journey back down to the fort on the Stinkingwater and had stopped to camp for a few days and enjoy the medicine waters. Your father was hunting one evening, and I was tanning a mountain sheep hide so that I might surprise him with a new pair of leggings. White Feather had found a very small black bear, whose mother was nowhere to be seen and must have become sick or died. We named him Growler, and White Feather asked to play with my medicine bundle, so that he might tie it around the bear's neck. After his pleading would not end, I finally gave my medicine bundle to him. I told White Feather to stay close to the lodge and to play out in a small meadow where I could see him clearly. I should have known the spirits were becoming angry, for the skies had darkened and the rolling of thunder had begun. Oh, I should have listened." She began to shake her head, tears rolling down her cheeks.

"Go on, Mother," Shadow said.

"I became busy with the mountain sheepskin and did not think about White Feather and the little bear for a time. Then I heard White Feather shouting, and I ran out of the lodge. White Feather was running across the meadow, yelling and looking into the sky. I could not see what he was looking at because of the trees, but I called for him to stop running. The river was in front of him. He did not stop but ran off a bank and fell down into the water. I rushed to the bank and into the water but could not see White Feather. He was very small and the waters took him under. Later I found him where the waters had taken him into a beaver dam. And he was dead."

Shadow took her mother into her arms. It seemed her sobbing would never stop, and Shadow could not keep her own tears from falling. After a time, Whisper continued with the story of the death of White Feather.

"I never did learn what happened to the small bear, Growler, or to my medicine bundle. I never saw either one of them again. Perhaps the spirits, in their anger with me, took the bear and my medicine bundle into the sky, and White Feather was running to catch up. He had placed the medicine bundle around the bear's neck while he was playing. I can think of nothing else, for White Feather would never have run without watching, as he did that day, unless something very unusual had happened. When I took him out of the beaver dam, there was thunder and lightning all around. It was very loud and popped as it struck the trees overhead. There would have been much fire if it had not been for the rain that also came." Here Whisper broke down again. "I could do nothing for my son. I could only carry him through the rain to our lodge and lay him in his bed. I shall never forget the deep pain in your father's eyes. Never. It haunts me each night during the Moon of the Huckleberry."

Shadow held her mother once again. Trying to control her own emotions, she said, "Mother, that time was past long ago. You cannot carry this burden throughout your life. You have told me many times that Amótkan chooses to take us from this world when He thinks it is best, and that we should not let ourselves be saddened for too long. The spirit of White Feather now rests in the Other Side Camp. He is happy there. We should be happy for him."

Whisper looked at Shadow. The tears were gone and anxiety had taken their place. "I am not sure if White Feather's spirit is truly at rest," she said. "Maybe this is why I remain troubled. Maybe this is why I feel the spirits remain angry with me. I should never have let White Feather play with my medicine bundle, a sacred thing. Someday you will also have a vision, and you will be instructed by the spirits to make a medicine bundle; and they will tell you what sacred objects to place in that medicine bundle. Yes, I believe the spirits remain angry with me. Otherwise there would not be so much trouble that threatens our family. The brothers of Ed Beeler wish to destroy our fort-lodge and take the life of your father. And you, yourself, have fought many times now since becoming a woman. I pray to Amótkan that you will not meet death.''

''Mother, do not worry,'' Shadow said. ''My medicine is strong. I have the power of the eagle and that of the good spirits with me. I shall remain in this life for many winters to come.''

''It is good that you have such confidence, my daughter. I feel there is much trouble ahead, that we have not even begun to understand what we have yet to face. Even though Walking Head has remained a very good friend, I do not feel good about traveling to visit the Blackfeet at Going-to-the-Sun Mountain. It is not that I feel Walking Head will turn against us; it is just that there is so much evil in these lands now that many things could happen to strain our friendship. The evil Beelers will do anything to get at your father. I feel I have little power with which to help our family. I have felt this way ever since the day White Feather was lost and my medicine bundle disappeared.'' She shook her head. ''I do not want to ask your father to turn back. He is so excited about talking trade with all the bands of Blackfoot peoples that will be there, and it would be an insult to Walking Head if we were to refuse his invitation. I just do not want to see our family suffer further.''

Shadow reflected on her mother's words with a more clear understanding of why she suffered such mental anguish. The death of White Feather had haunted her for so many years, and even discussing it now, which she had never done before, seemed of little solace to her. The roots of her torment were very deep, and it was difficult to change patterns of hurt that had been developed and nurtured by further unfortunate circumstances over so many winters. Now,

with changes coming ever more quickly to a land
which once knew only the rotation of seasons and use
by its peoples simply to sustain life, there was bound
to be added mental discomfort within her mother as
the life she once knew became lost.

At the heart of this concern, Shadow knew, was the
effect this would certainly have on their family struc-
ture. In her mother's eyes, Shadow could see one par-
ticular worry that overshadowed all others. That worry
took the form of the young Long Knife, Austin Wells.

"When I first met your father," Whisper said, "it
was during a battle. Men were killed. I, myself, killed
one of Walking Head's warriors, as we were enemies
then. I know you have heard this story before, but I
can see that you have met this young Long Knife in
the very same manner. I did not fight hand-to-hand
with your father, as you did this Austin Wells, for
your father was also an enemy of the Blackfeet then.
We are no longer enemies and this is why I have
learned their language and have taught it to you and
Little Bear but I wonder about Austin Wells and his
uncles. Do you think there will be trouble if this
young Long Knife wishes to see you again?"

This was a question Shadow had had on her mind
for some time. It would all be so much easier if he
was now on his way back to his homeland in the East
and she could forget forever that day when they had
met at the Gates of the Mountains. But this could
never be. Even after first meeting him, when she realized she could neither hate him nor get him out of
her mind, she knew there would be a great deal of
trouble. She wanted to be with a man who was blood
relation to her father's hated enemies, the Beelers.
And now that he was on the run from his uncles, there
would surely come a time when his uncles would
catch up to him, somewhere, at some place in these

lands. It was sure that the time would be when they were together.

"I do not want trouble," Shadow told her mother. "And perhaps trouble will not come to us. I do not know where Austin is. Since Father told me about hearing that he had run away from the fort-lodge called Benton, I have wondered where he might be. Maybe he has gone back to his home to the east."

"I doubt it, my daughter. If his eyes tell the same story that yours do, it is certain he is looking for you. It is very likely that he will be at the Blackfoot summer camp at the base of Going-to-the-Sun Mountain." She sighed. "I know the voice of the heart is very strong. I can only hope for the best."

Shadow thought about her situation many times during the next few days while they traveled from the waters called Two Medicine on toward Going-to-the-Sun Mountain. There was no doubt many problems could be avoided if only she could forget this young Kentuckian. The more she thought about it, the more convinced she became that the best solution was to avoid Austin Wells and keep him out of her life. Perhaps, as time went on, this would become easier, and she would someday forget about him completely. It would be hard, but it was certainly something she must do. There were already too many problems associated with keeping the family safe and having a good trade business at the fort-lodge. To consider going along with her heart, this time, would only invite more problems, many of which could possibly lead to death for her father. No, it would be better to suffer a loss of the heart than to chance the loss of her family and their happiness. She hoped the spirits would not bring them together again; but if she were to meet him, she would tell him that they could no longer see one another and that their lives must be lived apart.

They reached the Blackfoot encampment at Going-to-the-Sun Mountain the next day. They were invited to erect their lodge at the center of the village, near Walking Head's own lodge, as they were considered the most important of all the guests who were to come to the celebration. Shadow helped her mother erect the lodge while her father smoked the pipe of peace with Walking Head and other important members of the Blackfoot tribe. There would be much feasting and exchanging of gifts, for this was a memorable occasion. They would talk far into the night, Shadow knew, telling stories of war and talking of the upcoming fall hunt. Walking Head was glad that Shadow's father had decided to build his fort-lodge in the lands of the Blackfeet and would tell all his people that this man deserved much honor. Shadow could see that her father would gain a lot of trade business from this visit.

Little Bear had already found a number of boys who wanted to see how well he could shoot his bow. He went off gladly with them, knowing he must shoot well. All those in his family were known to be very powerful, and he had a reputation to uphold. Walking Head's wife, Laughs-in-the-Morning, exchanged warm greetings with Shadow and her mother and set in helping to erect the lodge. The entire village had heard of their coming and now looked upon them with staring eyes. It was well known among all Indian peoples of the mountains that Shadow and her mother were both possessed of great powers. Eagle's Shadow Woman, often called the Eagle Woman, and her mother, Whisper on the Water, who was known as the Spirit Woman, were now legends among those who lived in these lands. Many had seen Shadow's mother before and knew of her great feats as a young woman, but few had seen her daughter, the Eagle Woman, whom many said fought like five warriors and possibly possessed more power than even her mother. Shadow did not feel uncomfortable, though, for it had become a common thing to feel the searching looks and to hear the low whispers. Whenever she traveled, she expected it. Even after that first day of fighting, when as little more than a girl she had protected her family from the evil Beelers and the war party of Siksika, she knew her life would never be the same. Her mother had told her then that she had done something few others, either men or women, would have been able to do. Now for the rest of her life she would be known for her brave deeds, and all would look upon her as someone from the world of the spirits.

As the day wore on, Shadow found herself gazing through the throngs of people in the village, searching for a young Long Knife wearing a frontiersman hat. Although everyone else had gotten into the spirit of the celebration, Shadow could neither eat from the pots set out for feasting nor join in the many groups that were gathering for games and contests. Instead she wandered aimlessly about the camp, trying to formulate what she would say to Austin Wells when, and if, she ever saw him again.

During the evening of the third day, Shadow was sitting alone in the lodge when her mother came in.

"You spend a lot of time alone, my daughter," she said. "Why is it you do not talk with the women, or maybe join in some of the games?"

"I just do not feel like being with anyone," Shadow answered. "I do not know anyone here, and I guess I just feel uncomfortable."

"You have never been bashful," Whisper said. "It is unlike you not to want to meet new people. Why don't you come with me and show Laughs-in-the-Morning how you braided those shells and beads together in that necklace you gave me a few winters back? I have had many compliments on the necklace, and I'm sure all the women would like to know how you did such fine work."

"Maybe later, Mother. I do not feel like being with others right at this time."

"Have you seen Badger since we arrived?" Her mother then asked. "There is a story about you and him going around the village."

"No, I have not seen Badger," Shadow answered. "I understand he has been out hunting with several of the younger warriors. What is the story you have heard about us?"

"It is said that you are to become his wife."

Shadow straightened up suddenly. "What?" she asked, her voice filled with surprise. "What did you say?"

"That is what I heard." Whisper smiled. "It is all over the village. Badger and the warriors came in from hunting late last night, and he has been telling everyone this most of the day. You should get out of the lodge once in a while. You would then know more about what is going on around you."

"I see nothing at all funny about it," Shadow told her mother. "You know there is no truth in that. I cannot understand why he would say something like that. Has he been drinking the burning water again?"

"I do not know. I did not speak to him myself. The story is on the tongue of every woman in the village. It is said that he is painting buffalo hides for use as a lodge cover, and that you will likely go to his lodge before the sun has journeyed across the sky three times.''

Shadow became more angered with each additional word that her mother told her. She remembered how Badger had looked at her when he had come with his brother, Standing Elk, and their father to their fort-lodge on the waters of the Madison. In his eyes she had seen deep desire and a form of cunning that had told her to beware of this man, that he would certainly make himself a part of her life at any cost. It had been apparent to her then that he wanted to be able to walk up to her and announce that he was there to take her to be his, but the burning water was always on his breath, and more times than not he would turn away when her eyes met his. He no doubt felt deep shame for his condition, which made him less of a man. Shadow had known then that this man would try to find a way to bring up his own self-esteem. It seemed that a woman with as much honor as Shadow would certainly be right for a man who wished to have all those around him forget his past.

''I am going to find out what this is all about,'' Shadow said to her mother.

''Are you going to talk to Badger?'' Whisper asked.

''I will first ask Standing Elk what he knows about all this,'' Shadow answered. ''But sooner or later I will have to speak to Badger.''

Evening fires lit up the encampment. The entire village was in a festive spirit, as Badger and some of the other warriors had been successful in their hunt. They had brought back with them elk, deer, and mountain sheep, all of which would be excellent for feasting during the celebration. It was said also that they had located a very large herd of buffalo, which they had not disturbed, so that a large-scale hunt could be mounted after the festival. It was indeed a time for celebration.

Shadow made her way past games, dances, races, and other activities in her search for Badger and Standing Elk. Her mind was not on the excitement that was being shared by everyone else. Her concern was only to clear up the false rumors that had been started by Badger. Then, near a fire at the edge of the village, Shadow found Standing Elk in the company of a few other warriors sharpening arrows around a fire. He seemed to know why she would seek him out and walked over to where she stood. He made sign to her.

"I cannot speak for my brother," he told her. "I know nothing of what he has been saying, and I do not want to become involved. Please understand."

"Why does he speak words that have not truth?"

"I cannot say."

"Where can I find him?"

Standing Elk pointed over to another fire, not far away.

Shadow set her jaw and wasted little time in finding the fire where Badger was also working with his arrows. Upon seeing Shadow some of the warriors with him raised their eyebrows and made teasing comments to Badger. When Badger did not rise to greet her, acting as though he wished her to sit by him, Shadow quickly walked over and stood above him.

"It would be good if you and I had a private talk. I do not think you would want your friends to hear some of the things I am about to say to you."

Badger dropped his arrows and got up. His eyes were somewhat squinted, as if in a warning not to say or do anything that might embarrass him in front of the others. Shadow paid no attention to him and walked out from the fire. When she turned, Badger was standing behind her, his arms crossed in front of him.

"I have been hearing that you are to take me for your wife," she said. "Is it true that you have been saying this to everyone?"

"I think I said I would *like* to take you as my wife."

"Someone said that you bragged you would have me before the sun crossed the sky three times."

"We could shorten that if you were to come with me tonight." He laughed.

"Maybe you won't think it is so funny if I went before the entire village and told them that what they have been hearing from you is like the words of a small boy who, for the first time, becomes enchanted by a girl. Maybe I could tell them that you have those same kinds of feelings and cannot control them like a small boy would."

Badger stiffened in anger. "You wouldn't dare shame me in such a manner!"

"Why not? You have shamed me!"

"But I would like to have you as my wife."

"You have a strange way of showing it. And I believe your reasons for wanting me are not of the right kind. I believe you think you would gain much honor if I were to enter your lodge as your wife. It is not for love, as it should be. Honor is not a good reason to become married."

Badger thought for a moment. "I have told many that we are in courting. To change their thoughts would look bad for both of us."

"No," Shadow told him, "just for you. I did not

speak the lies. You spoke the lies. And if anyone asks, I will tell them that you must have spoken when your head was filled with the burning water.''

Badger raised his hand to strike her, his eyes wide. Shadow stood steadfast, glaring at him. Finally Badger lowered his hand and clenched his fists before he again made sign.

''I know what makes you not want me,'' he said. ''It is the Long Knife, Green Eyes. Yes, I know about when you killed the two Long Knives with him at the Gates of the Mountains but spared his life. I have heard the stories. Maybe you didn't know that he has left the fort-lodge called Benton. You will not see him again. It is me you shall have.''

''No, Badger, I shall never have you. The Long Knife you call Green Eyes has nothing to do with my feelings for you. When we were children and our parents would visit back and forth, I thought a great deal of you. But time and the burning water have changed you. I will never be your wife. Never.''

Badger considered striking her but noticed that the warriors at the fire were now all watching them. Instead he made final sign to her before leaving.

''You will be sorry that you have shamed me, Eagle Woman. The one called Green Eyes, if he is smart, will have gone back to his own lands to the east. He will have left these mountains. You, someday, will wish that your words to me this night had been different. Yes, the day will come when you will wish you had become my wife.''

Chapter Eight

———

GOING-TO-THE-SUN MOUNTAIN, THE best known of the giant peaks in these high mountains where the Blackfeet lived, stood bathed in the fiery glow of sunset as Shadow sat along the shore of a mountain lake nestled at its base. Nearby, a small stream of icy water trickled into the lake from where it fell over a series of small cliffs hanging with the deep green of watercress and moss.

Shadow had been here for some time, staring at the rocky face of the huge mountain, watching the sun color the large sheets of ice which clung to the ledges and crevices along the steep walls. Now the rays of late day bathed this secluded pocket high in the mountains with a rich brilliance, a subdued mixture of crimson and gold that shimmered from the surface of the lake and sparkled on the falling water that slid down the rock walls. Every tree stood still, and every flower faced the light, filling themselves with the gift of life itself.

Alone, Shadow continued to watch while small birds flitted to roost, and high along the rock wall a family of mountain goats bounced from ledge to ledge, making their way down to drink. But for Shadow the beauty of it all was lost to the deep longing within her. What she had wished for had come to pass. For seven days she had waited for Austin Wells, and he had not come. She had made up her mind to forget him. But she had succeeded. He was always there, deep within her. There was no way she could forget him.

As she gazed out across the lake, watching the small circles enlarge where trout and grayling surfaced for flies atop the water, her gaze was suddenly directed skyward when the mirrored image of giant wings appeared before her. Silent as the evening, a large eagle glided smoothly over the lake, riding the air until the bird made an upward thrust toward the high peaks. Shadow was startled and bewildered. It seemed much too late for hunting, and the eagle had made no descent toward the water to catch a fish. Shadow searched the horizon, shading her eyes against the sun's bright light over the peaks. But the eagle was gone.

Again she looked into the water as another reflection was cast up at her. There was the outline of a man's face, and a head covered by a broad frontiersman's hat. Shadow closed her eyes. The spirits were playing tricks on her this night.

She opened her eyes. The reflection was still there. The lips moved.

"Shadow? Is it you?"

Shadow gasped loudly. She jumped to her feet and turned around.

"Shadow." The voice of Austin Wells was soft and warm. "Shadow, I didn't think I would ever find you."

Shadow had heard his voice, had seen him there in front of her, but could still not believe it was he.

"I didn't mean to scare you," he said, removing his hat. "I've been wanting to see you again ever since we first met. A lot has happened since then."

"How did you find me so far from the village?" Shadow finally asked.

"I asked in the village and found your lodge. I talked with your mother, and she told me where you had gone. I can see where you got your beauty."

"It is getting late," Shadow said. "I should get back with the water I came after."

"Your mother had just come from one of the lakes below with some when I found her," Austin said. "So we don't have to go back yet. I think this is a nice place to be, to maybe talk. When we first met—I mean, it was hard to talk then. But let's forget that."

Shadow could not help herself. She was overwhelmed by his presence. Without the blood and scratches, he was even more handsome than she had remembered him. He was a dream come true. His eyes were a deeper green, his face more defined, his strong, rugged body an even more impressive figure than what she had seen and touched at the Gates of the Mountains. She could see in his eyes, by the way they searched deep into her own, that his feelings for her were equally as strong.

"Shall we just sit here for a time?" he asked, taking a step forward.

As she sat down with him in the lush grass and

flowers along the lake, Shadow hoped he could not hear the beating of her heart or see the excitement that must surely be evident in her eyes. His voice had a smooth tone that flooded her with warmth.

"It's really good to see you again. I don't know what to say, except that I'm glad I found you."

"My father brought word that you had trouble when you got back to Benton," Shadow said. "It was said that you might have gone back to your own lands far to the east."

Austin shook his head. "No, I wasn't about to go back to Kentucky. This is where I belong now. Nothing can make me leave here."

"But your uncles," Shadow said. "The two named Beeler now look for you, don't they?"

"I imagine," Austin answered. "I don't know what they think they're going to do once they find me. When I left Fort Benton, I told them I had fulfilled my obligations to them and that I was on my own. So they have no business meddling in my affairs from here on out."

"It was said that many of the company men were angry with you when you came back with the two dead Long Knives and you, yourself, were not killed."

Austin laughed. "Nobody could figure it out, that's for sure. But when some of the Blackfeet there saw your sign on the arrows, they became afraid of me right away. They all backed away with their hands over their mouths, pointing at me. I guess they thought I was some sort of spirit for not getting killed by you. But that worked out well for me. I told my uncles I was leaving, and there wasn't a thing they could do to stop me if they wanted to stay on the good side of Culbertson. With all the scratches that

you put on my face and neck, the Blackfeet thought
I had won a battle with a spirit eagle. Culbertson
wanted me gone so that I wouldn't scare his trade
away. And my uncles had to just sit and watch me
go.''

"Maybe your uncles will leave you alone now,"
Shadow said. "If the one named Culbertson does not
want you around his fort, you can do your uncles little
good.''

"They still have an eye on your father's fort,"
Austin said. "It's likely they'll try anything to get at
your family. But let's forget about them for now and
talk about something else, like how your mother knew
my name.''

Shadow tried to hide her embarrassment. "We
talked about the day you and I met and fought. She
was angry with me for doing what I did.''

"It would have been dangerous for anyone else but
you," Austin said. "There are a lot of stories about
you and how you've fought against your enemies.
And also about your mother. Is it true that she taught
you how to fight?''

Shadow nodded. "She was once a warrior. At my
age she fought many times against the Blackfeet to
protect her family. Now that I am a woman and she
is older, it is for me to fight in her place. So now all
consider me to be a warrior also.''

"You sound as if you wish people wouldn't think
of you that way," Austin said.

"It has made my life harder," Shadow admitted.
"I have but very few friends. They are all afraid of
my powers. I sometimes wish that people could see
me for who I am and not for what they hear about
me.''

The sun had left the sky, and the horizon in the

west was a deep crimson, with the silhouettes of the
jagged peaks looming high and black against the oncoming night. Below, the fires in the village dotted
the large meadow, and the sounds of evening songs
filled the valley.

"Prettiest country I've ever seen," Austin remarked.

"Amótkan made this land for all to enjoy,"
Shadow said. She watched as Austin pulled the stem
of a wildflower and smelled its fragrance. He then
fitted the stem into her hair so that the blossoms, a
cluster of miniature bluebells, fitted in just behind her
ear. Their eyes met and, slowly, their lips came together.

His kiss was long and deep, sending a rush of
warmth over her. When he had finished, Shadow
found herself wanting more but quickly rose to her
feet.

"I have been up here far longer than I meant to
be," she said. "I must get back with the water."

"Let me carry them for you," Austin said quickly,
beating her to the skin bags resting in the grass.

"I can carry them," Shadow insisted. But Austin
already had them and was starting down off the hill
toward the village below.

Shadow stopped him. "I will carry them. I thank
you for your offer, but I feel I should carry them."

"I'll tell you what," Austin said, resisting her efforts to get at the water bags. "I'll take them down
the hill to just outside the village. Then I'll give them
back to you. If you're worried about people seeing
us, we'll stay off the main trail. How does that
sound?"

Before she could answer, he had turned and was
making his way along the hillside, locating a game

trail that would come out below not far from the village. Shadow's feelings were again mixed, and she had become more confused than ever. Her desire to be with this man was uncontrollable, though she knew it was foolish to let herself become involved. He was determined to win her and was doing everything in his power to show her how much he cared for her. But it was a situation that would just not work. She could not justify letting herself fall in love with a man who worked for her father's enemies.

Though Shadow did everything in her power to hold back her feelings, she could not repress the flow of excitement that ran through her. Austin Wells had a strange sort of conquering force within him that left her helpless in his presence. As they traveled down along the trail, the light slowly began to leave the forest and the small shafts of red and gold that had filtered through the trees began to vanish. From nearby came the hoot of a great horned owl, and from the lake came the cries of loons as the moon rose over the still waters.

"I must confess," Austin said, "that I talked with your mother for some time before I went up to find you. It seemed like there were some things she wanted to know about me."

"What did she wish to know?" Shadow asked.

"I think she was wondering how loyal I was to my uncles, and why I'm not with them now. She never took her eyes off me for a minute when I answered her questions."

"Did you find it hard to talk to her?"

"Not at all," Austin answered. "At first we were both cautious. But then I think she decided that I wasn't a Beeler and that I didn't even like them."

"And what of my father? Did you see him?"

Shadow knew her father would not likely have been nearly as friendly right away. Anyone associated with the Beelers in any way would surely make him cautious.

"I did not see your father, though your mother warned me that seeing you would not set well with him. She told me that it was my choice and that she would not stand in my way."

They were nearing the village. Austin stopped in front of her and crossed over a fallen log, making his way carefully down a small embankment. He set the water skins down and turned to Shadow.

"Let me help you down," he said to her, his arms outstretched.

"I need no help," she said. "It is but a small bank."

Austin seemed not to hear her. As she started down, he first took her hand and then encircled her waist with a strong arm, pulling her into him.

Shadow lost her breath. Again her heart began to beat wildly, and the closeness sent a warmth through her.

"It seems like an eternity since we first met," he said to her. "I never stopped thinking about you. I spent my time wondering about you, where you were and what you were doing. What you were thinking. I wanted to come down to your fort, but I felt it was too soon. I guess I didn't want to get off on the wrong foot with your father."

He held her with his strong arms around her lower back, allowing her feet to touch the bank, leaving her face on a level with his. Shadow met his eyes with hers, aware that their lips were only inches apart. The pounding of her heart grew steadily more intense, and she was sure he could feel it against his chest.

"Tell me," he went on. "Tell me what I want to hear. Tell me that you also wondered about me and that you thought of me often." He looked into her eyes for a long moment, and it was all she could do to keep from pulling him to her. Then, softly, he said, "You are so beautiful."

Shadow let her eyes close as his lips came to hers, gently at first and then with more passion. She found herself losing control. Her arms encircled his neck, her fingers pressing into his thick hair. Her whole body grew more and more urgent, and she wished the kiss would go on forever.

"I've never felt so good," he whispered into her ear. "Never in my life." Then he pointed to a small game trail that angled off into a clearing nearby. "There," he said, "in those aspen trees, is where I am camped. Come over with me and we'll build a fire."

"I must go," she told Austin, arching away from him, pressing gently but firmly. "It's now dark and my family will grow worried."

"You are fully grown."

"Yes, but I seldom stay away from the lodge long after dark. Now, I must take the water skins and go."

"Let me take them," Austin insisted. "Let me carry them to your lodge for you and meet your father. Maybe I can get a job with him."

Shadow shook her head. "No, it is not a good idea. He will be angry to know that I was with you as it is. That would only make things worse."

"Don't you want to be with me?" Austin asked.

Shadow took a deep breath. "It is not that. You said yourself that the reason you did not come to our fort-lodge on the waters of the Madison was because of my father, because of your worry that he would not accept you. Why would you think that would change so soon?''

''We could at least give it a try,'' Austin said. ''It can't hurt anything.''

''No, it would hurt to try so soon. If my father did not accept you at first, it would then be very hard for him to ever accept you at all. Can you understand that? It will take time. You must meet him under different circumstances.''

''I can't understand why we don't just go down there and tell them both how we feel,'' Austin insisted. ''Now, let's go.''

Shadow grabbed him by the arm as he turned. ''No! If you do not understand what I have been trying to say to you, then you will understand that I do not want you to go to my lodge with me.'' She took the water skins from him.

Austin was quiet for a time. Finally he said, ''Maybe you're right. Maybe it's best if I don't go down with you. I don't want to cause you any trouble, and I certainly have enough troubles of my own without creating more.'' He then turned and was lost in the darkness.

Shadow wanted to call out to him, to find out what he was thinking. He had left without saying anything, really, and it bothered her. Certainly he was irritated; but had he become quite angry? Did he ever want to see her again? There was no way of knowing how he felt.

As Shadow made her way back to the lodge with the water skins, she became angry herself. He had no right to take anything for granted. He had no reason to believe she wanted to become seriously involved with him. This was the first time she had seen him since their initial meeting, when they had wanted to

kill one another. How could he be so bold in so short
a time?

But she had wanted his boldness; she had savored
his kisses. She knew this and was aware that he most
certainly had felt her fondness for him. This had only
served to make him more aggressive. She now felt
that she should have left the lake as soon as he had
found her. If she had only told him then that it was
too soon to give in to their feelings. But her feelings
had been so strong, so uncontrollable. No matter, it
was done. She had gotten close, too close, to him and
had felt the strength of his kisses. If she could have
only avoided it all. It was too late now to wish things
had been different.

"What is it, Shadow?" her mother asked as
Shadow dropped the skin bags inside the entrance to
the lodge. "What is the trouble?"

"Nothing, Mother."

"I see the young Long Knife, Austin Wells, found
you." Her eyes were on the bluebells in Shadow's
hair.

Shadow pulled the flowers out and tossed them outside. "Is there work to be done?" she asked her
mother. "I see father is over with Walking Head, talking in front of his lodge. Maybe they need more meat
for their pots in front of the fire."

"They have plenty. Walking Head's wife, Laughs-
in-the-Morning, has just given them fresh mountain
sheep. I am going over to visit her now, before the
dancing begins. Would you like to come along?"

Shadow shook her head. "I will try and finish the
dress I have been working on. It is a good time to do
that."

"During a celebration festival?"

"I do not feel much like celebrating tonight,

Mother. But I want you to enjoy yourself.''

Shadow began rummaging around in a leather pack for assorted colored beads and a collection of elk teeth. Her mother watched her for a short time and spoke again.

''I told your father that the young Long Knife, Austin Wells, had come to the lodge to find you.''

Shadow looked up quickly.

''I do not know what his feelings were,'' Whisper continued. ''He did not say anything, but his face showed concern. I did not see anger. Only concern.''

''I don't know if I will be seeing him again,'' Shadow said. ''Austin wanted to come down to the lodge and meet Father. I did not want him to, so he left. I do not know where he went or if he is even still here. He said only that he did not wish to make trouble. Then he was gone, and I did not speak to him again.''

Shadow could see in her mother's eyes a sort of conviction, a knowledge of what was happening. Shadow's mother certainly knew what Austin thought of her daughter, or he wouldn't have traveled up here to find her. He would have gone back to Kentucky if it had not been for Shadow. His presence was a definite indication of his determination to be with Shadow. And Shadow's actions showed her equally strong feelings for him. There was little doubt that their quarrel would soon be forgotten.

''You must understand, my daughter, that I talk to you about this young Long Knife only because I know what you feel for him. It is not I, but your father, who will not be pleased with things as they are.''

''I know he will not be pleased,'' Shadow said. ''I want to forget Austin in the worst way. I wish now I had never gone to the Gates of the Mountains. But that has already happened, and I now wish to be with him.''

''Do not say that you should not have met him,'' her mother warned her. ''The spirits were with you that day, and you were again given the power of many by your spirit guardian, the golden eagle. Do not speak against the decisions of the spirits. In time you will understand that meeting this young Long Knife was a good thing.''

''But it now makes things so much harder for our family. I don't know what to do.''

''You must always follow what the voices inside you say,'' her mother emphasized. ''The little voices that have power to help you are always talking. Listen to them.''

''I now hear so many voices,'' Shadow said, ''that I do not know which ones to listen to. They all tell me different things. There are those who want me to stay away from Austin and forget him forever, while other voices will not let me sleep because of my longing for him. Which do I listen to?''

''Which are stronger?''

''The voices of my heart. The ones that tell me to go to him.''

''Then listen to them.''

''What if they are wrong?''

Her mother's face became stern. ''Where is your faith, child? If you have no faith, you have nothing! It is easy to tell good from evil. Each morning when you pray, ask Amótkan in a special way to help you. Then listen! Do not concern yourself always when you are awake. Be happy. Think of other things. Walk through the mountains. The voices will come, and they will be right.''

"I will do that, Mother," Shadow said with a firm nod of her head. "I have known ever since I met Austin that he was someone sent to me by the she-eagle, the Watcher of the Skies. I knew when I met him that day at the Gates of the Mountains that we did not kill one another for a very special reason. He had come to me as Father once did to you. Yes, the voices have told me this."

"Then why are you fighting them?" her mother asked.

"You know the reason. Father is unsure of him. He is afraid that he is like his uncles, the evil Beelers. Until he learns that Austin is far different from them, he will not want us together."

"I know it will be difficult, my daughter. But you must do what you think is right. I, like you, have felt that there would come a day when our family would once again go through a very bad time. You know I still believe that it is my fault because I let your older brother play with my medicine bag and let him die because of it."

"Stop, Mother," Shadow said quickly. "That is all in the past, and I know the spirits are not angry with you. The spirits are angry only with those who refuse to feel sorrow for their mistakes. You are not like that."

"I still worry."

Shadow gave her mother a long hug. "I feel much better now that we have talked once again. I know there will be much trouble and it will be hard for us, but we have the good spirits with us and I will trust in them."

"No matter what happens, you must trust in them," Shadow heard her mother say, again becoming stern of voice. "Amótkan makes life very hard for those He loves. Happiness is something that must be worked at every day. We must remember that what he gives us and what he takes from us is done so with love. Good or bad, it can only make us stronger—if we will only let it.''

''Mother, I am so lucky to have been a child of yours,'' Shadow said, hugging her once again. ''I will always remember your words. They make it so much easier for me to face that which is hard.'' She nodded to herself. ''And I know now that, for a time, life will become very hard for me.''

Chapter Nine

—————

THE DOOR FLAP to the lodge opened, and Shadow saw her father and Little Bear enter. Little Bear, a broad smile on his face, was proudly displaying a new quiver for his arrows, made from the finely tanned hide of a bull elk. He announced that he had won this prize in an archery match with many of the other young boys in the village. Shadow could tell that her father's pride in Little Bear's accomplishment was darkened by his concern over Austin. But it was Little Bear who spoke first.

"The man who came to look for you," he told Shadow, "he seems to be strong. I saw him talking to Mother for a long time."

Shadow saw her father's eyes quickly go to her mother's, and her mother said, "I was going to talk to you about it, Jim. But you have been busy with Walking Head all day long."

"I'll listen now," he said. "This whole thing has got me worried, to say the least."

"His name is Austin and he is, I think, a good man," Shadow's mother said quickly. "He talked with me for a long time, and I do not believe he would have come clear up into this land if he did not wish to speak the truth."

Shadow watched her father as he seated himself and thought for a time. He had been successful in getting trade established with not only Walking Head but other bands of Blackfeet as well. Though the Beelers had not yet showed up, it was almost certain that they would come sooner or later. Shadow knew her father had a deep concern about her getting mixed up in any problems Austin Wells might have with his two uncles.

"Did you see him tonight?" he asked Shadow.

Shadow nodded. "He came up to the lake where I was getting water. We talked about his uncles, and he told me that he no longer worked for them, that they are wicked and evil men. He said that he wished to work for you." Shadow decided to tell him now, so there would be no misunderstanding about where Austin stood in the conflict between the Beelers and her father. She now wished she had listened to Austin and let him come to the lodge with her.

"He wants to work for me?" her father asked in surprise.

"He says he has become a part of this country and does not want to go back to his own lands toward the east," Shadow said. "Yes, he asked me to let him talk to you about working at our fort-lodge."

"And what did you tell him?"

"I did not think you would be pleased," Shadow answered. "I told him that it was too soon. Then he left. He did not say where he was going, or if he wanted to see me again. Maybe he has now decided to leave these lands.''

"I wish it was easier," Shadow's father said. "I just wish it was all easier. You don't know this man very well, and I don't know him at all. Now he wants to go to work for me. If that don't beat all I've ever heard." He was shaking his head. "I thought we had a talk after you got back from shootin' arrows into those other two at the Gates of the Mountains. I thought you understood that we had enough trouble then."

"I do not wish to make trouble, Father," Shadow said. "He came here to see me. We just talked. I know there is enough trouble with the Beelers as it is. And I know there will only be more if he were to work for you, but maybe he could be of help."

"It sounds to me like you two have gotten pretty fond of one another," he told Shadow. "If his uncles weren't Jake and Claude Beeler, I would say fine. But how do you know he's not just playin' up to you and maybe wants to do his uncles some good by gettin' to us from the inside?"

"Father, he does not care for his uncles. They have not been good to him. He has left them. You told me that yourself."

"That's only what I heard," her father said quickly. "Maybe none of it was true, and it's all a trick to get to us."

Shadow's mother spoke up. "Jim, you have become very distrustful."

"Can't be none too careful these days," he said in defense of his statement. "These mountains are gettin' full of men who'll say and do anything, just as long as there's some money in it."

"I wish you would not feel that way about Austin," Shadow said. "I believe his words are true."

Shadow watched her father get up and make his way back over to the door flap. "Just the same, I wish you'd stay away from one another. At least until I get a good idea what the Beelers are up to. They haven't showed up here yet, and that bothers me a little. I'd feel better if they would just crawl on out from under their rock and start something. That way we can get it all over with quicker and get back to tradin' robes for next spring's shipment to St. Louis."

"What if he comes back to see me again?" Shadow asked. "What if he has not left and still wants to work for you?"

"You can tell him that I'm worried about his uncles," her father answered. "Tell him once I get things straightened out with them, I will think about puttin' him to work. But not until then. See what he says." He turned to Shadow's mother. "I'm goin' out to talk more trade with Walking Head and his friends from up north."

When her father had left, Shadow picked up the dress she had been working on. The lodge was silent, as the eyes of both her mother and Little Bear were on her. She fought to hold back the tears, twisting the dress in her hands.

Shadow's mother stood at the door flap. "Are you sure you will not come with me now?"

Shadow shook her head.

The door flap closed, and Little Bear went over to where Shadow was sitting, still twisting the dress. He took a seat and made himself comfortable.

"I have never seen anything trouble you as this does," he said to Shadow.

"It is hard for you to understand," Shadow told him.

Little Bear smiled. "Maybe in time it will be better. It is only that Father does not know him at all. He has always been better friends with Indian peoples than those who are white. Maybe if he could know this man, he would feel better. This man seemed to me to be a lot like Father. In many ways."

"How do you know so much about him?" Shadow asked.

"After I watched him talk to Mother, I followed him out of the village for a ways. That was when he was going to find you at the high lake. I tried to sneak up behind him, but he knows the ways of the forest and heard me. He asked me in sign what I was doing. I told him that I thought he was a deer. He was not angry but only laughed and told me to look for an animal with four legs and not just two. I have not told this to either Mother or Father. But I think he is a good man. And I think maybe if Father knew this, he would understand that Austin Wells could help us against the Beelers. I am sure he knows them better than we do."

Shadow laughed. "Now you sound like a war chief. And I thought you didn't understand."

"Why don't you come with me and watch the dancing?" Little Bear then asked. "Maybe it would make you feel better."

Shadow shook her head. "I would rather not go to where they are dancing."

"Are you worried about Badger?" Little Bear asked. "There has been nothing more said about you becoming his wife since we first came. Maybe he was only joking when he said it."

"I just don't want to see him any more than I have

to,'' Shadow said. "Especially at night, when he has been drinking the burning water.''

"I think they drank all the burning water two nights past,'' Little Bear said. "I saw them break empty jugs then, and I have seen no new jugs. Maybe there will be no more drinking of the burning water. That would make his father happy, I know.''

"You are right, Little Bear,'' Shadow said. "Walking Head worries a great deal about Badger. It is too bad that Badger does not understand the burning water like his brother, Standing Elk. I have heard Standing Elk say many times that he does not like to drink the burning water because it makes him do crazy things. It makes him lose his head. If Badger understood that he, too, is poisoned by the burning water, he would stop drinking it.''

"I do not know a lot about these things,'' Little Bear said. "But maybe it is too late for Badger to stop drinking the burning water. Maybe he has drank it for so long that he now needs it, like many of the old Long Knives and other Indian peoples that we have seen who always ask Father for it and become angry when he says he does not have it. We have both seen this many times.''

Shadow nodded in agreement. Little Bear was very observant and could readily comprehend what was going on around him. They had been to the fort-lodge called Benton before and had seen the groups of broken-down men and women, Indians and old white trappers alike, who lingered around the fort to get whatever they could of the burning water. It had been the same at their old fort-lodge along the Stinking-water, far to the south, and now it was beginning to happen at their new fort-lodge along the Madison. They would straggle in, clothed only in badly worn

buckskins or tattered blankets, begging for the burning water, offering any sort of service they could
think of to get it. Many old Long Knives, who did
not want to go back to the lands in the east and were
too crippled and weak to be of service to those who
traded with the Indian peoples, spent their last days
trading sides of elk or deer meat for a jug of the
burning water. More than once Shadow had seen one
of them lying over a jug, either beside the fort-lodge
or along a trail, having died from what he had drunk.

"Maybe it would make you feel better if you came
with me," Little Bear again suggested.

Shadow shook her head. "No, I do not think dancing will help. You go ahead. I will be all right here."

After Little Bear had left, Shadow stared at her
unfinished dress, which she knew she was not in the
mood to work on. She thought it would give her
something to do as she tried to forget about Austin
and their meeting earlier. But the longer she lingered
in the lodge, the more she longed to be with him. She
remembered the trail near the small bank where he
had held her, which went around the hill to his camp.
She heard the sounds of the villagers laughing and
having fun around their own fires. It made her feel
even more alone. Finally, she could stand it no longer.
She had to be with Austin.

Shadow made her way out of the village, past the
singing and the laughing and the fires over which
meat of all kinds roasted and sizzled. Everyone
seemed to be having fun, and Shadow knew it would
go on nearly the entire night. It seemed no one got
any sleep during celebration festivals.

She hurried up the trail, making her way along the
hillside, until she found the small bank where the trail
forked. She hesitated a moment, wondering if he was

still camped in the aspens not far away or if he had left. She wondered how she would feel if he had gone and if she could bear it. She told herself to go ahead, she had come this far.

As she neared the small grove of aspens, her heart jumped. She smelled smoke from a campfire. He had not gone. Her excitement mounted and she entered the trees, seeing him seated near a small fire.

Upon hearing her, he stood up with his rifle and yelled out into the darkness, "Who is it?"

"Shadow," she answered. "I want to talk with you."

Austin lowered his rifle, and Shadow came into the light of the fire. His face was impassive, as if he did not know what to expect from her. Finally he put the rifle down against a tree.

"I'll be gone tomorrow," he said. "If that's what you want."

"No," Shadow said quickly. She came closer to him. He looked so rugged and strong in the light of the fire, his buckskin shirt opened halfway to the waist. "I do not want you to go. You should know that."

"I don't know what to think," he told her. "You let me hold you, then you tell me I'm not good enough to meet your family."

"No, I do not feel that way at all. It is only that I am torn between you and the worry of what your uncles want to do to my family. I fear that bringing you into this trouble could make things worse for my father."

"I don't understand," Austin said. "I think I could help your father a lot."

Shadow explained what she was thinking. "Maybe you could help if it were only your uncles that we must worry about. But there is also Badger.''

"You mean you and he—''

"No,'' Shadow said. "He is as much trouble as both of your uncles together. You know he does not like you after you beat him in the game of hands. He wants me to become his wife and will not want you to be with me.''

"We don't have to worry about him,'' Austin said with defiance. "He's got no right to think he can have you just because he wants you. There's no law that I know of that says you can't chose me over him, if that's what you want. He'll just have to get used to it.''

"It is not that easy,'' Shadow said. "My father wishes to trade with his father, Walking Head. They are good friends, and many of Walking Head's friends from other Blackfoot bands now also are thinking of traveling to our fort-lodge to trade. But if Badger sees you with me and my family, I know he will tell lies to his father and the other Blackfoot leaders. He will try to make them all believe that you are bad for his people. He will try to make Walking Head and the others angry with my father. This is what I worry about.''

Austin shook his head in frustration. "Together with all that, my uncles are bound and determined to get at your father and destroy his business. How many other problems can come into this?''

"My father will straighten it out,'' Shadow said. "He will have help from Walking Head. They are both wise men. I only wanted to tell you this so that you will understand that I do not want any more trouble if I can help it.''

Austin nodded. "I understand. I just wish things didn't have to be like they are.''

"It is not your fault," Shadow said. "I, too, wish that Badger and your uncles did not exist. But they do. There is nothing we can do about it."

"Well," Austin said with a smile, "none of them are here tonight. There is just you and me. They can't stop us from enjoying it, either."

Shadow let him put his arms around her, his green eyes shining in the light of the fire. He smiled. "You are quite a woman at that," he said. "You really do what you can for your father, don't you? Even if it means putting your own life in danger."

"He has been very good to me," Shadow said. "All in my family are very close."

Shadow felt his arms tighten around her ever so slightly. Being in his arms seemed to take away every care or worry she had. It was as if she were in a dream. She loved the sound of his voice and his gentle nature.

"You're the kind of woman every man dreams of," he told her. "So rare and so beautiful."

The flames in the fire danced, and a different warmth spread quickly through her as his lips touched hers. Shadow could feel his strength flowing from him as he held her against his body, and she molded herself to fit him. When he had finished his kiss, he took her by the hand, leading her to his bed of warm buffalo robes.

They sat down together, he wrapping a robe around them and drawing her close to him. Below the village rang with song and laughter. Where they were, the crickets and the crackling of the fire added life to the soft summer night.

"You have done something to me I can't explain," he said. "It's so wonderful."

Shadow felt herself raising her lips toward his,

reaching her arms out under the robe to encircle his broad shoulders. Their lips met, and she let out a sigh of hunger, a wanting from deep within that overwhelmed her. His lips were drawing from her the strongest sensation of desire she had ever known. His kiss went to her neck and the soft part of her throat. His hands were under her dress, slowly raising the hemline while he stroked her sleek thighs. She felt herself lying back with him, feeling his warmth ever more as his lips continued to spread fire along her throat and neck, and his hands worked their way along her stomach until they drove her wild with the sensation they brought to her breasts.

Her body tingled as she allowed him to carefully pull off her dress. His own buckskins removed, his lips continued to bring a fever to the very core of her being. Her nipples jutted tauter than she had ever known as his tongue danced across and around them. It took her mind from where she lay and carried her far beyond anything she had ever dreamed of. Desire overwhelmed her, and she felt her hands moving uncontrollably over his muscular body and through the coils of hair on his chest, feeling the ripples of his hard frame.

She pulled him to herself, gasping as he gently pushed himself deep into her. Her breath left her as he began a smooth, rhythmic motion that she fell into, rocking steadily faster with him until her passion rose beyond any limit she had ever known. She heard him and felt his hot breath in her ear. Together they cried out in an ecstasy neither had ever imagined, and Shadow held him tightly, getting all of him, wanting him forever.

She felt him kissing her lightly on her cheek as she caught her breath. He held himself over her with his strong arms, looking into her eyes as she ran her fingers across his face and through his thick hair.

"I will never be the same," he told her, giving her a soft kiss. He then rolled over and took her next to him, stroking her hair as she had his only moments before. "I never knew I could feel like this," he said. He held her close. "I love you, Shadow."

Shadow knew her feelings for him were also love. But their situation was so difficult.

"There are so many things that now work against us," Shadow said. "Perhaps, in time, all these troubles will be over and we can be together."

"We can't let that stop us," Austin said. "We can't let anything come between us. We've got to fight it. Together we can lick this thing."

"Before we can be together, my father must trust you," Shadow said. "He must understand that you are not with your uncles."

Austin set his jaw. "Then I'll just have to tell him. He won't accept it from you, so he'll have to hear it from me, personally. And now is as good a time as any."

"No," Shadow said quickly.

"Why not?"

"I am afraid. It troubles me that your uncles are coming, and it troubles me that Badger desires me in the way that he does and hates you."

"Listen," Austin suggested. "If we go down there right now, I can talk to your father before Badger even knows I'm around."

"I do not think so," Shadow told him. "My father is now with Walking Head and other high members of the Blackfoot peoples talking trade. We would not be able to see him now. And I do not want to take the chance that Badger will see us and cause trouble.

That would destroy everything and make the problem even worse.''

Austin threw his arms up in frustration. "We can't just go on like this. It's hard on both of us."

Shadow put her dress back on. "Be patient. It will take time to get things worked out. I will be back up to see you and tell you how things are."

When Austin had finished dressing, he took Shadow in his arms and held her close. "You are always leaving me," he said. "When will the time come when you do not have to leave? When can we stay together?"

"As soon as possible," Shadow answered.

He gave her a last, long kiss before she started back down the mountain. "Make it soon," he told her. "Very soon."

Shadow hurried back to the village, concerned that she had been missed and had possibly caused her family added worry. Though it was now getting late, the villagers continued with their dancing and games. It meant little that night would turn again into day; they had come to celebrate the gift of life with one another, and there was nothing of more importance during this gathering. They would all have to go back to taking life more seriously soon enough. The fall hunt would soon be upon them, and there would then be time only to prepare as much meat as possible for the upcoming snow moons.

Inside their lodge, Shadow found her father cleaning his Hawken rifle. His eyes showed that he knew where she had been.

"Your mother and Little Bear are both off visiting," he said to Shadow. "I wish you had gone with them."

Shadow took a deep breath and sat down. "I had to go, Father."

"I'm concerned," he said to her. "A scout came in not long ago and announced to Walking Head that the Beelers were camped less than a full day's ride from here. There's no way to tell when they will decide to come into camp, but you know as sure as a goose has feathers that they'll be here. I just don't want you and that young trapper friend of yours caught up in the middle of things when the lid finally blows off all this."

"I am able to fight," Shadow told her father. "You know that I am not afraid to help you against your enemies, no matter who they are."

"Yes, you can fight as well as most men," he said in acknowledgment. "But I'm just saying that when your heart starts to do your thinkin', your head don't always make the right decisions."

"Father, I understand what you are saying. And I will not let my heart rule my mind. I only ask that you have confidence in me to do the right things. I must listen to the voices inside me and obey them when they speak strongly to me."

"It's going to take all of us to overcome all this," her father said. "We're going to have trouble like we've never had it before." Here he looked sternly at Shadow. "And I'm going to have to count on you for the most help," he said. "You're going to have to be stronger than you've ever had to be before."

Shadow nodded. She had realized this for a long time. She knew there would be hard times for them before they could have true happiness. And now those hard times were upon them.

Chapter Ten

─────

THE SUN CAME and crossed the sky again while
Shadow stayed near the lodge to help her mother with
the cooking and other chores. She had found little to
be happy about since once again speaking with her
father late the night before. Their discussion had been
long and of a very serious tone. He had told her that
he wanted her to stay close to the lodge and not go
anywhere for a few days. Tension mounted now that
the Beelers were coming, and Shadow knew her father wanted to find out what they were up to as soon
as he could.

Having to stay in the village made Shadow feel like
a caged deer. She was used to roaming at will and
taking herself wherever she wanted to go, whenever
she wanted to. She knew very well her father's concern about the Beelers was not the main reason he
wished her to stay home: He seemed more convinced

than ever that Austin was still working with his uncles and was determined that she not see him for a time, at least until he knew for himself what the Beelers were planning. It made it doubly hard for Shadow, as her longing for Austin was again becoming strong and, at the same time, she realized her father's concern for her was very real. He had never before restricted her in any way, and it concerned her greatly that his feelings about this should be so strong.

More days passed and Shadow found herself becoming very temperamental. She tried to make things easier by joining in on visiting sessions to other lodges with her mother. But she found herself looking out from the village and toward the high peaks above, wondering if Austin were somewhere up among the rocks and timber, watching for her and wondering about her. She tried to dismiss the thought that he had become angry and, having become convinced that she no longer cared for him, he had decided to leave these lands after all. This thought haunted her often, though she knew deep within herself that he was still up at the high lake waiting for her to come to him.

"The Beelers have not yet come," she told her father that evening while they ate, "and it has been the passing of many suns since I last spoke with my spirit helper, the golden eagle. I feel I must go into the high country tomorrow. I shall return before the sun again returns."

Shadow's mother said nothing. Her father's eyes did not look up from his meal for a time. Then he nodded to her.

"Go ahead," he told her. "Maybe I've been a little overly worried. I don't know. I just have this bad feeling in my bones. Things have been going so well with Walking Head, and I would hate to see it all get spoiled." His face then became quite stern as he told her, "If you happen to run into the Beelers, just leave things be. No more stunts like the Gates of the Mountains."

"I will not harm the Beelers if they should happen to come," Shadow answered.

Shadow was up very early, so great was her eagerness to once again be off by herself. She brought water, chopped wood, and had meat already roasting by the time the others were just getting out of their beds. Her mother said with a little laugh, "I am glad your father decided to let you go off for today and be by yourself. I think he realized that you were just about crazy. And because of it, I think I *have* become crazy."

Shadow decided to go on foot and leave her horse with the herd. There were places she would go where she would need to leave the horse behind. And if she were to accidentally run into the Beelers, it would be much easier to hide without a horse.

It was near midday when she reached the shores of the high lake. The day was calm and the water was smooth and clear. She had known all this time that Austin's concern for her was as great as her own for him. She had brought with her a large skin bag filled with pemmican. Maybe this would better convince him of her love.

The lake was calm in the warm sunshine, with a small herd of mountain sheep drinking just off the trail. A huge ram, whose horns had grown down from its head in a perfect full curl, looked up at Shadow for a time before ambling toward the security of a nearby rock ledge. The shores of the lake were alive with ducks of all colors and sizes, most with families of nearly fledged little ones who all swam out toward the safety of open water.

Shadow then looked up toward the top of a nearby hill. There, standing beside a waterfall, was Austin, waving to her with his broad frontiersman hat, his face alive with a broad smile.

"It's been forever," he told her when they reached each other. "I was losing hope of ever seeing you again."

She savored the pleasure of his arms for a time, trying to put off what she knew she had to tell him. Finally, he said, "What's the matter? There is something troubling you. I can tell."

"My father is concerned about my seeing you," Shadow said. "He is still not convinced that you are now separated from your uncles. He told me that he believes that you are still with your uncles and that you are using me in order to help them destroy our family."

"I knew I should have gone down there the other night and found him," Austin said, slapping his hand against the side of his leg. "I shouldn't have let you talk me out of it. Now things are that much worse."

"He does not understand," Shadow said in her father's defense. "That is all. When he gets to know you, he will change his thinking."

"Your father and I need to have a long talk," Austin then said with a nod of conviction. "The best thing I can do is to get this all straightened out once and for all."

Shadow again went into his arms, feeling his strong caress. It felt so good to have him hold her close and cover her with his kisses. She did not wish to go back down to the village alone, but she was still not convinced that bringing Austin would solve anything at this time. The longer he held her the harder it would be for her to decide.

Then, from the trail nearby, came the sound of a horse coming at a fast gallop. Shadow and Austin looked to see Badger ride to a stop on his war pony. He was covered with paint from head to foot, and his eyes were deep slits of hate as he got down from the horse and buried the point of his lance in the ground beside him and spoke in sign.

"I see the Long Knife called Green Eyes, who is a dog and a thief, is now stealing my woman!"

Austin looked quickly to Shadow. "What does he mean by *his* woman?"

"A lie!" she told Austin. Then she stepped forward and glared at Badger, making her own sign to him. "I am tired of your lies and dishonest actions. You tell everyone that you own me, when you do not. I have told you before, and I will now say it to you again, I will never be a wife to one such as you. I will not give honor to him that seeks to control me and show me off to the people as one of his prize possessions. No, I will not allow you to cause more trouble for me. And I would like to know how it is you happen to be up here."

"It is easy to follow one who is in a hurry and does not look back," Badger answered. "You have no right to come up here and see the green-eyed dog who will soon die and be food for the wolves."

Shadow told Austin to remain calm while she continued to talk to Badger in her own behalf.

"Maybe you have trouble understanding what I have told you time and again," she made sign to him. "There will never be a time when I must ask your permission to do anything. I have every right to come to this place, or any other place that I choose. As for

you, there are no kind words that fit you. There is
certainly no goodness in your heart. You are indeed
without honor or you never would have followed me
up here, sneaking behind the bushes like a frightened
child.''

"Can you not hear the footsteps of a horse?"
Badger asked.

"No," Shadow quickly made sign back. "You
went back for your horse once you knew where I had
gone to. Then you painted yourself for war. But your
medicine is not good this fine day.''

Badger laughed. "My medicine is good. It is
strong. But I want to know why the green-eyed one
hides behind you and lets you speak. Is he not a man?
We shall see!" Badger then pulled his knife and began to walk toward them.

Austin pulled his own knife and quickly started forward.

"No!" Shadow yelled to Austin, grabbing him by
the arm.

"He came up here for a fight," Austin said to her.
"Now I aim to give him one.''

"Wait!" Shadow continued to yell, tugging at his
clothes. Badger, who had taken his stand, was now
laughing. Shadow finally made Austin hold up and
then continued to try talking him out of the fight.
"You know better than to do this!" she said with her
teeth gritted. "Even if you kill him, you will lose.
Why can't you see that?''

Austin took his eyes from Badger to Shadow.
"What do you mean?"

"It will be said in the village that you killed him
unfairly. Maybe that you and I killed him together,
so that he would not bother us. There would be no
one to say any different. Your life certainly would

then be in danger. And perhaps mine also. Let me talk to him again.''

Badger then made sign to both Shadow and Austin. ''It is funny to me that a woman must stand in front of a man. Yes, the green-eyed dog is afraid. I, Badger, have made him afraid, like a child when the sun falls and darkness comes to the land.''

''You make no one afraid,'' Shadow then told him. ''You only make them laugh. You come up here to fight but are afraid to make your challenge in front of all the people of the village, so that they may watch to see that all is fair. Why is this so? Why do you not make your challenge down among the people?''

''He has not come down among the people,'' Badger answered with a sneer. ''He stays up here and crawls through the grass like the snake that he is. He has been up here for the passing of many suns now, afraid to act like a man and show himself in the village.'' He laughed.

''I have told him to stay up here,'' Shadow told Badger. ''It is I who has not wanted him to come down. I knew if he did there would be trouble such as this. I did not want to involve my family in it. That is the only reason he is now up here. And if you had any honor, you would wait until he is in the village to make your challenge. Or maybe you know that he will cut your heart out for the black raven to feed upon, and you do not want the children of the village to laugh at you when you fall.''

Badger glared at Shadow for a time. Then he made sign again. ''You should not talk to your man that way. It makes him angry.''

''You are not a man,'' Austin told Badger in sign. ''You are a small boy who has yet to win a fight with those his own age. And he does not know that to fight a real man will cost him his life."

"Austin!" Shadow said quickly.

"Don't try and stop me this time," Austin said, moving forward and setting himself. "It's up to him now. If he really wants to fight, he'll come ahead."

Badger studied Austin for a time before putting his knife away. "No," he made sign, "the Eagle Woman is right. I will not kill you up here where the people of the village cannot watch. Though there is no glory in killing you, I will still let them see when I take your scalp and throw it to the camp dogs to fight over."

After climbing back on his horse, Badger then rode down the trail a short distance before turning around to stare at Shadow and Austin for a time. Austin quickly became irritated at Badger's insolence.

"Pay him no attention," Shadow said. "Put an arm around me."

Shadow and Austin then faced Badger with their arms around each other. Badger raised his lance in the air and screamed once before kicking his horse into a gallop down the trail.

"That really got to him," Austin said. "He and I had best get things settled right away. No use puttin' it off."

"That is not the answer," Shadow said. "It will only cause trouble with my father."

"Shadow, your father has got trouble, no matter what!" Austin said hotly. "And I don't want to play school-kid games with Badger. That won't make things any easier for anybody. It will just give Badger all the more reason to tell everyone that I'm a sneak and won't stand up to him like a man."

"You must wait to face him!" Shadow insisted.

"Damn!" Austin picked up his hat and slammed it against his leg. "I don't like any of this even a little bit."

"Please," Shadow said. "Try to understand. We must not make any more trouble than there already is. We cannot have the Blackfeet people angry at my father and us. It will ruin everything my father has worked so hard for. There would never be any chance for you to work for him or even be liked by him. I do not want that to happen, and I know you do not, either."

"What are we supposed to do?" Austin asked.

"I only know that we cannot do anything to Badger until all the people know that it is he who wants the trouble. And I do not know what your uncles will do when they come to the village. We can only wait and see what happens."

"But it could be too late by then," Austin argued. "If my uncles get the jump on things, they could cause more trouble than we could patch up. The same goes for Badger."

"There is nothing we can do!" Shadow emphasized. "When I killed the two with you at the Gates of the Mountains, I made things hard for my father. There are those who now say that he is fighting the American Fur Company, those from the fort-lodge called Benton. It is said he has started a feud with them, that he sent me to kill them so that there could be no goodwill between my father and those at Benton. Can you see what I mean by adding to the trouble there is already?"

"We'll lose for sure if I don't help you," Austin said. "We've got to do it together. And now!"

"Please," Shadow said, "try to understand. We must not make any more trouble than there already is. Stay up here. For me. For us. Wait until I can again come back and talk with you.''

''When will that be?''

''I cannot say. But wait. I will try and talk to my father. Perhaps I can bring him up here. Then you can talk to him and try to make him understand that you want to fight against your uncles, that you have been wronged by them and have a great dislike for all that they stand for. But we must not take the chance of you coming into the village and making the Blackfeet people angry. I do want you to talk to my father, but let me tell you when the time is right.''

''I'll go crazy up here,'' Austin said.

''I will talk to my father tonight,'' Shadow said. ''We will not have to wait as long to see one another as we did this time. But we must find another place to meet. Move your camp to the other side of the lake. Watch for me. And I will be more careful so that I will not be followed.''

''I still don't like it,'' Austin said, shaking his head. ''I'm just afraid that we'll lose before we get started against them.''

''I will talk to my father,'' Shadow repeated. ''Whether he is with me or not, I will meet you on the other side of the lake when the sun has crossed the sky twice.''

They held each other once again and Shadow left. Having spent more time with Austin than she had planned, she felt she must make her talk with her spirit helper short. She did not want to be missed again and cause concern for her family.

She made her way high among the rocks that overlooked the forest below. Taking her place on a rock ledge, she began to sing a song of prayer to the she-eagle. She hoped that the eagle would hear her and

come to give her strength and courage. Now that the
hard time for her family had come, it was very important to receive as much spiritual help as possible.

During her song, she looked down into the forest
and suddenly fell silent. Halfway up the mountain
was a column of Blackfoot warriors, led by Badger,
that was coming along a trail totally hidden from sight
off the main trail. Though only five warriors rode with
Badger, it was clear to Shadow that they meant to
find Austin and kill him. They all wore the paint of
war and were armed with their best bows and lances.
Shadow knew she must find Austin again quickly.

It took her little time to climb back down from the
rocks. She hurried to the lake where she had left him,
searching frantically in the vicinity of the waterfall
and all around where they had been together earlier.
But Austin was nowhere to be found.

Shadow tried to compose herself and think clearly.
Surely he was already moving his camp to the other
side of the lake. She would travel along the small path
that led from the main trail to his camp and hope that
she could reach him before he had already gone. Perhaps she would run into him along the way.

Shadow hurried through the forest, moving with
silence and grace toward the place where she had first
held Austin in her arms. She tried to breathe evenly
as she traveled quickly to prevent herself from becoming tired. It was hard for her to pace herself, to
keep from running all out, for it occurred to her that
Badger was traveling up the same trail they had used
to go back down to the village from the lake that first
night he had found her. After their confrontation earlier in the day, Badger must have found Austin's
camp. He was now leading his warriors directly to it.
As she thought more about it, Shadow became deeply

angered. Badger certainly wanted to be rid of Austin as soon as possible and no longer cared about honor in his quest for blood.

Finally Shadow broke from the trees around Austin's camp and found him packing his horse for the move to the other side of the lake. Not hearing her approach, he turned in surprise.

Shadow put her fingers to her lips and whispered, "Come with me, quickly! Leave your horse and belongings. Bring only your rifle."

Austin, realizing there was something terribly wrong, followed her into the trees behind his camp. Shadow then told him of seeing Badger and five warriors advancing up the hill, dressed for war. Austin then told her that Badger had indeed found his camp, for when he came back from meeting Shadow at the lake, he found a Blackfoot arrow had been driven through his sleeping robes and left as a sign. Now he knew that the arrow belonged to Badger.

There was no other escape for them but to climb up into the timber behind the camp and then, if necessary, higher, into the rocky crags along the face of Going-to-the-Sun Mountain. That would be only as a last resort, for the open rocks would leave them exposed to arrows from below and make them easy targets for Badger and his warriors.

Shadow and Austin settled themselves among the trees and rocks to wait. Below, the sounds of Badger and his warriors could already be heard in camp. Badger's voice was loud and angry. They had come in boldly, expecting to find Austin alone and surprised. Instead they had found only a horse left untied and a few meager belongings. It would not be enough, both Shadow and Austin knew, that the camp would be torn apart and destroyed. Badger would certainly want to find them. And he would know, by the horse left untied and the other belongings only partially packed, that Shadow had gotten to the camp and had warned Austin of his coming. Somehow she had seen him and his warriors. It was a sign of this woman's great power. But this would not be enough to keep him from finding her and the green-eyed Long Knife. He would kill this Long Knife and take the Eagle Woman for his own.

Austin checked his rifle. Shadow had only her knife; she had not thought it necessary to bring her bow and arrows. Even though Austin's rifle would be a good defense, Shadow knew he must not use it.

"Your firestick must stay silent," she told him. "You must not shoot. The sound would carry below and bring those from the village to see what was happening."

"This is a fine thing," Austin said in disgust. "Badger and his warriors are down there tearing my camp to shreds and will no doubt start up here after us any time now, and I can't even make good use of my rifle."

He hid it among a group of rocks and berry bushes nearby, saying that he would not worry about Badger's finding it. If they could not make a good stand along the cliffs above them, he would no longer have any use for the rifle anyway. From below came the whoops and shouts of Badger and his warriors as they started up the hill from Austin's camp. Her hopes that Badger would not realize that they had to be nearby were now shattered. Austin's words were true: If they did not have good medicine this day, there would be no need for them to worry about anything else.

Chapter Eleven

━━━━

SHADOW AND AUSTIN had no choice but to leave the cover of the timber at the edge of the high cliffs and begin their climb up among the rocks. At any other time this vertical garden would have been a scene of beauty, with its trails of green moss hanging under small streams of falling water along the face of the mountain, interspersed with rough formations of rock and wildflowers, all given life by the pockets of glaciers that melted slowly among the high peaks above. Now the jagged face of stone appeared stern and uninviting.

Austin removed his buckskin shirt and threw it aside, while Shadow made long slits along both sides of her dress. They would need as much mobility as possible to climb swiftly along the face of the cliff. Badger and his warriors were coming rapidly up the hill now, yelling war cries and urging one another onward.

"That Blackfoot wants you bad," Austin said of Badger. "And he thinks he will have my hair for a war prize."

"He will have neither," Shadow said with conviction. "He will be sorry he ever left the village this day and came up here to make trouble for us."

Shadow and Austin began to climb the face of the cliff, moving quickly, as their moccasins provided good footing for them. They found a slim, narrow trail etched in the cliff wall, a trail used by the milky-white mountain goat, whose home was these rocky crags high above the forest floor. This trail would serve them well, for they needed every advantage they could get.

Below, the yells of Badger and his warriors grew louder. They had come out of the timber and were now standing at the base of the cliff, pointing up at Shadow and Austin. Badger was laughing; he knew that the open face of the cliff served only to trap Shadow and this Long Knife with the green eyes, who stood in the way of his owning this woman he had desired since first seeing her. It would now be easy to rid himself of this Long Knife. It would take only one arrow, and it would not be a long shot.

Austin stopped on the trail and began to curse.

"What is it?" Shadow asked, watching below as Badger stood in a group with his warriors.

"The trail," Austin said. "It goes out along that steep wall of rock ahead. I don't see how even goats can stay on it."

"We have no choice but to go ahead," Shadow said. "There is no other way up from here." She clenched her fists in frustration, feeling very foolish for not having sought an easier way up the face of the mountain.

"Not one of them shot an arrow up here at me yet," Austin said in surprise. "What do you suppose they're up to?"

"They know we are trapped up here," Shadow said, "with no way to escape. They will not be in a hurry to try and kill you now. They will want to make a game of it." She looked below, and a shiver of fear ran through her. Each warrior was picking up a rock. It was clear to her that they meant to test their skill at trying to knock Austin off the face of the cliff.

"Go quickly!" she told Austin. "Move along the trail."

"I can't go any faster," Austin said. "What's the matter? Did they finally get their arrows out?"

As Austin worked for footing along the narrow trail, a rock slammed into the face of the cliff just above his head. He froze, fighting to keep his balance. A roar of laughter came up from Badger and his warriors below.

"Let them play their games," Shadow said through clenched teeth. "They will soon wish they had used their bows and not wasted the time it will take us to reach safety. Yes, this game will soon cost them dearly."

Austin had again caught his breath and was slowly moving along the wall, feeling for loose stones and carefully placing his feet in cracks and crevices. Another rock smashed into the face of the cliff near his left hand, shattering into fragments that stung his fingers. Again he held on tightly, knowing that to falter even slightly could mean death. More laughter came from below.

"I will get next to you," Shadow said to him. "Maybe they will stop if they have fear of hitting me."

"No!" Austin said. "I don't want to take that chance. Besides, they just might decide to forget the rocks and go to their bows."

Shadow, knowing he was right, could only nod in agreement. On his face was the terror of wondering when the next rock would come and if it would strike him. Shadow felt more helpless than at any time in her life. She could only climb along the face of the cliff with him and hope they did not hit him hard enough to cause him to fall. The continued laughter from below echoed in her ears, and she fought to control her feelings, knowing it would only make it harder to move her muscles if they were tight with the rage that seethed within her.

Austin then let out a loud groan as pain shot through his side and lower back. Shadow looked to see the large welt where the rock had glanced off his ribs. Loud cheering came up from below, and Shadow could hardly keep from screaming in frustration. Still, Austin refused to lose his nerve and continued onward, despite the rock that landed just under his right arm and the other one that glanced off his upper leg.

Shadow then heard his voice. It sounded strong and filled with hope.

"There's a cave just ahead," he told her, looking back and pointing with his head.

Shadow, with strength renewed, began to move behind Austin as he made his way toward the cave. Two more rocks came, both of them missing. The laughter below had stopped.

The cave was just above the narrow trail, back in the face of the cliff. Austin had just reached it and was beginning to pull himself up and into the opening when Shadow screamed at what she saw below. Badger's bow was drawn.

Austin slipped, a rock pulling loose from his grip. He slid sideways, digging and scratching at the face of the cliff, until he had regained his balance. Badger's arrow, meant for his back, struck the rocks where Austin had just been, splintering and driving a piece of the arrow's shaft into Austin's shoulder.

Austin continued to pull himself up into the cave, ignoring the blood that lined his shoulder and left side. Below, Badger had not even bothered to pull a second arrow from his quiver, so confident was he in his first shot. Now he yelled loudly and sent a second, wild shot caroming off the rocks beside the cave as Austin pulled himself in to safety.

Badger and his warriors screamed in anger as Austin helped Shadow into the cave. With a quick pull, she removed the large splinter of wood from Austin's shoulder and wrapped a piece from her dress around his wound to stop the bleeding. Austin seemed to be in no pain, so great was his relief to be off the face of the cliff and away from the rocks that could have meant his death.

"The spirits are with us," Shadow said with a broad smile. "You could have been struck many times but were not. We were led to the safety of this cave, when no other shelter is to be found along this cliff. It is a good day."

Austin took her in his arms and held her closer than he ever had before. Tears flooded her eyes. She now fully realized how much this man meant to her and how she would feel if she were to ever lose him. Never before had she known such happiness, and she could no longer know the joys of life without his touch and the warmth of his deep green eyes. She tried not to think of how it would be now if Badger's arrow had reached its mark.

"Badger will be on his way up here," Shadow then said. "Our time of danger has not yet passed, but we can now fight with the confidence that the spirits are with us this day."

"And we'd best get started with the fight," Austin said with renewed vigor and confidence. He peered out over the edge of the cave, and Shadow worked her way beside him, looking down to see what was now happening below.

Badger stood alone, directing his warriors as they spread out along the face of the cliff, each one looking for a place to begin their climb. It was clear that Badger's intent was to remain below and use his bow against Austin if he could. It would seem that Shadow and Austin would be trapped within the cave and then be easy prey for the warriors when they got up the cliff.

"What are you doing?" Shadow asked Austin as she watched him select a rock that was fairly large.

"I'm about to return a favor to our good friend, Badger," he answered. "He's busy with his warriors down there, and I am about to send him good wishes."

Badger had just finished instructing his warriors and was fitting an arrow to his bow when Austin released the rock. He looked up toward the cave to see Austin's face and the rock coming down at him, thrown with tremendous speed and force. Badger had no time to react before it landed squarely against his forearm, just above the wrist. The bones, shattered by the impact, splintered out in two different places along his arm.

"Didn't get a head shot," Austin said. "But he'll never shoot that bow of his the same again."

Badger had fallen sideways and was now curled up on the ground with his badly broken arm under him, vomiting in pain and shock. The other five warriors, now partway up the face of the cliff, could only stare down in disbelief. Austin then quickly heaved another rock down toward the closest warrior, who was climbing directly below them.

The warrior turned from watching Badger and looked up just as the rock reached him. It slammed solidly into the right side of his face, exploding the eyeball out of its socket and tearing flesh from the skull. The warrior pitched backward off the face of the cliff and tumbled along the rocks until he came to rest in a heap not far from the injured Badger. Still only half conscious from the blow to his arm, Badger did not even notice.

"There's four of them left," Austin said, leaning back inside the cave and holding his injured shoulder. "But now they will be a lot more careful about how they come up here after us."

"Maybe they will decide to leave this place now that Badger is injured and one of their number is dead," Shadow remarked hopefully as she looked down from the cave. The other four warriors had descended back down the cliff and were beginning to gather around Badger and their dead comrade.

Austin came back to the opening in the cave and watched with Shadow as the warriors helped Badger back from the bottom of the cliff and to the safety of the trees just below.

"We're still in a fix up here," he said to Shadow. "There's no place to go but up if the rest of them decide to come back up for us."

"It would not be wise for them to do that," Shadow said. "Surely they understand by now that it is not a good day for them. Badger's medicine is broken. There is no strength left in their power. It is gone, swept away by the spirits, who are with us this day. If they continue to try and kill you and take me for Badger, they will only meet with more harm."

It was hard to see through the trees below, but Shadow and Austin could make out Badger as he came to his feet, still doubled over his arm. In a short time he had straightened himself up and stood talking loudly with the other four warriors while he motioned his head toward the cave among the rocks where Shadow and Austin watched. He held his injured arm in front of him, but his body shook with rage as he spoke. Soon it was clear that the attack upon Austin and Shadow would continue, with renewed force.

"War songs," Shadow said to Austin as the four warriors began a loud yelling and chanting as they stood near Badger. "War songs of vengeance. They will soon come after us again. Now their hearts are filled with anger for Badger and for their lost brother. Our medicine will indeed have to be strong."

"I wish I had my rifle," Austin said, shaking his head. "I could put this all to rest right now."

Badger and the remaining four warriors climbed back up the hill toward the base of the cliff. They stayed just inside the trees, out of respect for Austin's accurate arm, and waved their weapons in the air, shouting oaths and insults to him.

"We can't stay here," Austin said. "We've got to get out of this cave, or we're trapped and at their mercy."

It was plain that the warriors intended to make a careful stalk of the entrance to the cave. They knew

what Austin could do to them if he had a chance to
throw rocks. Again they spread out along the cliff but
began their climb off to one side and not directly
below the cave. Shadow and Austin could only hear
them yelling as they began their assault; they would
not be able to see them until they had gotten up to
their position and had surrounded the cave. Then it
would be too late.

They waited until the warriors had gotten well off
the bottom before they started again out of the cave
and looked for a way up the rocks.

"Maybe we should make a stand here," Shadow
suggested. "Climbing will be very difficult. And I am
afraid for you with your injured arm."

"It's too easy for them to get above us," Austin
said. "We've got to climb and stay above them. I
can't think about my arm. We'll just climb. We have
to."

Again they began to work their way up along the
face of the mountain, searching for footing and avoiding the slick spots along the cliff where streams of
water fell from the melting ice above. Austin ignored
the warm flow of blood that soaked the piece of dress
tied around his upper arm and shoulder. Shadow
watched below for the warriors, all the while urging
Austin to move as quickly as possible and remember
that the spirits were with them.

Badger, now far below, screamed up at his warriors, pointing to where Shadow and Austin continued
to work their way up. Now there was no worry about
another warrior standing at the base of the cliff to fire
arrows at Austin. By the time one of the warriors took
the time to go back down and take position, they
would be well out of accurate range.

Austin stopped to catch his breath, his face showing torment from the pain in his shoulder. He was still losing blood, and Shadow worried that he would soon become too weak to either climb or keep his balance along the cliff.

"They're about to catch us, aren't they?" Austin said to Shadow. "How far back are they?"

"We cannot think about that," Shadow said. "We must continue upward. Maybe it is as hard for them to climb as it is for us. Maybe we are near the top and can make our stand."

Austin took a deep breath and blinked sweat from his eyes. "I just hope you're right and we're close to the top of this damn mountain. God, I hope you're right."

Time seemed an eternity for Shadow as she fought to keep her strength and, at the same time, give Austin support so that he could draw added energy from within himself. The mountain seemed to go up forever; the cliff seemed to become harder and harder to cling to. Rocks came loose and they would slip, taking strength away each time. She began a song to her spirit helper, the golden eagle, as they worked ever harder to make it up the face of high rock. Time was running out, as the cries of Badger's warriors grew ever closer to their position.

"There's a ledge above us," Shadow then heard Austin say. "We can't go any farther. We'll have to go around it."

As they began to transverse the face of the cliff, both Shadow and Austin became aware that one of Badger's warriors had somehow gotten above them and was now yelling to the others as he started down toward them. Perhaps he had found an easier way up the face of the mountain. It was hard to know. But it meant there was no hope now of gaining an advantage over any of the warriors.

"We've got to reach that ledge before he does," Austin said. "He's got us if we don't."

"He believes he has already won the victory," Shadow said as she listened to the warrior's cries. "He is crazed with the fires of war."

"I'm not done yet," Austin said. "I've got a lot left, and it will take a lot more than a bunch of yelling to get me off this cliff."

Shadow and Austin pulled themselves along below the ledge, searching for a place to climb up and over the edge. They worked with a renewed vigor and burst of strength. For Austin, there was the knowledge of certain death if they did not get to the ledge first. Shadow knew her own sense of worth and happiness would be destroyed if anything happened to this man whom she had come to love, she knew, more than her own self.

Finally they reached a place from where they could pull themselves up upon the ledge. Austin, finally able to peer up over the long, flat layer of rocks, turned back down to Shadow, his eyes wide.

"Damn! That Blackfoot is on the ledge and he sees me!"

Austin struggled to pull himself up. A piece of the ledge gave way, tumbling past Shadow's head and out into space. Austin yelled and fell sideways before again catching his balance. But he was lying awkwardly against the face of the cliff, unable to move for fear of falling. Shadow worked her way up next to him and, after securing herself, allowed him to use her as support to regain his footing.

The warrior was now working his way along the ledge toward them. He had placed his knife in his

mouth to allow himself better mobility. In his eyes
was a sense of control and confidence, a feeling that
he would sing a victory song very soon.

Then, on the ledge between the two of them and
the warrior, was a large nest of sticks in which two
half-fledged eaglets sat, watching intently as the warrior came ever closer to their home.

"It is a good sign," Shadow said, her eyes filling
with hope. "I was worried that my spirit helper had
not heard my prayers. Now we will have the she-eagle
fighting with us."

Shadow began a special song of thanksgiving and
deep appreciation for their good fortune. She knew
that the she-eagle was on the hunt for food to feed
her young, but that she was not far away and would
certainly hear the cries of the two eaglets when the
warrior reached the nest.

Austin worked ever harder now to get up onto the
ledge. The warrior had closed the distance between
them and had only to make it over the eagle nest
before he would be within striking distance. Another
piece of the ledge loosened, and Austin slipped once
again, catching himself before he fell. He held on
awkwardly as before, afraid to move.

The warrior, the knife held firmly between his
teeth, his eyes alive with the sense of the kill, continued across the last, short distance to where Shadow
and Austin clung helplessly to the face of the cliff.
He began to make his way across the nest, having no
regard for anything but his intent to get to Austin.
Terrified, the young eaglets raised their wings and
opened their beaks in defense, sending out shrill
screams of distress. They lay backward in the nest,
bringing up their talons to strike. The warrior planted
a foot directly in the nest on his way across to Austin

and felt one of the talons in his leg. He jumped, kicking at the young birds, which only made them scream louder.

Austin was yelling, "I can't move! Shadow, can't you get up here again?" But Shadow was herself helpless, having nearly lost her own balance when the ledge had once again broken off under Austin's weight.

The warrior came out of the nest and took the knife from his mouth, yelling a shrill war cry. He was answered from below, where the other three were rapidly closing the distance between themselves and the ledge. None of them saw the broad pair of wings appear from high in the sky, nor did they see them descending in a curving line toward the face of the cliff. Austin's face and hands, gripping rocks firmly for what little balance he could maintain, were now only a few feet from the warrior, who had flattened himself onto his stomach and was crawling the last, short distance toward Austin.

Again the warrior yelled. Then he grabbed Austin by the hair and jerked his head back, exposing the throat for the pull of the knife. The warrior was not aware of the huge wings that had folded in a dive for the ledge, nor could he see the piercing eyes alive with anger, the long talons poised for the strike.

The knife was nearly at Austin's throat when the she-eagle struck with tremendous force, her talons ripping deep along the warrior's spine, slicing long, ragged lines through skin and muscle, through tendons and ligaments that held rib to rib and rib to backbone. It was a quick, powerful strike meant to cripple, and the wings soared out and up for another dive.

Austin struggled to keep his balance as the warrior

jerked back, releasing the hold on his hair. The knife bounced down past Austin's face, rattling against the rocks as it began its long fall to the bottom of the cliff. The warrior, the breath driven from his lungs, his body arched in pain, struggled as streams of blood ran down from his back and down both sides of his arms.

"Help me up!" Austin yelled to Shadow.

"I can't!" Shadow told him. "I don't even know how much longer I can hold on!"

Shadow looked up to where the warrior was regaining his senses. His eyes were on Austin, and in them was a terrible sense of purpose. That purpose was to kill the green-eyed Long Knife and take her back down to Badger. Shadow knew his intent would soon overcome the pain in his back; and with Austin helpless, his mission would bring him glory.

Chapter Twelve

———

SHADOW SEARCHED THE skies in earnest for the she-eagle's return. She would certainly come again to strike, Shadow knew, but it would have to be within the next few moments to save Austin from death.

Austin was helpless, trying to control the terror of knowing that the wounded warrior was now beginning to regain enough strength to make his way back over.

In an effort to borrow time, Shadow yelled at the top of her lungs.

"Eagle! It's the eagle!"

There was no eagle yet, Shadow knew, but her trick worked, and very well. Terrified, the warrior immediately forgot about Austin and rolled sideways, his eyes bulging and his arm crooked over him to shield himself from the attack he thought was coming. But there was no eagle, and the warrior turned back to

Shadow and Austin, his teeth gritted and his eyes alive with hate. He was losing strength, he knew, and the added fear that had shot through him for no reason had cost him precious energy.

The warrior screamed in defiance of Shadow's trick, again working himself up for the kill. He again lowered himself in front of Austin, grabbing him by the hair once more. Without the knife, the warrior had to use his fists. Austin tried his best to dodge a blow that opened a cut over his left eye. He would have fallen had the warrior not kept hold of his hair to strike again.

Then the broad wings appeared once more, riding the mountain air currents along the face of the cliff. The warrior had once again raised his fist, and Shadow wanted to cry out. But this time she would not; she would let the she-eagle come once more in surprise.

Suddenly Shadow froze, gripping the face of the cliff with all the strength she could muster. She dared not look below for fear of losing her balance. She dared not move or kick out at the warrior who had grabbed her ankle.

In that instant, the she-eagle struck again, ripping once more through the bloody back of the warrior near her nest. The warrior screamed, his pain far more intense than the first time, the shock registering with more force inside of a body weakened considerably from the first attack. The warrior now found himself off balance, sliding over the edge of the rocks above Austin.

Shadow and Austin squeezed themselves into the cliff as close as they could. Again the spirits were with them: The warrior had blacked out from the pain and now slid over Austin's head and back in a limp heap.

Suddenly the other warrior below Shadow released his grip on her ankle as the unconscious warrior dropped headfirst into his face, knocking him off the rocks. Together they fell, one twisting and screaming, the other already appearing lifeless, as they tumbled and bounced off rock outcrops on their way to the bottom of the cliff.

The remaining two warriors, both very close to Shadow and Austin, began to immediately start back down, calling out to their own spirit helpers for protection against the wrath of the Eagle Woman, whose power was destroying them. They traveled downward as fast as they could, their eyes going back and forth between the bottom and the ledge above, where the she-eagle had taken her place at the nest beside her young and was now looking down at them, her wings raised out from her body in anger and her beak open, calling down a stern warning.

Shadow took a deep breath and moved down to a spot where she could rest and not worry about slipping. The terror of being caught between the warrior on the ledge and those coming up from below had not left her. Austin, too, shook with the release of long-held tension.

"We'd better get down," he said, "before my arm starts to tighten up."

Going down, in many ways, proved more difficult than the climb up. It took deep concentration to keep their footing and fight off the fatigue that was building up within them now that the danger had passed. The remaining two warriors were now close to the bottom, and it was plain that they wanted no more of the Eagle Woman and the Long Knife they called

Green Eyes. Even when Badger shouted at them, they shook their heads, threatening to leave if he wanted them to fight any more this day.

Shadow and Austin finally reached the base of the cliff. Austin found his shirt and his gun, paying no attention to the hateful stares of Badger, who stood not far away, holding his injured arm. The other two warriors stood behind him, almost afraid to cast their eyes on Shadow or Austin, now and again looking up at the face of the cliff to see if the eagle had again taken wing.

"Now is your chance to kill me, Eagle Woman," Badger said defiantly. "You would be wise to do it. If you do not, the day will come when you will lie beneath me and tell me that you like it and that you are proud to be my woman. I will own you, Eagle Woman. And the green-eyed dog will no longer have life but will have long since rotted and left his bones for the wolves."

"Maybe we should grant his wish," Austin told Shadow. "If that's what he wants, it's sure as hell what I would enjoy."

Shadow looked at Austin, knowing he spoke from deep anger and would not bring himself down to take the life of a man who could not fight back.

"Your words bring no fear to anyone's heart," Shadow said. "Your medicine will never be strong. It only grows weaker. And I will not relieve you of your burden of guilt by killing you. You have caused many needless deaths this day, and I would like to know how you will answer to your father for it. No, to kill you would make it easy for you. Living to face your father and your people is a more just thing."

Shadow and Austin left, returning to Austin's camp

to get his horse and retrieve whatever belongings Badger and his warriors had not destroyed. Shadow would now have to return to the village and tell her father what had happened along the cliffs of Going-to-the-Sun Mountain. She knew he would be angry and would tell her that she had been foolish to once again see Austin. But she knew that Austin might not now be alive if she had not left the village to find him. Her father would not understand, but she would tell him that the day would soon come when he would be glad that she had met Austin. She knew now that the spirits certainly wanted them to be together and that he would be of great help to her and her family. They would all be together and nothing could overcome them.

Shadow stood with her mother among the villagers, who had formed a long line at the edge of a meadow to watch horse races and other tests of skill at horsemanship. Everyone was shouting and yelling, jumping around and urging the riders on as the events took place. But her mind was not on the racing. She was deeply troubled.

Three days had passed since Shadow had last seen Austin after their fight with Badger and his warriors. Badger himself had appeared in the village only once, and it was said that his broken arm had been the result of a fall from his pony while hunting buffalo. Badger had convinced the village that the others had been killed while hunting also, when a stampede had broken out while they were chasing the herd. Shadow had spoken once with Standing Elk and knew that he did not believe his brother's story. It was not often that so many warriors from one hunting band would meet such a tragic fate.

What concerned Shadow even more was the fact that the Beelers had arrived and were camped at the edge of the village. The one time she had seen Badger, he had been talking to them, and it had given her a very uneasy feeling. She had known they were talking about her family, and the knowledge that something bad would soon happen caused her great worry. They had not seen her and had laughed and joked about something they were planning to do. Shadow had watched the large one called Wolf lead a pinto horse from the herd. The horse looked very similar to a horse that her father owned, except for the markings of brown along the forelegs. What they were going to do with the pinto they had was not clear to Shadow. But she knew something was being conceived that would cause trouble for her father.

The three days without Austin also bothered Shadow. She knew he would certainly understand why she had not yet gone back up to the lake to see him, but being away from him was hard to bear. She had already grown to need his strong arms and gentle caress. He was a part of her now, like one of her arms or legs, or maybe a part of her heart that could never be lost without deep pain and scarring. He was something that would be part of her life, now, from this time on, until her spirit was no longer within her in this world.

Now, as she watched a group of men and horses gather for another race, she became aware of the brown pinto she had seen a few days earlier. But no, it was not the same pinto. It was, instead, her father's horse! The smaller of the two Beeler brothers, Jake, was riding the horse, and it appeared as if he was betting something with Badger, who stood just off to one side with the huge Beeler named Wolf. Shadow pointed this out to her mother, who instantly became angry. Though they could not see her father, Shadow knew he would become blood mad when he saw what was happening. Men fought to the death for the sake of a good horse. Shadow decided to quickly get her bow and arrows from their lodge.

The horses began to run wildly across the meadow, and as Shadow returned with her bow, she could see her father limping noticeably to the area where the race would finish. Shadow's tension turned quickly to anger as she realized the bad leg her father was now living with had been caused by the very same two men who were once again trying to make trouble for her family. She vividly remembered that day she had fought in the forest as a young woman against these two evil men and the warriors they had brought with them to kill her father. They had only succeeded in wounding her father badly that day; they had not been able to kill him. As Shadow rushed toward her father, she became ever more determined that they would again meet defeat this day.

"Get off that horse!" Shadow heard her father yelling as Jake Beeler crossed the finish line well ahead of the rest. "I said get down off my horse!"

Jake Beeler waited until his brother, Wolf, and Badger got there to back him up. Then he finally got down from the pinto.

"What's the matter with you, Ayers?" he yelled, laughing.

"What the hell do you think you're doing with my horse?" Shadow's father yelled back.

"He ain't yours!" Wolf bellowed. "Jake won him from Badger, here, in that last race. Fair and square!"

"Like hell!" Shadow's father yelled again. He

started for the pinto. "He's mine and I aim to claim him!"

Wolf quickly stepped between him and the horse. "You got no call comin' out here after what's ours!" he growled.

Then Jake, who was walking around behind Shadow's father, said, "It looks to me like he was fixin' to steal that horse from us, don't it? What say we teach him a little lesson? That way he'll know better than to cause trouble with us."

"Why don't you just take a hold of him once," Wolf told his brother, Jake. "I'll commence to pound some reason into him."

"Maybe you would like to die, evil ones!" Shadow spat the words at them. Her bow was drawn and pointed directly at Wolf.

"You're makin' a mistake, there, Injun woman," Jake said, backing away from Shadow's father a ways. "Killin' don't set good with our friend, Badger."

"Why don't you ask him about killing?" Shadow said. "If he is smart, he will have no part in this."

Badger's eyes narrowed. He knew very well that Shadow was referring to their fight on the cliffs of Going-to-the-Sun Mountain. The last thing he now wanted was to have the deaths of his warriors brought up again before the council. His broken arm, bound tightly against his side, was still causing him pain, and he used that as an excuse. He told one of his warriors near him to translate the words he would speak in Blackfoot into sign so that all could understand.

"The Eagle Woman is right," came the translation. "This is not so serious a matter as to fight over. There no doubt has been some mistake."

Wolf and Jake looked at him as if they had been double-crossed in some manner. This was a turn of events they had not expected. By now, a group of dog soldiers had arrived. They were a group of warriors from the Brave Bears Society whose sole responsibility was to police the events of the summer festival. They had undisputed authority over the people, and it was they who kept order. Already word had come to them that a fight was taking place at the end of the horse race. They had come to investigate and restore order. When they saw Shadow with her bow ready to shoot, their eyes grew wide.

Badger spoke to them, explaining the mix-up and the problem with the pinto horse. Shadow learned through the interpreter that the dog soldiers had instructed three young horse tenders to go out from the village and bring back from the horse herds all the brown pintos that bore any resemblance to the one over which the argument had started.

"Ain't that something, now?" Wolf said to Shadow's father while the horse tenders were out looking through the pintos in the herd. "You've got to have that girl of yours around to save your hide. Seems to me that you're pretty yellow down your back."

"It seems to me that you can't fight a man square off without your little brother to help," Shadow's father retorted. "So I wonder who it is that's got the yellow streak?"

Wolf's one good eye flashed. He stepped forward with his fists clenched. Shadow's father set himself on his good leg and waited. One of the dog soldiers rode his horse over, with his war club raised, and yelled a stern warning that there would be no fighting.

"Lucky for you, Ayers," Wolf mumbled under his breath, his fists still clenched.

Two of the horse tenders then returned with a pinto that looked strikingly like the one who was the subject of the dispute. Shadow recognized it immediately as the same horse she had seen with Badger and the Beelers only a few days before. Now it was clear to Shadow what they had done: They knew there would be trouble when they took her father's horse from the herd to race; they knew there would be so much trouble that someone might get killed. After they had killed her father in the quarrel, they would say that the horses were so close in color that they had made a mistake.

"Can't hold a man to blame for this, now can you?" Jake was telling the dog soldiers in sign. "These two horses are plumb alike, they are. Just like two twins, I'd say."

One of the dog soldiers frowned and asked Badger, "Why did you not go out to the herd and get your own pony? Why did you have the Long Knife do it?"

Badger pointed to his injured arm.

The dog soldier shook his head. "The two pintos are not so close that one should have been mistaken for the other." He then looked at Jake, who had been the one to go out and get the horse for the race. "Are you blind?" the dog soldier asked him. "Are you like the big one called Wolf, who is your brother? Can you not see very well?"

The other dog soldiers laughed, eager to enjoy a joke over someone's poor knowledge of horses. Badger joined in, making sure he was looked upon in good stead by the dog soldiers. Jake and Wolf both realized they were being played for fools but could only try to control their anger and say nothing.

Before they left, the dog soldier warned Badger
that there should be no trouble. But Shadow knew
from the look on Badger's face that the dog soldier
was warning him that there should be no trouble concerning the Long Knives called Beeler, even if they
were his friends. Badger could say nothing back to
the dog soldier. It did not matter that Badger's father
held a very important position within the tribal con-
figuration; the dog soldiers were an elected group of
elite individuals accountable to no one when it came
to discipline. In a case such as this, when lives could
have been lost and a general disruption of the summer
festival could have occurred, strict disciplinary action
could be expected to restore order. If someone needed
punishment, there was no amount of influence that
would save him. Badger could only be quiet and listen
to what he was being told. Shadow knew very well
that the dog soldier thought it very strange that
Badger would lose a bet on so valuable a horse as the
pinto during a single race, and also not notice that the
horse did not even belong to him before the race had
even started. And why had he not stopped the fight
to say that the horse was not his? The dog soldier
knew something was not right but would let it go this
time.

Shadow wanted to step forward and speak to the
dog soldier herself, to tell him that the Beelers and
Badger had tried to make trouble for her father and
then kill him. It would be an opportunity to possibly
cause trouble for the Beelers themselves, and maybe
even have them driven out of the village. But then
she thought better of it. There would have to be a
meeting of the council, with all the elders present. It
would mean that her father would have to say that
Badger, too, was an enemy for being with the Beelers

and going along with their plan. This could turn many of the Blackfeet people against him, Shadow knew, and possibly hurt his chances to establish trade relations with them. No, she would not say anything. She would let it rest as it was.

When the dog soldiers had left, Wolf squinted with his one good eye and said to Shadow's father, "We ain't done yet, Ayers. One of these times we'll catch you without the girl and her arrows. You'd best watch your back trail if you've got a lick of sense."

Badger, who had been staring at Shadow for some time, told her through the warrior with him, "And there is no need for you to think of the Long Knife called Green Eyes any longer. The warriors with me that day have taken their revenge." He smiled as he saw the look of concern come over Shadow's face. "If you do not believe me, look out among the horses and see if his pony is not among those I call my own." He laughed as he walked off with the Beelers.

"What is he talking about?" Shadow felt her father nudging her as he spoke, trying to get her to answer him. She continued to stare after Badger and he repeated, "Shadow, what does he mean about the other day? What is all this?"

"I did not want to tell you, Father," Shadow began to explain, "for fear that you would become very angry. When I left to see my spirit helper, I also saw Austin. Then Badger and some of his warriors came and tried to kill Austin. There was a fight on the cliffs of Going-to-the-Sun Mountain. Badger has told the people of this village that his warriors died while hunting buffalo, that they died under the hooves of a stampede. He has said that his arm was broken in a fall from his pony during that stampede. None of it is true. His warriors died in the fight along the cliffs.

Badger's arm was broken when Austin threw a large rock at him." Shadow took a deep breath, relieved to see that her father was more concerned than angry.

"Did you kill any of them yourself?" he asked.

Shadow shook her head. "It was mainly the she-eagle who fought for us. My spirit helper came to me that day. The fighting was near her nest, and she killed one of the warriors, who then fell on another, sending them both down to the bottom of the cliff. Besides breaking Badger's arm, he killed the third warrior with a rock, also."

"Things have really gotten started now, haven't they?" he said.

"Do not blame Austin," Shadow said. "He fought them only when there was no other way. Only when they would have killed him to get me. Badger wants me very badly."

"I can see that," her father said. "I guess I've known that for some time. That Austin must be some kind of fighter."

"The spirits were with us, Father," Shadow said. "The spirits told me that Austin and I are to be as one. The she-eagle saved his life. For me, this happened. I know it, Father."

"What about this story Badger just told?" he asked Shadow. "What does he mean about the revenge and now having Austin's horse in his herd?"

"I don't know," Shadow answered, her concern growing. "The sun has crossed the sky three times now since I have last seen Austin. I must go back up to the lake. I must talk to him again." She hesitated a moment and asked, "Father, will you come with me this time? He has wanted to talk to you for a long time. I have told him no. But now I know it is time that he told you what is in his heart. Will you come?"

"I've thought about all this for a time," he said. "It's been on my mind a lot, you and this young Kentuckian. I guess it brings to mind your mother and I when we were both young. Nothing could keep us apart. Maybe he is the right one for you."

"I know he is," Shadow said, wanting to show excitement but afraid of the words Badger had just spoken. She had to know where Austin was. "We must leave right away," she told her father.

"We'll take horses," her father said. "We can get up there faster and maybe find out what Badger was saying."

Badger had been right about having Austin's horse. Shadow saw it immediately when they went out to the herd to get her horse. Her breath left her for a time while she wondered what had happened to Austin. She tried not to think the worst: that Badger had been telling the truth. She started off with her father up the trail that would lead to the high lake at the base of Going-to-the Sun Mountain. They had to find him up there waiting for her. They just had to.

Chapter Thirteen

As THEY RODE, drawing nearer to the high lake whose waters had mirrored the face of this man she loved so dearly, Shadow's eyes wandered far over the forest, looking for any sign that might tell her where Austin would be. Afternoon was growing steadily into evening, and already the nighthawks were swooping and diving above the flat, open meadows back from the lake. They would have to find him soon, Shadow knew, or the day would be ended, and they would have to go back down to the village, where she would get no sleep until she knew for sure where he was or if he had been killed by Badger's warriors.

They had passed Austin's old camp earlier, and Shadow had taken her father to the base of the cliff to show him where the fight had occurred. There was still blood on the rocks at the base of the rock wall where the warriors had fallen. High above the ledge,

the she-eagle had been circling, her piercing cry echoing out across the forest below. Her father could now
better understand how the spirits must have smiled
down upon them that day when they had fought
Badger and his warriors, for it was hard to believe
that anyone could have the strength to climb so high
among the rocks and still be able to fight an enemy.
Without the help of the she-eagle, they most certainly
would have died. Shadow was glad to see that her
father was becoming convinced more and more that
Austin was a man of great honor and would certainly
be a good husband to his daughter.

As the light in the west grew ever more dim, and
the sun fell farther and farther down toward the horizon, Shadow began to feel the horrible sensation of
panic. They had now ridden all around the lake, with
no sign of a camp anywhere. No tracks from his horse
could be seen anywhere around the lake or at any of
the small streams and springs that were everywhere
among the high meadows.

"Shadow, we've got no choice but to go back
down and hope he's camped out from here, maybe in
some other part of the mountains," her father finally
said. "Maybe he'll show up before long."

"What if Badger's words are true?" Shadow
asked, trying to control her emotions. "What if he
has been killed?"

"There is no way for us to really be sure about
that," he said, "one way or the other. If he's as good
in the hills as he appears to be, I doubt if anyone
could get a good jump on him, Blackfoot or whatever.
He's too smart to get himself in a bad way, especially
after that run-in with Badger and his warriors that you
two had the other day. I'd rather think he's just layin'
back out of sight for a time."

Shadow felt somewhat better, wanting to believe that her father's words held good meaning. Austin was as good in the mountains as anyone, and he most likely would not let anyone surprise him. But Badger's words and the way he had said them were haunting. She would hear them over and over again, hoping they were just lies, but the doubts remained.

The ride back down to the village was for Shadow like a dance with no music, a sky with no blue. She wanted Austin to just come out of the forest and find them, to somehow materialize in front of her. But she knew it would not happen and that the closing night would soon make the land as dark as her spirits now were. Though her father repeatedly tried to lead her from her despair, Shadow could not help but wonder if she would see Austin ever again.

Three more days passed and still there was no sign of Austin. Badger was around her often now, staring at her and speaking whenever he got the chance, telling her that the green-eyed Long Knife was gone and that she should submit herself to him. His arm was out of the sling, and though it was still heavily wrapped and surely painful, he seemed to delight in making sign to Shadow and annoying her as much as possible.

At the end of that third day, Shadow made another trip up to the lake, taking a roundabout way that made it hard for Badger to follow her. She searched for most of the afternoon and well into evening with no sign of Austin or any camp. She could not understand what had happened to him. She was less certain now that he was dead, since Badger could produce no scalp when she had demanded proof of his death. But it was indeed Austin's horse that was now among

those in Badger's herd, and it seemed very strange
that Austin would go anywhere on foot.

Two more days passed and still not a sign of Austin. Though Shadow had talked at length with both
her father and mother, and even Little Bear, there was
no bringing her spirits up. After she had finally gotten
her father to admit that he thought Austin was right
for her, it now seemed that Austin had himself
changed his mind about her. Shadow tried not to face
that possibility, but it seemed apparent now.

"There is to be a dance tonight," Shadow's mother
told her that evening when the sun had fallen behind
the high peaks to the west. "It would be good for you
if you would join the other women your age. You
have always liked to dance."

Shadow shook her head, preferring to remain inside
the lodge. Then, after a time, she said to her mother
and father as they were preparing to leave, "It is
strange. I feel as if the spirits are trying to play tricks
on me."

"The spirits play tricks on you?" her mother
asked. "How?"

"It is as if voices are telling me to go out and join
in the dancing. I cannot understand why I should
dance this night. I have nothing to be happy for, nothing to celebrate. It is strange."

"It would be good if you would go to the dance,"
her mother said. "It is hard to forget someone, but to
meet others can always help."

After her mother and father had left, Shadow sat
and thought for a time. Finally she went out of the
lodge to where the people of the village were gathered
to dance. It was a dance in which the women displayed their availability for marriage. To dance with
a male partner did not signify that marriage would

take place, but only that these two people were attracted to one another and that their union might be a good one.

A large circle of drummers, facing inward, had assembled near the center of the village where the fires burned brightly. Into this circle of drummers came the women who wished to participate, while the men stood outside the circle and waited for the dancing to begin. All the dancers, men and women alike, were dressed in their brightest, most colorful costumes. Shadow wore her new antelope dress, beaded and trimmed with elk teeth. The other women also wore their finest, and they presented an array of sparkling color and gloss as the firelight caught the beads, shells, mirrors, metal earrings, and various other bracelets and charms. Many of the women wore different ornaments made from coins used by the Long Knives, and some even had shells obtained in trade with other peoples from lands far distant, where the giant waters go on forever.

The men also wore their most appealing combination of dressware. Special paint and feather arrangements adorned their hair and clothing. Articles of war were placed in special places on their shirts so that the women might see them and realize that they were honorable warriors and worthy of their attention. Many of the men carried pouches of flower pollen and love charms made up for them by special elders within the village in hopes they might use them later in the evening. It was an evening all had waited for.

Shadow, still not sure of why she had decided to come, took her place with the women as the drums began a rhythmic beat. Shadow, with the other women, began to move in time with the drums, raising and lowering her head, moving her feet in a slight shuffling pattern. The drummers worked at a continuous, steady beat, singing a song that was meant to depict the beauty and grace of the women, as well as their abilities in keeping a fine lodge. It was also a song about the strength and virility of the men.

The dancing continued, and the women began to get caught up in the words and music, feeling the power of the dance itself begin to come over them. With the other women, Shadow began to twist and sway to the sound of the drums and singing, her movements becoming ever more pronounced as she danced. She let herself relax more and found herself totally caught up in the ritualistic sensation of the ceremony.

The men began threading through the drummers, working their way in among the women. They would offer themselves by dancing in a circle around the woman they wished to be with. If she wished it also, she would then dance a circle around him.

Shadow saw Badger making his way toward her, and she was suddenly filled with fear. She began to ask herself over and over again why she had even come out of the lodge to join in the dancing. She should have known this was going to happen. And there was no other young warrior in the village with whom she wished to dance. What had been her reason for coming? Could the voices she had heard been real or only imagined? Were the spirits indeed playing tricks on her? It seemed that way now, and she knew it would be hard to stay away from him.

Shadow worked her way in and around the other dancers to avoid even letting him near her. He kept coming, trying to dance his way to her, working to corner her as best he could. No matter where she went or how obvious she made it seem that she did not wish to be with him, he continued after her.

Shadow finally decided that she would have to leave the circle of dancers entirely if she wished to be rid of Badger. She had tired of this game of avoidance. It was plain that Badger was not going to give up trying to dance with her, no matter what she did to stay away from him.

By now many of the dancers had come together as couples, moving themselves around one another, touching and rubbing as the drums and singing continued. As she worked her way toward the edge of the dancers, Shadow was aware that Badger had given up trying to get close to her in the manner of the ceremony, but was now walking at a fast pace to cut her off before she could get out of the circle. She could see that he was filled with the burning water and that it had complete control of his thoughts. His eyes had become wild, and his desire for her was etched into his expression.

Shadow was now sure that the voices had been wrong. Surely they could not have been telling her to couple with Badger. This could not be. Perhaps the voices had been saying something entirely different than to come to the dance, and she had heard them wrong. It was too late now to know for sure. She now wanted only to get as far away from Badger and the dancing as she could.

Badger was upon her, reaching out for her. Shadow spun quickly away from him, colliding with a dancing pair. She stumbled and caught herself just as Badger grabbed for her again. She lunged ahead, twisting away so that his hand could not grab her dress. She was now at the edge of the circle and was beginning to fall again when she felt a strong arm around her waist. She struggled to get free.

"Shadow, take it easy. It's me."

Startled, she turned and looked into the green eyes she had missed seeing so much.

"Shadow, what's wrong?" he asked.

"Austin," she finally said. "What are you doing here in the village?"

She felt a pull at her arm, a savage pull that hurt and partially tore her away from Austin. In one quick movement, Austin had lunged around her and had slammed his fist directly into Badger's face, splitting his lip and knocking him back into the dancers.

"Austin, don't!" Shadow told him.

Austin stood glaring over Badger while the drums hushed and the crowd looked on. Immediately three dog soldiers came through the dancers and surrounded Austin, their lances pointed directly at his chest. Badger quickly rose to his feet and brought his arm up to strike. One of the dog soldiers grabbed his arm and yelled at him in Blackfoot. They had not come to help him fight the Long Knife but only to restore order in the village.

Walking Head and a few other elders in the village then arrived and spoke with the dog soldiers in Blackfoot. Badger was pointing at Austin and yelling.

"Austin," Shadow said, "I am very glad to see you, but you should not have come into the village. I told you there would be trouble."

"Shadow, I haven't been able to see you," Austin explained. "I just couldn't stay hiding out any longer."

"Why did you not stay at the lake, where we agreed to meet?"

"Because Badger's warriors were up there looking for me all the time. They stole my horse and would have killed me if it hadn't been that I was out of camp after meat. So I had to go clear out of the area. I just finally said to myself that I was going to come into the village and see you, and just let things happen as they may.''

"Well, bad things have happened," Shadow said. "Now you will be taken before the council, and it will be decided whether or not you had a right to strike Badger."

Shadow's mother and father stood beside her now, both looking at Austin.

"I don't have to ask if you're Austin Wells," Shadow's father said.

"I didn't aim to make any trouble," Austin said. "It's just that Shadow was getting her dress ripped off by that damned crazy Badger."

"They've got their own system of order here," Shadow's father explained to Austin. "You're going to have to come up with a real good reason why you hit Badger or there could be real trouble for you."

"You know why I hit him," Austin said.

"Maybe so. But that won't hold up with the council. He's one of theirs and you're a stranger they don't even know. Just hold tight and don't do any more to rile them. Things are bad enough for you now."

Shadow stood and watched the dog soldiers take Austin away. He would be tied and held until a decision could be reached by the council as to what his punishment would be. It could be decided that he had acted in self-defense, but it would be hard to prove since Austin had struck first and had not even spoken a warning.

Shadow began to take heart as she watched her father take Walking Head aside and speak to him. She knew her father would speak for Austin and that his influence would surely be beneficial in helping to get this situation cleared up. Austin would be taken to a lodge to be held instead of being tied to a stake within the village. He would be far better off within the lodge, safe from the pokes and stones administered to those captives who were left out for all to torture as they saw fit. For this Shadow was deeply grateful.

The next day Shadow's father worked things out for Austin even before the council was set to assemble and hear the case. He convinced Walking Head that Austin had meant no harm and that Austin had come to the village to work for him. There was no mistake that Badger had been drunk on the burning water. He was now sick, and it was apparent to all that he did not even intend to speak before the council in his own behalf. Shadow's father gave Walking Head presents for himself and for Badger to show that the unfortunate incident should not stand between any of them. There had been no harm done, and in the future Austin would stay away from Badger.

"You are mighty lucky, Austin," Shadow's father said as they all sat inside the lodge after Austin's release. "They could just as easily have decided to string you out somewhere for the wolves."

"I owe you a great deal, Mr. Ayers," Austin said. "I only hope that I can measure up to what you expect of me. I have wanted to work for you ever since I left my uncles, but things just didn't seem to work so that I could meet you and talk to you about it."

"I think things will work just fine," Shadow's father said. "But, the way I see it, we can avoid more trouble if you go on down to the fort on the Madison and wait until we all get back down. Stayin' here with us will just be rubbin' salt into Badger, and we don't need any more run-ins with him."

"What about my uncles?" Austin asked. "They

will be a lot of trouble for us. You can count on that.
I heard about what they tried with your horse the
other day. I wouldn't put anything past them.''

''I plan to just stay clear of them until we leave
the village. Another two days and I will have met all
the leaders of the different bands. I've got a good
relationship started with the Blackfeet now, and I
want it to continue. Walking Head and our family go
back a long ways, clear back to when beaver was big
business in these parts. Things have changed a lot
since then, but he and I know each other real good.
That's what got you out of that mess you were just
in. But I don't want any more messes.''

Austin nodded in understanding. ''But I was just
thinking: If you want to stay here just two more days,
why not let me stay on here with you? It would be
good if I met the leaders of the different bands with
you. That way they would all know me as a friend of
yours. That would make it easier if I was ever to
travel to their villages to trade.''

''He is right, Father,'' Shadow added. She did not
like the idea of Austin's going back down to the Madison alone. ''He should also meet all the leaders, so
that they will know him.''

Shadow watched her father think for a time. Finally
he said, ''I guess it would be good if you met the
leaders with me. But I don't want you any place
where Badger shows up. If he decides to come back
from the Beeler camp with a belly full of whiskey, I
don't want you out where he can hound you. I don't
want any more fights between you two.''

Austin nodded. ''I don't aim to bring any trouble
on anyone. I guess I just get riled up once in a while.''

''I think you will do me some good,'' Shadow's
father said, ''but these Blackfeet are touchy when it

comes to folks they don't know too well. Walking Head is well respected, and he is the only reason I can get along with the rest of them. If it wasn't for him, I wouldn't be any different to them than any other white trader who's come out here to the mountains and wants their furs. They would demand the same of me as they do all the others, and that means a lot more presents, more whiskey, and no free room and board at their ceremonies. I can't let that change now. I know you've got a hell of a problem on your hands with Badger, but you've somehow got to just let it ride. Understand?''

''I don't want any trouble with any of them,'' Austin replied. ''I've got to tell you that I love your daughter, and I just couldn't stay up on that mountain without seeing her. She means a lot to me, which I am sure you already know. And after the two of us survived that fight with Badger and his warriors, I don't ever want to lose her.''

Shadow felt much better now that everything was beginning to work out with Austin and her family. It would make things much easier for all of them, and Shadow would not have to worry about Austin's safety and whereabouts.

Later in the evening, Little Bear came back from playing games with the boys his own age and sat down in the lodge next to Austin, his eyes wide.

''I remember you,'' Austin said with a laugh. ''You were sneaking along the trail behind me one day not long ago. If I remember right, you had a good reason for it, too. You were hunting deer, or some such thing.''

Little Bear laughed then himself. ''You have a good mind for remembering. Did you know then that I was the brother of Shadow?''

"No," Austin said. "But you are pretty tricky, just like your sister."

"His name is Austin," Shadow said to Little Bear. "Can you say Austin?"

Little Bear struggled sheepishly for a time. Finally he said, "It is a funny word, but I will learn to speak it plainly."

"Yes, you will learn to speak his name as well as your own," Shadow said to Little Bear with a smile. She was beginning to feel even better about things now, seeing that Austin and Little Bear had taken an immediate liking to one another.

Later that evening, after they had eaten, Austin sat down with Little Bear near the fire and said, "Why don't you and I play a game of hands. I'll bet I can beat you, even though your mother tells me you are better than all the boys your own age."

Little Bear jumped with enthusiasm. It was true, he had beaten almost all the boys in the village, even some who were older than himself. He had many items such as arrows and small knives and slingshots which he proudly displayed as proof of his skill.

"I will bet these three knives against your hat," Little Bear said, his eyes shining in the light of the fire. He had a pair of small bones in his hand.

"Very well," Austin said with a grin. "I accept. You go first."

Little Bear began to shift the bones deftly back and forth from one hand to the other, chanting a victory song he himself had made up. He spent time trying to trick Austin with fakes and quick movements, but he could see right away that Austin would be a hard one to beat at this game. He did not try to watch every movement of the hands but instead watched the eyes.

Austin then guessed right away which hand held

the notched bone. Little Bear shook his head with a sigh while Austin moved a stone over into his row. When it was Austin's turn with the bones, Little Bear grew intent. Austin then began, shifting the bones from hand to hand in a flurry of movement which made Little Bear's mouth drop open. When Austin began to juggle the bones, Little Bear was even more impressed. He had witnessed many hand games, but none of the players, whether they were boys his own age or even adults, could match the skill that Austin possessed. He was mesmerized.

"Which hand is it in?" Austin then asked.

Little Bear looked from one hand to the other and up into Austin's eyes. Austin was trying to keep from laughing. Little Bear then pointed to Austin's right hand. Inside the grip was the bone with the notched center.

Little Bear's eyes lit up and then he laughed. "The spirits are with me," he said, "for it was not my eyes that saw the right bone."

"I'll tell you what would be fair," Austin suggested to Little Bear. "I can play the game of hands better than you and I am sure that you can shoot a bow much better than I can. If I teach you how to juggle the bones, will you teach me how to shoot a bow?"

Little Bear readily agreed. When first light came, Austin would go out with Little Bear and they would set up targets to shoot at. Austin would learn skill with a bow. And for now it was Little Bear's turn to learn. He could not wait to show the other boys in the village the skill he would soon learn, the art of juggling. Yes, it was good that this Long Knife and his sister had come to love one another. This Long

Knife was quite interesting and would be a good teacher.

Shadow was happy as she watched her brother and Austin get to know one another. It was now plain that her family had accepted Austin completely, even her father. It was now a matter of completing what they had come to do among the Blackfeet. Shadow knew her father was still very anxious about how the trading would go this coming season, for it would be this first season which would decide whether or not the fort-lodge along the Madison would make money for her father. Shadow knew that with Austin, her father's chances of success would be far greater. Watching Austin and Little Bear, she began to realize how lucky she was that he had come up to these lands to find her. Now she wanted him never to be out of her sight.

Chapter Fourteen

———

THEY WATCHED A pair of swans settle on the lake and thought of the happy days that had been passing for them. Austin had been with Shadow's father talking trade with Walking Head and all the heads of the Blackfoot bands. He presented himself well, and Shadow heard from her father that the Blackfeet people seemed to like him. He was kind and patient, two qualities that were held in high esteem among true warriors. Austin was beginning to make a place for himself beside Shadow's father as a respected trader.

Shadow had found things easier for them than she could have imagined. Badger had left the village for a time. It was said that he was on a vision quest, that his medicine had failed him many times during this season of the warm moons and that he wished to make restitution with the spirits and once again have the power he had come to know as a warrior within his band. There was still a great deal of dissent among the people over the deaths of the three warriors who he had said died under the hooves of a herd of buffalo. The two other warriors who had also been with them would not speak on the subject, even to the elders. It was being said that the elders wanted to know more about the hunt and the reason no one was speaking about it. Some were even talking of leaving under Badger to form a new and different band of their own. But nothing was settled.

Because of all this trouble, the Beelers had moved their camp and had not been seen or heard from in nearly a week's time. After the trouble they had started, they had no doubt realized more trouble could end all hope they might have of taking trade away from Shadow's father. But Shadow knew that the Beelers would now try even harder to get to her father; his good fortune in making friends with the Blackfeet had only served to make them even more determined to stop him.

The celebration festival drew to a close, and it was time to again return to the fort on the Madison. Everyone was in good spirits for all had gone well since Austin had come into the village. Shadow was especially happy and wanted to give thanks to her spirit guardian, the golden eagle. She would travel up to the lake and then to the cliffs above the water along Going-to-the-Sun Mountain, where she would spend time in prayer for the happiness that had now come to her.

It was early in the evening and Shadow was nearing the lake above the village. She stopped suddenly where the trail broke from the trees into a meadow near the water's edge and caught her breath. From out of the forest had come Badger, and he was standing right in front of her.

"It is good that I have found you." His cheeks were hollow and his mouth was drawn, his lips cracked. He held his broken arm, still wrapped in skins for support, with his good hand and looked at her out of eyes that were dazed from hunger and lack of rest. His quest to gain power had taken a great deal of strength from him.

"Badger, I do not wish to see you," Shadow said. She began to walk around him.

"Wait," he said. "I think the spirits have sent you to me."

Shadow was surprised at the comment and also at the tone of his voice. It was not harsh and arrogant but almost pleading. It did not seem like Badger at all.

"What is it you want?" Shadow asked with hesitation, watching him closely and from a distance to avoid being tricked.

"I mean no harm to you," he said. He remained where he was, standing still with no movement forward, seeing that Shadow was like a deer ready to spring away if he was even to blink. "Do not fear me," he said assuringly. "My heart is good. I swear by the spirits. I mean you no harm."

Shadow was taken aback by his strange nature.

"Come closer to me," Badger urged, "so that we might speak easier."

Shadow was hesitant. "I know better than to be tricked by you," she said. "I can hear what you have to say from where you stand. And hurry; I must go up and say my prayers before night comes to the land."

"I want you to think of me differently from what

you now do," Badger said. "My heart has changed and I want you to help me."

Shadow became even more confused. If Badger was trying to fool her, he was disguising his voice very well. The pleading tone still seemed very real.

"I do not understand," Shadow said. "What is this talk of change, and what do you mean by asking for help from me? Help in doing what?"

"I want to once again have honor among my people," he said. "I want to become who I once was. Can you understand?"

"I yet do not understand your words to me," Shadow said, still maintaining the distance between herself and Badger. "I know who you are and what you have done. Now I hear you tell me that you no longer want to be the person I know."

"Yes, you *do* understand," Badger said quickly. There seemed now to be a touch of eagerness in his voice, as if he felt headway was being made. "I want the past to be forgotten. I want to become one of honor now, and never be like I once was."

"You try to deceive me," Shadow said. "I know better than to believe you. I will not forget the day on the cliffs of Going-to-the-Sun Mountain." She turned and pointed high above the lake. "It is strange to me that you would speak to me of forgetting when all your words before have been nothing but lies."

"Hear my words, Eagle's Shadow Woman," Badger said. "The cliffs above the waters here, along Going-to-the-Sun Mountain, haunt my sleep each night. I see the rocks over and over again, and I see the warriors who were my friends falling far down to their deaths. I will never forget that day, and I will always know in my heart that I did the wrong thing. I knew that my medicine was not good, yet I told the warriors with me that I felt very strong. I told them they would gain much honor if they would help me to take you for my wife. They believed I had power that day, even after the stone from the green-eyed Long Knife struck my arm. They climbed up among the rocks to get you and to destroy the Long Knife. But I was not to have glory that day. Instead the she-eagle came and destroyed the victory that I had nearly won.''

"How could you ever have thought of it as a victory?'' Shadow asked him. "Even if you and your warriors would have succeeded in killing Austin, you would never have gained me as your wife. You would see me die at your hands first.''

"I do not want to hear anger in your voice,'' Badger said. "I have paid for my foolish desires. And I will always pay each time night falls, for the spirits of the dead warriors are very angry with me.''

"That is something you, yourself, must live with,'' Shadow said. "Even if I wanted to, I could not make their spirits rest and leave you alone in the night.''

"This I understand,'' Badger said. "But now I must make my life different and try to find a way to make their spirits rest.''

"I hope you do not intend to avenge them by trying to kill Austin again,'' Shadow said.

Badger shook his head. He held up his broken arm. "When the spirits of the dead warriors do not come, then it is the pain of this arm that keeps sleep from my eyes. If I had not tried to kill the green-eyed Long Knife, then I would never have lost my warriors, and my arm would now be strong. Instead it will never be strong again. No, I do not wish to kill anyone. I only want to gain back the power I once had, to be a respected warrior once again.''

"Why do you tell me this?" Shadow asked.

"I need you to help me."

Shadow studied him carefully. His eyes were not hateful and burning, as she had seen them so many times lately. Nor were they the eyes of obsession and desire that she knew so well when he had looked upon her in the past. Now they were soft and held sadness.

"You want me to help you?"

Badger nodded.

"Then you want me to be wife to you?"

"No. I have told you that I will not be the same person I was before. I know you have much love for Green Eyes. I know that you will never love me. I only want you to help me change."

"I do not know how I can help you," Shadow said.

"You have much power," Badger said. "You are favored by the spirits. Someone like you could help me become the warrior I once was."

"Have you not gone to seek the spirits yourself?" Shadow asked. "It is said in the village that you had come up here to find your own power."

"Power will not come to me." Badger said it quickly, turning his head away from her as he spoke. It was a very hard thing for him to admit to anyone. It was plain to Shadow that he had spent a lot of time looking hard at his past, or he would not have been able to admit it even to himself. To have once had a great deal of power, only to lose it and now suffer from the fear that he might never regain any of it was a source of great shame to him. He was now desperate. Now his voice turned to insolence. "I do not understand the spirits at all," he said with a huff. "They look upon me with disfavor. I have spent the passing of three suns without food or water, yet no vision or even any sign that the spirits hear me has been sent. I have spoken prayers; I have burned the sacred sage and the juniper. Still I am left alone.''

"Maybe you do not have the right feelings when you ask the spirits to hear you," Shadow said. "They will not hear you if they think you want power for the wrong reasons."

"I want only to once again have honor among my people," he said. "I believe the spirits will not hear me because I have not spoken with them for so long. Maybe they no longer hear my voice. But I know that they hear you, Eagle's Shadow Woman. You, who have even more power than many brave warriors.''

His tone had become desperate, and it bothered Shadow. He was now grasping for a way, any way, in which he could once again regain the honor he had once held within the band. His honor was still there in the eyes of some of the warriors, but for many it was slipping away each time he appeared before them.

But it seemed his desperation had taken on a new form. It was plain to her now that he had not been drinking the burning water for some time, possibly even since the Beelers had moved their camp away from the village. Now that he had gone for three days without either food or water, his entire system was no doubt rid of most of the burning water. His drive for power was not caused now from the burning water but from the knowledge that the burning water had robbed him of dignity and favor in the eyes of many of his people. His determination now came from knowing he must become respected without the burning water. He knew this but did not want to have to wait for it.

"I believe you now," Shadow told him. "And I think it is good that you want to once again gain favor among your people. But you must be willing to let the spirits help you do this without telling them to. Maybe the time is not yet right. There will be another mountain to climb in some part of your lands. Maybe if you wait and climb another mountain the spirits will then look upon you with favor.''

"I have no more time,'' Badger said. "I must have power. I must have it now.''

"You know that power can come only when the time is right,'' Shadow told him. "You know very well that I cannot help you gain power. That is a very personal thing between each one of us and the spirits.''

Badger took a deep breath, knowing very well that what she had said was true. If he was to gain special favors from the spirits, it would have to come from them without help from another. In fact, rarely could another give that kind of help. So he would take another approach.

"It would be good if I had something of yours through which I could gain power,'' Badger said. "You could give me one of your arrows. If I could have one of your arrows, maybe the spirits would favor me as they do you. Maybe then some of your power would come to me.''

"I do not think it would be good to give you anything of mine,'' Shadow said. "I do not think the spirits would like that. I do not want to have something bad happen, either to you or me.''

"No bad things will happen. The spirits look upon you with favor. There would be no bad thing that would come to pass, only power to me.''

"No,'' Shadow answered. "I cannot take that chance. If you do not wish to return to your people until you have gained power, then you should stay on this mountain until it comes to you.'' She looked at him, realizing suddenly that she was not afraid of arousing his anger. ''I want you to understand,'' she said, ''that I cannot help you gain favor with the spirits in any way.''

Badger would not give in so easily. ''Then you are saying that you do not wish to help me become the warrior I once was?''

''It would be very good if you could change back to the person you once were,'' Shadow said. ''Only you can make that happen is what my words to you mean. I cannot tell the spirits to help you, nor will I try to transfer any of my power to you.''

''I only wish you would remember the days when we were children,'' Badger said. ''Do you know the time when I held the black horse so that he would not run away with you? And can you remember the time when I told you about the rattlesnake along the trail just in front of you?''

''I am grateful for those things,'' Shadow said, ''and it would be good if we were friends now as we were then. I would be very happy if you could call me just friend, as your brother Standing Elk does, and not wish to possess me for your own.''

It was plain to Badger that Shadow was not going to give in to his wishes. She was glad that he wanted to change and become the warrior he had once been, but she would not accept him as that person now. She would have to see it happen first. Her lack of confidence angered him. He thought it would not be this way if she had not met someone else.

''Why do you want the green-eyed Long Knife?'' he asked. ''When I have once again regained my power, I will have more honor than he.''

''You told me that you do not wish to have me for

your own," Shadow said. "But I can see that your words have no truth to them."

"I cannot help it," Badger admitted. "I do understand that you could never want me, so I will someday accept that you will never be mine."

"I do not think that we should speak anymore about it," Shadow said. "I hope you can become the man you were once, but that is for you to do. I do not wish to see you anymore; it can only cause more trouble between us."

"I told you that I wanted things between us to change," Badger insisted, "that we should be friends, as we were as children."

"If you want to be friends with me, then you must also be friends with Austin."

Badger hesitated.

"We can never be friends ourselves if you hate Austin," Shadow went on. "You know that."

"I will try to make friends with him," Badger said. "I will try."

"Maybe too much has already happened between you," Shadow said. "You have told me that you wish the fight on the cliffs of Going-to-the-Sun Mountain had never happened. You show me your broken arm, which was struck by a stone from Austin's hand, and you say that it happened because you were foolish. But I wonder how you would now feel if Austin had not hit your arm with the stone, and he had died from one of your arrows, or your warrior's knife. What if you had been victorious and none of your warriors had been killed? How would your heart be now if you had taken me down from the rocks with the intent of having me as your own?" Her eyes were hard and her tone filled with the bitter memory of that day.

"I have no more words left to speak about that

day," Badger answered. "I have told you that my heart is sad; I can say no more. I only want to make my life better now than it has been."

Shadow stared at him for a moment. She had suddenly realized what he had been trying to say to her all this time. He had been saying that he wanted power, but it had really been a call for help. He did not want power to become a great warrior again. No, he first wanted the power to stay away from what had caused all the trouble he was now paying for. He wanted the power it would take to stay away from the burning water.

"I can help you by telling you two things that you must do," Shadow then said.

"What must I do?" Badger asked.

"If you stay away from the two evil Long Knives called Beeler, and also never drink the burning water again, your life will once again become happy."

"This I understand." Badger nodded. "It is true, I wish never to drink the burning water again. Both my father and my brother, Standing Elk, have told me that the burning water has ruined my life. They feel bad for me. My mother cries in the lodge each night. She prays to her spirit helpers for me, and to Napi, the Old Man, asking him to save her son. I want never to drink the burning water; I want to be free of it and not let it control my thoughts. This I want very badly."

Shadow could see in his eyes a plea for help, a reaching out for support. It was certainly true that the nightmares and the guilt of what he had done were affecting him more and more each time the sun crossed the sky. Deep pain had found its way into his face, and without the burning water inside of him to influence his thinking, he had told himself he would never again know happiness until he could stop the evil drinking.

"If you really wish to help yourself stay away from the burning water, then I will help you also," Shadow said. "As children we were very good friends. I would like to again become friends."

Badger bit his lip hard, until a thin trickle of blood showed on his chin. Shadow went over to him, realizing now that he had been hiding behind what was left of his honor, unable to admit that he wanted her now more as a mother than a wife. She went up to him and they embraced.

Shadow felt good. She knew the real Badger had been driven out long ago by the burning water and that the person who had replaced him was now gone, leaving the place open for that Badger she had once known to return. As long as there was no burning water to again bring back the evil person, the good Badger would find more and more strength.

"You must be very strong about this," Shadow said. "It will be very hard, but you must not give in."

"I will be strong," Badger said. "Now that I know your power is with me, I will be able to bring the spirits into my life once again."

Hearing something behind them on the trail, Shadow turned to see Austin staring at her. In his eyes were both hurt and anger, mixed with confusion. Badger stepped back from her and looked at Austin for a time. Neither of them spoke, and Shadow suddenly felt like her whole world had fallen apart.

Chapter Fifteen

━━━━━

SHADOW WATCHED AUSTIN as he came toward them.

"What is this?" he asked.

"I will go now," Badger said quietly.

"No, stay," Austin said. "I want to know what this is all about."

Badger started back down the trail, and Shadow quickly moved in front of Austin.

"Let him go," she said. "There is no need for trouble."

"No need for trouble?"

"It is not what you think."

Austin threw up his hands. "Not very many days back he was trying to knock me off the face of that mountain up there. Now I catch you with him up here all alone, and you want to protect him. I'm afraid I just don't understand all this."

"Let me tell you what happened," Shadow began.

Austin, without hearing her, kept on talking. "It is really hard for me to make any sense out of things anymore. You haven't wanted to come up here to the lake with me ever since I moved into your family's lodge down in the village. And it doesn't bother you a bit to sleep in a different robe from me, either. I guess I can see why now. Maybe there is someone else you feel better with now than me."

"What do you mean?" Shadow asked. "What are you saying to me, Austin?"

"Maybe I was wrong about us. Maybe you just want me to help your father, since he's getting up in years, and don't really want me at all. Is that what is going on?"

"Austin, that is very cruel!" Shadow said, blinking back tears. "And you are very unfair. You know how much love I have for you. I cannot understand how you would ever speak to me like that."

"You had your arms around him," Austin said. "You don't know what that did to me, to see you with him like that. And after all we've been through together, just because of him."

Shadow pulled him close to her. "Please do not think that anyone could ever take your place. No one ever could. Not anyone. I understand that seeing us must have made you feel strange. But if you will hear my words, then you will know that Badger came to me because he wants to become our friend."

Austin was still shaking his head. "I've got to have time to put this all together. What I just saw was the last thing in the world I ever expected."

Shadow drew his head down and his lips to hers. "You know how I feel for you," she said. "And I know that it has been hard sleeping in the same lodge, but not next to me. It has been hard for me, also."

She put her hands under his buckskin shirt, letting the tips of her fingers glide across the rippling muscles of his chest and back. She let him press into her, his mouth again eagerly seeking hers.

Together they found a grassy opening near a small spring, hidden among the fragrant blossoms and leafy branches of juneberry bushes. The ground beneath them, warm from the sun that shone down through the forest, was welcome to the touch as they pressed tightly together in a long embrace. The want within Shadow had welled up strongly, and she pushed her hand down into his buckskin pants, hearing his gasp in her ear and relishing the touch of his lips which were against her breasts, searching and working their way to her firm nipples, now alive with passion.

They then took time to remove one another's clothing, enjoying the sight and touch of their bodies, making this time of pleasure between them last as long as possible. For the first time, Shadow felt even more desire as Austin's hand stroked her inner thigh and found its way higher, bringing to her a sensation that surpassed anything she had ever known. No longer able to control herself, she held his manhood tightly, rubbing him with the fierce desire he had brought to her.

Swiftly and gently he was atop her and had entered her. Her ecstasy immediately reached its peak, as did his, and Shadow felt herself exploding with the force of her release. Waves of total, incredible warmth flooded through her, reaching into the core of her very being. Though she had known the fires of passion with Austin before, she thought nothing could ever compare with what they now had between them.

After they had lain together for a time, Shadow put her dress back on and watched Austin pull his buckskins over his lean, hard body. Such controlled power. No other man could ever be like this one.

"I am sorry I got angry with you," he said. "But you can surely understand the surprise I felt."

"I can," Shadow said, making herself comfortable against his shoulder as he sat back against the trunk of an aspen. "I held him as a mother does her son, when she wants him to know that he has her support. He is a sick man and very sad and lonely. When we were children, he was very kind to me. Now he has come to me for help."

"Are you sure this isn't some kind of trick?" Austin asked. "I wouldn't put anything past Badger. I believe he would try anything to get you and get rid of me."

"I really believe that he wants to change," Shadow said. "But I can understand how you would doubt his word. At first I thought, also, that he might be trying to play a game with me and I told him so. Then as he talked I could see that his heart was filled with sadness and that the many evil things he had done were haunting him each time the sun left the sky."

"Does he just feel sorry for himself?"

"It is more than that. He is to blame for the deaths of the warriors who were with him the day we fought on the cliffs. This will stay with him always. He wants to change his life now, he has said, and I believe his words are true."

"I still worry about one thing," Austin said. "He wants you. He wants you desperately. I can't see how that will change."

"He has told me," Shadow said, "that he understands that I will never become his. He says he wants just to be friends, like when we were children. He needs a lot of help to overcome the burning water, and he feels my power will do this for him.''

"I don't know," Austin said. "I just want you to
be careful. It would be good for all of us if Badger
is sincere. We would certainly be better off having
him with us, like his father, and not against us. We're
going to have enough troubles with my uncles. If you
can help Badger with his drinking problem, maybe
the other warriors who follow him will come to our
side, also. Then we can turn everybody against the
Beelers.''

"That would be very good," Shadow answered.
She was starting to get excited, feeling that maybe
now they were getting closer to that day when the
two of them could enjoy happiness with her family,
a total happiness without the worry that now held
them in its grasp. "But your uncles are the worst part
of Badger's problem. It is they who bring the burning
water to him and to the other warriors that follow him.
I will need your help, Austin. You will have to be
sure that your uncles do not destroy what we are going to do for Badger. It is certain that they will do
everything they can to keep Badger with them.''

"I'll do what I can," Austin said. "But I don't
have a lot of confidence in Badger. I just hope he will
listen to you.''

Shadow gave Austin a warm hug. "I am so lucky
to have found you," she said to him, her eyes filled
with love. "Your understanding makes me very
happy. I only hope that Badger can stay away from
the burning water. I hope that very much.''

The celebration festival ended, and all the different
bands of the Blackfeet nation began to move out from
the mountains and back down into the river valleys
below. The Hunting Moon would come soon, and

though the warriors hunted at all times of the year, this was when the main hunting took place, the time when the most meat for the lodges was taken so that there would be plenty to last through the cold moons.

Shadow's father was happy for an invitation from Walking Head to join his band near another range of mountains called the Big Snows. Here the buffalo were plenty, and they would take much meat for their winter camp. It was indeed an honor to receive such an invitation, for it meant that Shadow's father and his family had not only been accepted as friends with whom they could trade, but also as extended family and relation.

Austin traveled back down to the fort on the Madison with Shadow and her family. He exchanged many stories with both her father and Little Bear, and there was much laughter and fun. It seemed to Shadow that her happiness had come early for her. It seemed much too wonderful to be true.

Shadow's father was especially happy to see how fast Austin had learned the ways of the trade business and the manner of communication with the Indian peoples of the mountains. He seemed also to have a natural sense about working with the men who worked for Shadow's father and had made many friends among them in a very short time. He was soon accepted as the next in command below Shadow's father and took over many of the duties of everyday operation with none of the men showing any resentment. Shadow knew that Austin treated each one fairly, and they saw him to be as understanding and considerate as her father.

Austin also showed his ability to maintain order under a situation of stress. When a band of Shoshones from the south came to trade on the same day as a

band of Piegan Blackfeet, he talked both sides out of
a bloody conflict. He told them that it would not be
good to kill one another and have mourning in the
lodges instead of happiness, especially just before the
Hunting Moon, when all warriors would be needed to
make meat for the winter camps. He gave both sides
presents to show that his heart was good for all of
them and that he did not want to see the sorrow such
a battle would cause to all their families. So the elders
of both the Piegans and the Shoshones came together
and smoked the pipe of peace and shared meat from
the same pot, forgetting, at least for that time, the
bitter hatred that had torn their two peoples apart for
so long.

Their love became a binding force between them,
and Shadow wanted never to have this man out of
arm's reach. He was now her total life: The air she
breathed and the water that she drank gave her no
more life than the touch and the embrace of this
man with whom she had once fought in a deep forest.
She thanked her spirit guardian, the she-eagle, and
Amótkan, the All-Powerful One, who ruled over all
the earth, for her total happiness. Never had her life
been so wonderful, with each day fresh and bright.

When the Hunting Moon came, it was decided that
Austin would lead a group of men from the fort up
to the mountains of Big Snows. There he would meet
with Walking Head and join with his warriors in the
fall hunt. Austin would take with him many presents
for Walking Head's people: cooking pots, beads,
sugar, coffee, and many things for their comfort and
happiness. He would tell Walking Head that there
would be knives and guns, and more blankets and
cloth from which to make clothing, all waiting for
them down at the fort. The buffalo robes from the

hunt would be tanned and ready to trade.

Shadow remained at the fort, happy to be working on a lodge that she and Austin would soon call their own. Upon his return, they would have a wedding ceremony. After the cold moons had passed and the lands were again, warm and green, they would journey to the land of the Salish, her mother's people, and would then join in on the annual wedding ceremonial dance, marking the beginning of their lives together. It would be a joyous time for Shadow and Austin, and both her parents and Little Bear would share in the honor of their lives as man and wife.

The days remained warm and pleasant as the time of the Hunting Moon came on, but the nights had brought coolness. The colors of the trees were already beginning to change from the green of the warm moons. Soon one of the nights would bring a cold that left the frost across the land, and there would come the many shades of crimson and gold, mixed with the orange and brown that also came. All the trees whose leaves fell with the snows would wear their finest robes, and the colors would mix with the deep green of the pines and the firs and the juniper, to make the mountains beautiful to see.

Shadow thought of Austin nearly always now as she continued to work on the new lodge for them. She peeled the bark from the long lodgepole pines which would support the buffalo hides she so carefully stretched and tanned. She could not wait until the lodge was up and the hides were sewn together for the cover. She would then paint the signs of her love and happiness all around the outside of the lodge. There would be the she-eagle, the symbol of her power, and the mark that symbolized the sun. Even the blue of the small, bell-shaped flower of the mountains would be drawn, in honor of that first night at the high lake at Going-to-the-Sun Mountain, when Austin found her and showed his love for her. There were so many things she would paint upon their lodge.

The sun had crossed the sky four times since Austin had left with her father's traders from the fort. In the distance, out in the valley, Shadow could see three riders. Shadow could see that two of them were hurt, one very badly. He had been shot with an arrow through the lower stomach and was in a great deal of pain. Shadow knew them. They were the three who had left with Austin.

Shadow stood beside her father, very concerned.

"What happened out there, Will?" Shadow's father asked the trader who had not been injured, while the other two were taken for treatment.

"We were jumped by Piegans," he answered. "They were full of trade whiskey. Leading them was Jake and Wolf Beeler."

"Where is Austin and the others who went out with you?" Shadow could sense the deep anger in her father's voice. Something like this was bound to have happened sooner or later.

"He's waitin' back up where we had the fight, at the Valley of White Medicine. He wants me to bring more trade goods. The Beelers and the Piegans with them stripped us clean. We're lucky we got away with our horses and our hair."

"I wish he had come back down with you," Shadow's father said. "Who else got hurt?"

"Just Jenkens and Conner," the trader answered. "We were damn lucky, and I guess we shot good and drove them back. But they got away with our whole pack string."

"Why didn't you all come back?" Shadow's father asked.

"Austin is madder than a wet hen. He don't aim to let his uncles stop him from the hunt with Walking Head."

"Did you see Badger, Walking Head's son, among the Piegans you fought?"

The trader shook his head. "Just Piegans. But Austin figures his uncles are lookin' for Badger so they can fill him full of whiskey, too. He wants me back with the supplies fast so that we can beat the Beelers to Walking Head's camp."

Shadow's father took a deep breath and slapped his buckskin pants. "Damn, this gets under my skin!" He turned back to the trader. "Austin ought to know that you can't go back up there alone. That's just askin' for more trouble. And I can't spare that many more men from here, not with the Shoshones and the Nez Perce both comin' in to trade every day."

"I will go back with him, Father," Shadow said quickly. "We will reach Walking Head's village before it is too late to stop the Beelers."

"I don't like that, either," her father told her. "The Beelers could be anywhere out there, just waitin' with them Piegans. I don't want you in danger like that."

"I must go," Shadow insisted. "I cannot rest now, not until I know that Austin is safe. I must be with him. I have to go; I have to find him. You must understand how I feel."

Shadow's father was thinking, a deep frown on his face.

"I will need but two others beside myself," Shadow went on. "We will travel fast and reach Austin at the Valley of White Medicine soon."

Finally he nodded, knowing to argue with her

would not change her mind. He did not want her taking off alone again like she had when she had left for the Gates of the Mountains.

"Don't take any chances, any at all," Shadow heard her father say. "If the Beelers show up again with those Piegans, just hightail it out and don't try to save the supplies. A few beads and blankets don't measure up to your life. Understand?"

Shadow nodded. She prepared herself for the journey to find Austin while her father and some of the men packed horses with more trade supplies. It was easy to see that the Beelers had started their work to destroy her father's business and would try to take Austin's life. The trader named Will and one other, who was very good with a rifle, would go with her, and they would travel a different trail than the one that followed the waters of the Madison into the Missouri. They would instead use one of the lesser traveled trails that would keep them up in the forests and out of the open valleys and meadows of the lowlands. It would be a harder journey, but much safer.

As she finished packing her own horse, Shadow turned to see Little Bear beside her.

"Take these, my strong sister," he said.

Little Bear held out his bow and quiver of arrows. They were the same bow and arrows that she had used to help her father and save her family from the Beelers and the Siksika. It did not seem that long ago to Shadow now as she took the bow from her young brother and slung the quiver of arrows across her back. They had served her well then, and she knew the power was even stronger within them now.

"I thank you, my brother," Shadow said. "I know I will be protected from harm."

"I do not fear for you, my sister." There was pride

in his dark eyes as he looked up at her. "You have made that bow and the arrows with it very powerful in my hands. You will now only bring more power to them. There will be nothing that can stop you."

Shadow's mother, with deep concern on her face, hugged her and said, "I am still paying for the death of your older brother. It is because of that day such great unhappiness now comes to us. I fear it will become much worse. I am frightened, my daughter. You must be sure and watch out for yourself and Austin. You must both be strong and overcome the evil that has come because of me."

"Mother, you cannot blame yourself," Shadow said. "None of this is any of your fault. The Beelers are the ones who are evil."

"Yes, they are evil," her mother replied. "But the good spirits do not shield us from them. No, it is because of me. The spirit of your long-dead brother still does not rest."

"Mother, you cannot do this to yourself. You will become sick."

"If I had listened to the voices of the spirits," her mother continued, "I would have not let him play with my medicine bundle that day. He would now be alive, and we would all be happy."

"Dry your tears, Mother," Shadow said. "You are a strong woman. It pains my heart to see you feel so sad."

"My medicine is now weak," she said. "The spirits look upon me with disfavor."

Shadow thought for a moment. She remembered the discussion she had had with her mother about the death of her older brother. It had happened in the Valley of White Medicine, she remembered her mother saying. Though she had never seen this place,

Shadow knew she must go there after meeting with
Austin. Yes, when the Hunting Moon was over, she
would visit this place. Maybe then she would know
why her mother blamed herself for all the trouble that
befell them.

"When I go to the Valley of White Medicine to
find Austin," she said to her mother, "I will also pray
to the spirits there. I will talk to them and ask them
to release you from the pain you have suffered for
the passing of so many snows."

"Are you not afraid to go there, my daughter? I
see things of evil each time I think of that valley."

"When the Hunting Moon is ended and Austin
journeys back with me from the village of Walking
Head, I will spend time in that valley," Shadow told
her mother. "Then I will ask them to once again give
you happiness."

Little Bear then spoke. "I wish to also know of my
lost brother, who would have taught me many things
about the forest. Talk to the spirits in that land and
tell them that I wish to know how he was and if he
laughed as I do, and if he liked to run among the hills
and climb the trees. Ask the spirits these things, and
tell them that I want badly to know."

"I will do that," Shadow said. "I will talk to the
spirits in that land. You must listen for their voices.
If they hear me, they will surely speak to you."

Shadow noticed her mother, who was now looking
far out of the valley toward the north, toward the
lands that led to the Valley of White Medicine. Her
mind was there now, and she said to Shadow, "Tell
them I am sorry, my daughter, and I hope they will
hear you. I pray they will hear you."

Chapter Sixteen

SHADOW LEFT WITH the two traders, following the trail along the river until it reached the Three Forks. They then crossed the waters called Madison, and before them lay the broad valley of the Missouri. They traveled the worn trail, the path used by buffalo, elk, deer, and even the fleet antelope, until they came to a smaller flow of water that led into the forest to the east. All the Long Knife traders were calling it Sixteenmile, the distance between these waters and the Three Forks. Here they would leave the main trail and travel up into the mountains, reaching the divide that led into the land that held the spirit of her lost brother, the high land called the Valley of White Medicine.

Shadow's mind rested very little during the journey. Though they stayed hidden along the trails through timber and rock, her eyes were ever open for the Beelers and their war party of Piegans. She wanted badly to find Austin safe. She then wanted to reach Walking Head's village and find them all happy and waiting for them. And as they came over the divide into a land she had never seen, she worried about the spirits who lived here and what they thought of her. Before her was the Valley of White Medicine, and it scared her.

She had traveled down toward the valley with the other two traders only a short distance when they found Austin and the others camped in the trees below a steep hill. They had built no fire since stopping here after the attack and were glad to see more provisions, some of which were food and coffee.

"I am so happy to see you," Shadow told Austin. "I have worried much about you ever since the day when the traders came back down to the fort-lodge and told of your uncles and the Piegans."

"They'll pay for what they did," Austin said with a deep conviction. "They jumped us from ambush, the Piegans." He showed her a gash in his saddle where the steel point of an arrow had buried itself. "I guess they got scared when we dropped four or five of them right away. They turned and took off into the trees with their dead and wounded, yelling about broken medicine. I never did get a shot at either of my uncles. They both stayed back in the trees and let the Piegans do their fighting for them, the cowards. But they'll get theirs. I'm through with the games now. As quick as I can get my sights on them, it's over."

The valley was long, with high mountains on both sides and snow atop the peaks.

"It is a beautiful land," Shadow said to Austin as they began to cross through it. "But this valley is doing something to me, making me feel strange."

"How do you mean?" Austin asked.

"I have told you the story of how my brother drowned in the waters that flow through here," she explained. "And you know that my mother feels the spirit of my brother is unhappy. She feels that the spirits here are causing bad things to happen to her and to us, her family. I told her I would speak to the spirits here. I believe they want me to be here for a time. I cannot understand."

Shadow looked high above to see a number of eagles circling the valley. There seemed to be a great number of them. It was a sign to Shadow. It meant that this was a special place.

"Shadow, are you afraid of this place?" Austin asked.

"I do feel fear," Shadow answered. "But there are voices that are telling me not to be afraid but to remain here for some reason."

Austin began to stare at her. She could see on his face a look of concern for her.

"It is nothing to worry about," Shadow assured him. "I do not feel evil here. I only feel strength and power and the calling of my lost brother. I believe there is something he wants to tell me."

Austin was holding his breath. He began to look around as they rode on through the valley. They had come to the place from which the valley took its name: It was a large meadow filled with bubbling pots in the ground, from which steam rose in dense clouds off boiling water and mud. The ground was bleached white and the crust broke under the weight of the horses.

"Do you actually hear his voice?" Austin asked her.

"It is not actually a voice," Shadow answered. "I

cannot explain it. I can only try, but I have no words which can explain this to you. It is a strange feeling I have deep inside of my body, far back in my mind, past the thought we know as beings of this world.''

Austin continued to watch around him while they rode on through the vapor-filled bottom along the river. The pots bubbled and popped, filling the air with a strange smell. It was not fear of the land which made Austin uneasy. He knew there was volcanic activity beneath the valley which heated the rocks below and sent the water and mud rising through cracks and fissures until they boiled out at the earth's surface. Nor was it the smell of the sulphur in the water which now made him cringe. Shadow was now singing a strange song, and her eyes seemed to be in contact with something he could not understand.

When she had finished, he asked, ''What was that all about? You've even got the men spooked now.''

''I am talking with the spirits, as I promised my mother I would do,'' Shadow answered. ''But a strange thing has happened to me: I did not know that song until I entered this valley.''

''What does it mean?'' Austin asked. ''Weren't you singing in Salish?''

''Yes, it was my mother's native tongue. And I can remember her singing it once when I was a little girl, though she never did teach me the words.'' She looked at Austin and her eyes held tears. ''I believe it is the song she was singing the day my brother was lost in the river. I have no way of knowing for sure, but I feel this to be true.''

''I don't know what all this means,'' Austin said, ''but I'm more than a little uneasy right now.''

''There is nothing to fear,'' Shadow said. ''I only wish I could better understand why the song has come to me and what the spirits are trying to say.''

"We'll be out of here tomorrow," Austin said. "Then it's not far to Walking Head's camp. Maybe in time you'll understand what happened to you."

"I feel, somehow, that I should try and understand now," Shadow said. "I feel I should hear the voices clearly before I leave this valley. Maybe I should stay here and let you go on to Walking Head's village."

"I don't think you should be alone in this country," Austin said. "What if my uncles and the Piegans found you?"

"I do not think the Piegans would come in here to fight," Shadow said. "They would think there were spirits after them if I were to again sing the song I just finished. This is a strange land, and though there might be times when they have no fear of the boiling pools, I know they would become afraid if they heard voices here."

"Well, I've never seen anything like it before," Austin said. "I've heard you speak of the geysers way south of here, in the high country of the Yellowstone. That country must be similar to this. I've heard it called Colter's Hell."

"The place you speak of is in the Burning Mountains," Shadow said. "Yes, it is high up where the waters of the Yellowstone begin. But there are a great many of the burning holes in the ground there. Many, many of them cover a big valley."

"It must be some place to see," Austin said.

"I have been there, and it is a land like no other," Shadow said. "I have been there often. My mother and father spent much time there when they were younger. It was there that she once saved her own life and the life of my father as well. I will take you to that place when the warm moons again return to the land.''

They camped at the far end of the valley that night, and Shadow felt very strange about leaving the following morning. There was something holding her. Austin told her that she could not stay alone, and she turned her back on the valley to travel on to the mountains of Big Snows with Austin and the other men. It troubled her deeply, though, and it was hard to put the valley out of her mind for a time. She would return to this place when the Hunting Moon had passed, she told herself, and then she would learn the secret of this place.

They traveled on into another valley that took them farther east. They had come to the waters called Musselshell, and this land was also new to Shadow. As all the lands of the mountains, there was the same great beauty in this place, but somewhat different in that it led out into the open grasslands that would become the wide plains. It was this valley that broke out of the high mountains and found its way into spreading, rolling hills of high grass. In the distance, marking the sweeping vastness of the open grasslands, were the mountains of Big Snows.

They had turned north to reach Walking Head's village, traveling toward a large, high ridge which took them over and into the land where the hunt would take place.

''They call this land the Judith,'' Austin said to Shadow. ''This whole, broad basin drains into a river named by those two men, Lewis and Clark, who came out here fifty years ago. I heard the story that Clark had a girlfriend he married when he got back from their journey out here, and he named the river and this whole country after her. Judith. Kind of a pretty name, isn't it? Suits the country." He turned to Shadow. "If I ever find a piece of ground that hasn't got a name, I aim to put yours on it."

Shadow smiled. "I am honored that you would think of me that way, but it matters only that I am with you."

They traveled on, across the high plateau that the traders in the land had come to call the Judith Gap. They were going into one of the best buffalo regions of the entire Rocky Mountain area. Surrounded by mountains on three sides, this high basin was a solid sea of grass through which sparkling pure waters ran on their way to a large creek named for the wolf, which, together with the waters of the Judith, flowed north into the Missouri.

Shadow pointed far out across the rolling grassland to where a small chain of mountains in the distance marked the end of the basin. At the far end of the mountains were two lone peaks which stood off by themselves. "That biggest butte," Shadow said, "which looks to be square and stands alone at the end of all the mountains, is a place my mother has spoken of to me in many stories. Though I have seen it just now for the first time, I know that has to be the mountain she talks of. It is a high place from which the Blackfeet peoples look for the buffalo, and many snows past, my mother was taken there by Walking Head after he had stolen her from her people. He wanted my mother for his wife, but my mother loved my father very much and refused Walking Head. That happened in the days when the beaver was plenty and the Long Knives had first come into these lands to trap."

"Those must have been some days," Austin said. "The old-timers, and the others like Jim Bridger and

Kit Carson, and your father, they're a breed of their own.''

"Strong-willed," Shadow said. "There will be no more times like those."

They skirted the north end of the mountains of Big Snows and found Walking Head's village. It was just below a giant spring of water that flowed like a large river out of the hillside. It was much the same as the springs that flowed into the Missouri, near the place called the Great Falls, but the hills here were much steeper and were green with timber. The area in and near the springs was lush with grass and covered at the water's edge with dense clusters of red flowers, all of which grew under huge golden willow trees filled with birds of every size and color.

Walking Head greeted them and welcomed them into the village. Badger and Standing Elk were also there. Both Shadow and Austin were relieved to hear that the Beelers had not yet come with the burning water. Badger assured them that he had quit drinking and never wanted to see any of it again.

That night they feasted and talked of trade and the coming hunt. The buffalo had come in great numbers this year, and there would be many robes. Badger felt it was a good sign for both him and his people. Since they had last met on the trail leading to the high lake of Going-to-the-Sun Mountain, he had had a successful vision quest and had received power. "The spirits told me that it would stay with me only if I do not drink the burning water," he told them. His arm was nearly healed, and he now had it out of the sling, wrapped only in a thick piece of badger fur, the animal from which he received his power. This would be his special, personal medicine, and the wrap would remain around his wrist even after it had healed completely.

The next day a scout from the village who had been out searching for signs of buffalo returned singing a song of the hunt. The people of the village, upon hearing this song, became excited and welcomed the scout back with a large gathering near the central lodge of Walking Head. The scout had found a stone a little smaller than his hand in a dry wash just north of the camp. He held the stone, still singing, in a sacred way, for he had found a buffalo stone.

It was laid out on a dark robe for the people of the village to see and also pray to. It seemed to have a hump and a head with little bumps for horns. Black markings on the face of the stone, though somewhat out of place, were eyes. It had no legs, but the warrior who had found it said that the buffalo stone was lying down, with its feet under it.

That day the warrior began to organize a hunt, for it had been his power which had led him to the stone, and it was believed he would then be successful in finding a herd when he returned to the place where the stone had been found. It would be a good hunt, with most of the warriors in the village going.

Shadow and Austin decided to stay in the village and let the men who had come with them go on the hunt. Austin wanted to talk further with Walking Head and the other elders about trade and the trouble that was sure to come when his uncles, the Beelers, found their camp. The word had already come that the Beelers were somewhere near the mountains of Big Snows, and Austin wanted to warn them to keep their warriors away from them.

The hunters left the following morning very early, and as Shadow stood near the entrance to the lodge they had been given to share as special guests, she watched Austin send off the traders who had come with them, wishing them all good luck. When he returned to her, she greeted him with a smile.

"It is good to be with my man in the same lodge when I am able to lie with him."

"You and I like it," Austin said. "But have you noticed Badger? I don't think he cares for it a bit. The way he looks at us bothers me. I told you he would never get used to seeing you and I together. It's bound to make him crazy again. Mark my words."

"You need not worry," Shadow said. "He will again accept the way things are in a few days. It has been some time since he last saw us together. Now that his power has returned, his will has returned also. It will just take time for him."

"I'm still worried," Austin said. "I see that Standing Elk is getting ready to take a wife from among the young women of this village. But Badger is not. What does that say?"

"Only that he is not ready yet," Shadow answered.

"No." Austin shook his head. "Only that he wants you."

Austin smoked and ate and sat in council with Walking Head and the elders throughout that day and two more that followed. Shadow visited Walking Head's wife, Laughs-in-the-Morning, who was her mother's good friend, and other women in the village as well. Then often she would go off by herself up into the hills, for she needed to speak to her spirit guardian daily now.

Shadow worried some about what Austin had said regarding his feelings about Badger. It was true that the stare was returning more and more into Badger's eyes, and there was no doubt that he did not want to see Shadow with Austin at all. Now he was gone with the hunters, and Shadow tried to convince herself that there was little to worry about. Badger would accept the fact that she belonged to Austin and not him; it would only take time. But the more she said it to herself, the less she believed it.

Early the next morning the hunters returned, and the villagers shouted and cheered as they entered. The hunt had been very successful, and there were a great many buffalo down for the women of the village to dress and butcher. The hunters had brought back with them many of the choice cuts of meat: tongues, hump steaks, livers, hearts, and even the brains. That night there would be a gigantic feast and celebration, and there would no doubt be dancing. The entire village was jubilant.

It was just after midday when Austin found Shadow. His face was clouded with concern and anger.

"We'd best round up the men and move out, just as soon as possible."

"What is it?" Shadow asked. "What has happened?"

"My uncles. They've been camped out near the area where the hunt took place. Badger and some of the other warriors have been in their camp."

"What?" Shadow asked, not wanting to believe what she was hearing.

"It's true," Austin went on. "Some of our men were telling me. In fact, it sounds as if Badger didn't even take part in the hunt at all, that he was drinking my uncles' whiskey the whole time."

"Oh, no!" Shadow said. "I must find him and help him."

Now it was Austin's turn to be surprised. "What did you say?"

"I must help him," Shadow repeated. "Do you know where your uncles are camped?"

"Listen, I wouldn't go out there if I had to. My hair would be gone in a flash. And I can't figure all this talk from you. You can't really mean that you think you can help him now."

"But I must."

Austin's anger continued to grow. "What is the matter with you? Didn't you hear me? I said he's been drinking for over three days. There is no way you are ever going to talk to him now. If I thought I could get away with it, I would take the men out to my uncles' camp with me, and we'd just bury those two today and be over with it. But I can't take a chance on getting some of the warriors mixed up in the middle of it. We've got to just get out now, while the getting is good."

"Maybe they would want to kill you," Shadow said. "But I might have a chance."

"Will you please forget Badger?" Austin yelled. "Give up on him, will you?"

"Austin, if I give up now, he will become our enemy once again. We cannot let that happen. Do you understand?"

"No," Austin answered, "and I don't think you do either. As long as there's a jug of whiskey within arm's reach, Badger is going to put it up to his lips. He's gone, Shadow. He doesn't have any way he can stop himself. You can't do anything for him."

Shadow stood silent for a moment. Finally she said, "I think I can help him."

Austin took a deep breath. "I was afraid it would come to this sooner or later," he said. "You are going to have to choose between Badger and me.''

"What do you mean choose between you?" Shadow asked.

"Just that." His face was hard and serious. "I've heard enough about Badger. So far you haven't told me anything about us. Or is Badger more important?"

Shadow looked at him. He had become very angry and was waiting for her answer. It seemed to Shadow that no answer that she could give would make him understand how she felt. But she would need an answer, and it must be thought out carefully.

Chapter Seventeen

SHADOW CONTINUED TO feel Austin's intent stare. She had never known his fury to reach such a level about how she felt toward Badger. Even along the trail below the lake at Going-to-the-Sun Mountain, when he had found her embracing Badger, even then his anger had not been this intense. Standing with his arms folded in front of him, it seemed to Shadow that she was being forced into a decision which could mean her happiness.

"Surely you do not still worry that I have any feelings for Badger like I do for you," she finally told him. "You do not think that, do you?"

"I don't know," he said. "When you aren't visiting with the women of the village, I don't see you. You're gone somewhere. And Badger never did go on the hunt. Now you want to stay here when it seems real plain to me that my life could be in danger. What am I supposed to think?"

Shadow blinked rapidly. He had to try to hurt her feelings each time they argued, it seemed. It was not fair, nor was it right for him to accuse her that way.

"You know I speak to my spirit guardian each day," Shadow said quickly, biting her lip. "It is not right that you say I am seeing Badger secretly. There is no truth to that and you know it yourself. You are just angry with me because I wish to follow the voices that I hear."

"Sometimes I think those voices of yours are pretty farfetched," Austin blurted out. "Sometimes I think they are just plain crazy!"

"I do not care what you think!" Shadow yelled, suddenly angered greatly by his last attack. "I have feelings that I must obey. And I will obey them!"

"You've got to be the most mule-headed woman in all these mountains!" Austin said back. "You would tell me night was day, just to disagree with me. Well, I don't cater to that. Now, I'm going to round up the men and bid farewell to Walking Head. I want you to be ready when I come for you."

"I am going to try and help Badger one more time."

"You are leaving with *me*!"

"I am *not* leaving!"

Austin stood back from her, his hands on his hips. "You really mean it, don't you? You've taken Badger over me."

"I only want to *help* Badger. I don't love him. I promised him I would try and help him. Now I must do that."

"Then you'll do it alone," Austin said flatly. "I told you I aimed to clear out just as soon as I could.

Now is as good a time as any.'' He went inside the lodge and began to gather up those things that were his.

Shadow followed him in. She fought the tears which sprang from her eyes and wiped them away quickly while she talked.

"What about the men? Are they leaving with you?"

"No, they work for your father. They wouldn't want to go with me."

Shadow fought the tears again. "Where will you go?"

"I don't know." He shook his head. "Just anyplace but here."

He had finished gathering his things and went back out of the lodge. Shadow followed him out, the tears streaming down her face.

"Wait!"

Austin kept walking.

"Wait!" she repeated.

Austin finally stopped and turned around. She did not run up to him but talked from a distance.

"Why are you doing this?"

"I told you. I don't feel safe here. And if I fight and kill somebody, then I will have wrecked everything your father and I have done the whole summer."

"You don't have to leave. I can control Badger."

"No you can't."

"But what will I tell my father?" Shadow ran her hands through her hair and wiped again at the tears on her face, hoping that this was only a bad dream but knowing it was not. She fought at the hurt deep inside that was now tearing at her.

"Tell him what you want," she heard Austin answer. "It's been hard for me, living minute to minute, wondering all the time if you had more feelings for me or Badger. Now I guess I know." He turned and continued walking out of the village, past the people who were already laughing and celebrating, paying no attention to either him or Shadow.

It was hard to stand and watch him disappear among the villagers, but she could not move herself from the spot where she stood to go after him. The tears welled up in her eyes, and she let them fall as she looked out past the village, over the heads of the people, and to the horse herd. She finally saw him again, walking toward the horse he always rode. Holding back a sob, Shadow then turned and rushed back into the lodge. She could not bear to see him ride away.

She let the rest of the day pass, staying alone within the lodge while outside she could hear the noise of the happy villagers. Laughs-in-the-Morning, Walking Head's wife, did not see her among the others and came to invite her out, as did other women she had met. She thanked them all for their kindness and told them that there was no happiness in her heart and that she would stay within the lodge and get ready to leave the following day. When some of the men came to find Austin, she told them he had gone and that she would take them back to the fort the following day.

Finally she decided that it was not good to remain in the lodge; Austin had already left and there was nothing she could do now to bring him back. No, she would go out and begin what she had decided she must do: She would begin her efforts to try to help Badger once again. She would succeed and then she would show Austin that he should have believed in her.

Shadow came out of the lodge and began to walk through the village. She was looking for Standing Elk, for she felt it would be good to have his help when she talked to Badger. Standing Elk could be with her and add his support.

She found him at the edge of the village among a group of warriors. They were all laughing and telling stories of war among themselves, making a lot of noise. When Shadow reached their fire, Standing Elk saw her and stood up. He yelled her name and drew attention to the others that he thought she was very beautiful. Shadow stared at him in disbelief.

"Standing Elk, what are you doing?" she asked. "Why are you drinking the burning water?"

Standing Elk laughed and came closer to her. His face had a strange grin across it, and his eyes seemed to be those of someone else, someone strange and evil.

"What has happened?" Shadow could hardly bring herself to believe what she was seeing.

"I lost a bet." He continued to laugh, weaving as he stopped beside her. "But I am glad that I lost the bet, for the burning water is good. It is very good." He tilted a jug he was holding and closed his eyes as the whiskey spilled from the corners of his mouth.

"No," Shadow said, reaching for the jug.

Standing Elk finished swallowing and offered her the jug.

"I didn't mean I wanted any," Shadow explained. "I just want you to stop."

"I lost the bet," Standing Elk repeated.

"What bet?" Shadow asked him.

"It was with my brother, Badger," he answered, "and the two Long Knives, the ones called Beeler. They told me if I could beat my brother at the game of hands, he would leave their camp and come with me and not drink any of the burning water. They said also if I lost to Badger, I would have to drink from his jug. I lost.''

"Let me have the jug, Standing Elk." Shadow reached for the jug, and Standing Elk quickly pulled it away. "Give it to me," Shadow then demanded.

"It is mine!" Standing Elk yelled. His eyes were squinted at her.

Shadow backed away from him. He had told her before many times that he became a different person when the burning water was in him. She could now see what he meant.

"You told me you would help me keep the burning water from your brother," Shadow said. "Instead I find you drinking it, also. Why did you listen to the evil Long Knives named Beeler? Why didn't you just leave their camp? You knew you could never beat Badger at the game of hands. Why didn't you come to find me? I would have gladly helped you."

"The burning water is good," was all that Standing Elk could answer, tipping the jug again.

Shadow turned and made her way back into the main part of the village. Again she fell into depression, feeling helpless and alone at finding Standing Elk drunk on the burning water. Now she began to wonder if she shouldn't have listened to Austin's words to her. Maybe he had been right about all of this. It would be very hard now, if not impossible, to make Badger listen to her if Standing Elk was also drunk. She felt almost crazed with anger and frustration.

Dancing had begun in the center of the village, another dance much the same as the one in which Badger had tried to get to her before she had bumped into Austin. Shadow worked her way around the circle of dancers, looking for some of the men who had come with them from the fort. She thought it strange not to see any, not even one of them. As she looked around the village, around all the fires where there was food, where hand games were being played, and even where stories were being told, she began to become very concerned. She could not see any of them.

Quickly she made her way back over to where Standing Elk was still drinking with the group of warriors. He seemed very angry with her.

"Why do you leave me?" he asked.

"Where is your father?" Shadow asked.

"He is high in the mountains of Big Snows. He went there to pray for a successful hunt. He has not yet come down. But you have not told me why you left me."

"I wanted to find the men who came here with Austin and me," she answered. "I want to know where the other traders are. Do you know?"

"Do not worry about the Long Knife traders who came with you," Standing Elk said, throwing his free arm around her and drinking from the jug. When he had finished, he added, "They are in the camp of the Long Knives called Beeler." He grinned. "They will go nowhere."

Shadow caught her breath. "What do you mean?" she asked. "Are Badger and his warriors holding them?"

"That is right." Standing Elk nodded.

"Why?" Shadow asked. "Where is the camp?"

"Do not worry about them," Standing Elk said, still holding Shadow with his free arm. "It is for you and I to now enjoy the night."

"I want to know why the traders I brought with

me to this village are being held in the camp of the evil Beelers," Shadow demanded. "I will speak to you no more unless you answer my question."

"It was the Long Knives called Beeler who wanted them to be taken and held," Standing Elk said. "It was today when they were taken. And the one called Green Eyes, why does he not look for them with you?"

"Austin?" Shadow asked.

Standing Elk nodded. "It is said that Green Eyes is no longer in the village. I cannot remember if he was taken or not. One of these warriors here at this fire came from the camp of the Beelers and said that he thought he was there."

Shadow fought the strange feeling that was now welling up from deep in her stomach, a knotting, twisting feeling that made her want to scream. Standing Elk was drunk and making little sense about what had happened to Austin and the rest of the men. It sounded as though Austin had been taken as a captive with them.

"Try to remember what happened," Shadow said. "Do you know if Austin is with them or not?"

"He is not with them," Standing Elk finally said. "Badger told me that the Long Knife with you had been taken to the Beeler camp after the hunt. But I did not know that the Green Eyes was no longer with you. I am glad to learn this. Now you can be with me, for when Badger learns that Green Eyes is no longer here, he will want to claim you for himself."

Shadow backed away from Standing Elk, trembling with anger. He was certainly someone else when he drank the burning water. Shadow could think of nobody, not even Badger, who was as evil as this man when he was drunk. What he had been saying about

Austin had been just an evil trick to learn if Austin had left the village for good. Now he was going to try to take her for his own pleasure. She turned to leave and felt his hand grasp her arm.

"You cannot leave me again," he said to Shadow. "You have already left me once this night. The warriors with me think that it is funny. I do not think that it is funny. I do not want to be shamed again. I want you to go to the circle of dancers with me."

"I do not want to dance with you," Shadow said forcefully.

"You will."

"Would your father be proud of you if he knew you had been drinking the burning water?"

Standing Elk released Shadow's arm. He stared at her a moment before rejoining his friends around the fire. Shadow knew he would think about it, but the burning water would then take control of him again.

The night wore on, and the moon climbed high into the sky. The dancing continued, with the fever of the drums building within each of the dancers. More and more the young couples dancing together were disappearing from the broad circle of firelight and into the darkness beyond.

Standing Elk, having now consumed more trade whiskey, again approached Shadow.

"You will dance with me now," he demanded.

Shadow shook her head. "I do not wish to dance with you, Standing Elk. I have told you this. You are my good friend, but I do not wish to dance with you."

"Why do you shame me in front of my people?" Standing Elk asked.

"I am not shaming you," Shadow said. "There are other young women who have said no to other warriors who have asked them to dance."

"My brother, Badger, said that you would surely dance with me," Standing Elk told her, his eyes glassy in the light of the fire.

"What?" Shadow asked.

"Yes, he told me that you would dance with me and that you would want to go out into the bushes with me. Green Eyes, before he left the village, is said to have been telling stories about you, about how you like to go out into the bushes. Badger told me about those stories. Now dance with me."

Shadow turned sideways to hide the tears that filled her eyes. Was this true? Did Austin say those things? He had certainly been mad when he had left the village, but it did not seem right that he would have spoken to anybody. No, this was surely another evil trick by Standing Elk to break her down into submission. It was a bad thing now that he knew that Austin had left. She could only hope he hadn't told Badger.

Standing Elk took her arm and started for the circle of dancers. Shadow pulled away from him, crying frustrated tears.

"No, Standing Elk, I do not wish to dance!"

Shadow fought to control herself, to keep from breaking down completely in front of Standing Elk. Then in an instant her tears were suddenly changed to fear and anger as she felt herself being taken from her feet. Standing Elk then hoisted her up over his back and began to carry her out into the darkness.

"Maybe you do not wish to dance," Standing Elk said to her angrily. "Maybe you just want to go out into the bushes."

Shadow was taken completely by surprise. He held her by the waist and her legs as he quickly moved with her out to the river. "No!" Shadow yelled, struggling against him. "Listen to me! Hear me through the burning water that clouds your mind.''

It was no use. Shadow knew he was paying her no attention. He grunted something as he resisted her struggling, hauling her with the added strength of his arousal. In a patch of tall grass just up from the river, he forced her down and then situated himself atop her.

Thrashing violently, Shadow slammed the heel of her hand flush into his nose, feeling instantly the warm flow of blood that burst from his nostrils and onto her arm. Standing Elk growled in rage and pain, holding his face with both hands.

Shadow quickly pushed herself out from under him and then strained against his sudden grasp just above her left elbow. He squeezed hard and twisted her around to face him. Shadow gasped as he pressed his knife up close to her face, his breathing coarse and uneven.

He forced her back down, the knife close to her throat. She tried to make her mind work correctly, to shake away the cloudiness. It was not a dream, a nightmare of horror; it was real.

Suddenly, anger welled up within her. The combined effect of hearing slurs reported to have come from Austin, together with the thought of Standing Elk's having been given trade whiskey, made her feel total rage.

Though her arm was now growing numb from Standing Elk's grip, she brought her free hand into play, drawing from herself a crazed strength. With incredible force, she grabbed Standing Elk's wrist and sprung it backward until the knife slid free from his hand. It happened in an instant, taking Standing Elk totally by surprise. Furious, he hit her across the face and began searching for the knife. He held her other arm in his tight grip, but Shadow still had one free hand and two free legs.

Shadow did not even feel her cut lip and the blood that smeared her face as Standing Elk again struck her. Instead, she grabbed a handful of his hair and with all her strength, twisted his head sideways. He yelled, releasing her arm and, at the same time, striking at her again with his fist. Shadow held the hair, twisting his head sideways all the more while he flailed at her.

Gaining additional confidence now that both arms were free, Shadow slammed a fist into his midsection. He jolted but was not stopped by the blow. Instead he raised his arm, pushing it directly outward toward Shadow.

Arching herself sideways, Shadow avoided direct contact. But a sudden, warm and sticky wetness invaded her ribs just under her dress. Somehow Standing Elk had found the knife and it had just grazed her side.

Totally maddened and driven by the instinct for survival, Shadow grabbed Standing Elk's wrist, feeling the blade scraping the back of an arm. With all her might she slammed her knee into his stomach. She heard the breath go out of his lungs and pulled herself away, releasing his wrist, as he fell forward. From his mouth there came a funny squeak as the knife, pinned blade upward between the ground and his body, entered his upper stomach.

At first Shadow did not know what had happened until Standing Elk twisted sideways with a grimace on his face. He then came to his knees, staring at the handle which slumped down from his stomach at an awkward angle. As if Shadow were not even there, Standing Elk then brought himself to his feet and began to walk off aimlessly into the night. He began a high-pitched song in Blackfoot, which Shadow knew surely was his death song.

Shadow forced herself out of shock and started after him. "No, Standing Elk," she was saying. "No, do not sing your death song. You will not die." She finally reached him and turned him around toward the village, leading him in toward the fires.

Standing Elk quit singing and stared at her. His eyes had lost the strange glare from earlier. It seemed as if the burning water had suddenly left his mind, and he had become the Standing Elk that Shadow had always known. It was as if he couldn't believe what had happened to him.

"Hold still," Shadow said. She pulled the knife from his stomach and threw it aside. Standing Elk jerked with the pain, faltering until Shadow helped him again gain control. He held his stomach, the blood running between and under his fingers. Some of the villagers had noticed them and there was a general cry of alarm.

"Maybe I will not die," Standing Elk said. "At least I hope I will not die."

Shadow helped him through the throngs of onlookers and into his lodge. She let his mother attend to him, making him comfortable on his robes as best she could. He would certainly become sick and would need the attention of one of the village shamans. He did not seem to have bled a great deal, but the knife blade had gone deep into his stomach, and it was hard to tell how much damage had been done inside.

Feeling cold and alone, Shadow explained to Walking Head what had happened. He was not angry at her, but he knew very well where the burning water had come from. He would send warriors to the camp

of the Beelers and tell them to leave and bring back
the men who had come with Shadow. Badger was
now standing among the younger warriors in the village. It was certain that he was blaming Shadow for
his brother's injury. It was certain there would be a
council held to determine what had taken place. Until
it was decided what would happen to Shadow if
Standing Elk died, she knew she would be held and
not allowed to leave the village, together with the men
she and Austin had brought with them for trade talk.

Throughout the next three days, Shadow could only
sit within a lodge and pray to her spirit helper that
Standing Elk did not die. Outside, in the center of the
village, Standing Elk was being cared for by a shaman
who danced over him and blew the smoke of the sacred sage in his face. The cries of Badger for justice
could be heard throughout each lodge, and Shadow
knew the time of the council was not far off. She
would be held accountable whether Standing Elk
lived or died.

Also on her mind was Austin. She wondered where
he was now, wishing they had not had the harsh
words between them. She wondered if he had told
Badger that she liked men. Each time she thought of
it, the pain welled up again within her. Surely Badger
had just said it to Standing Elk to urge him on toward
her that night of the dancing when he had been
stabbed. Surely Austin would never say such a thing
to anyone, no matter how angry he was with her.

Another day passed, and that night Shadow was
summoned before the council. Standing Elk was still
critically ill from his knife wound. Death could come
at any time. Badger had convinced the elders of the

village that they needed to know what had happened. Feeling as alone as she ever had during her entire life, she left the lodge to face what the council fires might bring.

Chapter Eighteen

━━━━━━

SHADOW SAT SILENT as the council began discussion about the incident involving her and Standing Elk. Only those members of the council, with the exception of Walking Head, who did not know Shadow were allowed to sit at the fires now. They would be brought in later, after other things were first said. Shadow knew that Badger would be among those to join the circle later.

She knew also that it would be some time before she would be asked anything. Her mind went to Austin; he was gone, and she had no idea if he was still angry or if he now wished he had stayed. Shadow knew that the chances were good that he would have gotten into a fight with Badger or some of the warriors if he had stayed. She wondered if the traders who had come with her were being treated well. They had been brought over from the Beelers' camp by order of Walking Head when he learned that they had been taken without any reason. He had been angry, and he had warned the Beelers to never come to his village again. It had made Badger angry, for this meant he would have to leave to get the burning water that had once again taken control of him.

Shadow thought about all these things, happy to have heard it from Walking Head's wife, Laughs-in-the-Morning. Shadow felt bad for this woman, who now understood that she might well lose both of her sons: Standing Elk from the knife wound and Badger from the burning water. It was becoming more and more plain to all that the burning water was very bad for the body. News had come from the Piegans that two warriors had been poisoned by trade whiskey, though it was not certain where they had gotten it. Shadow had told Laughs-in-the-Morning that most certainly it had come from the evil Beelers, for they had been with a war party of Piegans and had tried to kill Austin and the other traders just before the hunt.

Walking Head and the other members of the council made sacred preparations for the upcoming sessions that would determine what had happened between Shadow and Standing Elk. The pipe that was used by the special society that governed all council events was lit and passed many times within the circle. It was important that the spirits be a part of these proceedings so that the truth might be learned.

"We will hear from Eagle's Shadow Woman," Walking Head announced after the final rites had concluded before the formal council was to open. "Her story will be heard first."

Morning had come to the land and the early light mixed with the slim columns of smoke that drifted up from the sage that burned on the coals. Shadow knew her story would be heard, and then later she would have to tell it again. But now she worried little about the outcome of the council; the truth would come, for the day had broken clear of clouds, and the spirits would receive the smoke from the sacred sage.

Shadow began her story but was stopped by Walking Head when a runner came to the council and spoke into Walking Head's ear. A smile broke across Walking Head's lips and he made an announcement to the council.

"I have just learned that Standing Elk's fever broke sometime during the darkness. He has been eating until now and has heard that Eagle's Shadow Woman sits before us to account for his wound. He wishes to speak himself."

The council quickly approved Standing Elk's request to be heard. He was brought out on a travois so that his wound would not break open again. He looked weak and tired, but his eyes were again like those of the Standing Elk Shadow had once known. But before he was allowed to speak, Walking Head again turned to Shadow.

"It is still the decision of this council that you speak first. We wish to hear what you think happened."

Shadow began her story with great composure, showing to the members of the council that she was confident and sure of her words. It showed that she was not afraid to speak of the incident and that her words contained truth. Although she felt uneasy about discussing the burning water, she knew that it was the main cause of the trouble. She felt it important to address this in the right way.

"I do not believe Standing Elk would have been

hurt if there had been no burning water in the village," she began. "It is my feeling that there was a lot of trouble that night because of the trade whiskey that came with the Long Knives called Beeler. When Standing Elk drank the burning water, he did not know what he was doing. When he does not drink the burning water, there is no finer man in this village."

The members of the council nodded among themselves. Everyone realized that Standing Elk became someone else when he drank. But that was a thing that the individual chose to do, if he wished. No one could tell him he could not drink it. It was up to the individual to know what he would face if he acted foolishly.

"It is known that the burning water has caused my son to do bad things," Walking Head said to Shadow. "But you must tell us exactly what the bad things were, so that we might understand exactly what happened that night."

Shadow glanced over at Standing Elk, but he was looking down at the ground. It was plain that he felt shame and was sorry that any of it happened at all. Shadow could see that he must have remembered most everything he said and did that night and knew he must now relive it again.

"I did not want to dance with Standing Elk," Shadow told the council. "He became angry and forced me out from the village into the darkness. We fought, and he was stabbed by accident when he fell onto his knife."

"Why did my son force you from the village?" Walking Head asked. "He has never shown that kind of interest toward you before."

"He told me that he had heard from Badger that I

liked to go out into the night with men and that I would surely want to leave with him.''

Then one of the other council members spoke up. ''Is this true? Did you want to go out into the night with someone? It could have been this wanting within you that brought Standing Elk over to ask you to dance.''

''No,'' Shadow said quickly. ''This is not true. I did not want to go out into the bushes with anybody. I was preparing to leave the village and just wanted to find my men. I had told Austin, the green-eyed one, that I wanted to help Badger stay away from the burning water. He became very angry with me and left. When I found Standing Elk, to ask him to help me with Badger, he was also drunk. So I decided to leave with my men. But Standing Elk wanted me to go out into the bushes with him.''

Having heard from Shadow, the council then turned to Standing Elk.

''What do you wish to now say with regard to how you have been accused?'' Walking Head asked his son.

Standing Elk spoke with his head bowed. ''The Eagle Woman is good to me with her words. She does not wish to do me dishonor. But I acted very unjustly against her that night and wish to tell her that my heart is sad. It is not right that she should defend herself before this council. It is just that I defend myself, and that my brother, Badger, also defend himself. I do not see him here.''

''Then you put no blame for your wound upon the Eagle Woman, the one called Eagle's Shadow Woman by her people?'' Walking Head asked Standing Elk.

''I put my knife in her face,'' Standing Elk blurted

out. "I would have forced myself upon her. How would any one of you in the council act if it were your own daughter?"

Walking Head and the other members of the council nodded in understanding.

Walking Head then turned to Shadow. "It is the decision of this council that you bear no guilt for the injury to Standing Elk. Any action you might have taken against him was justified. I can only hope that your heart remains good and that you have no bad feelings for this council, Standing Elk, or my people."

"That night will forever be with me," Shadow said. "I can only blame myself for what happened, for Austin told me there would be trouble if I were to stay. It would have been better if I had left with him, as he asked me to do. My heart will not change toward my good friend, Standing Elk, or toward the people of this village."

A pipe of peace was lit and passed around to each of the council members, to Standing Elk, and then to Shadow. Shadow let the smoke rise to the heavens, giving homage to the four directions, and to earth and sky. There were only good feelings within the hearts of all, and this would carry on throughout their lives.

When the ceremony was finished, Walking Head again turned to Shadow. "I must ask you to remain in council with us," he said to her. "The matter will not be pleasant, but it is very important. It concerns the matter of my son, Badger."

At the announcement, a runner was sent to bring Badger to the council fires. It was plain that he was still under the influence of trade whiskey. He took a seat and glared at Shadow before stating his name to the council members. He took the pipe and smoked before passing it around the circle.

"It is the intention of this council to determine what part you played in the incident which led to the wounding of Standing Elk," Walking Head told Badger. "Your name has been brought up as being a part of this problem."

"How could I be responsible for any of it when I was not even there?" Badger asked indignantly.

Shadow could see immediately that the members of the council, including Walking Head, were already annoyed by Badger's attitude. He was becoming defensive, a sure sign that he had something to hide.

Walking Head cleared his throat and prepared to question his son.

"Where were you on that night when Standing Elk received the knife wound?" he asked.

"In the camp of the Long Knives called Beeler," Badger answered quickly.

"What were you doing there?"

"Talking trade. They have better presents and trade items to offer than the father of Eagle's Shadow Woman. I think we should trade with the Beelers."

"Who we trade with is not a matter of concern before this council," Walking Head reminded him. "While you were in the Beeler camp, did you drink any of the burning water?"

"Yes," Badger answered. "But so did Standing Elk. So did many of the younger warriors who were with me."

"Are you saying that Standing Elk was also in the Beeler camp?" Walking Head asked.

Badger nodded.

"Did Standing Elk drink any of the burning water while he was in the Beeler camp?"

"Yes, I have already told you that."

Walking Head cleared his throat again. "It does not matter how many times you are asked a question, Badger. You will answer what you are asked each time you are asked. Do you understand?"

Badger nodded reluctantly.

Walking Head continued. "Did Standing Elk drink any of the burning water in the camp of the Beelers?"

"Yes, much of it," Badger answered.

"Did you speak with him about anything?"

"I spoke with Standing Elk a great deal. He drank from my jug, and I drank from his."

Walking Head nodded. "Did you ever speak together about Eagle's Shadow Woman?"

Badger hesitated. Finally he nodded his head, turning to look at Shadow where she sat silent, knowing that he must now account for the evil he had caused to happen to his own brother.

"What did you say to Standing Elk about Eagle's Shadow Woman?" Walking Head asked Badger, looking at him closely.

Badger was twisting his fingers together. "I only told him what I had heard from the green-eyed Long Knife when he talked to me."

"What do you mean?" Walking Head questioned him. "You are accountable for what you say to another. It does not matter that you heard something from someone. I want to know what you said to Standing Elk about Eagle's Shadow Woman. Even if you repeat what someone else has said first, it can only mean that you also believe it to be true. Now what did you say to Standing Elk about Eagle's Shadow Woman?"

"I told him that Eagle's Shadow Woman wanted

to go out into the bushes with him, that she liked to go out into the bushes with men.''

Shadow stared straight ahead while Badger continued to tell about the rumors he had heard. Then, as he finished, he turned to glance at Shadow before he again spoke to the council.

''I want you all to know that the green-eyed Long Knife told me these things in order to save his life. He was afraid I would kill him.'' He looked again to Shadow for a reaction.

Shadow tried not to smile. She glanced at Standing Elk, who looked at Badger in disbelief. Shadow remembered the evil trick Standing Elk had played on her that night: He had tricked her into saying that Austin had left, and Standing Elk knew very well that Badger had not known this. He had even told Shadow that he must go out with her quickly before Badger learned that Austin had left, for Badger would then surely claim her as his own. Now Badger was lying to the council by saying that Austin had spoken against Shadow's virtue, and that he had spared Austin's life. Standing Elk was still looking at his brother; for when the council came to him to ask questions, they would learn that Badger had not even spoken to Austin at all that night.

Badger then added, ''So that I would not kill him, he told me that I could have Eagle's Shadow Woman for my own.''

The council sat silent for a moment. Walking Head asked the others present if there might be questions from them. There were none, and Walking Head proceeded.

''You have told us that you spoke to Standing Elk in the Beeler camp, and that you drank the burning water with him. Is this true?''

"It is true," Badger acknowledged.

"And you have also said that you told Standing Elk that Eagle's Shadow Woman liked to go out into the night with men, and that it would be good if he went to find her and take her out into the night himself. Is this true?"

"Yes."

"Finally, it was said by you that you saw the green-eyed Long Knife named Austin and that he told you that you might have Eagle's Shadow Woman for your own in return for his life. Is this true?"

"Yes, and it was he who said that Eagle's Shadow Woman would be happy to go out into the bushes with Standing Elk. I told this to Standing Elk only after I had heard it from Green Eyes."

Shadow had by now stopped feeling sorry for Badger and his hopeless fight against the burning water. She could see that supporting him had only made it worse. He would need to learn for himself how the burning water put lies into his mouth and made a fool of him. He would be able to see this only by falling far, far down and suffering a great deal for his evil. He would have to want to stop drinking on his own; no amount of help would do him any good until he, himself, had made up his mind to change. Shadow could see now that the time for his falling was near.

Walking Head now turned to his son, Standing Elk.

"Badger has told this council that he saw and spoke to you in the camp of the Beelers, and that you both drank the burning water together and talked about Eagle's Shadow Woman. Is this true?"

"Yes." Standing Elk nodded. "We saw each other and spoke of Eagle's Shadow Woman."

"Badger has also said that he spared Green Eyes his life in exchange for Eagle's Shadow Woman,"

Walking Head continued. "He has stated before this council that Green Eyes told him that Eagle's Shadow Woman liked men and that you should go and find her in the village. Is this true?"

"I did not see Green Eyes in the Beeler camp," Standing Elk then said.

There was a silence in the council.

"You did not see Green Eyes in the Beeler camp?" Walking Head asked.

Standing Elk shook his head, ignoring the glaring eyes of Badger. "I saw the other Long Knives who came to this village with Green Eyes and Eagle's Shadow Woman, but I did not see Green Eyes."

"Don't you remember?" Badger then asked. "Does your wound make you too sick to remember?"

"Silence!" Walking Head's voice boomed across the council fire. His jaw was firm, and the lines in his face had squeezed together in anger as his eyes burned into Badger. "You were not asked to speak. You are to remain silent until you are again called upon. Do you understand?"

Badger was trying to control his anger. Finally he nodded.

"You did not see the one called Green Eyes in the Beeler camp?" Walking Head asked Standing Elk.

"I did not see him there," Standing Elk answered. "But I was not there for very long. It is possible that he was there when I was not."

Again there was silence among the council. Badger seemed to relax a bit.

"There were other warriors at the camp of the Beelers," Walking Head said. "I want to know their names."

Standing Elk gave him many names. A lot of warriors had gone to the camp and had been drinking the burning water. A runner was sent to gather these warriors and bring them to the council. While they waited, Standing Elk was questioned again by his father.

"When Badger told you that Eagle's Shadow Woman liked men, did he say that he had learned this from Green Eyes?"

"No," Standing Elk answered. "He spoke very little about Green Eyes. Only that Green Eyes would be angry when he learned that I had taken his woman out into the bushes."

The silence among those in the council was now one that made Badger very tense. All eyes were upon him. He did not look at Standing Elk or he would have seen the pain on his brother's face. Badger looked at no one; he kept his head bowed and could only hope that the council took mercy upon him. He had not committed a crime worthy of death, and he knew they would not allow Shadow to take any action against him, but his situation was very serious, and it might mean banishment from the tribe for the rest of his life.

When all the other warriors who had been drinking in the Beeler camp were found and brought before the council, they, in turn, testified that they had not seen Austin at all that night. There was no question in the minds of the council members that Badger had lied about seeing Green Eyes and sparing his life in return for Shadow. Badger had only been trying to cover up the fact that he had made up the dishonorable statements about Shadow's virtue so that he could claim Shadow as his own.

Standing Elk was taken back into the lodge of a shaman who continued to administer to him. Shadow was also allowed to leave for a time while the council decided Badger's fate. He was taken away under guard and made to remain ready to go back to the council fire whenever called.

Shadow was allowed to visit Standing Elk and found him feeling guilty.

"It is not your fault," Shadow told him. "It was wrong for you to drink the burning water and to make the bet with Badger when you knew you could never beat him at the hands game, but you are not responsible for Badger's lies or his evil mind."

"I wanted very badly to stop him from drinking the burning water," Standing Elk said. "And I was willing to do anything to make him stop. I guess I felt I would have enough power to beat him at the hands game."

"But you knew Badger would never have stopped his drinking even if you had won," Shadow said. "So you never should have consented to taking drink yourself if you lost."

"I only know that my brother has gone too far this time and that he will be punished by the council. It will cost him much influence in this village, and he will never again have the power he once had among my people. I am afraid that he will now break away from this band and form another band of his own. There are many warriors in this village who think as he does: There are many who wish to drive the Long Knives from our lands completely and allow no more of them to travel here. If the council decides to banish him, I believe he will go off with those who will follow him."

"That would be bad for all of your people," Shadow said. "If they begin to kill Long Knives, then all the Blackfeet will be blamed and not just those who are truly responsible."

"I understand this," Standing Elk said. "It will mean that someone will have to try and stop Badger. The village will want me to talk to him, and I know already that he no longer listens to talk."

"I know that what is coming is not good," Shadow said. "But you and I will always be friends, and we will always have good in our hearts for one another."

"I would smoke the pipe with you if I could," Standing Elk said.

"You should now rest and become strong," Shadow said. "There is much for you to do for your people. And I have heard that you have found a young woman in this village whom you wish to marry. This is good."

"She is now out with the other women cutting up the fallen buffalo," Standing Elk said. "I only hope she is not unhappy with what happened the other night. I could take her for my wife no matter how she felt about me, but she is good and kind and I know that she loves me. I do not want to make her life unhappy."

"You will not," Shadow assured him. "But you must make a pact with your spirit helper that you will never again drink the burning water. You must never again drink it."

"I have already made that pact," Standing Elk told her. "The spirits gave me life again in return for my promise not to drink the burning water. That promise will always be kept."

"I will see you another day," Shadow said to Standing Elk, "perhaps when the snows have once again left the land and the warm moons have come. If you come to my father's fort with your wife, I would like to meet her. And I wish you happiness with her, and I wish for you many children."

Shadow went out into the village and found the traders who had come with her and Austin. She put the one called Will, who had brought the two wounded men back down to the fort-lodge, in charge of the rest. Though she wanted to leave with them right away, Shadow knew she must stay and smoke the pipe again with Walking Head to insure the peace between her family and his. This was important; she did not want to leave the village and insult Walking Head and those in the council without a formal farewell.

But Badger was already leaving the village. It had been decided that he was to leave the band and be banished for the duration of one season of the cold moons. He would be allowed to return when the grass was again green only if he could show that his heart had changed and that he would drink the burning water no more. Though it was rare that the council would ever impose personal restrictions on anyone, this case was different. It had been decided that Badger's behavior when drinking imposed a threat to others in the village. They felt it just to make these demands on Badger so that the village as a whole might be better off.

Shadow's anger was mainly directed at the Beelers, though. It had been those two evil Long Knives who had caused all the problems to begin with, and somehow they had managed to slip away and escape having to account for their part in these bad incidents. They would cause even more trouble, Shadow knew, and they would be glad to take Badger with them over the cold moons. He could help them a great deal in their fight against her father.

Though she had tried hard, Shadow could not drive Austin from her memory, either. He was there always, and Shadow hoped that it was possible she would find him waiting for her back down along the waters of the Madison at her father's fort-lodge.

Now, just before she was to join the council and smoke with them in farewell, Shadow met with Badger for one last time.

"Wouldn't it have been much better if you had told the Beelers to leave?" she asked him. "Don't you now wish that you had never taken the burning water?"

Badger laughed in her face. "I am only glad that I am leaving this village and all the foolish people who listen to my father and the council. No, they did not win; they did not succeed in making me feel that I have done any wrong, for I have not. It is they who are wrong, and you, Eagle's Shadow Woman. Yes, you all will someday wish you had not plotted against me. I am not leaving this village alone, as the council thinks. No, there are many warriors who are going with me. They are also tired of being weak and child-minded. We will answer to no one. And you, Eagle's Shadow Woman, will soon be in my lodge with me."

Shadow shook her head, feeling foolish to believe she could have thought her efforts to help this man were ever appreciated. Badger had taken her for granted all this time. She was sure now that she should have listened to Austin and been aware of what Badger was really like. It was time she forgot the past, their childhood when life was different and somehow much simpler. All that had changed. And now Shadow knew she must face that fact or forever live her life shunning reality.

"I will never be in your lodge, Badger," she said to him without emotion. "I will never think of you as a friend again, either. If you and your warriors cause any more problems for me or my family, I will surely travel the path of war against you.''

"Sing your war songs," Badger answered. "For that time has already come.''

Shadow watched him turn and join his other warriors, who were ready to leave. He had been very sincere, and Shadow knew there was no question that she would have to stop him or he would destroy her life. She wanted to go up to him now, to challenge him, to get it over with. If she lost her own life, so be it; at least she would not have to face the mental torment that she knew lay ahead. She already stood upon the path of war.

Chapter Nineteen

━━━━━

THEY HAD CROSSED the mountains called Gallatin and were nearly to the valley of the Three Forks. The days had passed slowly for Shadow, without the company of Austin, and she felt as cold and alone as she ever had. She had not gone back into the Valley of White Medicine; she felt its whispering voices would only bring her discomfort, and this would only make her long for Austin's arms that much more. It was best now to just go back to her father's fort-lodge and hope to find Austin there. If he had decided to leave for good, she would just have to face it and try to forget him.

They crossed the river called Gallatin, now beginning to ice up along the small reaches where the sun's light never fell. The time of the cold moons was fast approaching, and soon the skies would be filled with snow. The leaves were nearly gone from the trees, and the grass was brittle under the hooves of the horses. The peaks high above were again smothered with the snows that had come with the beginning of the Hunting Moon, and now the Story-telling Moon—November—had come to the land. These days would be the last of the fleeting warm moons, and Shadow did not even feel happy enough to enjoy them.

The fort-lodge would come into sight soon, and Shadow looked down the valley, seeing smoke rising from where the fort-lodge should be. It rose in a thin wisp but kept getting thicker. Shadow began to discuss it with Will, the trader she had put in charge of the men.

"The smoke," she said, "seems too thick to be that of a campfire."

"I've been watching it myself," he said. "I think we'd best be getting to the fort as quick as we can."

They rode at a gallop, their horses moving along through the trees and brush just up from the river. It would be faster traveling than if they stayed on the main trail, which wound along the bottom next to the river. As they drew nearer, Shadow became well aware that the smoke was coming from the fort and that it was not a campfire.

She kicked her horse into a run across the last flat stretch before the fort. She could see Siksika warriors circling the fort, screaming and yelling. They were led by Badger.

The traders charged behind Shadow, pulling within good range of their Hawken firesticks before dismounting and firing. Badger's warriors began to fall from the backs of their horses, and Shadow could see Badger yelling to them, rounding them up to retreat from the fort.

Shadow was screaming, urging her horse toward

the form of Badger as he continued to order his warriors back from the burning fort. The Beelers were also there, sitting their horses near the edge of the trees, waiting for the others so that they might all get away together. The warriors were picking up the dead and wounded now, trying to get away with their fallen comrades while the traders with Shadow continued to fire at them with their Hawken firesticks.

Shadow saw nothing but the form of Badger. This was her time to end his evil ways and to never worry about him again. She was filled with rage and frustration at seeing her father's dreams now burning ferociously. Men from inside the fort were now running out, helping those who had been injured and shooting at the fleeing warriors. Some of the dead and wounded fell from the grasp of the warriors who held them, while others held on and made their way to safety. Shadow pressed on toward Badger, her mind set for the fight she would have with him.

Then the trader named Will yelled at her. His eyes were wild. "Shadow, your pa!" he said, pointing at a man who was running from the fort toward the river, his buckskins aflame.

Shadow screamed and jumped off her horse next to him. She made him roll in the dirt until the flames were out. With Will's help, she took him to the river and laid him in the shallows next to the bank.

"Father," she cried to him. "Father, can you speak to me?"

He was waving her back to the fort. "Forget about me! I'll make it! Go find your mother and Little Bear. Find them! They're both still inside the fort!"

Shadow rushed to the fort with Will behind her. Will sent a couple of the men to the river to attend to Shadow's father while they went inside the burning walls. Shadow looked desperately through the blinding, choking smoke, screaming for her mother. Timbers fell from the fort walls, throwing flame and sparks everywhere. There were other men screaming and running, fighting their burning clothes. Then, next to a burning storehouse, Shadow saw her mother. She was in a twisted heap on the ground, unconscious and bleeding from a shoulder wound.

Suddenly a large pile of buffalo robes that had been stacked beside the storehouse slid sideways and over onto the fallen form of Shadow's mother. Shadow screamed and rushed over to her. Partially blinded by tears, Shadow struggled to pull her mother out from under the pile of robes that were now catching ashes from the flaming walls of the storehouse. Will found a pole only partly in flames and used it to brace the nearby fort wall, which was alive with flames and ready to collapse at any instant.

"Pull her out!" Will was coughing. "I can't hold it! I can't hold it any longer!"

With superhuman strength, Shadow moved some of the robes, now beginning to burst into flames. She took her mother under the arms and pulled her out from under the remaining robes and clear of the wall, just as it fell. Will was under the heap of flaming wood. He screamed for only an instant before he was silent and lost among the towering flames.

Shadow screamed again and again, shaking her head in horror and disbelief. She felt a hand on her shoulder as another one of the men jolted her into helping him with her mother. Shadow was yelling, "Little Bear! Where is Little Bear!" while she struggled with her mother.

Finally her mother was free of the flaming inferno that was now the fort. The fire had already reached the powder kegs, spreading it so quickly and with such deadly force. Shadow, burned herself and delirious with grief, kept screaming for Little Bear. She turned to go back in and look for him but was held back by two of the men. A third came to help when it became apparent that Shadow would soon struggle past the first two. Then, in defeat, Shadow twisted over onto her stomach and buried her face in the grass and dirt.

"No!" She sobbed uncontrollably. "No, it can't be! It just can't be!"

Shadow continued to sob in frustration and despair. It seemed all had now been lost. Then she heard the voice of her mother, who was now kneeling down beside her, shaking her to make her listen.

"Hear me and be strong," her mother said. "I want you to listen to my words."

Shadow sat up, taking her mother in her arms, careful not to bring more pain to her injured shoulder. Her mother's face was black with soot and ash, streaked through with sweat and tears.

"Little Bear did not die in the fort-lodge," her mother announced. "I was shot by one of the Beelers when they took him. They gave him to one of Badger's warriors and they rode away with him."

Shadow was happy that he had not died in the flames, but was now very concerned about why the Beelers had taken him. She had been so intent on getting to Badger that she had not even noticed that Little Bear was among those whom the warriors were carrying on their horses. But he was not that far away, if she rode swiftly.

"It would not be good to try and catch up to them now," Shadow's mother said, as if reading her mind. "Your father is burned very badly and needs our attention. You would only cause his death should you try and fight them now. You must prepare yourself, my daughter. It will be your greatest test.''

Shadow looked out toward the valley where they had gone with Little Bear. Her feelings were mixed with the almost uncontrollable urge to try to rescue her brother and the deep concern for her injured father.

''Where is Austin?'' she then heard her mother ask. ''It is strange that he is not with you. Did he remain with Walking Head and his people for some reason?''

''No, Mother,'' Shadow answered. ''He thought that I cared more for Badger than I did for- him. He has gone and I don't know where he went. I had hoped to see him here. But if you have not seen him, then I do not know where he is.''

''His love for you is strong,'' her mother said. ''He will come again for you.''

''Why has he not come before now?'' Shadow asked. ''The sun has crossed the sky as many as the fingers on two hands.''

''I cannot say,'' her mother answered. ''But you must not give up hope. Your love is too strong.''

''It is my fault he is not here with me now,'' Shadow said. ''He was right about Badger; I could not keep him from the burning water. Austin wanted me to take the men and leave Walking Head's village, for he was afraid there would be a great deal of trouble. He was right.''

Shadow went on to tell the story of her trouble with Standing Elk and the affair with the council. She told of how Badger had lied and had been banished from his people for the duration of the cold moons. It was evident now that his words to Shadow that day in the village after the council had banished him should have been taken as a warning. She was angry with herself for not having realized that he would surely come to the fort-lodge first. The extra time she had been forced to spend in the village saying good-bye to Walking Head and the council had given Badger enough headstart to get down into the valley of the Three Forks ahead of her. But this would be his last raid against her family, Shadow promised herself. He had told her to sing her war songs. She would now, and she would never stop chasing him and his evil friends, the Beelers, until she had gotten Little Bear back from them and they had all left this life.

Shadow knew very well now that Badger would not allow the Beelers to kill Little Bear. He was no doubt using her brother to gain her for himself. Little Bear would be returned when Shadow had agreed to become Badger's woman. But there would be no lodge for Badger to take her into, nor would there be any village where he could call himself war chief. Shadow would see to that.

Shadow and her mother helped her father up from the shallows of the river and out of his burned buck-skins. There were some places along his lower back where the scorched skin came loose with the clothes. It was not easy to see whether or not the burns had gone through all the layers of skin, but all along his back and arms was black and deep red. He would drift in and out of blackness with pain. Once, when he came to, he tried to laugh. He said, "It'll take a barrel of bear grease before I let someone slap me on the back."

It would be the passing of many suns before he could be moved. They would go into the land of the Bitterroot, where the Salish would welcome them and give them food and shelter during the cold moons.

There was nothing left for them here where the fort-lodge had once stood. All that now remained were smoldering ashes that the men now searched through to find the bodies of the traders who had been trapped inside. The memory of Will and how he had held the flaming wall up so that she could save her mother would remain with Shadow forever. He had given his life for theirs.

Shadow and her mother spent the day making a bed for her father from the remaining buffalo robes that had not been inside the fort, and also preparing an herb for him to drink. Shadow went to the banks along the river and stripped what leaves were left on the snowberry bushes that grew under the trees and in pockets where the floodwaters of spring always settled. From these leaves she would make a poultice to cover his burns and a tea which would help reduce the fever which was sure to fire his head. Though the leaves were brown with the coming of the cold moons, they had remained soft from the water which fed them, and they would still contain the medicine to help heal the burns.

Though the days passed slowly and there were many times when it seemed her father was near death, Shadow felt good that the men who worked for her father had remained to help guard against another attack, if it should come. They were angry at what had happened and did what they could to help by collecting many leaves up and down the river from the snowberry bushes, as well as others that helped with sickness and swelling. They made sure that there was plenty of meat to eat and that firewood was always ready to warm them all. They would stay with her father, Shadow knew. They would go to the village of the Salish and guard against attack along the way.

Then, when her father had recovered from his burns, they would journey back here with him and would again build a fort-lodge called Madison.

Shadow worried that the cold moons would come upon them before they reached the Salish villages. Her father was now ready to move; his burns had developed a crust over them and he had stopped losing the fluids from his body. His strength was returning, and he was talking each day about rebuilding the fort before the snows came. Finally he agreed that it would be best to wait until the warm moons again came to the land: There were no supplies to take them through the winter, no robes from the buffalo or different kinds of food that they would need in great amounts to feed themselves and all the men. And there was no protection if Badger should return with the Beelers and his warriors. It was certain that to go and stay among the Salish was the best way to spend the cold moons.

They talked about Little Bear each day, wondering, worrying about where he was and how he was being treated. It still seemed certain that they would not do him great harm, for he would then be no good to them in bringing Shadow into Badger's lodge. It seemed strange that none of Badger's warriors had come with a message of some sort, telling them what Badger wished in return for Little Bear. If they had intended to kill him, surely they would have done so without carrying him off when they escaped.

Now, just before they were to leave for the Bitterroot, Shadow spent time alone on a mountain above the river. She held Little Bear's bow in her hands and offered it to her spirit helper, the golden eagle, so that she might receive a vision and learn where Little Bear was being held. But the vision would not come, and

Shadow knew that in order to have the spirits help her, she must spend time fasting and praying until she felt the time was right. She knew now that the mission ahead of her would be far harder than she had expected. It would be the hardest time of her life. She only wished she had Austin beside her to help and love her. She still loved him so, and she would never forget him, never. He would remain in her heart forever.

The Salish village welcomed them and was angry to learn of what had happened along the waters of the Madison. They were doubly angry now, for it was clear who had killed three of their scouts hunting for buffalo. Two other warriors had come back to the village with the dead, telling of a young Siksika war chief whose medicine was the badger. When Shadow described the badger fur wrapped about his wrist as his personal medicine, the warriors nodded and yelled war songs. His medicine would not save him.

So intent on caring for her husband, Shadow's mother neglected her shoulder, and it was now very sore. She had never mentioned it to Shadow; it was much more important that her husband receive more care.

However, now it was time for Shadow to give her mother the broth that came from the leaves of the snowberry. She had taken to bed with fever, though it was not nearly as severe as the one her father had endured. Still, Shadow worried and stayed by her bed. Her father, who rested nearby, could only talk about Little Bear and wanting to go out to find him soon.

Late during one night, Shadow heard her mother's voice in the darkness.

"Shadow, my daughter, hear me. Light the fire in

the lodge so that you might hear my words."

Shadow lit the fire and went to her mother's side.

"You must rest, Mother. The fever makes you speak. Do not worry. Rest." She adjusted the robes around her mother's arms.

She then sat back quickly as her mother angrily pushed the robes off again. She sat up and said to Shadow, "I do not speak with the fever in my head. If you would touch my brow, you would see that the fever has broken."

The fever had broken, and Shadow made a shout for joy. Her father, who had already awakened, sat up in his bed.

"You say you're feelin' better now?" he asked.

"I feel much better," Shadow's mother answered.

"Then maybe you could slip over here to my bed," he suggested. "It's been quite a spell."

"First thing you would think of, isn't it?" Shadow's mother told him. "It would be better if you saved your strength. Go back to sleep while I speak with our daughter."

Shadow laughed while her father grumbled about how things change after so many years together. Then she became serious as she heard her mother.

"I want you to do what I ask," her mother began. "This is the beginning of a hard time for you, and you will need my help. I have dreamed these past days, many times I have dreamed. The spirits have sent these dreams to me, I know this. They are to help you."

"What is it I am to do?" Shadow asked.

"When the sun comes again to the land, I want you to go out from the village, far out from the village. You must go to a sacred place, my daughter. You must find the Medicine Tree. Do you hear me?"

"Yes, Mother." Shadow nodded. "How will I know the Medicine Tree? I have never been there."

"You traveled there with me as a very small child," her mother said. "Even then you looked upon it with wonder. If you go out from the village and follow the river upward, you will find it. Yes, you will know it when you see it."

Shadow thought a moment while her mother said a prayer. When her mother had finished, Shadow asked, "Tell me of the Medicine Tree. I know this tree is special to you and has been a place that is special in your life."

"I will tell you of the Medicine Tree," Shadow's mother said. There was a mist in her eyes as she spoke. "It has always been a holy place to my people, the Salish. You are of my blood, and it is therefore a holy place to you, also. All who go there can learn from the spirits if their heart is good and open to what they might hear. But you must believe." She turned to Shadow, the mist still in her eyes. "I know you believe, my daughter. That is why I want you to go there. You will receive power and you will learn many things. The spirits have told me this."

"It makes me feel good to hear this," Shadow told her mother. "It makes me happy to know that the spirits have talked to you and that they have said to you that I might learn from them."

"Yes, my daughter." Shadow was intent now on the words that her mother was saying. She seemed to be convinced of something and wanted to share it with Shadow. "Many snows have passed since the death of your older brother in the Valley of White Medicine. Since that time I have grieved and been afraid. Now I am no longer afraid. I am only ashamed that I have not been able to see and enjoy life as much

as I should have. I think of you and of Little Bear."
Here she paused, and the mist in her eyes welled to
tears.

"Little Bear lives, Mother," Shadow assured her.
"Do not mourn him. He is not dead."

"I believe your words are true," Shadow's mother
told her. "But now I think of the time that has passed
and how I could have enjoyed it more with him. I
feel ashamed. Instead of seeing him, I always saw
your lost brother. That is not the way it should have
been."

"Do not worry, Mother. You will see him again.
He has not left this world."

"Yes, I know he lives," her mother said. "The
spirits have told me this. I just want him to be here
so that I can hold him and tell him that I love him. I
want to let him know that he is very special."

"The day will soon come when you will again see
Little Bear," Shadow answered. "What more must I
know about the Medicine Tree?"

"You will learn what you must do when you get
to the Medicine Tree," her mother said. "When I was
near your age, I went to the tree to gain power. My
life then was much the same as yours now. I wished
to find my mother, who was called Little Grasses. She
was your grandmother."

"I remember her," Shadow said, thinking back on
the small Salish woman of many, many snows who
held her as a child and sang songs to stop her crying
when she was hurt or put her to sleep when the darkness came. She had been special. "Yes, I remember
her well. And the old Long Knife who was father's
dear friend, the one called Fiddler."

"Yes," her mother continued. "I have told you the

story of how my mother was lost from me during the raid by the Siksika.''

Shadow nodded.

''I went to the Medicine Tree to ask for power, to ask the spirits and my spirit helper, the small owl of the forest, to help me find my mother. At that time I also loved your father. But I was being chased by Walking Head, and your father did not approve of my coming to the Bitterroot to gain power.''

Shadow shook her head in disbelief. It was so similar to what she was now going through herself: Austin was gone, yet her love for him was still strong; and she knew she must now stop Badger from destroying her life totally. The only difference was that she knew she must also find Little Bear, as her mother had looked for the woman called Little Grasses, her grandmother, and that he was in danger of being killed by Badger and the Beelers.

''My dreams these past days while I lay sick with fever have taken me back to the Medicine Tree,'' Shadow's mother continued. ''I saw that time when, as a young woman like you, I went to the Medicine Tree and saw many things. The fever showed me the face of my older brother, Rising Wolf, who had been killed in a raid by the Siksika when I was but eleven winters of age. I had loved him very much, and his loss had hurt me deeply, just as the loss of your older brother again hurt me deeply. But most of all I remembered words that Rising Wolf had said to me when he was alive. He had heard them from an elder in our band: 'Loneliness is a thing that comes to all of us. We must learn what it means. We must learn that loneliness is a sign that tells us we are not giving ourselves to others. To feel loneliness is to know there are things we can be doing that will make our hearts glad. Then loneliness cannot enter.' Now that I have had these dreams and those words have come back, I can see that I was lonely for a long time, even though you and your father and Little Bear were always there to be with me. You tried to make me happy many times, but I would not forget my loneliness. When you fast and say your prayers at the Medicine Tree, remember those words.''

''I will always remember them,'' Shadow told her mother. ''I am glad that you are helping me.''

''I will let you get some sleep before you leave for the Medicine Tree,'' Shadow heard her mother say. ''But first there is one more thing I want you to do.''

''What is it, Mother?'' Shadow asked.

''Come close,'' her mother said.

Shadow leaned over and felt her mother's arms pull her in tight against her. They held one another for a long time, each feeling the warmth and love of the other. No words had to be spoken; it was a special thing that was happening.

''Be strong,'' Shadow's mother finally said. ''You have a hard time ahead. I will speak to you again when you return.''

Chapter Twenty

———

SNOW HAD BEGUN to fall as Shadow continued up the valley called Bitterroot. This entire land, its mountains, its waters, and the valley itself, had taken its name from the small flower that comes with the warm moons, whose brilliant pink blossoms bring a beautiful color to the mountains and hillsides. It was also a main food item for all the Indian peoples of the mountains, who boiled its root for stews and mixed it with meat and other plants. This land, ancestral home to the Salish, held mystical power for Shadow's people. Now she hoped this power would come to her.

Her steps were slow as she walked, for she had not eaten for the passing of the sun twice across the sky. She had prayed the entire time she had been looking for the Medicine Tree and hoped that when she found it, the spirits would look with favor upon her. She had found a sweat lodge along the river, one that had been built many snows past and left for journeys such as hers. She had gathered wood and made a fire, heating the stones within the lodge. She had filled elkskin bags left inside the lodge with water and had poured the water onto the rocks to give off steam. She had done all these things in the sacred way, and she had prayed to Amótkan and to her spirit helper, the golden eagle. She had done all things in the manner the spirits wished; she could now only hope that they heard her.

The sun crossed the sky once again, and the snow continued to fall. It came down in big, soft flakes that were wet to the touch and made a soft blanket upon the ground. No wind blew, but only the falling of piled snow from trees could be heard. All was silent but for the singing of Shadow as she continued to talk to the spirits.

They came that night, visions and dreams which made her mind afraid and made her cry out in the sweat lodge near the waters called Bitterroot. She held her head as she sat upright near the steaming rocks, sweat pouring from her body. She could see Badger shooting an arrow, and the arrow running its way through Austin's shoulder. She could see the blood on his buckskins and hear the cry from his lips. She saw his rifle spit fire, and then she saw another warrior fall, clutching his chest.

The vision continued, and Shadow still swayed to and fro, holding her head as the terrible scene continued to unfold before her. She again saw Austin, with the arrow buried deep in his shoulder, swing his rifle with his good arm; she saw the stock crash into the head of another Siksika warrior. She saw the warrior fall and the splinters from the gunstock fly into the

air. Austin's eyes, wild as fire, bore into Badger. His
knife in his good hand, he swung in a vicious arc, the
blade glistening and Austin's screams of war loud and
eerie to hear. Shadow tried to shake the vision free
of her mind, but it would not leave. She did not want
to see Austin die.

As her vision continued, Shadow became more relaxed. She now saw Austin, still yelling, the knife still
reaching out toward Badger. She saw Badger raise his
arm quickly to fend off the knife. The blade ripped
through the badger skin wrapping around his wrist,
slicing into skin and muscle. The wrapping fell in
half, and Badger's eyes grew wild and filled with
panic. His medicine now lay on the ground. He was
helpless. He backed away from Austin, yelling to his
warriors. Austin came ahead, trying to finish Badger,
but was struck by a war club. Before going down,
Shadow saw Austin swing the knife again, opening
the stomach of the warrior who had struck him. She
saw Badger, holding his badly cut wrist, yelling for
his warriors to leave that place, for the green-eyed
Long Knife fought with the spirits that day. He could
not be killed, this Long Knife whom the Eagle
Woman called her man. He had broken the medicine
of the badger and would surely kill all of them, no
matter how many arrows would go into his body or
how many blows he might receive from their war
clubs. They must leave or die with the spirits who
were angry with them.

The vision was nearly over. The scene was fading
in her mind. Shadow saw the warrior whom Austin
had cut with the knife, his eyes dazed, holding his
stomach so that his insides would not fall out, while
another warrior tried to help him onto a horse. She
saw them leaving, Badger and the remaining warriors,

while Austin stumbled forward and fell to the ground. The ground was white where he lay. It was white but not with snow. No, it was white with the medicine that comes from the water that boils up from the ground. He was there, in the Valley of White Medicine! He had been there waiting for her to come after the hunt with Walking Head's people. He had remembered her saying that she must return to that valley to find out why it held her in its grasp.

Tears flowed from Shadow's eyes. She got up from her seat near the hot rocks within the lodge and rushed outside. The snow had stopped falling, and the valley was filled with fog and low clouds. The snow was soft and wet on her feet, and the air felt strangely warm on her body. She found her doeskin dress and put it back on, forgetting the robe she had also brought. The air was so warm, she would need nothing more. She wandered for a time. It was not clear to her which way she would need to go to again find the village. She looked into the waters of the river, but her mind would not tell her which way the current flowed. It was hazy and seemed to be running in a strange motion which made her dizzy. She stepped back from the bank so that she would not fall in. She turned and looked back up from the river into the forest. All the trees had melted together. All was a solid, strange green.

Shadow wandered onward through the valley, falling at times into the snow, finding it harder to rise each time she found herself lying in the mantel of white softness. It seemed ever warmer to her, and as inviting as the robes of the buffalo on a cold night. But each time she rose once again to her feet. Her mission was not yet complete.

The clouds fell closer in around her, and once again

snow began to fall. It settled on her hair and on her dress the soft flakes seeming to wrap her in a blanket of white. A song came to her head, the same song she had sung while with Austin in the Valley of White Medicine, the song her mother had been singing the day her older brother had been lost.

Shadow continued the song, seeming to gain more consciousness as she sang. It seemed strange to her that these words should again come to her, and here, in this place. Strength seemed also to return to her, and she knew the spirits were now reaching her. She had reached the second plateau, the level of consciousness the dreamers often spoke of. It happened when one's body had given up all of its strength, yet the will of the mind was so strong as to bring on a second surge of energy, a state different from that of life as it is ordinarily known. Shadow knew she had arrived at a higher level of awareness, where the mind lived totally and the body was forgotten.

But it did not frighten her, and when she saw the giant tree in front of her, standing alone from the others, she realized why the song had come to her and why the spirits had now brought her out of her weakened condition. She had found the Medicine Tree.

She stood for a time, the duration of which she could not comprehend, and stared at the huge tree. She began to look closely at the limbs, where the snow had settled and had given the tree a robe of white. But on one of the lower branches was something small and brown, and it seemed to be drawing her to it. She got very close and to her amazement, she saw that it was a tiny owl, no bigger than her fist. He was the tiny warrior of the forest who hunted by night and was seldom seen by anyone. He was her mother's spirit guardian.

This was a very special sign, Shadow knew. From the little owl would come the answer to her mother's anguish. Yes, she would now learn why her mother had for so long lived in despair.

Shadow felt a strange feeling overwhelm her as she watched the little owl who appeared to fly directly into the tree. The tree seemed to open before her, and she found herself following the owl into another time and place, another life where she had never been before. Shadow did not know whether to feel fear or relief at knowing that soon she would understand the deepest of her mother's thoughts.

The owl had placed itself upon the limb of a tree near a campfire. Near the campfire was a woman who sang a song as she sewed a dress. Shadow knew the song well, for it was the same song her mother had sung when she was but a child, the same song she herself had just sung before finding the Medicine Tree. Shadow knew that the woman sewing on the dress was her mother, those many snows past, when her older brother had died in the Valley of White Medicine.

Shadow looked down upon the scene as if she were suspended in the air above the fire. She now felt fear as she watched the woman, whom she knew to be her mother, give a small boy her medicine bundle. The small boy was her lost brother, White Feather, and he took the medicine bundle with glee, holding it next to him and running off to play with it. Shadow tried to turn away from the scene, but the small owl flew up at her, and it became plain to Shadow that she had to watch.

White Feather then took the medicine bundle to an

open meadow near the river. Tied to a leather leash in the meadow was a tiny black bear, not over a few weeks in age. The little bear had been playfully chewing at the leash and had nearly chewed it in half. White Feather put the medicine bundle around his neck, and with his knife, which he had made himself under instruction from both his father and his mother, he began to pretend that he was a mighty warrior who was conquering the bear with his bare hands.

White Feather and the small bear romped together for some time, with White Feather pretending he was stabbing the bear. Often he would stand up and raise the medicine bundle that hung around his neck, holding it up so that the spirits could see that he had gained power from it. Then he put the medicine bundle around the bear's neck and continued his mock fight. After a time he tired of the game and left the bear with the medicine bundle still tied around its neck.

Shadow then saw the little owl suddenly leave the branch of the tree beside the woman who was sewing and singing. Shadow thought this very strange, for it was time for her to learn what had happened to her brother. But the vision before her had turned murky gray, and the figures were melting away from her senses. Instead she was again following the little owl through the depth of the Medicine Tree, until she finally felt herself in the snow once again, standing in front of the tree. The little owl was gone.

"My sister, I have found you!"

Shadow could not believe what she was hearing. She asked herself if she was still within her dream, still in contact with the spirit world. But she was not, and it was the flesh form of Little Bear who stood beside her, putting his arms around her.

"I prayed to Amótkan that I would come upon you somewhere," Little Bear said, overcome with emotion. "But the snow is coming so heavy that I was afraid I would not see you."

It was several moments before Shadow could speak. Finally she said, "Where did you come from, Little Bear? Did the spirits send you to me?"

Little Bear, knowing now that Shadow's mind was only just coming back to this earth, said, "I have come from the Valley of White Medicine. I have escaped from the camp of the Beelers. It is so good to see you, my sister."

Shadow held him for a long time. She was overjoyed that he was safe. Though she was very weak and was now becoming sick from lack of food, she somehow found the strength to return to the village with Little Bear. She gained added strength when she heard Little Bear's words about Austin.

"He is as great a warrior as has ever lived," Little Bear said. "He was in the Valley of White Medicine when the Beelers and Badger took me there. Badger's warriors are many and still, when Austin saw that they held me, he charged them with his firestick. He was wild and his medicine was very strong. Though he was shot by an arrow from Badger's bow and struck by the war club of a warrior, he still fought like a spirit and killed four Siksika warriors before he drove them away. I jumped from my horse and hid in the trees among the pools of boiling water. Badger and the Beelers did not try to find me. They were happy just to get away with their lives. Once again the Beelers showed themselves to be cowards, for they stayed back with me and did not try and fight Austin. They thought there were many warriors and that they would surely kill him easily. But he would move in and out and around among the pools of boiling water, through the steam where they could not find him nor see him. After a time they thought he was a spirit and fled in terror. Badger lost his medicine skin that was wrapped around his wrist. He will never get it back, and I am sure that the Beelers now wish they had gone to fight Austin themselves with their own firesticks, for they are marked for death.''

''Is Austin back in the village?'' Shadow asked. It seemed odd to her that he had not come with Little Bear to find her.

''He waits for you in the Valley of White Medicine,'' Little Bear answered. ''He would not come with me. I went to help him after the Beelers and Badger had left with the warriors, and he was very glad to see me. He was hurting from the arrow through his shoulder and from the blow on the head that the warrior had given him, but he is very strong and was even able to walk around though I told him he should not. I helped him get food, and we built a shelter from willows and covered it with bark from the cottonwood trees. I stayed with him for the passing of many suns, and he told me that I was his brother. It was good to be with him, for I finally beat him at the game of hands. He said it was not fair because he could not move his arms as well as he usually could. He felt good when I left and said that he would not worry about me coming here by myself. He was worried a great deal, though, about you and Mother and Father.''

''Why did he stay in the Valley of White Medicine?'' Shadow asked.

''He would not tell me,'' Little Bear answered. ''He said only that you would understand. He said that the valley was holding him as it had held you.''

Shadow did understand. She knew it had something to do with the spirits who lived there and that they were trying to tell Austin something about the valley. She now knew that his love for her was very strong, and that he had never meant to leave her for good. He had only wanted to meet her in the Valley of White Medicine after she and the men left Walking Head's village. He had been waiting for her, no doubt, when Badger and the Beelers had come through with Little Bear as their hostage.

At the Salish village, Shadow was greeted by her mother and father, who were both anxious to know if her vision quest had been a success.

"It is hard to know if it was complete or not," Shadow answered. "I do not believe my time with the spirits will be over until I again have Austin with me. I know I must go again to the Valley of White Medicine, where he waits for me."

Shadow's mother nodded. "This I know, my daughter. That Austin has also been touched by the spirits is a good sign. This means that his mind is open to those things which are more powerful than we as human beings. I only hope that you will not take chances going to the Valley of White Medicine. You would stand no chance against the Beelers and Badger by yourself."

"It is not yet time to go after the evil Beelers and Badger," Shadow said. "I must first find Austin and learn the answer to the visions that I have seen. Then it will be time to stop the Beelers and take the path of war against Badger."

"I will go with you, my sister," Little Bear said. "I know where the Beeler camp is, the place where they make the burning water. They have much of it at this camp, and only I can take you to it."

Shadow nodded. She knew both her mother and father would be very worried and might not allow Little Bear to go. But they all knew that the Beelers had nearly killed each one of them already and would surely try again if they learned that her mother and father had survived the destruction of the fort-lodge on the waters of the Madison. There was no choice now but to destroy their camp and break up the newly formed band of Siksika led by Badger.

"I know it is important to get rid of Badger and the Beelers," Shadow's father said, "but I don't think any one of us is in any condition at this time to go out after them. It's time we all got our strength back. Then we can think about rebuilding the fort and starting over."

"I will have my strength back soon," Shadow said. "Then I must go to the Valley of White Medicine. I know this is the only way to gain lasting happiness in our family. I will find Austin there, and together we will learn what the valley wants to tell us."

"I want you to come back here as soon as possible," Shadow's father instructed. "You can't go up against all of them, not just the two of you."

"I only want to find Austin," Shadow told her father. "I will let the spirits tell me when the time is right to journey on the path of war. I am sure that Austin will want to take with us many of the Salish warriors from this village. Their hearts are filled with the cries of war, and they will surely remember the death songs of their lost brothers at the hands of Badger and his warriors. But the snows have come, and it is not a good time for war."

Shadow rested and regained her strength, her mind constantly on Austin. She worried that the Beelers had returned to find him, and that Badger had regained his power in some manner. But her worries seemed always to take comfort in the knowledge that the spirits were smiling on him; he had been chosen to learn the secret of the Valley of White Medicine along with her. She could not fully understand why this had happened but was very glad for it.

When Shadow had finally prepared herself for the journey and had packed her horse with many robes and blankets, she told her parents that this journey might well be the most important one of her life and also of theirs. It would mean their happiness and the end of all the problems they had had to fight for so long. It would mean the end of her mother's torment over the loss of White Feather, the older brother Shadow had never known. Shadow hoped beyond all measure that this journey to find the truth and the light would be her last.

Because this journey was so important, Shadow told her parents that she had to stay in the Valley of White Medicine until she had learned the secret of the valley. She must complete the vision she had started at the Medicine Tree; there could be no leaving the valley now until she had learned the secret and had then gotten the power she would need to end her family's troubles.

"If I have not returned with Austin by the end of the cold moons," she told her parents, "then you can send the warriors from this village to find me. Send them when the grass-that-opens-like-the-fox's-tail can be seen in all the meadows and valleys. Send them to the Valley of White Medicine. Austin and I will meet them there."

"If you feel you will stay through the cold moons," Little Bear said to her, "I want to go with you now. My medicine is strong."

"Come with the warriors," Shadow told him. "I cannot let you come this time, for I do not know what lies ahead. I have begun to have dreams again. I know the dreams will bother me until the time when I can again have a vision quest. I don't know when that time will be, but I must stay in the Valley of White Medicine until that time comes. Strange things might happen to me, and I want you to remain here where it is safe. You were in my dreams, and now you have returned. I do not want to worry about you anymore."

"I worried about you, also," Little Bear said. "And I worried a great deal about Mother and Father. I knew that they were still inside the fort-lodge and that it was burning when I was taken by the Beelers. I saw Mother get shot; but I knew they did not kill her, for she held her shoulder and stood screaming for a time when they were taking me."

"All of that is behind us now," Shadow said with conviction. "None of that will ever happen again. Now it is our turn to try and destroy their lives." Shadow was looking out toward the distant mountains to the east while she spoke. "And we shall succeed."

Chapter Twenty-one

THE RISING MIST parted, and Shadow could clearly see Austin's lean, hard-muscled form as he stood in the grass at the edge of the river. It was warm here in the Valley of White Medicine, and though the snows had fallen in the high mountains above the valley floor, the steam from the boiling waters made this place lush and comfortable.

At first he did not see her, and Shadow relished for a time the sight of his strong body, the wound in his shoulder now scarred over. He was dressed only in a thin loincloth, for he had been bathing in one of the warm pools. Now he stood tall and straight, praying to the sun, which was a round, misty yellow ball through the dense clouds of rising steam. He had been alone in this land for the passing of nearly three full moons, and he had become, in thought and action, the same as the Indian peoples who lived in the mountains.

Shadow watched him for a time longer, thinking of how good it would feel to once again be in his arms, knowing that to have him touch her again would bring a sensation she had longed for since far back during the time of the Hunting Moon. It had been far too long since she had looked into his deep green eyes, too many nights without his warm caress. Now all of this was over, she knew.

When he saw her, his face lit up like a beam of light. Shadow went over to him, and his arms encircled her, sending through her body the greatest feeling of warmth and closeness she had known for a long time. Little Bear had given her his brotherly love in the Salish village, and when she hugged her mother and father, there was a special feeling there, also. But that was the closeness of family, a natural thing that comes with the bloodline. The sensations she now shared with Austin made her heart pound heavily.

"Little Bear told me," Shadow said. "I feel as if I have traveled a thousand miles to find you." She felt his kisses smother her lips, face, and neck.

"I should never have left you in Walking Head's village," he said. "I felt like going back as soon as I had left, but I guess I was afraid I would lose face."

"It is just as well that you were not there," Shadow said. "Many bad things happened. But they have all passed now, and there will be no more times like those."

"What happened?" Austin asked.

"Your uncles, the evil Beelers, set up their camp not far from Walking Head's village," Shadow said. "They filled Badger and his warriors with the burning water. Then they took our men captive. But they were all released by Walking Head's order, and none of them were hurt."

"Why did they do that?" Austin asked.

"I think they were trying to make you angry," Shadow answered. "They did not know that you had left the village. Even Standing Elk took the burning water."

"Standing Elk?" Austin said, unable to believe it. "Standing Elk started drinking?"

"Yes, but he is not going to drink again. He has talked with his spirit helper. But a bad thing happened between us while he drank that night."

Shadow went on to tell Austin of that night and how Standing Elk had tried to take her out into the darkness. She did not even bring up the notion that Austin had said anything regarding her virtue. She went on to talk about the council and how fair Walking Head had been, even though both of his sons had been involved in the incident and the resultant shame it brought to his family. It was past now, and the days ahead would be good ones, just as soon as Badger and the Beelers were stopped.

"I could not believe what I was seeing," Austin said as he recalled his fight with Badger and his warriors. "They were riding right through the valley, as big as you please, and I saw Little Bear on a horse in the middle of their group. My uncles were riding on either side of him. Little Bear wasn't even tied up. I guess they figured he was not going to try and escape."

"He told me of his escape," Shadow said. "And how you fought like many warriors that day. You have always had a special place in his heart, but now you are a figure of strength, also."

"Badger was drinking from a jug," Austin went

on to say. "Right then I knew that I had been right about him. I wasn't sure what had happened to everyone at the fort, and I guess I just went sort of crazy. I didn't figure I had anything to lose."

"It is good that they came through this valley," Shadow said. "It is hard to say now what would have happened if they had decided to cross through another pass over the mountains."

"I just want to be able to rest easy without worrying about Badger and my uncles," Austin said. "Little Bear told me the whole story about the raid on the fort and how you and the men showed up just in time to keep Badger from making sure everyone was killed. Little Bear knew your mother had been shot and knew your father had been badly burned, but he didn't seem to worry about it any. I guess he figured once you showed up, things were pretty well under control. How does it feel to know someone thinks that much of you?"

Shadow smiled. "He is a special brother. And he thinks a great deal of you, also."

Austin nodded. "He stayed here with me a long time. I told him to go ahead and find all of you, but he wanted to be sure that I could make it by myself. He was a real good help to me for the better part of three weeks. I couldn't hardly move my shoulder, and he did a lot of things for me. I spent a lot of time in these hot pots, and I think that helped my shoulder heal faster than it would have otherwise."

"It is good that you are strong once again," Shadow said. "For only the spirits know what lies ahead of us. You told Little Bear that they have touched you, also."

"They have," Austin replied, and nodded. "I've got this feeling about this valley. It's like you said when we first rode through here on the way to Walking Head's village: There is just something here that holds the answer to a lot of things, especially the link between your mother's peace of mind and the past."

"My mother told me that the spirits must have chosen you especially for me," Shadow said. "We first met trying to kill one another, which is an unusual thing. Then so many things happened that would have separated many others for the rest of their lives. But now we will never again be apart."

They had talked throughout the afternoon, sitting near the warm waters, and now the evening had settled in around them. The clouds had lifted from the mountains to the west and the sun was falling behind them. The rising mist from the valley had taken on a red glow, and flocks of ducks and geese, out searching for food, were now flying down through the mist to settle onto the river for the night.

"It is time that we let you relax from your long journey," Austin said to Shadow. "The horses are cared for, and you have eaten well. Now we will spend time in the warmth of a medicine spring."

Shadow was aware that he was unlacing the strings at the front of her dress. He began slowly encircling his fingers into the cords and loosening them one by one. His lips caressed her neck and found the lobes of her ears. She was aware of the tautness that had developed in her breasts and the sense of desire that was coming over her. Finally her dress fell free.

"I have some laces that need undoing," Austin then told Shadow.

Shadow's fingers then went to the buckskin loincloth. Soon the leather thong that bound it was undone, and it fell to the ground. Together they entered a warm pool, finding a place that was shallow enough

to sit down. "Remember the first time I did this?"
Shadow heard him ask as he began to gently work
the muscles of her shoulders with his fingers. She
thought back on that day and how strange it had
seemed then to have felt suddenly drawn to this man,
to have been so quickly and so very forcefully cap-
tured by his eyes and his boundless strength. It was
so good to have him back.

They sat in the warm water for a long time. They
laughed and talked of days past and days to come.
They discussed rebuilding the fort and once again
having a good trade business along the waters of the
Madison. The fort would be built this time of mud
and grass, Austin said, just like the fort called Benton.
That way no fire could burn it down again. He seemed
anxious to start over and glad to hear that the men
from the fort had stayed with Shadow's father. The
business would most certainly start up again, Austin
promised, and it would be better than ever.

The moon came out overhead, only one day ahead
of being full. The night was cloudless, and the huge
ball rose yellow-orange into the sky, glistening off the
river and the pools of water and the geysers.

Austin was kissing her deeply, pulling her next to
him in the warm water of the pool.

"You are something beyond imagination," he told
her as he looked into her eyes. "There could never
be another as beautiful as you. Never."

He carried her out of the water and placed her onto
the buffalo robes they had brought to the pool for
drying and lying on. The steam settled on their bodies
in tiny drops that the moonlight made sparkle. He
kissed her again, his hands caressing her lovingly,
drawing from her the uncontrollable passion she always felt when he touched her. She gave herself to

him completely, letting her own fingers explore his strong muscled frame.

Once again she felt the tremendous, controlled power of this man as he became one with her, taking her breath away. Once again he carried her up and up, beyond life itself, to a wonderful height of sheer ecstasy, unmatched by any feeling she had ever experienced. He carried her into a world of pleasure she knew she could now never reach with another. His strength seemed to encompass her very being. She felt totally feminine and totally in love.

They held one another throughout the night, enjoying the closeness. It was a time of joy that had now come to Shadow, and she felt confident now that this man would always be with her. She knew they would both face very difficult tests, but the tests would be easier to bear together. Shadow let sleep come, knowing she could conquer whatever might stand in her way of complete happiness.

Light had only begun to streak into the sky when Shadow was awakened by the sound of war drums. She and Austin gathered their weapons and looked out from cover across the valley. There were many warriors, painted in their medicine colors, wearing their finest shirts of war. They were mostly warriors who had been with Badger, along with some Piegans.

"A lot of the Piegans out there were among those who attacked our column on the way to Walking Head's village," Austin said as he studied the different faces and war ponies through his spyglass. "That warrior with the antelope headdress, he led the Piegans that day." He continued to look with his spyglass. "I see a lot of warriors," he added, "but I don't see my uncles or Badger anywhere."

The warriors continued to sing their songs of war. They knew they had found the Eagle Woman and the Long Knife called Green Eyes. This was their day for glory, and they would gain much honor.

"We've got our work cut out for us now," Austin said. "I just hope they don't decide to rush us all at once."

After watching them for a time, Shadow said, "I believe there are a small number of them who wish for glory but not all of them. It was an accident that they found us, and some of them seem as if this is not a good way to die."

"There are still a good number of them who do," Austin said. "But maybe I can scare them a little. Maybe I can show them the badger skin that I cut from Badger's wrist and get them to thinking."

"It is a strange thing that this has happened," Shadow commented. "It seems as if they are on their way to war across the mountains and have just found us as they traveled through. The few who want glory are telling the others that it will help them when they reach their enemies, while some of them are worried that this might be a bad sign. If those who want to fight are defeated, they will likely turn back and leave the path of war."

"I see what you mean," Austin said, noticing that there was arguing going on among them. It seemed as if there were two main leaders who had decided to raid across the mountains, but they did not agree on whether or not it would be good to try to kill Shadow and Austin or wiser to leave them and go on ahead. They all knew of the Eagle Woman's power. If it was not broken this day when war was made upon her, then she would surely cause them many deaths across the mountains when her wrath followed them.

Shadow pointed out toward the warriors, where a group of six were breaking off from the main group toward their camp. They were led by the warrior with the antelope headdress.

"They will test their medicine this day," Shadow said. "For them it is a good day to die."

"I'll talk to them," Austin said. "I want them to be sure and understand that they *will* die today if they don't just ride on out of this valley in peace."

Austin walked out into the open from the trees where they were camped and raised his hand in peace. The warriors stopped their horses, but none of them raised a hand in greeting. The one with the antelope headdress began to speak in sign.

"Are you ready to die this fine day?" he asked. "I will have the scalp of the one called Green Eyes to show to my people. Then I will take the scalp of the Eagle Woman also."

"Where is Badger?" Austin asked, disregarding what the warrior had said. "Why does he not ride to war with you?"

"He saves his medicine," the one with the antelope headdress answered. "He wants to gain more power so that he might someday conquer both you and the Eagle Woman. But he will not get that chance, for I will show your scalps to him."

Austin then held up the ripped badger skin that he had taken from Badger. "Badger will never again have medicine," Austin made sign, "for I have taken it from him. He is lucky to still have life in this world. And as for you, you with the antelope headdress, who speaks of things he cannot do, it would be good if you led these warriors out of this valley, for I will surely take your medicine and your life."

The warriors all appeared stunned at first by Austin's boldness. But they had prepared for war in the right manner, and these six were certain that the spirits looked down upon them with favor this day.

"How is it that only one speaks with what he thinks to be so much power?" the warrior with the antelope headdress asked. "You would be easy to kill."

"You had better stay out of range of my rifle," Austin answered. "It will be you who will fall first. And then my woman, the one who has the medicine of the eagle, she will drive her arrows through the rest of you."

Now some of the warriors who had stayed behind began calling to the warrior with the headdress of the antelope. It was plain that they were telling him that it would be better to go on toward the mountains and forget about the green-eyed Long Knife and the Eagle Woman until Badger was with them. Shadow now came out and stood near Austin. She had an arrow fitted to her bow. The warrior with the antelope headdress yelled something back to the main group of warriors and turned again to Austin.

"Do you feel more brave now that you have a woman behind you?" the warrior made sign to Austin. "I knew you were a coward."

"You speak like a child," Austin made sign back. "And I am sure, in hand-to-hand fighting, that you are most certainly a child. Maybe it is best if you now go back into the lodge of your mother, so that she can wipe your nose and put you into your robes for the night."

The warrior with the antelope headdress sat up straight on his horse, enraged at the remark. He had made the first insult, and Austin had returned one of his own. It was now this warrior's turn to prove whether or not he was worthy of the insult he had given Austin.

"I see no marking on your war shirt to show that you have been victorious in hand-to-hand fighting," the warrior said to Austin. He pointed to his own war shirt, which bore the red imprint of a hand across his heart.

"I will before this day is done," Austin said. "And I will cut your heart out for the wolves."

The warrior got down from his horse and stripped off his war shirt and his leggings, singing a war song as he prepared himself to meet Austin. Shadow took Austin's shirt and pants, leaving him also with only a loincloth. The two men strode forward, meeting in the open between the warriors and where Shadow stood, her bow still armed with an arrow.

Austin knew the fight would be short. He had brought with him the piece of badger skin and had tied it around his own wrist. This was sure to make the warrior feel very strange, fighting someone with the same medicine as Badger, with whom he had ridden to war many times. When the other warriors saw this, they began to point and talk loudly among themselves.

Austin faced the warrior with the antelope headdress. "There is no need for you to die this day," Austin made sign to him. "You know this is not a good day to die."

The warrior took his stance in front of Austin. In one hand he held a knife, in the other a war club. His eyes were intense, and he set his jaw.

Austin pointed to the scar on his shoulder. "This was done by an arrow from Badger's bow. He was no further from me than what you are now. The arrow went clear through, and still I cut his medicine from his wrist. Maybe you have seen his wrist now. I'll bet he can't even move the muscles in his hand now.'' He held up the wrist with the badger skin tied around it and added, ''You do not have to die this day. You can take this back to Badger and tell him that you took it from me, and that I was alive when you did it. That is a far better coup than you have ever before counted.''

''I will take your scalp with me, also!'' the warrior cried out. He lunged at Austin with his knife.

Austin dodged the knife and ducked quickly as the war club whizzed past his ear.

''I am much too fast for you,'' Austin said to the warrior. ''I will ask you once again if you do not want to take the badger medicine from my wrist and take it back with you. It would be a victory for you; but if you try and fight me, your woman will wail for you in your lodge.''

The warrior was standing just as he had before when he had lunged first with the knife and then swung the club. Austin waited for him to thrust with the knife, and then, as the club came up, he reached in with his own knife and cut a deep gash in the warrior's chest.

The warrior staggered back, blood running in a series of thin streams down his painted chest. His eyes rolled wild, and he again lunged for Austin.

The blade of Austin's knife tore straight up through his stomach and chest, opening him up like he was a fallen deer that was being dressed in the field. The warrior gagged on his own blood and stumbled forward to his knees. His breath was gone, and he could not speak, nor could he sing his death song, though his lips moved as though he were mouthing the words.

Now it was for the other five warriors to want revenge and they rode forward, yelling and singing war songs. Shadow was prepared though, and her first arrow took the lead rider just below his throat. It threw him backward off his horse and under the riders behind him. Two of the horses, stumbling over the warrior who had fallen under their legs, squealed in panic and tumbled off balance, throwing the warriors on their backs underneath. One lay still, and the other hobbled back toward the main group of warriors.

Shadow had loosed another arrow, and one of the two remaining warriors fought to stay on his horse as the shaft ripped through the left side of his chest. The last warrior, unable to believe that those with him had already fallen, turned off to the side and rode back to the main group, who all stood in disbelief.

Austin walked up to the warrior with the antelope headdress, now lifeless and doubled over in his own blood. He looked out to the group of warriors who were now calling to their spirit helpers.

"This warrior did not listen to my words," Austin told them all in sign. "He was to have glory this day, and all he found was death. This did not have to happen; you saw me tell him that it was not a good day for him." Austin then took the badger skin from his wrist and dropped it into the blood of the fallen warrior. "When you come over here for your fallen brother, take this with you. Show it to Badger. It will be marked for death. Tell him that he must understand that what he has done to the fort-lodge along the Madison will be avenged. Tell him to talk to the spirits and to sing his death song, for he will soon leave this life."

Austin then went with Shadow back into the vapors and the mist that rose from the geysers along the river.

They watched the warriors come up and pick up the body of the warrior with the antelope headdress and the bodies of the other two who had fallen along with him. Never was there any doubt that they wanted to just pick up the fallen and take them out of the valley and away from this Long Knife with the green eyes who had most certainly gotten medicine from the Eagle Woman. There would be no road to war for them, and they would certainly tell Badger what they had seen. Now Badger would have cause for even more worry: He would think about his attack against the fort-lodge on the Madison, and he would wish his medicine was stronger than that which he now got only from the burning water.

That night Shadow went out by herself into the forest near the river. The coming of the warriors this day had been a sign, and she knew that the reason for her strange feelings in this valley would be revealed when the snows had vanished. This time was not far off now, for already she could hear the sounds of the geese high in the night sky as they made their way north. She would know when the time was right, for she knew the dreams would come again.

The dreams began to come again, and for the passing of many nights, Shadow saw the little owl of the forest, and it was leading her again to some strange place, a place she had never seen before. It was not the camp where her mother had been sewing the dress and where she had seen her lost brother, White Feather, take the medicine bundle and play with the bear. This place, the place of her dreams each night, was a far different place than the peaceful camp beside the river. This place was a large meadow surrounded by the rocks of the high mountains, and in this meadow were many dead trees. No dreams had ever scared her like the dreams of this strange meadow of dead trees. No dreams of any kind.

The dreams continued to haunt her, much the same as the ones she had before she had gone to the Medicine Tree. But there was an urgency associated with these dreams that Shadow could not explain. They left her cold and afraid each morning when she awoke. It was a very real sign which she could not ignore.

"I must find this meadow of dead trees," Shadow told Austin. "I must go there and find whatever awaits me. I do not know what that might be, but there is something that I must know about this place. I will take the trail that goes up from this crossing near the river toward the high meadows above the valley."

"You cannot go alone," Austin told her. "We have been apart far too long, and I do not want to risk having you apart from me again."

"You cannot go up there with me. There is something up there that calls me, and it will not allow me to rest until I have found it. It is a personal thing."

"I want to go with you," Austin said. "I love you. I don't want anything to happen to you."

"Wait for a time," Shadow instructed. "Let the sun cross the sky as many as the fingers of one hand. If I have not returned, then come up and find me."

"That is a long time," Austin said. "A lot of things could happen to you."

"Nothing will happen that I cannot face and conquer," Shadow told him. "You and I both know that there have been no ravens laughing at us. Death is not near for us. The spirits are calling me, and they want me to go alone. I will see you when the sun has crossed the sky for the fifth time."

Austin took her into his arms and held her close. Shadow let his warmth seep into her very being. She had found a man like no other.

"I love you more than I can say," Austin said to her. "And though I know death is far away at this time, I still do not want harm to come to you, even if it is in the form of strange happenings."

Shadow looked into his concerned face. "Between us we have had many strange happenings," she said. "And there will be many more. That is the way of our lives. We have been chosen to have our faith tested. Now we must show strength. Do not fear for me. This is something I have wanted to do for a very long time, ever since my mother finally told me why her life has not been a happy one for many winters. Soon we will all be happy."

"If there comes a time of struggle for you up there," Austin said, "I want you to think of me and how much I love you. Always remember that you are to me like the sun is to the creatures of the forest and the flowers that bloom in the meadows—you are the gift of life. You are my life."

"I will remember," Shadow told him. "I will always remember."

Chapter Twenty-two

———

SHADOW BEGAN HER ascent up into the high mountains. She prayed as she walked, moving slowly and deliberately, telling the spirits that she was ready for whatever lay ahead.

She climbed higher and higher. The hillsides, with the coming of the warm moons, had become filled with color. Flowers of every description were in abundance, and the air held their fragrance. Shadow knew she must learn the secret of this place now, for down below the grass-that-opens-like-a-fox's-tail would be grown up across the meadows and valleys, and the Salish war party would have already left the Bitterroot Valley for these lands.

Shadow began to get a very strange feeling as she came to a meadow far up into the mountains above the valley floor. It was now late in the evening, and the air was cooling off. The day had been warm, and

Shadow thought this meadow to be unusually warm as she walked out from the trail. Coming down from the high peaks just above was a large mass of rolling dark clouds, and Shadow knew that a thunderstorm was on its way.

She said prayers ever more fervently now, for a storm could mean many things: It might mean that the spirits had become angry and that they were getting ready to show their power. Shadow certainly did not want them to be angry with her now, especially when she needed so desperately to have them with her.

The rumbling from the clouds had now started, and Shadow worked her way deeper into the meadow, following the small stream that was surrounded by dense forest on both sides. The trees along the stream were all gigantic in size: aspens that had been growing here for many winters and were fed from the waters underneath the ground. Shadow could now see that those waters were warm, for steam rose out of pockets along the bank where the water flowed in a thin, twisting stream.

As she continued on, Shadow noticed that the opening between the trees along the stream and the dense forest suddenly grew tighter. It was as if the mountains had suddenly closed down around the meadow and had swallowed it up. The sun had fallen behind the peaks above the meadow, and eerie shadows began to appear in the steam and among the aspens around her.

The rumbling from the clouds grew louder, and a quick flash of lightning burst down from the sky and into the forest ahead of her. Shadow took a deep breath, continuing her songs, and went on to where she knew she must go.

Again the sky broke apart overhead, and a loud crack of thunder was followed by a jagged spear of light. They would come ever more often and more violent now, Shadow knew. But she must go on.

Then, as if her eyes had been playing tricks on her, the forest that had closed in around her seemed to suddenly fall away again, and she saw open meadow in the twilight on both sides of the stream. She continued on, seeing the black mass of clouds boiling overhead, rumbling, as if angry voices were calling down. She must ignore the storm, she told herself; she must not let those spirits who were against her stop her from doing what she must do.

Shadow made her way ahead along the small stream and through the giant aspens. The meadow had grown more broad, and there seemed to be even more streams that now flowed independently of one another. The steam rose in dense clouds here, and Shadow knew there was even more warmth below the ground in this place than in the valley below.

Shadow sang ever louder as the Thunder Voices from the sky grew more violent and the lightning came faster. The night was closing in quickly now, and the trees had become filled with strange forms that danced in the steam and mist.

As she became aware of where she was, Shadow's breath caught in her throat. She had come to the most unusual place she had ever seen. The giant aspens here had no leaves, and Shadow quickly realized that they were all dead. They were spread out all over across a strange, broad flat that was covered with the white medicine from the hot, boiling waters. But the waters had also left, and all that remained were sunken holes and pits where the waters had once risen to the surface.

Shadow began to tremble as she looked across the vast aspen graveyard. The meadow was filled with dead trees, their gnarled and twisted branches reaching out toward the sky at strange and awkward angles. They stood like starkly grotesque silhouettes against the bank of rolling clouds that threw fire from above.

Suddenly a bolt of lightning, reached down from just above and struck the trunk of a dead tree near Shadow. The ground at the base of the tree sizzled, and a strange, pungent smell filled the air. Shadow was knocked to the ground, stunned. She shook her head and rose to her feet, looking up into the tree where small licks of flame danced along the trunk and branches.

Filled with terror, Shadow turned to run from the meadow. But she realized that the many holes and pits from which the boiling waters once came were everywhere and to run would certainly mean falling into one and possibly being swallowed up.

Darkness had now fallen everywhere, and only the flashes of light from above showed her the strange meadow. She struggled through the dead trees, leaving the burning one behind her and working her way past the many empty holes that were everywhere. Once the crust broke beneath her, and she lunged forward to avoid falling into an underground cavern. She told herself she must control her terror and not panic. The evil spirits did not want her to learn the secret of the valley.

Shadow struggled on, hoping to find a way out of the meadow. The storm had grown even more violent, and lightning, with a loud crash of thunder, came down into the meadow, striking trees and putting flame into them. Then, as if frozen to one spot,

Shadow came to a sudden stop and stared in rigid fright. Directly in front of her was a dead tree whose jagged, spreading branches held what appeared to be the transformation of a spirit.

Unable to move, to even breathe or scream, Shadow could only stare. Each time the lightning flashed she would see it, huge and horrifying. Caught in the branches of a large tree was the skeleton of a giant eagle, its wings spread wide amidst the twisting branches. With each flash of lightning and crash of thunder the eagle would glare down at her through eye sockets in a skull long since void of life. The huge beak hung open, the head bowed, as if the tree had caught the great bird in its last moments of life, holding the struggling wings open across its own gnarled and lifeless limbs.

She continued to stare at the skeleton that hung within the tree, noting that the talons of the giant bird were longer than her own fingers. As the lightning continued to flash, Shadow could see another, smaller form in the grip of the talons. It was the skeleton of a small animal. She then saw a piece of weathered leather thong entangled around the neck of the small animal and the left talon of the eagle.

Shadow shook her head back and forth in disbelief. as she saw, caught between two rib bones of the eagle, the blade of a knife. Suddenly it was as if she were back at the Medicine Tree in the Bitterroot Valley, watching the peaceful scene with her lost brother, White Feather, and the small bear, still growling as it played with her brother and chewing at the leather thong around its neck. Now she could see it all clearly.

She saw her brother, White Feather, yell in disbelief as the small bear he had been playing with was crushed and torn beneath the weight of a huge eagle which had dropped down from the sky. The eagle then became entangled in the leash around the small bear's neck. Struggling to rise from the ground with its prey, the giant eagle fought but could not ascend. White Feather, trying to save the small bear, summoned all his courage and power, rushing into the eagle, slashing with his knife.

The huge eagle, rising again with the knife stuck into its ribs, snapped the leather thong where the small bear had been chewing. It then rose above the treetops, mortally wounded but still clutching the bear firmly in its talons. White Feather, frantic at the loss of the little bear, began to run after the eagle, hoping it would drop from the sky with his knife in its side. His eyes on the sky for any sign of the eagle, White Feather then ran over the bank of the river and was carried away in the current.

Tears flooded down Shadow's cheeks as the scene in front of her gave way again to the thunder and lightning of the storm. She began to climb the tree. A flash of lightning struck the tree next to her and again the force of the bolt stunned her. But she caught herself as she began to fall through the branches. Again she started up to the eagle, the branches of the tree nearby ablaze with jagged orange flame. The light from the flaming tree nearby allowed her to see more clearly what she had gone to find. If she could reach the little bear, held in the talons of the eagle, she would then be able to look for her mother's medicine bundle. She must find it there. She must.

Shadow finally reached the branches where the eagle had been caught. The light from the flaming tree nearby and the flashes of electricity from the sky showed the outlines of the eagle and the small bear clearly. Shadow fought to control her fear, and her mind began to grow hazy from the power of the moment. She called upon Amótkan and the living members of the eagle clan, her spirit helpers. This large skeleton that rested in the tree before her was once alive and flew with them among the high peaks. Soon Shadow felt her strength returning.

From her place among the dead tree limbs, Shadow began to search through the weathered leather thongs and strips that were twisted about the eagle's talons and the neck and facial bones of the small bear. Her hands trembling, she gently removed a small leather pouch that had been punctured by the tip of one of the talons. Hardly able to breathe, Shadow pulled to her breast the small pouch. She had found it; she now held her mother's long-lost medicine bundle.

Still trembling, Shadow continued to clutch the medicine bundle to her heart. She thanked Amótkan and the spirits for her good fortune and for giving her the strength to endure the storm and find this tree. This would mean new life for her mother and happiness for all her family. Shadow knew she could now make her mother understand that White Feather had been lost those many winters past and that there was no way he would return. It was something that could not be. But now that she had her medicine bundle again, good things would be a part of her remaining winters in this life.

As Shadow started down out of the tree, a heavy wind began to blow. The fires that had started in some of the dead trees began to burn more brightly, and the entire meadow was like day. Shadow's hair blew across her face and into her eyes, blinding her as she continued to work her way down from the tree.

When she reached the ground, Shadow turned in all directions to see the fires in the trees spreading all around her with the tremendous wind. She was quickly becoming trapped in a wall of flame.

Shadow turned her face to the sky and screamed in anger.

"Here me, Thunder Spirits, I will not be devoured by you! I will not leave this life until I see my mother happy again! Hear me!"

Shadow continued to scream, pointing to the skeletal form of the giant eagle in the tree.

"Bad things will come to you if you destroy the remains of my spirit helper! Hear me, Thunder Spirits, the good spirits will have revenge!"

The wind continued, and the fires in the trees had now spread around her entirely. But now she could feel drops of water stinging her face through the wind. The drops came more frequently and in more abundance. Shadow, with her face directed upward, stood still and rigid as the sky opened, and torrents of rain descended with the wind into the forest.

She stood for a long time, feeling the wetness and the strength of the storm, letting its power roar through her. The fires in the trees turned to smoldering plumes of dense smoke, and the meadow was filled with the sizzling and crackling of fires being doused by water. It was good that this had happened, Shadow knew, for it had tested her strength to the fullest and enabled her to more fully believe in the powers of the good spirits who worked for her. She knew now that she could not be conquered by evil in any form, nor could she be intimidated by it. The strength of her faith had endured.

*   *   *

Shadow found Austin waiting for her at their camp, worried and anxious to see her. From below he had been able to see the fierce storm that had dropped in over the top of the high peaks. He had been ready to come and look for her, for he had known that the coming of the storm had been a test of her courage.

"I'm glad you found what you went up after," he said to her. "But there is something more to be done. You have left something up there."

He was looking up toward the high meadow, and Shadow noticed a strange look had come into his eyes. She was not afraid but glad for this. It meant the spirits were now talking to him once again.

"I've always known there was something up there," he said to Shadow. "Now I feel it pulling me, just like it pulled you."

"Am I to remain here?" Shadow asked.

Austin shook his head. "No, you are to come with me. You would have understood yourself what it is that remains up there if you had not been so intent on finding your mother's medicine bundle. But it will become plain to you when we reach the meadow and the tree with the eagle in it."

Shadow left sign for Little Bear and the Salish war party to read if they should arrive before she and Austin had come back down from the high meadow. They would know that she and Austin were on a sacred mission and that there was plenty of meat in camp to eat while they waited. Shadow was sure that Little Bear and the war party would be there any day, for now the grass-that-opens-like-a-fox's-tail had fully opened.

Austin followed her up the trail, intent on knowing for himself why he had also been drawn to this place by the spirits. He now understood very well that those who seek power must withstand many tests before they can be chosen. Austin knew now that he also had been chosen to receive power and that he must face a stern quest in order to receive it. He had learned the art of self-sacrifice from Shadow, and he would soon have the chance to offer himself up to the spirits.

"This is a strange place," Austin said as they worked their way up the small, steaming creek through the giant aspens. "There is a feeling in the air here. Something not seen."

"It is a spirit land," Shadow said. "They are all around us, both good and bad. You must believe that the good spirits are more powerful than the bad, for they are. But if you doubt this for even a single moment, your power within your mind will be destroyed, and you will become too frightened to learn or receive."

"It is only natural to feel fear," Austin said.

"But it is something that must be controlled," Shadow told him. "We must learn to make ourselves believe what we know to be true, even though it is not plain to us. We must understand that which is spoken inside of our minds. That which is bad will usually bring us earthly gain while that which is good will usually take something from us. When we learn that giving brings far more joy than receiving, then we can fully understand the power of good over evil. Fear is the reaction to that which we do not understand and have no power over. Fear can be conquered by letting good work for us and believing that good will always be our helper. Do you feel that now?"

Shadow felt Austin take her hand in his own and

then draw her close to him. In his eyes was no fear but only deep love.

"How could anyone be afraid with someone like you at their side?" he asked. "You are my strength, my rock in times of need. You are everything to me, Shadow, and nothing will ever change that."

Shadow felt his warm kiss and his strong arms giving her that unspoken feeling of deep commitment. She wanted more than anything to make this man happy and to be his wife forever.

"It is now my turn to become as strong as you," Austin added. "Then and only then can I say that I have sacrificed as much as you have. Then I can say I have given all I know how to give to you."

"You have given much already," Shadow said. "You have given of yourself, and that is enough for me. You have nothing to prove to me."

"I did not bring you back up here to prove anything," Austin said. "I brought you here because of something inside me that says we can be stronger together as one, after I, too, have come to know this place of the spirits."

The sun had reached the top of the sky when they came to the place where the dead trees covered the meadow. Though it was not filled with the eerie shapes that come with the end of the day, to Shadow this place seemed every bit as strange and foreboding.

Upon entering this place, Shadow had to again fight a strange fear that now tried to overpower her. She pointed to an area at one side of the big meadow, near the base of a rocky cliff. She saw something there she had not noticed when she had come here the first time. Maybe it had been the near darkness that had hidden it from her, or maybe it was a trick

the spirits were now pulling on her. It did not matter
now, for what she and Austin were seeing was perfectly real.

Shadow walked over with Austin to a flat below
the cliff to look closer. Scattered along the base of
the rocks for a long ways were the skeletons of many,
many elk; they had found an elk burial ground. The
huge racks of the bulls lay at all angles, together with
the ribs and the other bones, all mixed in jumbled
piles, the antlers sticking up from skulls half buried
like thousands of forked sticks.

The herds of the valley had used this part of the
meadow for many winters, and the old bulls would
come here to die, making their final resting place
with others of their kind. Even now, in the full light
of day, it seemed like a place meant to be visited
and left quickly. Here and there ravens sat on the
dead branches of aspens, having fed that morning
on bulls that had died with the coming of the warm
moons.

"I never knew anything like this existed," Austin
said, mesmerized by the scene.

"It is a sacred place," Shadow said. "Come, we
must go on to where the giant eagle rests."

They made their way on through the meadow, passing the open holes and depressions where the water
once boiled out as geysers and hot pools. Shadow
could realize now, in the light of day, the magnitude
of this unusual place. The dead trees spread all across
the meadow, which seemed as big as a sea. It looked
as though the stream had gone underground here, for
there were gurgling sounds beneath the white, crusted
earth.

"Do you remember where the eagle was?" Austin
asked Shadow.

Shadow looked all around the meadow, searching the tall, dead aspens with their high, jagged branches that all looked alike. Many of them had been struck by lightning and bore the charred marks of fire. But they were scattered, and there were so many that it was impossible to determine where she had exactly been.

"Perhaps if I can find my footsteps," Shadow suggested, but then thought otherwise as she remembered the storm that had certainly washed out all of her traces. "Maybe it is best if we let the spirits lead us where they will."

They continued to search throughout the day, wandering across the large meadow time and time again, searching through the maze of giant aspens for the skeleton of the eagle. Day wore into evening and Shadow, refusing to give up hope, took the medicine bundle from around her neck.

It was badly weathered, and Shadow handled the medicine bundle with great care so that it would stay together. She held it high above her, for the spirits to see, and began a song.

When she had finished, Austin said, "Maybe it would be good if I were to also hold the medicine bundle. I believe the spirits could speak through me and help me find the eagle."

Shadow hesitated.

"What is it you said about doing this together?" Austin asked her. "You must surely know that the bond between us can only grow stronger if you will trust me with the most precious, most sacred item you have ever held in your grasp."

Shadow knew immediately that he was right. The medicine bundle was so much a part of her that she had not even thought about whether or not she could allow Austin to gain from its power.

"You must have the right thoughts," Shadow said, her tone tinged with a hint of warning. "You must have no doubt in your heart."

"I do not doubt, Shadow," Austin said. "But it seems as though you have your doubts about me. You know as well as I that we must both understand one another and have the greatest of confidence in one another if we are to succeed." He looked at Shadow for a short time and then added, "Maybe it is best if we go back down the mountain and leave the eagle alone. If you do not have the same confidence in me that you did in yourself, then only bad things will happen if I take the medicine bundle from you."

Shadow listened to him, seeing again a strange look in his eyes. The spirits were indeed speaking through him.

"Maybe that is what happened to your mother when she gave the medicine bundle to your brother to play with," Austin continued. "Maybe it was not the fact that she had given him the medicine bundle that caused the misfortune, but only that she had the wrong attitude when she let him play with it. If she had not worried and felt only that the power of the medicine bundle would be as strong with her child as it was with her, then she would not be grieving even to this day. She was wrong to let him play with her most sacred item if she felt she was doing wrong, for negative thoughts will always bring negative reactions."

"Then you think my mother worried so much about a bad thing happening that such an event actually occurred?" Shadow asked.

"I am sure that this is the case," Austin replied.

"If she had been confident that she was doing no wrong in letting your brother play with her medicine bundle, then nothing bad would likely have happened. But he knew that your mother did not want him to lose her medicine bundle and he could see that she was very upset with herself for giving it to him, so he did a very irrational thing to try and keep the eagle from flying away with it."

Shadow blinked with the revelation. It all seemed so clear to her now: If her mother had felt so uneasy about giving the medicine bundle to White Feather to play with, then she should have been very forceful and told him that this was something she was not to let anyone have, for any reason. She was now facing the same situation. She must now ask herself if she had the confidence in Austin to give him this sacred object.

"The spirits are testing you once again," Austin told her, "but not by force of thunder and storm this time. You are getting a real test of the mind."

Shadow looked into Austin's eyes. They were smiling; and so was his entire face. He was so confident in her that he felt no apprehension whatsoever about how she felt about her decision. Shadow then knew that his love had crossed the boundary beyond life as was known by mortal beings on this earth. He had transcended the space of just human love to that of eternal love.

Shadow's eyes misted. She knew without a doubt now that the spirits had chosen this man to be with her for a special reason. He had come to bring her through the last leg of her journey to happiness for all time. This man was certainly more than she had ever dreamed he could be, spiritually as well as physically. She could never thank Amótkan enough, and the wisdom of her spirit helper, the golden eagle, was without bounds or measure.

"Take this sacred item," Shadow told Austin as she held the medicine bundle out to him. "Take it and lead us together to the truth, lead us, for we are one."

Chapter Twenty-three

AUSTIN HELD THE medicine bundle, and Shadow stood beside him while they both looked up into the tree at the skeleton of the giant eagle. It was even more massive in appearance than when she had seen it during the night of the storm. It still seemed to be something from another world, and it was hard for Shadow not to tremble at the sight of it.

"That bird must have possessed tremendous power when it was alive," Austin said. "And to think that in a single moment, your brother ended that power with a single thrust of a small knife."

"Even a giant must someday fall," Shadow said. "But if the spirit is good, it will go on forever."

Austin climbed up into the tree, making his way through the gnarled and twisted branches. From the moment he had first seen the eagle, he had known what he was after. When he reached the eagle, he pulled the knife from between its ribs and set to work removing the talons from the giant bird.

"These contain the power of many eagles," he told Shadow. "With these the two of us can never be defeated."

When he had finished, Austin came down from the tree and stood before Shadow with the talons. The years of weathering had bleached them white, but the bones were still sturdy and the talons long and sharp.

"Now we must go and let ourselves be filled with the power," Shadow said. "These, together with the medicine bundle that I found that night of the storm, will bring us great favor from the spirits."

They climbed above the meadow and into the high rocks above the valley floor. Evening had now become early nightfall, and the land was again cast in twilight. The peaks shimmered in the last glistening rays of the sun, and the air was calm.

Shadow had brought with her the special woods that she would need to make a fire to the spirits: She had sage and juniper branches, which she would lay together when the fire had begun to burn well. The smoke would then reach high into the sky and be received by Amótkan, and all the spirits would know that the hearts of both herself and Austin were good and that they, together, wished for the power to hold them together and make them strong through the trials which lay ahead.

The night passed, and Shadow sang songs to the spirits and burned the sage and juniper. She had smeared herself and Austin with white clay, so that the spirits might know they were pure and wished to be heard in their prayers. It was a good night for burning the sacred woods for the moon had just passed full and shone down onto the land with a warm white light that made the skies open to the smoke. Wolves howled, and coyote moved around the rocks where Shadow and Austin had taken their place. This was good, for it meant that all the creatures of the forest knew they had come high into these mountains to pray and the fact that they could see and hear them meant that there was no evil present to drive them away.

The ledge on which Shadow and Austin sat became warm from the fire, and the heat moved through the rocks. The light attracted many night birds of prey, and they would swoop past, their wings silent in the darkness. There was the large owl, who came over many times, and the smaller nighthawk, whose journey through the air was not smooth like the owl's but zigzag, bringing illusions to the eyes.

Finally light came over the peaks in the eastern sky, and Shadow began to sing a morning song. She added more sage and juniper to the fire, and once again the smoke rose high into the air. Within Shadow was a special feeling this morning as the sun slowly began to climb above the mountains. It was a feeling that told her this day would be special in the lives of both herself and Austin. It would be even more special than the days previous, when she had learned the secret of the valley and had come to be one spirit with Austin.

Though it was hard to imagine what could now come that would be an even greater event, Shadow knew that the spirits had heard them and that they would now become among those chosen to rise above the flesh and blood of the mortal being.

Shadow took one of the large eagle talons and held it in her left hand. She gave Austin the other talon, and he took it with his right hand. The two then joined hands and held the talons high above their heads, facing the sun, which was now a large yellow ball that had risen just above the rocky peaks in the east. Still grasping hands, Shadow and Austin raised their arms to the sky, reaching out toward the sun with their fingers interlocked and the talons of the eagle facing outward. The sage and juniper smoke rose around them, and the song from Shadow's lips grew more intense.

Then, from the high cliffs behind them, came a loud, piercing cry. It was a call Shadow had heard many times, the call that was now a part of her inner being. It was the cry of the golden eagle.

The shrill cry echoed again, and the eagle soared majestically overhead, not far above the outstretched hands and talons, soaring out over the valley. Frozen in the moment was the vision of the eagle, huge and dark in silhouette, wings spread full and wide, as the bird crossed before the round, yellow glow that was the sun.

Shadow gasped, her muscles rigid, her whole body taut. Then she began a loud wail, throwing her head back as she slumped to her knees, still holding the talon high in the air. She remained in that position for a time, her eyes closed. She began a prayer of thanks:

"Oh, eagle, source of my power, I feel the gift of strength that you have given to me and the man I love. Within our bodies is the magic that you possess, the courage that is in your heart. I give thanks that you have come to us this day. Your power will remain within us always."

The eagle, now far out over the valley, was joined by others who flew over Shadow and Austin as they began their morning hunt. It was as if the manifestation of their power was being concentrated over this one spot, this one ledge on which there burned the sacred woods of sacrifice and vision. Shadow and Austin embraced, holding one another close and rejoicing in their unity of spirit, which had now been accepted by Amótkan and the powers above. Together in mind and body, they would be as one and would have twice the power of their enemies.

Shadow greeted Little Bear with a warm hug, and Austin held him as a man does his brother. It was a glad time, and they all sat with the Salish war party to feast and enjoy the day. Little Bear and the war party had come a long way across the mountains, and there was much to tell of their journey.

"Father has left for the place they call St. Louis," Little Bear announced. "They are going to bring back supplies and trade goods to start a new fort. Father was so anxious that they left well before the snows were gone, so that they might meet us back at the waters of the Madison early in the season of the warm moons."

"That means he might be back at any time now," Austin said.

"Yes, and Badger has learned of it," Little Bear said. "We met a small war party of mixed Siksika and Piegan warriors who fought us. Many of their number were killed, and only a few of our warriors were even slightly injured. Their medicine was very bad. One of their warriors spoke to us before he died, so that we would not cut him apart after his spirit left his body. He told us that Badger is now using the burning water as his only medicine and that he waits for the day when Father returns with the men from the place called St. Louis."

"How did Badger learn of this?" Shadow asked.

"The evil Beelers heard of it from some of the Long Knives at the fort-lodge called Benton. Some of them came into the Salish village where we were staying over the cold moons. Their leader's name was Culbertson, and he was surprised to see Father and Mother there. But there was no fighting. He said he had heard that our fort-lodge had been burned, and Father told him not to feel too happy, for the fort-lodge would be rebuilt as soon as he and the men returned from St. Louis. So he and his men left, for they knew they would get no trade from our people. But they told the Beelers, and now the Beelers surely are glad that Badger wishes to stop Father and his men."

"It is good that you have learned all this," Shadow said to her brother. "It is very important that we now find the Beelers and Badger."

"I know where they have their camp, for they took me there when they burned our fort-lodge," Little Bear said. "I know we must hurry, for there is little time before Father will return from St. Louis with the men; but I am worried about the warriors who are with me."

"Why are you worried about them?" Shadow asked.

"They are afraid of fighting the Beelers," Little Bear answered. "They are afraid that the Beelers have more power than Austin does. They know that Austin was once made to do what the Beelers wanted, and for this they feel the Beelers have power over him."

"Do they feel the Beelers will turn against them in battle?" Austin asked Little Bear. "Don't they understand that I left the Beelers because they are evil men, and I don't want to be around them anymore?

Can't they see that if I had the power to leave them, then I also have the power over them?''

"Maybe this is something they cannot see," Little Bear said. "But I am afraid that their medicine will not be good against the Beelers if they are with Badger."

"You can be sure they will be with Badger," Austin said. "They will want to grab all those supplies, just like they did last fall when I was on my way with the men to Walking Head's village."

"If I stop Badger, then maybe the Beelers will leave these lands in defeat," Shadow suggested.

"No," Austin said. "As long as your father is alive, they will be after him. They thought they had gotten the job done last fall when they burned the fort, but now they know they still have to finish things. There is too much hatred in those two; we can't expect them to ever give up."

"Then I will fight them alone," Shadow said. "I do not wish to lead these warriors if they have no medicine. They will be killed."

"I will give them medicine," Austin said. "Let me show them that I have more power than my two uncles."

Shadow looked into Austin's eyes and saw there a look of strong determination. It was mixed with the faraway look he had gotten in the meadow up along the mountains. Shadow also had the same confidence he had, for they were now one. She did not worry nor did she ask what he would do to give the warriors the medicine they needed against the Beelers. It would be something, she knew, that would give them strength to fight boldly.

Austin turned to Shadow and said, "I will need the talons from the eagle and also the medicine bundle that you found in the grasp of the great eagle. I shall return them to you after the passing of three suns.''

Austin brought the warriors around him and told them that he had heard from the spirits and that he was to do a sacred thing.

''If there is any among you who is a drummer,'' he said, ''then let him step forward. He who drums for me during this time will receive great honor, for the spirits will also be with him.''

Shadow watched as Austin led not one but seven drummers who had volunteered to assist him out to the river's edge. He removed all his clothes but his loincloth and placed the medicine bundle around his neck. Even though she had reinforced it with another piece of leather, Shadow knew that the medicine bundle that her mother had owned so many winters past was still very sacred and very powerful, for she had not looked inside the bundle, thereby preserving its power.

She continued to watch Austin as he instructed the drummers in what they were to do. It made her proud to see that her man had become one with the land and now listened so closely to the voices within him, having no fear whatsoever in what they had told him to do. He would certainly gain the confidence of the Salish warriors who had come so far to fight for one of their people, the Eagle Woman, even when they were afraid of the power they thought the Beelers possessed. Austin would now change that; he would show all of them that he was far stronger than they, for he heard the voices of the spirits, as did all those who listened and were close to the land.

Shadow and Little Bear watched together as the sun crossed the sky for the first time. Austin had built a small, round lodge out of willows and had covered it with buffalo hide. As in the manner of sacred purification, he had built a fire and had heated stones inside the lodge. Again the smell of sage and juniper was thick in the air, and the steam covered his body as he fasted and prayed within the lodge. At times he would come out from within the lodge and immerse himself in the waters of the river, raising his hands and his head to the sky when he came out of the water. The spirits were with him, and it was plain to see that the Salish warriors knew this.

"His love for you is far deeper than life itself," Little Bear told Shadow, understanding clearly that his sister and this man, whom he had come to call brother, were now two spirits in one. "It is a very unusual thing to have found someone like him."

"You speak beyond your years," Shadow told her brother. "I was led to him by my spirit helper, the golden eagle. Yes, he is very special."

"Mother and Father have such a love," Little Bear said. "But their love was formed in a time far different than this. It is a love of the old days. Yours is a love that will stand the test of change. Yours is a love that can withstand hardships that many people do not have to face. I only hope when I am of age that I can find a love of this kind."

Shadow sat listening to her brother, ever more amazed at the wisdom of his words, wisdom way beyond his years. He had a depth of understanding that many do not achieve even as adults. There was no doubt that he would grow up to bring his wisdom to his people.

Austin came out of the sweat lodge when the sun was straight above the second day. He was taken toward a special place prepared by the drummers beneath the trunk of a large cottonwood tree. Descending from one of the limbs of the tree were two rawhide ropes. At the end of each rope was attached one of the large talons from the giant eagle.

With a medicine pipe in his hands, Austin sat down at the foot of the cottonwood and began to smoke, offering the pipe to the heavens and to the earth, and then to the four directions. He smoked the entire afternoon with his head lifted to the sky. Shadow sat a distance behind him, singing songs to the spirits to help insure the success of his sacrifice.

The drummers continued to sound their rhythmic beat, and Austin spent the night smoking and sitting beneath the cottonwood, and burning the sacred fire. At times he would get up and return to the sweat lodge and then dive into the river. When the sun once again returned to the land, he was ready to fulfill his sacrifice and, for a time, the drums stopped.

One of the drummers came over to Austin, who had now seated himself under the cottonwood, facing the east. The sun was climbing into the sky, and the light on the land brought warmth. All the Salish warriors had gathered in a circle around the tree. All were chanting songs to give Austin confidence and tell him that they wished him success. The drummer now knelt beside Austin, a knife in his hand.

"I am strong," Shadow heard Austin say to the drummer who knelt beside him. "Make the cuts deep."

Shadow held her breath while the warrior pinched the skin and muscle above Austin's left breast between his thumb and forefinger. He made two deep incisions, one on each side of the skin and muscle he was holding. He then reached up and took one of the eagle feet suspended on the rawhide ropes and inserted two of the long black talons through the wounds. He pushed the talons far through the slits so they would not come loose.

Blood streamed out and mixed with the sweat on Austin's body, but his face remained hard and determined. The drummer then repeated the procedure on the other side, and Austin sat facing the rising sun with the eagle talons hanging from his chest.

Shadow began to sing once more, and Austin returned to smoking the pipe for a time. Finally he rose to his feet when the sun had risen fully and nodded to the drummers. Two of them came over to him while the others began their drumming. The two who had come over to Austin prayed, and each took hold of one of the rawhide ropes that hung over the bough of the cottonwood. Together they began to hoist Austin up and off of his feet.

Austin made no sound as they pulled him up. His head fell back, and he bit his lips as the skin and muscle in his chest stretched tightly with the pull of the eagle talons. He began to spin in a slow circle, and the blood from his wounds began dripping to the ground from where it had run down his chest and onto his legs and feet.

The drummers tied the ropes to stakes in the ground and took their places with the others in the circle around Austin. They began to chant as they drummed, calling to the spirits on behalf of this man who was certainly worthy of great honor. He was indeed one of them, and there was no doubt that he had fully accepted the life of one who lives with the earth. He wished to gain the confidence and support of those who would follow him into battle.

Shadow watched the sun climb ever higher into the sky while Austin struggled to make the talons tear through the skin and muscle of his chest. It was a test

of strength and endurance, a matter of the mind block-
ing out the pain and conquering the overwhelming
desire for relief. It was a test that only the very strong
passed. And those who passed were held in high esteem.

Shadow watched while Austin continued to twist
and jerk against the ropes until he was exhausted.
Blood had caked his chest and the entire front of his
body. The talons were tearing through, but they had
been implanted deep, and there was a lot of tissue to
cut before he would fall free.

Austin blacked out, and the drummers came and let
him down. He came back to consciousness but would
take no water. Instead he shook his head and stumbled
to his feet. He staggered for a time, waving the drummers back from him. He would do this alone.

Shadow sang more songs to the spirits as the two
drummers again hoisted him off his feet. Austin hung
suspended once again, spinning and kicking to tear
loose from the talons.

"He will either succeed or die," Little Bear said
to Shadow as he watched Austin. "His pride is great,
and he wants more than anything to have the confidence of our warriors."

"I believe he already has their confidence,"
Shadow said. "I do not think many of them have ever
seen such a display of strength and courage. I only
hope the spirits smile down on him soon. He has lost
a great deal of blood."

"He will break loose soon," Little Bear said. "The
skin and muscle have stretched far, and if he can be
strong for just a short time longer, he will have com-
pleted the sacrifice."

Shadow began to think about their union and how
important this man truly was to her. He was now her

whole life, body and spirit. She knew she could help him greatly by showing her support to the fullest. He had already heard her songs and knew she was calling on the spirits for him, but if he could see her standing beside him, maybe it would give him the added strength he would need to complete his sacrifice.

Shadow had the drummers lower him to the ground once again. She spoke to him as the ropes became loose.

"I know that you will be successful," she told Austin as he stood on wobbly legs before her. She felt her eyes wetting with tears but fought them so that he would not be worried. "You are as strong a man who has ever lived, and all the warriors who see you this day are talking of your honor."

Regaining his breath, Austin looked down at the wounds in his chest where the talons held him. He was aware that very little skin and muscle remained; but it had been stretched so far that it would take a terrific jerk to pull through.

Austin then looked up at where the ropes crossed over the cottonwood bough. He told the drummers to tie the ropes to the stakes. When it was done, he took a series of long breaths and stared for a while at the ropes. Then, with a sudden burst of energy, he pulled violently against the ropes.

Shadow saw him fall sideways as one of the talons ripped completely through. The drummers had taken up a loud chant, and their drumming had reached a fevered pace. Nearly unconscious, Austin struggled to his feet, now aware that the other side hung only by a thin shred of skin and muscle.

He twisted sideways, pulling free, and fell upon his back, his chest heaving. The drummers and all the Salish warriors gave loud cheers and chants of thanks to the spirits. Shadow then came with a skin filled with water and helped him to a sitting position.

"You have gained great glory," she told him. "The warriors all cheer you. They all know that you have more power than any Long Knife in the mountains. They will gladly ride with you to war against your uncles."

The sun was nearly down when the fires were built and the feasting began. Shadow had sewed Austin's wounds closed with deer sinew, and he would heal quickly. His strength was returning rapidly, for his mind was strong, and he knew well that he had become a man of great courage and dignity in the eyes of the Salish. Now that he was feared by Badger's warriors and respected by those who would fight with him, the path to victory would be easier to travel.

Shadow gave thanks to all the spirits herself. It would have been very difficult to have fought without the numbers they would need to conquer Badger and his warriors. But now their strength was great, and they were about to seek out their enemies.

Chapter Twenty-four

SHADOW PAINTED HERSELF for war. With her fingers she made red lines across her cheekbones in the pattern of an eagle's wings. Then she made long lines down each side of her chin, and turned them under in the form of talons. In her hair she placed two feathers taken from the tail of an eagle. While Austin had rested, she had made a medicine shield from the buffalo hide that he had placed over his sweat lodge. Shadow knew that this hide had been hardened from the smoke of his sacrifice fire.

On the face of her shield, she had painted the sign of the great eagle with a large beak and talons for added power. To the shield she had then attached the talons of the eagle in the meadow, the talons which Austin had used in his sacrifice. She was now ready for battle and would have more power than she had ever before possessed. She would need this power, for waiting in the open beyond their camp was a large group of warriors led by Badger and the Beelers.

They had come the night before, and their war drums had sounded throughout the time of darkness until the light broke into the sky. They were more confident than either Shadow or Austin had imagined them to be. The Beelers had brought a wagon into the valley, no doubt filled with kegs of the burning water, and they had remained within the circle of dancing, screaming warriors, confident that they would see both Austin and Shadow die before the morning had grown very old.

"So we meet again," Austin yelled out to his uncles from in front of the line of Salish warriors. They were sitting on horses near their wagon, flanked by Siksika warriors from Badger's village. "Where's your war paint, or are the two of you too yellow to fight?"

It was Jake who answered with a laugh. "If you keep your hair and get by all of these murderin' redskins around us, then we'll see what you can do."

"You and Wolf sit tight and say your prayers," Austin yelled back. "We'll eat them up like so much sugar candy. Then you'll get your turn. Plan on it."

Neither Jake nor Wolf seemed too concerned and they continued to sit their horses near the wagon. Finally Jake spoke up again. "You had best get out of our way so we can cross the valley. We've got a meetin' to make with Jim Ayers and his men. They're bringin' supplies clear out from St. Louis, just for us."

"This is the end of the road for you," Austin told him. "You might as well forget about Jim Ayers and the supplies. You didn't get him when you went down and burned his fort, and you won't get him now."

"We'll see," Jake yelled back. "We'll just see about that."

"I look for one warrior and one warrior only," Shadow made sign to the Siksika. "I do not see him here. I want to fight him, for he has done much evil to my family."

A warrior then moved out from the ranks of the Siksika and sat his horse to speak.

"I am not Badger," he made sign. "I am blood brother to a warrior you killed when the green-eyed Long Knife killed the one with the antelope headdress in hand-to-hand fighting. It is I who will take your heart this fine day!"

It did not seem strange to Shadow that a warrior had ridden forward to avenge the death of his brother, but she could not understand why Badger was nowhere to be seen. And none of the warriors would say whether he had even come with them. She continued to listen to the warrior who, in the tradition of war, was now trying to build his own confidence while tearing hers apart.

"I have killed many whose power was far greater than yours, Eagle Woman. Nothing of what they say about you is true. You are but a small girl who still plays with the stick dolls your mother has made for you. No, you will die easily this day."

Austin was on his horse near her, and Shadow could hear his rifle click as he pulled the hammer back.

"This is my fight," Shadow told him. "No one else but him will come. This I know. They want to see how good their medicine is. He is the most powerful, and if he dies, there will be many of their warriors who will also sing their own death songs."

"I'm looking for Badger," Austin said. "I don't trust him."

"I will face this warrior," Shadow said. "Then we will look for Badger."

When the warrior had finished trying to shake Shadow's confidence, she made a sign back to him.

"It is said that your brother had much more power than you, and he died easily. How do you think you can fight me when your brother was clearly no match for me? Sing your death song, for you cannot possibly win this day."

The warrior stripped off his war shirt, exposing arms and shoulders smeared solid with yellow and black paint, set in stripes. Across his chest was a bone breastplate, made from the fingers of his conquered enemies. He leveled a Hawken rifle as he screamed a war cry and charged Shadow, his eyes round and wild.

Shadow raised her shield and screamed her own war cry, kicking her horse into a dead run. When she had seen the bone breastplate, she had fitted an arrow to her bow tipped with a point made from the steel of a Green River knife. This Siksika warrior would soon feel the point of death as it drove through his best medicine.

Shadow heard the boom of the Siksika warrior's big rifle, an explosion over the pounding of the horses' hooves across the meadow. The impact of the ball against the shield stung her arm, but it glanced off, and the warrior pulled his horse up in disbelief.

Shadow was now upon him, her bow drawn as if running toward a buffalo. The arrow zipped the short distance between her and the startled warrior, splitting through his fingerbone chest protector and driving itself clear out through his back, carrying bits of heart and lung tissue with it.

The warrior's horse reared skyward as he pulled hard on the rope bridle. His mouth was stuck open, as if trying to gasp for breath that wouldn't come. The horse jerked sideways with the strain of the bridle, and the warrior fell onto the ground. He twisted for a time until the glaze of death came over his eyes and he lay still.

Shadow jumped from her horse's back, her knife in her hand. This was the day when she would stop her enemies for good. With her knife she cut a circle around the top of the warrior's head and ripped his scalp free. She screamed a war cry as she held the dripping scalp up for the other Siksika warriors to see. Suddenly she heard Austin's voice behind her.

"Get down!" he was yelling. "Shadow, get down!"

Quickly she lowered herself, holding her shield in front of herself again for protection. She heard the boom of a rifle and the whiz of a lead ball as it passed just over her head. She then heard Austin's rifle and heard him shout.

She looked toward the line of Siksika warriors, who were now starting forward. Near the wagon she could see the big Beeler with the one eye, the one called Wolf. He was still standing but was holding his side. Shadow knew he had been hit by the shot from Austin, but he was so large that he would certainly not go down with just one lead ball.

Austin pulled Shadow up on the horse he was riding, and she struggled to hold on as he took her back where she would not be overrun by the charging Siksika warriors. The battle had begun to develop, with warrior against warrior on horseback and on foot,

fighting one-on-one, yelling the cries of war and hatred.

"That damned Jake shot at you," Austin said.
"But he got under the wagon too fast, and I had to
unload on Wolf. I just wish I had gotten Jake instead.
It would sure make things a lot easier."

"I still do not understand what has happened to
Badger," Shadow said. "It is strange that he is not
here leading his warriors in battle. This I cannot understand, for the last time I saw him he promised me
that he would someday take me away from you and
then have me as his woman to do with what he
wanted. I feel there is something wrong, or he would
be here to fight."

"He's here," Austin said. "I've got little doubt
about that. I don't know just where, but he's here
someplace. Just keep your eyes wide open. I don't
trust him at all."

Shadow and Austin talked again to Little Bear as
they went back into the fight. He would do as he was
instructed and stay away from the battle area, but he
would keep his bow ready. He never took his eyes
off his warrior sister, who was scattering Siksika warriors before her like leaves before the wind. She used
a war club as well as her bow, and there was none
who could stand before her.

Austin, too, fought savagely, with the power he had
obtained from his sacrifice and from his union with
Shadow. The Siksika began to run from him also, and
it was only a short time before their medicine was
completely broken, and they began to run for the shelter of the trees back up from the meadow, taking their
dead and wounded with them whenever they could.
It was a good day for the Salish; the spirit of the eagle

was powerful and had looked upon them all with great favor.

The warriors had left the meadow entirely now, and only the wagon with the two Beelers under it remained. They had shot two Salish warriors who had tried to get to them and had many rifles with them. It would be hard to get them out.

Then Shadow saw Austin charging toward them on his horse. He rode at an angle, holding himself against the side of the horse away from the line of fire. But the Beelers shot his horse, and it went down, trapping his legs underneath. Shadow then saw the Beeler called Wolf come out from under the wagon. The one called Jake yelled for him to come back, but he would not listen. Wolf continued to hold his side where Austin had shot him. Swinging a hatchet he had taken from the wagon in his other hand, he walked out ever closer to Austin, his eyes round and crazy.

Austin struggled to pull his legs out from under the fallen horse while Wolf came closer, swinging the ax back and forth. Shadow rode up toward them on her horse and had to jump aside as a ball from Jake's rifle whizzed past her shoulder. Shadow then jumped down from the horse and sent it off before it, too, was shot and killed. She then fit an arrow to her bow and got ready to take aim at Wolf before Jake could shoot at her again.

It was then that Little Bear sprang from where he had been among the trees along the river. He ran screaming at Wolf, who was now nearly upon Austin, the ax raised. Jake quickly turned his aim from Shadow to Little Bear, but he was running in a zigzag pattern, making it impossible to get a good shot off. Shadow then quickly released an arrow that went under the wagon and sliced across Jake's back. He screamed in pain and rolled back farther under the wagon.

Little Bear was now shooting arrows into Wolf as fast as he could fit them to his bow. The huge man roared in pain, now with three arrows sticking from his chest and stomach. He had reached Austin and had tried to strike him with the ax, but Austin had grabbed his wrist and was struggling to keep his grip. Little Bear shot another arrow into Wolf, but the crazed man was so large that it would not stop him.

Finally, shooting from behind, Shadow placed an arrow at the base of Wolf's neck, paralyzing him. He slumped forward to the ground, off of Austin, unable to move, his eyes wild and unseeing.

Shadow turned to the wagon but did not see Jake. She looked all around the open bottom. Salish warriors were still fighting the Siksika here and there, while others were stripping the dead. But nowhere could she see Jake. He was no doubt inside the wagon, for she would have seen him running if he had tried to leave for the cover of the trees.

Shadow helped Little Bear get Austin out from under the horse. He had pulled muscles and possibly strained a knee some, but there were no broken bones. When he could get to his feet, he took his rifle and started for the wagon where Jake was hiding. A short distance away, he stopped.

"You might as well come on out, Jake," he yelled in to his uncle. "You've got nowhere to go. You can't go anyplace."

"Why don't you just come in and get me?" he yelled. He then punched a hole in the canvas of the wagon and stuck his rifle out.

Austin ran to one side as Jake set off a quick, erratic shot and pulled the rifle back inside. Shadow yelled for him to get back, and he retreated to the fallen horse, where they all took cover.

"I will get him out," Shadow said. "I do not believe he will like it when I loose an arrow covered with flame."

"I want to do something first," Austin said. "He's so fond of that rot-gut trade whiskey of his. I think I'll spill some of it for him."

Time and again Austin fired into the wagon, hearing the heavy *thwok* of the lead balls as they tore into the kegs. After a time, the whiskey began to run through the floorboards and drip out onto the ground under the wagon. Austin laughed and mocked his uncle the entire time, telling him what a shame it was that all that whiskey was going to waste. He could hear his uncle cursing, and often he would fire wildly from the hole in the canvas. But he was trapped and could do nothing.

The Salish warriors began to come back from the battle, talking of the deeds they had accomplished. They saw what was happening with the wagon, and all joined together out of rifle range to watch. One, who had built a fire, brought a piece of flaming wood over when Shadow motioned to him. She quickly tied it to the shaft of an arrow and fired it into the wagon through the hole that Jake had made to fire his rifle.

Flames immediately roared up within the wagon, fueled by the spilled whiskey that still flowed from the holes. Jake tumbled out the back screaming, his buckskins ablaze. He got up and ran crazy, swatting at the flames with his hands and arms. Running in pain and blind panic, he turned around and fell, rolling, then picked himself up and ran straight for the wagon.

He crashed into one flaming wheel and fell back,

then stumbled forward and under the wagon just as it exploded in a ball of fire from the sudden additional fuel given by other kegs that had split from the intense heat. The wagon crashed down on Jake's body, a wall of towering flame and ash.

"Well, I guess we don't have to worry about the whiskey or my uncles now," Austin said, turning from the scene.

Two warriors then approached Shadow and Austin. They looked to Shadow and one of them said, "The one who is called Badger. He calls for you to come to him."

The warrior pointed to a cliff above the valley floor.

"You will find him there," the warrior said. "He awaits you. He is yours, Eagle's Shadow Woman, for you to kill if you wish."

Chapter Twenty-five

THEY WALKED TO the base of a high, rocky hillside that pushed up into a cliff. The ledge overlooked the valley below and was near the trail Shadow and Austin had taken to reach the high meadow of dead trees. Sitting high among the rocks on the cliff was Badger, staring out across the valley with his hands extended in prayer.

"What is he doing?" Shadow asked. "The fight is over. His medicine will do no good now."

The Salish warrior who had spoken to Shadow before said, "It is a strange thing. His warriors say he has been up there since before the fight." He pointed to the remaining Siksika warriors, now gathered together with their dead and wounded, silent in defeat. "They say he will not come down, not even when one of them asks. And they will not say why he has remained up there."

Shadow thought for a time and then looked to Austin. "The spirits have told me that this is the day when we will have total happiness. So I must go up and either bring him down here or fight him."

"I do not have any worries about it," Austin said. "But it would make me feel a lot better if I understood what he was doing up there. I want you to be very careful; you can't tell what he will do."

"I will return soon," Shadow said. "It is for me now to finish this thing."

Shadow started up the trail into the mountains which would take her to the cliff where Badger sat. She sang songs to her spirit helper, the golden eagle, and felt more at ease when she looked high into the sky and saw a number of the large birds circling overhead. Her medicine was very strong this day and now was the time to face Badger.

She reached the cliff and found her way among the rocks to the level where Badger was seated. She looked across and saw him sitting on a broad ledge overlooking the valley below. Shadow looked down to where Austin and Little Bear stood with some of the Salish warriors, all looking up at her from below. She then turned and spoke to the man who had told her he would someday own her.

"Your time to pray has ended," she said to him. "Your warriors sit silent in defeat and the evil Beelers lie dead." She had fitted an arrow to her bow, making herself ready for anything he might do.

Badger heard her and stopped his chanting. He brought his arms back in at his sides, but he did not get up or even turn to her.

"I knew you would come up to this place," he said to her. "Now you can help me again gain favor with the spirits, for you have power beyond any limits."

"I did not come to help you gain power," Shadow said to him. "I came to face you as an enemy. I came to make you see that you will never take me as your own. Since you have told me that you will not accept this, then it is for me to face you in battle, for I would rather die than live as your woman."

Badger was silent for a moment. Finally he said, "There is no longer war in my heart. I have learned that the path of evil is the path of destruction."

Still Badger did not turn and face her, nor did he rise from his place on the ledge. What he had just said seemed very strange to Shadow. It was as if he had once again stopped drinking the burning water, though she knew very well that he hadn't. She maintained her distance from him and kept her bow ready to use.

"Did you hear me, Eagle's Shadow Woman?" Badger continued. "Did you hear my words?"

"Yes, but they are hard to believe. Words such as those that pass your lips sound to me like lies. I do not believe your heart has changed since we last met in your father's village. I do not believe you have forgiven your father and the council for banishing you, and I do not think you will ever leave me alone to live in peace."

"Hear me, Eagle's Shadow Woman," Badger said in a louder tone of voice. "My life has changed since we last met. It has had to change. I have no choice now but to live differently than I once did."

"What do you mean?" Shadow asked.

Badger continued to sit facing the valley. He would not turn to her as he spoke.

"My life is now filled with much sorrow," he explained. "I have taken the path the bad spirits wished me to follow. Now my life as it is supposed to be lived is past, and I must suffer and be less than a man.''

"Turn to me," Shadow said to Badger. "Turn to me, so that I might understand what you are saying."

Badger reluctantly turned his head to face Shadow. She began to move among the rocks toward him, but his head remained still. Shadow could see now that his eyes did not follow her movements. *He was blind!*

"You cannot see me, can you?" Shadow said to him. "You have lost the use of your eyes!"

"It is true," Badger said. "All is nearly darkness for me now. The world is a mixture of shapes that I cannot bring my eyes to put lines upon. All is jumbled together in gray and black. My brother, Standing Elk, has told me that it is the burning water which has done this to me. He says that the burning water is poison and that it has killed the part of me that lets me see. All I know is that the evil spirits have had their way with me and now they cast me off, laughing at me. For me there is no more life. A man has no more life when his eyes are dark and will not see."

Shadow was stunned. She stood for a time without speaking but only stared at Badger. This was the reason he had not come with the war party that was on its way over the mountains, when Austin had killed the warrior with the antelope headdress, and this was the reason he had not fought this day with his own warriors and the Beelers. It seemed strange to Shadow that he did not feel anger toward the Beelers.

"It would do me no good to try and take revenge on the Long Knives called Beeler," Badger said to Shadow when she asked him this question. "I cannot see. How would I be able to do this? They would easily kill me if I tried to do this thing, and it would not be a proud death. No, my spirit would not reach

the Other Side Camp where there is always peace. I
truly wanted to take revenge very badly, but I know
it would have been very foolish.''

It was plain that Badger had become very frustrated
throughout his life and had turned to the burning water for support, a support that never came. The burning water had robbed him of his dignity and his power
among his people.

''Perhaps you can now become very close to the
spirits,'' Shadow said to him. ''It is said that those
who are blind can see things others cannot. It is certain that you now will have much time in which to
seek the voices.''

''I cannot go to the places where the voices speak
from,'' Badger argued. ''I was helped to this place
by two of my warriors. I felt very foolish. There was
a time when they all looked upon me as having great
honor and power. Now they must place my food in
front of me and lead me where I want to go. Now
that the land has no light, there is nothing left to my
life.''

''That is not true,'' Shadow said. ''You can still
feel the warmth of the sun and hear the birds sing
nesting songs. And when you take a wife, you can
then hear her voice. Someday you will feel the touch
of your children and hear them speak to you.''

''That day will never come,'' Badger said bitterly.
''There is no woman who would want a man whose
eyes are dead. How could he put food in the lodge or
gain glory in war? How could he be looked upon with
respect when those who see him walking blind know
that he was foolish and caused it himself?''

''Do not worry about your honor,'' Shadow said.
''You will gain even more honor if you learn from
your mistake and then teach others what you know,

so their lives will remain complete and without trag-
edy.''

"It is easy for you to say these things, Eagle's
Shadow Woman, for it is not you who is blind."

"That is true," Shadow said. "All I am saying is
that life can still be good for you. You can still speak,
and hear, and you can walk across the land."

"I do not want to walk!" Badger yelled. "I wish
to run again! There was a time when I could run. I
cannot now. I can see no meaning to life if I cannot
run once again!"

"That is for the spirits to decide," Shadow told
him. "I do not have that power."

"But you can talk to the spirits for me," Badger
said. "You can tell the eagle who flies in the sky that
you wish to have me look upon you once again with
eyes that can see!"

Shadow shook her head. "That would not be wise.
The spirits look upon each of us as individuals. It is
for each of us individually to please them. It would
be better if you came down from this place and returned with your warriors to your village. Another day
will come, and you can decide if you want to ask for
your sight back."

"I cannot go with my warriors," Badger said.
"They now look upon me with disfavor."

"They will help you," Shadow said. "Do not think
because you have become blind that they look upon
you with disfavor."

"That is not the reason," Badger said. "It is because I have caused many deaths this day. I told them
that even though I could not see, I felt I had power
this day and that they would be victorious against
you. They believed me and came into this valley with
war in their hearts. There was one warrior who told

me that he felt he now had the power I once had when I could see. I told him to lead the warriors when I should have said that he must get his own power. He wore a breastplate made of finger bones.''

''I remember that warrior,'' Shadow said. ''He has sung his death song this day.''

Badger bowed his head. ''How many others?''

''A great many,'' Shadow answered.

''And the Long Knives called Beeler, you said they have also met death?''

''They have.''

''What is there for me to go down for?'' Badger asked. ''What is left for me? My warriors will now surely hate me. If I regain my eyesight, perhaps they will see that I once again have power and will follow me.'' He raised his head to the sky and again started to chant songs.

Shadow turned and started away from him. There was no way she could ever talk to him; she had never been able to talk to him. It was useless. But she would now have to worry no more about Badger chasing her.

''Where are you going, Eagle's Shadow Woman?'' she heard him ask.

Shadow turned quickly. ''How did you know I was leaving?''

Suddenly Badger was up and rushing across the ledge toward her. Shocked beyond belief, Shadow could not move for an instant. When she finally turned again, it was too late. Badger had jumped upon her and was holding her.

''You lied to me!'' Shadow yelled at him. ''You are not blind at all!''

''I am not yet blind,'' Badger admitted. ''But my eyes are failing me. There are days when all is very blurred. My sight will someday leave forever if I do not get your power.''

"Let me go, Badger," Shadow demanded.

"You will first sing to your spirit helper, so that I may get power," Badger insisted.

Shadow struggled against him, but it only served to anger him and make him hold her tighter.

"Maybe there are other ways in which I can receive power from you." He laughed.

Shadow felt his hands reaching under her dress. She screamed at him and pounded him with her fists. She could smell the burning water on his breath and knew that he would never release her now unless she fought him, as she had prepared to do.

Then, just overhead, an eagle cried out as it passed across the face of the cliff. Badger turned to look up, and Shadow pushed her way out from under him, slamming him savagely in the throat with her fist.

Badger choked as Shadow worked her way off the ledge and into the steeper rocks along the face of the mountain. He had ripped her dress, and she had lost her bow and arrows, and also her medicine shield. After getting a firm foothold, Shadow then stopped and turned to Badger.

"You are a fool!" she yelled to him. "You will never gain the favor of the spirits."

Badger was now standing on the ledge, holding his throat. When he was able to speak, he yelled back in anger.

"Maybe you, yourself, have gotten away from me, but your power remains here."

Badger then picked up her medicine shield and placed it on his arm. He then took her bow and arrows and held them up to the sky, screaming a war cry.

"Put down my weapons!" Shadow yelled in rage.

Badger continued to scream his war cry and held the bow and arrows to the sky in one hand, raising the shield which was attached to his arm. Shadow watched in rage as he sang to the spirits with her weapons. He began to dance and wave his arms, the talons on Shadow's shield bouncing to the rhythm of his movements.

Shadow was no longer able to control her anger. She pulled her knife and started back across the rocks to the ledge. Badger continued to dance, not paying attention to anything but his songs to the spirits. Then, at the last instant, he saw Shadow come onto the ledge with her knife raised.

Badger put Shadow's shield out in front of himself, laughing.

"The Eagle Woman cannot harm me. She cannot fight against her own power."

Shadow stood back, trying to control her anger so that she might think clearly. She remembered that his right wrist had no strength because of the bad break he had sustained from the rock during the celebration festival, now nearly a full year past. She wished she had let Austin come with her but knew that she must do this thing on her own if she wanted true happiness.

"What is wrong with the powerful Eagle's Shadow Woman?" Badger taunted her. "Now I, Badger, have the favor of the spirits and you have nothing!!" He set her bow and arrows down and pulled his own knife. Then he started forward, holding her medicine shield in front of him. "Since I now have your power," he said, "I no longer need you, for now you are nothing."

Badger lunged at her with the knife, and Shadow quickly grabbed his wrist and twisted. He grunted in pain, and the knife fell from his grasp. He grabbed her by the throat with his good hand, squeezing with all his might. Struggling for breath, she twisted to one side and plunged her knife into his ribs. The pain and shock of the knife had thrown Badger off balance, and he fell facedown onto Shadow's medicine shield. He began to yell loudly as he struggled to his feet, twisting his head away from the shield. He had fallen on the talons, and they had embedded themselves in his face and throat.

Badger screamed as he jerked back wildly from the shield, ripping the talons loose from himself, large gashes appearing across his mouth and all along his neck. He threw the shield aside and began to stumble about in a state of wild frenzy. In a matter of moments he had fallen from the ledge and was shrieking as he tumbled through the air toward the valley floor.

Shadow stood numbed for a time with shock and horror. She did not look over the edge but took up her shield and her bow and arrows and made her way across the rocks to the trail, which would take her back down to the bottom.

As she started back down, she could see many of the warriors running to the base of the rocks. In a short time, she met Austin and Little Bear, who had started up to find her. They had seen Badger jump up from where he had been seated and knew something had gone wrong.

"I was afraid we wouldn't see you alive again," Austin said to her. "I learned from some of the warriors that Badger was going blind, and I knew you would most likely take pity on him. But when I saw him jump up like that, I knew he could see better than what he was leading everyone to believe."

"It does not matter anymore," Shadow said.

"There is now no one left to keep us from total happiness."

"That's true," Austin said. "Nothing can ever keep us apart."

"Then you will stay as my brother?" Little Bear asked, his eyes alive with joy.

"I'll stay," Austin replied. "You'll have to play the hands game with me every day."

Shadow smiled and let Austin take her into his arms. It was true, and she could hardly believe it: They would now share total happiness for all time. She would never again be without the warmth he brought her with his love. They would be together forever, as one.

Epilogue

SHADOW AND AUSTIN met her father and the men as they returned from St. Louis with supplies and trade articles for the new fort-lodge that would be built just up the river from where the old one had been burned. Little Bear had gone back to the Bitterroot with the Salish warriors to tell their mother that all was well and that Shadow had a special surprise for her when they met again where the fort-lodge was to be built.

The surprise had brought great happiness and peace of mind to Shadow's mother, for to get her long-lost medicine bundle back once again surely meant that the spirits again looked down on her with favor. Now her life would be filled each day with the warmth she had lost those many snows past, and she could rest in knowing that the spirit of her lost child now dwelled in the Land of Eternal Summer.

But the memory of the Beelers returned to Shadow

now and then, and she heard of other problems now occurring throughout the land because of the burning water that was so prevalent in trade. It made her concerned to think that many others were now suffering the same problems that had taken Badger's life. But she knew that evil was a very powerful weapon, whether it was used by Indian peoples or Long Knives.

Shadow could understand, though, that there would soon be many more Long Knives in these lands. She would hear of them from time to time as they came up the river on the fireboats to the fort called Benton. And it was said that they traveled now along the trails to the south in wooden wagons covered with white cloth, many of them who wished to make their homes in these lands. It would not be long before they would call these lands their own.

Shadow had many times thought of this and even talked about it with Austin and her family. No one would be happy when this time came, for it would mean a change, and something would be lost that could never again be found. It made Shadow sad to think that the land she loved so dearly would become something that she didn't know. But she would always take heart at the words of her father, who seemed to have a mind that could sort out that which was acceptable and that which was not. And there was her husband, Austin, whom she loved beyond all measure. In his arms, all seemed to be good and problems seemed to melt away.

Though her father fussed and fumed about things, saying his health was fine, Shadow was happy to see that Austin had taken over the majority of the work that needed to be done, together with the day-to-day operations of the fort. Walking Head had again brought his people down to trade, together with three other bands of Siksika Blackfeet and one band of Kainah. There had been a feast and all had gone well. Standing Elk had taken a wife, and though Badger was gone, it seemed a relief that his suffering was finally over. Life with their good friends among the Blackfeet was once again happy.

Happiness for Shadow had now finally come, and as she looked far down into the valley from a high ledge among the rocks, she felt a deep fulfillment and warm sense of security. She had found the only man to whom she could give such love and receive more in return. His strength had helped her overcome the terrible dangers that arose from time to time. And, most of all, she owed life itself to her spirit helper, the she-eagle of the skies.

Now, as the warmth of the sun settled her thoughts and the approaching night made the land calm, Shadow continued to look out over the broad expanse of the valley below. The Moon of the Chokecherry— September—was nearing its end, and all the rivers and grasslands were painted their strongest colors. The leaves of the trees, nipped by the cold that now came with the darkness, clung to the branches in layers of red and gold. The birds had now come together in flocks and flew along the ground in swift, darting masses as they looked for food before the night came. Shadow knew that before long she would look into the skies and see the long V-formation of the geese as they made their way to the warm lands far to the south. It was the time when all living things prepared for the cold moons.

It was now with contentment that Shadow looked back on her life, knowing she would now live in peace and happiness. Though she, like her mother,

would always be known as a fierce fighter with the
powers of the spirits, the time had now come when
she could put her bow aside and enjoy life to the
fullest. And it was good to again see her mother with
a happy smile, singing morning songs as she prepared
herself for the day. She was now also content with
her life and had no more fears about the spirits. That
time had now passed and only good things lay ahead.

But Shadow had become a legend throughout all
these lands, and the stories could still be heard around
campfires. In the villages of her people, the Salish,
the warriors who had come to know her sang the song
an elder had taught them:

> The wind calls, the day has come.
> Upon the clouds the warrior sails.
> Her heart is strong;
> She holds the skies.
> And her call is heard throughout the land.

Yes, it was time to merely listen to the song and
remember it, but never to try to become the woman
warrior she had been. She had a new life now, and
the smiles from her mother the past few mornings had
been followed by the question "Did you get sick
again when you went for water?" Shadow had told
her she had become sick. It was a sure sign. So now,
this night, she would go into the lodge that she and
Austin had shared as man and wife and would tell
him that he would become a father after the cold
moons had passed. She would tell him that when the
deer hid their fawns along the river's edge, and when
both the elk and the buffalo nursed their calves while
feeding in the new growth of grass, then he would be
able to hold his child next to him. She would not tell

him if it would be a boy or a girl, for she did not
care. And she knew he would not care, either. He had
told her this when they had talked of children before.
She only knew that he would be very happy.

The sun was now close to the high mountains in
the west, ready to fall behind them. From among the
rocks above came a high, shrill call, and Shadow
turned her face to the sky. Crossing just overhead was
the she-eagle, the image of power and majesty,
Shadow's spirit helper. "Thank you for all you have
done," Shadow said in final tribute as she watched
the giant bird sail out across the valley, gliding gracefully on golden wings that carried her far out toward
the high peaks in the distance.

Westerns available from